THE
PARADISE
REHEARSAL
CLUB

A NOVEL BY

MARGARET CRONIN FISK

AND

ALAN FISK

SUMMIT BOOKS
NEW YORK

Copyright © 1982 by Margaret Cronin Fisk and Alan Fisk
All rights reserved
including the right of reproduction
in whole or in part in any form
Published by SUMMIT BOOKS
A Simon & Schuster Division of Gulf & Western Corporation
Simon & Schuster Building
1230 Avenue of the Americas
New York, New York 10020
SUMMIT BOOKS and colophon
are trademarks of Simon & Schuster
Manufactured in the United States of America

10   9   8   7   6   5   4   3   2   1

Library of Congress Cataloging in Publication Data

Fisk, Margaret Cronin.
    The Paradise Rehearsal Club.

    I. Fisk, Alan.   II. Title.
PS3556.I81458P3   813'.54   81-16545
ISBN 0-671-40023-1   AACR2

"First Fig" by Edna St. Vincent Millay is reprinted from Collected Poems, Harper & Row,
copyright 1922, 1950 by Edna St. Vincent Millay.
    Excerpt from "Tea for Two" by Vincent Youmans
and Irving Caesar reprinted by permission.
    Excerpt from "It's a Walk-in for Walker" by
Irving Berlin on page 32, copyright 1925 by Irving
Berlin, copyright renewed 1952 by Irving Berlin,
reprinted by permission of Irving Berlin Music
Corporation.

We'd like to give special thanks to:
Andy Geller and Connie Rosenblum, for their friendship and unflagging faith; Larry Fallon, for his memories; Norma Vavolizza, Barrie Samuels, Barry Gross, Peter and Debbie Goodman, for being there when we needed them; Chris Steinmetz, for believing in us in the beginning; Howard Crook, Jan Andrews, Bill Ridley, Phil Bieber, Red Smith, the boys at the By George, Tony Betts, K. R. Murdoch, the New York Public Library; and finally, Mary McCarville, for leading the cheering section.

To our parents, Margaret and John Cronin and Ben and Ann Fisk; to Barbara and Bill Hamill; and of course, to our dear friend and agent extraordinaire, Freya Manston

"I seen my opportunities and I took 'em."

—GEORGE WASHINGTON PLUNKETT
*Tammany boss, public servant,
millionaire on a salary that
rarely exceeded $40 per week*

1925

MONEY.

The city throbbed with it, lusted over it, built on it. The sense of it hung in the air like a fine stinging mist, constantly reminding people that it was just around every corner, up every block.

Money.

It was a fever, a phenomenon the likes of which New York and America had never seen before. Let one barber make a half-million dollars in six weeks dabbling in the stock market (as one did) and a million barbers and cabbies and clerks said to their wives: Why not me? The next day people who did not even have radios owned a hundred shares of RCA. New York was a thousand California gold rushes exploding at once. Fortunes loomed over every horizon. A trucker taking a load to Montreal picks up a case of liquor for a friend. In New York the trucker finds the liquor is worth ten times what it cost. Five more trips to Canada and the trucker is a rich man. Twenty trips and he owns half-share in a speakeasy and is written up in the papers twice a week as a Broadway swell. Invent a better sewing machine and the best people beat a path to your door. Politicians croon in your ear, gamblers give you only sure things, long-legged women assault you with tantalizing scents.

The twenties were already roaring with the joy of throwing off social shackles, with a universal laugh at flagpole sitters and stockings rolled at the knee. It was the American Dream gone wild with excess to a jazz beat. It was Xanadu rushing to joyous oblivion on the back of a dollar.

1

THERE WERE A LOT of rich suckers at the table, but only two gamblers. The suckers were easy to spot. In the glare from the bright light over their heads they looked baggy-eyed, their tuxedoes disheveled. They mopped at their brows with already grimy handkerchiefs. Each stared at his cards with a desperate intensity as if, with enough willpower, deuces could be persuaded to evolve into aces. Their piles of money had steadily dwindled as little hills of cigar and cigarette ash grew around them. Collars loosened, they breathed noisily in the smoky air that enveloped the room. There was no other world for them now. No families, friends, jobs, businesses. Just the white light and the reality of losing.

The real gamblers stuck out like cactus in a rose arbor. George McManus had a smile on his face as he picked up his cards, spread them slowly, then sat back to see what the man on his right would bet. There was no sweat on McManus's brow, his tuxedo was as neatly pressed as when he had left his suite Saturday night. The red carnation in his lapel, McManus's trademark, was still fresh. Women called his face fascinating. Perhaps unfinished would have described him better; he looked as if an artist had carved him out of wood but neglected to finish the job with sandpaper. The result was a long, deeply-lined face, deep-set eyes, a strong chin with a prominent cleft, all under jet-black oiled hair. An old ragged scar ran over his right eye, the result of an enemy's once offering McManus a drink but declining to take it out of the bottle first.

He rubbed the scar lightly as he surveyed the losers at the poker table: two fat and very successful Wall Street speculators, an insurance executive with the look of a prosperous mortician, a dignified steel magnate from Pittsburgh, and the only son of a lumber baron who owned enough of Maine to start his own state. They had lost heavily, and the insurance man was even running out of paper to write IOUs. A good chunk of their money sat on the table in front of McManus, perhaps $70,000. It had been an exceptionally good night and morning, McManus thought. He could see sunlight sneaking through the cracks between the elegant red curtains. Muffled traffic noises came from Seventh Avenue, but none of the others seemed to notice.

"What's your pleasure?" The lumber heir, Frank Sturgis, a smooth-faced twenty-three-year-old whose mouth was screwed in a perpetual smirk, looked at McManus.

"Two," McManus said, throwing a hundred-dollar bill onto the pile of money in the center of the table. He gave Sturgis two cards and received two others.

"How about you, Mr. Rothstein?" Sturgis turned toward the man on McManus's left.

The man shook his head, indicating he wanted no cards. He shifted in his seat, sat up, and stared intently at the other players, his cards carefully pressed to his chest. He absent-mindedly rubbed the back of his card hand, stopping occasionally only to pluck at his eyebrows. For all his mannerisms Arnold Rothstein could not be called nervous as much as intense. Now and then, without thinking, he would reach down to his shin and snap his garter. Behind his thin, sharp, deadpan face Rothstein was enjoying himself. This was the kind of poker game he liked. The others had begun playing for the sport of it, unmindful of the money they were losing. They drank, laughed, told stories, bragged about women. Only after they had been playing for hours had they begun to realize what was happening. Rothstein and McManus were steadily cleaning them out. Gradually, the heartiness and cheer had gone out of the evening, like a picnic being covered by rain-clouds.

McManus dropped out on the next raise and sat back, watching Rothstein. The gambler was studying Sturgis like a mongoose stalking a cobra, McManus thought. All night long Rothstein had been playing the youth, letting him win a game here and a game there, complimenting him on a good hand, consoling him on a loss, praising him when he bluffed successfully. It had reached the point where Sturgis was looking

16

at Rothstein for a sign of approval on every hand. Rothstein nodded with appreciation as the boy won another pot. And Sturgis beamed. The kid was snowed by Rothstein's reputation, McManus thought. The big-time gambler and loanshark, the man who had half of New York City in his back pocket. The kid was a fool.

McManus had seen many like him at the poker games he ran in his expensive Park Central Hotel suite. He had developed a sixth sense for finding bored men with money. The speakeasies were full of them, men who quickly tired of the music, the booze, the forced laughter. Their only reason for living was making money, and many found an almost sexual attraction in its pursuit, as if the adrenaline that throbbed through them was issued by the U.S. Mint. The signs were unmistakable. At the 300 Club, Salon Royal, Helen Morgan's, El Fay, and a thousand other joints they tapped their fingers impatiently to the easy runs of the piano players, smoked incessantly, doodled figures on tablecloths. Their eyes strayed restlessly about the rooms as wives and girlfriends uselessly strove to get their attention. They didn't always know what they were looking for. But McManus knew.

"Last game, okay George? It's getting late," said the insurance man. Under his white hair his face was even redder than usual and his eyes were rheumy. He had lost close to $50,000. A nice guy, McManus thought, who shouldn't play cards.

"Late hell, it's getting early," Sturgis joked with a strained laugh, looking at Rothstein. "And I'm just starting to get hot. Won the last two hands, didn't I?"

"Last game," McManus agreed flatly, not even looking at Sturgis. He could see what was coming. It was the bottom of the ninth for the kid and Sturgis was only too ready. There was a tension in the air that hadn't been there before as McManus dealt the cards, something between anger and suspense.

For three rounds the betting was heavy, heavier than it had been all night. McManus dropped out on the second round and by the fourth, with over $80,000 in the kitty, only Sturgis, one of the fat stockbrokers, and Rothstein were left. Rothstein raised again and the fat man gave it up. He threw his cards down with a look of disgust. Staring at his lost money he breathed heavily, his mouth puckering like a fish gasping for air on a dock.

Everyone looked at Sturgis. He scratched at his brown hair, carefully parted in the middle, then flipped a bunch of bills into the center of the table. "That's all I've got, Mr. Rothstein. See your four thousand and raise you a thousand." His hands shook slightly.

Rothstein sat stiff-backed behind a pile of bills big enough to derail a train. Carefully, knowing all eyes were on him, he counted out ten hundred-dollar bills and put them in the center of the table. Then his hand fell on a stack of bills in front of him. Slowly Rothstein pushed the stack away.

"Raise you a hundred thousand," Rothstein said quietly.

Sturgis sat stunned. He pulled at his collar and it snapped open, the button rolling slowly across the table. His lips moved but no words came out.

"I don't . . . no money . . ." Sturgis was sputtering now.

"You can write, can't you?" Rothstein never took his eyes off the boy's face.

"Huh?"

"An IOU. Your signature's good, ain't it?"

Sturgis looked about wildly but none of the other players would meet his eyes. The youth's strong fingers were nervously twisting and bending his cards. A lone drop of sweat sat precariously on the ridge of his nose, as if it also was deciding which way to go. McManus felt he could almost hear Sturgis's mind working, trying to make a big decision for the first time in his life. Sturgis desperately looked at Rothstein and the gambler's eyes seemed to hold him. Then, slowly, Rothstein smiled for the first time that night. A great, benevolent, warm grin. A salesman's grin. As McManus watched, Sturgis's shoulders slumped slightly. He seemed to relax, to gain confidence, always watching Rothstein's eyes. And that smile. He's hooked, McManus thought. He thinks Rothstein is going to let him win. He thinks Arnold Rothstein likes him.

As if in a dream, like some bizarre slow-motion ballet, Sturgis reached for a pad and pencil across the table. He scribbled slowly on the pad, tore off the top sheet carefully, and threw it onto the pile of money. When he finally looked away from

Rothstein his hands were so wet the pencil almost slipped out of his fingers.

"Call," Sturgis finally said. Then, without waiting for Rothstein, he threw his cards on the table. Three kings stared at the ceiling.

"Nice," Rothstein said emotionlessly.

Sturgis whooped and threw his arms in the air, running his fingers through his hair. The others at the table let out a collective sigh as Sturgis stood and stretched, elation on his face. He bent and began to rake the pile of money toward him.

"But . . . ." Rothstein left the word hanging in the air. He leaned his elbows on the table, turned the cards toward Sturgis, and spread them with his fingers—three sixes and a pair of twos.

"A full house," someone muttered. "The kid loses."

Sturgis picked up the three kings and slowly, carefully, tore them in half, then in half again. The ripping of the cardboard was the only sound in the room.

"You cheated, you goddamn Jew," he shouted, and everybody jumped. "You cheated. I don't know how, but nobody wins the way you do. You fooled me." Sturgis was screaming now. He leaned over the table and threw the scraps of cardboard into Rothstein's face.

Rothstein stood up quickly, knocking over his chair. Nobody saw his hand move, just the quick flash of light off his pinky ring and then the sound of the slap dying away. A little drop of blood ran down the kid's cheek where Rothstein's ring had cut him.

Sturgis's knuckles whitened as he gripped the table. For a moment McManus thought the boy might either leap at Rothstein or bawl. McManus touched his arm and Sturgis suddenly collapsed back into his chair, like a sail gone slack when the wind has died. McManus pulled Sturgis away from the table, got him into his coat, and led him out the door. The other players sat without speaking for a long minute. Then they rose together and, thanking McManus, left.

When McManus got back to the table Rothstein was pouring himself a drink at the bar on the sideboard.

"You were pretty rough on the kid, Arnie." McManus sat down and idly shuffled the cards.

19

For the second time that night Rothstein smiled. He was feeling expansive. "He needed a lesson and I gave him one. When bums like that lose they can never admit a better man beat them. It's always bad luck or a dame on their mind or the other guy is crooked. Then they get mad and do something stupid. You tell me how come people can never face the truth."

"Fuck the truth, Arnie. You broke that kid. He was bouncing off the walls when he walked out of here."

"Don't be a jerk, George. Taking knocks is the only way that kid will grow up. I did him a favor." Rothstein was standing in front of a mirror, adjusting his tie. "And let me tell ya, the sob story sounds pretty funny coming from a head-cracker like you used to be. What was the name of that Hell's Kitchen gang you used to run with? Every one of them had a record longer than a fat man's belt. When did you ever give anybody a break?"

"That was ten years ago. I grew up. I make my living at gambling, but I don't suck blood."

"What are you, the mick Robin Hood? Listen, you feel so bad for the kid, I'll make you a little proposition." Rothstein held up the IOU and a match. "I'll put the torch to the kid's paper. Then you and me, we cut the cards just once. High card takes everything. What do you say, Georgie?"

McManus studied Rothstein's impassive face. All or nothing. It was McManus's favorite game. All or nothing. McManus looked at the money still on the table. Rothstein had to have won over two hundred thousand in cash, he thought, as against his seventy thousand. Three to one odds on an even bet. Gambler's heaven. And McManus remembered the look on the face of Frankie Sturgis as he had stumbled out the door. There were some things, he mused, that were even more imporant than money. But not many.

"You've got a bet, Arnie. And I hope you walk out of here with your pockets emptier than that kid's eyes."

Rothstein's lips moved in what could have been taken as a thin smile. McManus watched as the corner of the paper slowly turned brown then black as the flame caught it. Rothstein dropped the paper into an ashtray. It turned blue for a moment, then it was nothing but ash.

McManus shuffled the cards once more and laid the deck on the table. He lifted off about half the cards and turned them over. On the bottom was the nine of spades. He put the cards back on the deck, shuffled, and handed them to Rothstein. With no hesitation Rothstein cut and showed the bottom card. The jack of spades.

"You know why you'll never be big-time, Georgie?" Rothstein said matter-of-factly, bundling the money into two thick piles. "You're no better than all the other greedy suckers. You don't know when to quit." He put rubber bands around the piles and slipped them into his coat pockets. "Next time you have a game, Georgie," he said from the door, "be sure to let me know."

Alone, McManus sat at the table, his hand still on the deck. He listened as the street noises grew louder. In the distance, a church bell tolled for the faithful.

2

THE PIANO MUSIC tinkled slowly through the room, coming to George like pebbles drifting through water. The saloon was hot, noisy, the air full of laughter and smoke and the smell of the girl next to him. She was very close to him now, her thigh pressed against his, her breast brushing his arm when she leaned over to laugh with the people across the table, people he could barely see. She smelled wonderful as her hair wisped past his nose, George thought. She smelled of perfume and soap and beer and sweat and excitement. He wished he could think of her name. But it had been too long now, too many hours of beer and whiskey. How long had he been here? George wondered idly, trying to bring the room into focus. A day? A week? His head ached suddenly with a burst of noise. He could remember the card game. He could remember he was broke. Then he stopped remembering.

She was back, nuzzling his ear, her lips on his neck, her breath hot. He looked into her face as if he had never seen her before and was pleased with what he saw. It was a comely, slightly plump face, framed by tightly curled blond-brown hair. A little blue fan was stuck behind one ear. Her mouth smiled up at him, as ripe and red as an old tomato. She giggled—he could remember that she giggled a lot—and ran her hand up his thigh, brushing his groin. He tried clumsily to put his arm around the girl, to squeeze her, and she finally had to help him. Now his hand brushed her soft arm, then her side, feeling the warmth through the silky material of her thin dress. His fingers caressed the curve of her breast and the girl giggled into his ear until the pain behind his eyes returned.

Someone was laughing at him across the table—high, loud laughter. He turned from the girl and squinted, trying to make out the mocking faces. There was a girl and a man across the booth and he wondered that the girl looked so much like the girl next to him, who was now chewing on his ear again and squeezing his hand as it was squeezing her breast. George was torn between passion and curiosity, trying to make out the man's face. But he couldn't bring it into focus. His eyes could only take in the bright yellow sport coat with the broad blue stripes that the other man wore. And his tie, bearing a brown girl, naked except for a grass skirt. Slowly, he realized it was Izzy the Stub across the booth because no one else could get away with wearing anything like that tie. Izzy the Stub raised his arms, stuck two fingers into his mouth, and whistled for another round of needle beer. The piercing whistle cut through George's skull as he watched the girl in the grass skirt sway.

The girl next to Izzy the Stub looked so much like the girl next to George—who was now halfway on his lap—that George thought at first he must be going insane. Then slowly it came back to him, how Izzy had found him walking the streets after the card game. Izzy's remedy had been a drink or two, and twelve hours later Izzy had started talking about a pair of twins who liked a good time more than life itself. And now George's twin was licking his stubbly cheek, slipping her tongue between his half-numb lips, and he found his hands rubbing her buttocks and she just couldn't stop giggling.

"Let's go somewhere, love," she whispered to George, her tongue doing figure-eights on his ear as George looked at Izzy, who was laughing like a madman and shouting about rookie cops and City Hall and cleaning up Times Square or something. Through the fuzziness around his brain George was trying to listen to Izzy the Stub but the girl was now undoing the studs of his formal shirt and slipping her hand inside to caress George's chest. Slowly George became aware of other men standing around their table and laughing with Izzy. He heard someone talking about Mayor Hylan and how he was so stupid he couldn't remember to say "Ladies and Gentlemen" at the beginning of his addresses unless someone wrote it on top of his speech.

But it was no good anymore, because the girl was rolling George's nipples between her fingers like vintage cigars. He was writhing so much in the booth that he couldn't listen and filled his hands with any part of the girl's body he could grasp. He was mumbling now to Izzy the Stub, saying he had to go, the girl half dragging him from the booth as she tried to tuck her half-bared breast back into her dress at the same time. He stumbled on someone's chair leg and the girl pleaded into his ear to hurry up, for God's sake, because she couldn't stand it anymore. George got off the floor and dusted the knee of his tuxedo trousers while the other men laughed and the girl pulled at his arm. But Izzy the Stub told them to shut up and beamed at George and told him to try and not get pinched.

The girl pulled him through the crowded saloon and to the street. She practically threw herself in front of a taxi to stop it as he tried desperately to remember her name because someone had once told him that gentlemen never forgot a name. She quickly shoved him into the cab and told him to give the driver his address and then half leaped on George, her tongue deep in his mouth, as the cabbie shrugged in resignation and drove off. Jesus, Mary, and Joseph, but he was loaded, George thought, his brain swimming. He finally stumbled from the cab in front of the hotel while the girl tore through her purse for the fare because George managed to say he didn't have enough money left to make a stack of two coins.

She rushed him through the lobby where he staggered into a potted palm and several annoyed hotel residents before they found their way into the elevator. The operator tactfully looked straight ahead as the girl pushed George into the corner of the elevator and pulled his face into her sweaty breasts, moaning into his ear and wriggling against his hips. He licked her tit while trying valiantly to stand up.

"Fourteenth floor, if you care," the elevator operator sniffed, and George would have swung at the man but he could barely move, and his hands felt like overboiled sausages. The girl pulled him down the corridor and then ripped the key from him as he fumbled with the lock, shoving him into the suite. He managed to turn on the light before he fell onto the heavy sofa, but the girl flicked the light off and then swirled around and around in the center of the dim room, giggling again, making herself even dizzier. As she swayed before him George thought of the dancing girl on Izzy the Stub's tie, hips twitching with every breath. What was Izzy talking about? George tried to remember. Cops, Times Square, the mayor. Something, something there.

And now the girl came to him and he could see the lights dancing in her eyes as the huge five-story neon sign on the hotel across Seventh Avenue flickered on and off. She pulled him to his feet and kissed him hard on the mouth while she ground her hips and stomach against him. He put his arms around her and ran his hands down her back and cupped her buttocks through her thin dress until she writhed against him even harder.

She sat him down again, then unbuttoned her dress and let it fall to her feet. She slipped off her underthings, then came to him languidly, sitting on his lap and pulling his face to her bare breasts and cooing in his ear. For a time George did not touch her, just reveled in her delicious beery smell and smoothness. And then his hands came up and squeezed her swollen nipples clumsily and he felt a shudder go through the girl. Suddenly George was sorry he was so drunk. It didn't even matter that he was busted. He just wanted this girl very much. Through the haze that enveloped him he tried to caress her again but his hands were still thick and heavy and would not do what he wanted. She only giggled again and helped him off with his jacket. Then she knelt in front of him and fumbled with his pants, finally getting her hands inside and enveloping his heat in her cool fingers. George wanted to talk to her now, to say something, but all he could think of was to ask her name and he was ashamed of being that drunk.

Finally she pushed him back on the couch. Still holding him in her hand she straddled George and guided him into her. God, she hardly weighs anything, he marveled, as she began to gyrate above him. Slowly, then ever faster she writhed and pushed down on him and he heard the giggles give way to sighs and moans. Spent for the moment, she leaned over him and kissed him gently on the forehead. As she lingered, stroking George's hair, one breast touched his lips. Without thinking he took her nipple in his mouth and sucked gently. He could see the white of her teeth above him as she smiled serenely, her breasts swaying. But where was her grass skirt? George wondered, Izzy the Stub suddenly racing through his mind. And where was the mayor? In Times Square? He must get a tie like Izzy the Stub's, George decided, his tongue teasing the girl's nipple. A wonderful tie.

Finally she pulled her breast away and sat up again. Now, as she worked on him, he began to feel the heat rise in him in earnest. There was a sudden madness in the girl as she ground away, lost in her pleasure. He watched her as she joyously hovered over him, breasts bouncing and hair flying. There it was again in the back of his mind, the thought like a cat creeping through the shadows. He reached for it but couldn't quite touch it, giving in to the girl instead. He pulled her breasts to him, oblivious to anything else, the stars exploding behind his eyes. She gave a short shriek and George moaned and, rising to meet her push, burst into her. Tammany. Cops. Then he knew what he was reaching for. And suddenly they were both giggling as the neon sign lit them up, then plunged them back into darkness.

3

TAMMANY HALL loomed squat and bulky over the bustle of Fourteenth Street, like a fortress impervious to the woes of the outside world. In many ways Tammany *was* a fortress—a citadel of political power as strong as any European monarch's castle. But instead of stone ramparts and moats and drawbridges, Tammany was protected by its far-flung influence, its mercenaries directing the battle in every precinct and on every block in New York City.

There was an air of supercharged activity about the building as George McManus stepped out of his cab in front of the Tammany Wigwam. Intent-looking men rushed in and out past other groups of men, their heads together in earnest conversation on the sidewalk and low front steps. Still other men swarmed over the front of the building draping red, white, and blue crepe and American flags across every inch of stone, preparing for the Tammany Society's annual Decoration Day celebration, which would attract every Democratic officeholder of any importance in the five boroughs. This year in particular, George knew, none of the viceroys and captains and precinct stooges of Tammany would dare miss the Decoration Day extravaganza. For this was the year that Tammany was finally coming back. Tammany's boy, State Senator Jimmy Walker, was going to be the next mayor.

George pulled his lapels straight, fiddled with his tie, adjusted his fedora over one eye, and took a deep breath. Then he took the steps two at a time and walked into the cool, dim lobby of the Wigwam. Around him the dark and somber faces of the old Tammany sachems going back a hundred years stared reprovingly from paintings on the walls, as if they knew what was on his mind. You got yours, George thought, looking around. Now it's my turn. He picked his way past workmen in the lobby and climbed a flight of stairs to the second floor where a bored-looking clerk behind a desk took his name, then trotted toward the other end of the corridor and disappeared into an office.

George stood restlessly, waiting for the clerk to return, his hands kneading the brim of the hat he now held. George rehearsed in his mind what he was going to say. He wiped the sweaty palms of his hands with a handkerchief. Funny, he thought, but he could lay out thousands on one card without blinking an eye, and here he stood nervous as a schoolboy. He fought to keep control, to keep that steadiness that people took for nervelessness. Too much was at stake, he told himself, to slip now.

When was the last time he had felt like this? he tried to remember. Certainly he had been afraid in Hell's Kitchen, where growing up with a constant sense of fear was the best insurance policy. But there had been no fear shooting craps and playing cards in alleys and basements, something he knew he was good at. And then he'd graduated to running poker games in smelly rooms in cheap hotels with grimy players who bent and sweated on the cards until they were equally worn and world-weary. There'd been fights, even knives drawn over little more than pennies. The players had sat hunched around the scarred and ash-strewn tables. And when there were no chairs they sat on the beds until the bedsprings played a symphony of greed and sagged in surrender. No, he had never been frightened then, because there was no way to go but up. He had taken dimes from high school boys, dealt to drunks. And dreamed of something more.

The bored-looking clerk returned and jerked his head toward an open door, which George took as an invitation to go in. His footsteps echoed noisily as he walked down the corridor. The office he turned into was big, wood-paneled, and expensive-looking, with hundreds of law books carefully ranked on shelves on one wall. Sunlight streamed through a big window that faced south—toward City Hall. Jimmy Walker sat slouched in a leather chair behind a huge mahogany desk that had nothing but a telephone on top of it. The desk was so big George could only see Walker's head and shoulders and a derby hat that he spun playfully on one finger. Walker was unmistakable—thin, dapper, with narrow, bloodless lips and eyes as calculating as they were friendly. He half danced out from behind the big desk and pumped George's hand.

"So you're McManus." Walker looked genuinely happy to see him, George thought. Every inch the politician. "I hear you can make the queen of hearts jump up and dance the black bottom," Walker went on. "I know a couple of gents you skinned in one of your card games. They had nothing but admiration for you, strangely enough. Do you do hypnosis as well as card tricks?"

"I make a living," George answered.

A barking laugh erupted behind George and he quickly turned to see a small mountain of a man sitting in a huge, overstuffed armchair. James Hines, Tammany's West Side boss, was massively powerful under his florid, falling face— powerful as the blacksmith he had once been. He was almost bald but bushy-browed. Under his broad nose one of Havana's finest jutted from his mouth, unlit. He liked to twirl a cigar when he was thinking. He was twirling it now.

"Damned if all you Hell's Kitchen boys aren't alike," Hines said in his best boisterous Irish politician manner. "As cheap with a word as a Scotsman with a dollar." He beamed benevolently at George. Of all the racketeers and gamblers and bootleggers from Harlem to Hell's Kitchen that Hines protected, George McManus was one of his favorites. His poker games never caused any trouble, and George was always right on time every month with his gratitude. So when George had called and asked for this meeting, Hines had been quick to agree, asking no questions. After all, Havana cigars weren't cheap. A man could always use a few more dollars.

"I thought it was going to be just you and me, Hines," said George, shaking the old man's hands.

"Well, Georgie, if you can't trust the next goddamn mayor, who can you trust?" Hines looked over at Walker. "Besides, Jimmy and me have the Tammany tiger by the tail now."

"So what's on your mind, McManus?" Walker said, sitting on the desk and going back to spinning the derby on his finger.

McManus looked from one man to the other, wondering how much to tell. And how much he'd have to tell. "I guess you know about Hylan and his cleaning up the rackets in Times Square," he began. "I've got an idea that could make a lot of money off it. A game."

"Come on, McManus. Every mayor cracks down on the rackets in the Tenderloin every four years. It's as big a reelection ritual as kissing babies. How can you make money out of that?" Walker sounded disappointed, as if he had expected more.

"This time I want to use it to my advantage," McManus

countered. "But I'll need a little pull in the right place at the right time."

"I thought I'd been taking pretty good care of you, Georgie." Hines was twirling his cigar like mad. "You never had any trouble with the law, did you?"

McManus shook his head. "That was paying off a few cops to look the other way. I've got bigger plans now. This calls for more protection."

"How big?" Walker asked, laying the derby on the table.

"I need a judge. And someone who'll play ball for a long time, not just one quick court appearance." McManus knew they were watching him now, measuring him.

"You certainly talk a good show, McManus," Walker said slowly, "but Hines here tells me you had some bad luck at cards the other night. Are you sure you can afford the kind of hefty, uh . . . campaign contribution that your idea calls for?"

McManus was surprised. He knew Rothstein liked to brag when he had hurt someone, but he hadn't expected the word to spread all the way to Tammany and Hines this quickly. He had been too busy drinking, and then sobering up, he realized, to hear the whispers. A fine sweat broke out around his hairline.

He was thinking quickly now, watching Walker closely. How could he get back in this game when they knew he didn't have any money?

"I'm not asking for charity," McManus said, turning to Hines. "I've always made good on my promises in the past."

Hines shrugged and settled back in his chair. "But that was yesterday, George, and yesterday doesn't count. This isn't a candy store where you can get credit."

"Look, I'll tell you my idea. Just hear me out. I want—"

"I like you, McManus. You're no dope and you're loyal, and Tammany respects loyalty above all else. But I don't think we can do business. Not now," Walker said.

George started to protest but Walker cut him off. "And no, I don't even want to know about your plans. I'm going to be the next mayor, once the primary is locked up. And as this city's highest elected official I will not tolerate any corruption that I know about. So I don't want to know about it. Now maybe someday, when you're back on your feet and you still want to add to my war chest . . ."

Suddenly Walker was interrupted by shouts in the hallway, then a tremendous crash and a banging on the heavy door. Abruptly the door flew open and a tall, burly, red-faced man in his sixties wearing an expensive gray business suit barged into the office. The man was carrying a fine leather briefcase with one arm and fighting off the skinny clerk who hung around his neck with the other. With a final heave the big man threw the clerk to the floor.

"Goddamn, I will not be treated like kitchen help, Walker," the burly man shouted, his eyes red-rimmed with anger. He pulled a handsome watch on a heavy gold chain from a vest pocket and brandished it like a papal decree. "Ten minutes, damn it, ten minutes I've been cooling my heels outside your office like some third-rate lackey. Well, maybe this will buy me some of your time!"

He rushed to the desk and before anyone could say a word turned over his briefcase. Money in dozens of neat bundles rained out, covering the desk and overflowing onto the floor with a plop. For a long minute everyone in the room stared, transfixed, at the green heap.

"I tried to stop him, boss," the clerk finally said, picking himself off the floor. Hines quickly waved him out of the office.

"I thought this would get your attention, Walker," the burly man said, calmer now, pleased with the effect he had created. He pulled a silk handkerchief from a pocket and mopped his face. "It's all there, the whole two hundred thousand we discussed. Now let's talk about what it's going to buy me."

Walker picked some of the packets of bills off the floor and placed them on the desk almost reverently. "This is hardly the time or place, Wainwright, although I have to admire your business sense. You know how to get action, all right."

"That's not what I want to hear," replied Horace Newkirk Wainwright, slightly mollified anyway. "If I want compliments, I'll buy them. I want to hear about that subway contract. Do I get it or not?"

Walker looked at McManus, then at Hines, who nodded, indicating that it was all right for McManus to hear what was being said.

"Let me say, Wainwright, that your most generous campaign contribution will certainly stand you in good stead in my new administration," Walker began. He went behind the desk and sat down, almost hidden by the mound of money, then popped up nervously. "And when it comes time to let that tunnel job, well, we shall certainly remember our friends."

Wainwright snorted and fixed Walker with his stare. "Cut the political babble, Walker. The day you take office I expect you to start steering that contract through the council and the appropriate city agencies. I want to break ground before spring, or there'll be no more where that came from." He poked a thumb in the direction of the money, a look of satisfaction on his face.

George was trying to remember what he knew about Horace Wainwright, but all he could conjure was another wealthy businessman on the society pages. Europe each spring. Newport in the summer. Debutante balls in the fall. And money year round.

Walker came around the desk with a placating gesture but Wainwright was already pulling on a pair of gloves and moving to the door. "Enough talk, Walker. Now let's see some action. When I shell out good money, I expect to see people jump."

Walker dashed to the door as Wainwright walked out. "Good to see you again, Horace," he called to Wainwright's back. "And congratulations, I hear your little girl's getting married." The red-faced man turned and gave Walker a queer look, then marched stiffly down the hall.

"Well, isn't he one sweet old son of a bitch," Walker said slowly, going to the desk and weighing a packet of bills in the palm of his hand.

Hines took George's arm and led him out of the office into the cool corridor. "You embarrassed me, Georgie. You should have told me on the telephone what was on your mind. You don't come to Tammany like a pauper with your hand out. I thought better of you." He looked at George earnestly, then punched him lightly on one shoulder. "But now you know, huh? Now you see how it's done. Don't make the same mistake twice."

31

The older man turned and started to go back into the office when George touched his arm.

"Don't count me out yet, Hines. I'll be back with enough money to cover Walker's desk twice over."

Hines looked at him for a second. "I'll look forward to that, Georgie."

He closed the office door behind him. George could hear the two men's voices, murmuring as from a great depth. He couldn't make out the words. George pulled on his fedora and walked slowly down the hall. He wasn't going to let this beat him, he thought. The problem was simple—but where do you get that kind of front money in a hurry? And now that the word was out that he was broke it would be doubly hard. He might be able to put together a few thousand here and there, but he knew the funny looks he'd get. Maybe McManus is finished this time, the hustlers would be thinking. Maybe the luck is gone. Maybe Rothstein was too much for him.

He walked past the clerk at the desk, who was still nursing his injured pride, and down the stairs. The bustle in the Wigwam's main hall was even greater than before. He picked his way through the workmen and Tammany functionaries and reached the sidewalk, squinting in the sudden sunlight. He was debating whether to head back uptown, maybe try Izzy the Stub, when the clerk suddenly materialized beside him, tapping George on the shoulder.

"Boss Hines told me to give ya this," he shouted over the traffic noises on Fourteenth Street as he handed George a note. The clerk disappeared as George unfolded the paper. He read in Hines's scrawl: "Big Bill Dwyer."

George folded the paper again, then one more time, and creased it carefully before putting it in his pocket. As he turned to walk up the street he could hear some children singing in an upstairs room of the Wigwam. They were rehearsing a campaign song that Irving Berlin had written especially for his pal Jimmy Walker:

> Why it's a walk-in with Walker
> It's a walk-in with Jim
> He's a corker—and one of the mob
> A real New Yorker—who's fit for the job.

32

4

THE GIRL in the wedding gown took a long slug from her silver-plated hip flask and coughed only slightly. She pulled another hatpin from her dressing table drawer, wound a small rubber band around the base of the pin for weight, then flung the makeshift dart hard at her father's portrait on her bedroom wall. She smiled as the pin hit Horace Wainwright's bulbous nose, stuck for a moment, then fell to join the other hatpin darts scattered on the floor below the painting. Elizabeth Wainwright smiled again, this time smugly, as her father resumed pounding on her bedroom door. Elizabeth was already two hours late for her own wedding. Five hundred restless members of New York's upper crust were milling about the Wainwright mansion, getting quietly smashed on the subway baron's liquor, waiting for the bride to show. But she was in no hurry.

Elizabeth Wainwright had declared war on her father. She hadn't announced it to him yet, but it was war just the same. Her father had tricked her into this marriage and the only way she was going to go through with it was if Wainwright broke down the door and dragged her out. In the meantime, she prepared another dart.

Elizabeth was not quite twenty-one, at an age when she obeyed nothing but the impulse of the moment, heeded no opinion but her own. Her short, auburn hair framed a soft, pale face—a face that lacked the angularity and aloofness of many women of her class. Her intense, intelligent eyes were the color of paper money. She had a small, upturned nose, a sensuous mouth, and a slightly undershot chin. Her chin was her only physical imperfection and in her vanity she hid the flaw by insisting that all photographs of her be taken full-face. It was a measure of her charm with the newsmen who haunted nightclubs that not even the worst scandal sheets had a profile shot of Elizabeth on file.

This was not the first time she had declared war on her father. It probably would not be the last. They had been in a nearly constant state of hostility for as long as Elizabeth could remember. Her mother said it was because they were so much alike, and certainly Elizabeth had acquired many of the traits that had turned Horace Wainwright into that most respected of all Americans—a multimillionaire businessman. She was tenacious, often devious, and had a total inability to accept anything less than what she wanted when she wanted it. But their disputes went much deeper than that. Horace Wainwright wanted to possess his daughter, to control her as he controlled every other member of his small family. Unfortunately, Elizabeth Wainwright was uncontrollable.

For that, Wainwright had only himself to blame. Horace had raised Elizabeth to believe there was nothing she couldn't do, no one on earth who could rule her. He had meant, of course, that she could do anything as long as *he* approved. But Elizabeth accepted no such qualifications. She cared nothing for social conventions. She rejected all authority, raced cars, flew rickety airplanes, insulted her father's closest business associates, stayed away from home for days at a time, and was once found by her father's detectives in a happy daze in a Chinatown opium den. She was reckless, careless, and fearless—and old Wainwright adored her.

Now he cooed softly through his daughter's locked bedroom door. But Elizabeth wouldn't answer. He glanced around the hallway, assured himself that no one could see him, then peeked through her keyhole. He breathed a sigh of relief as he spotted her white-gowned form. She was still there. She was also already dressed. That could mean only one thing, Wainwright decided. Elizabeth intended to go through with this marriage. She was merely making a final show of defiance before bowing to the inevitable. Not that he could blame her. He had tricked her into this.

Wainwright checked the time on the grandfather clock at the end of the hall and sighed. While he could understand Elizabeth's petulance, he could accept no further delays of this wedding. Several guests were already talking about leaving. His supply of champagne was nearly exhausted. He rattled the solid oak door. "You've made your point. Now come out." No response. "At least let me come in so we can talk," he pleaded.

To his surprise, Elizabeth crossed to the door and let her

father in. Wainwright quickly sucked in his breath as he got a good look at his daughter. Her grandmother's wedding dress made her look like a queen out of a fairy tale book. The off-white gown was silk over satin, with Spanish lace at the bodice and on the sleeves. Small but brilliant blue-white diamonds had been pasted on the waistline and hemline and in streams down the long full skirt. The waist was drawn in. The full, low-cut bodice daringly accentuated Elizabeth's breasts. She looked, Wainwright thought with great fatherly pride, nothing like the brides at the other weddings this season, those hawk-faced child-women with their faddish boyish-cut, flat-chested, low-waisted wedding gowns. His pride abated somewhat when he spied his pin-punctured portrait.

"I see you've kept yourself busy," he said gruffly. "Don't you think your guests have waited long enough?"

She turned away from him and began pulling a diamond clip from her hair. "You can tell them all to go home," she said airily as she tossed the clip on her dressing table. "I'm not getting married today."

Wainwright took her shoulder and spun her around gently. "Oh yes, you are, young lady. Do you want to make us both the laughingstocks of New York?"

"You're a cruel, mean, heartless, arrogant old tyrant and I hate you."

"This is no time for chit-chat, Elizabeth. We'll talk about my good points later—after your honeymoon. I understand young Cooper is taking you to his family hunting lodge in Canada. Very romantic." Wainwright sat on the big bed and watched his angry daughter.

"Oh yes, we're going to slaughter a few helpless ducks, maybe bump off a moose or two. Very romantic." She pulled off her diamond tiara and threw it on the floor. "How could you do this to me? You said I had to get engaged to Bobby to get your old steel contract. But what about our contract? I was going to get a new Stutz-Bearcat, remember? Not a spare tire for life."

Wainwright checked his pocket watch again, picked the tiara off the floor, and tenderly placed it back on his daughter's head. "Would you believe me if I told you this was for your own good? After all, child, you're almost twenty-one.

Most of your girlfriends were married ages ago. It's time for you to become a wife and mother."

"Boring, b-o-r-i-n-g," she cried. "And please don't tell me how this is for my own good when you are making several million dollars selling my body to the highest bidder." Her eyes blazed at Wainwright as he went to the door. "There's a name for men like you."

"Yes, child. They are called rich." He started through the door, then looked back. "You have five minutes to pull yourself together and appear downstairs. And for God's sake, you might smile. It is your wedding day."

"I don't suppose tears would help?" she called after him. But Wainwright laughed and closed the door.

Now what, she wondered, looking desperately around her huge, cluttered bedroom. With the bridesmaids and the servants gone, she finally had a few minutes to think. A very few minutes. How could she marry this Bobby Cooper? He was a fop, a lounge lizard. Oh, he was handsome enough, and funny when he had been drinking—which was most of the time. But he lacked character and drive. Bobby was a well-dressed, overeducated sloth plodding through drawing rooms with a cocktail in each well-manicured hand. If he hadn't been born rich the world would have chewed him up and spat him out long ago, she knew.

Elizabeth heard the orchestra downstairs warming up for the Wedding March, and the assembled guests buzzing loudly in anticipation. There was always her mother, Elizabeth thought. Maybe an appeal to her. . . . But she quickly dropped the idea. Flora Wainwright was a leaf in Horace Wainwright's hurricane. She was tiny, exquisite, but almost lighter than air. Most people hardly realized she was in the same room. Elizabeth's memories of her mother were of a woman most concerned about aspic and table garnishes and next week's high tea. She always seemed to be caught up in opening or closing one of the three family mansions, arms aflutter, giving orders to the servants, then changing them again. She could almost see her mother downstairs now, fussing feverishly over the flowers. No, there was no help there. If she wanted to stop this wedding, Elizabeth decided, she had to do it herself.

Elizabeth locked the door and then, for good measure,

pushed a chair under the handle—something she'd seen in the movies. She'd have to go through the garden. It was her only chance of escaping without being detected. She took one last look at herself in the mirror and sighed. It was a shame so few people would see her in this dress, she thought. She wished she had time to change. She hated the idea of climbing through the garden in her grandmother's dress, but there was no time for sentiment.

Elizabeth rushed to the large French window, slid the panels open, gingerly slipped out onto the terrace, and down the long steps to the garden. She hiked up her gown as she made her way between two rows of stunted rose bushes. As usual the garden was dark and gloomy. The stone walls around the Wainwright grounds combined with the gothic-style mansion to create shadows that lifted for only an hour each day. That hour had long since passed and Elizabeth could barely see where she was going.

"Goddammit," she said as a lone prickly bush caught her skirt and ripped loose several of the tiny diamonds sewn in the hemline. She pulled her dress free and frantically glanced around, checking if anyone had seen or heard her. But she was totally alone in the garden. And a clump of overgrown fern—the only plant that seemed to thrive on the Wainwright grounds—made her invisible to those few guests standing nearby in the conservatory.

A spot of sunlight shone from beyond the garden gate and Elizabeth tried to run toward it but the bejeweled dress was so heavy her long legs moved as if in slow motion. She was flushed and perspiring as she rushed through the gate and onto Sixty-fifth Street. Quickly Elizabeth spotted a crowd at the corner of Fifth Avenue. Before anyone had a chance to discover her she darted back to the safety of the garden. She cautiously peeked around the garden wall and stared at the group encamped across from the mansion. She had completely forgotten the rabble. Every social event along Fifth Avenue drew the celebrity-mad working class like piranha to naked flesh. They would camp out across the street for hours, waiting for mere glimpses of people with money. For a moment a wave of despair passed through Elizabeth. There was no way she could get out of the garden without someone

37

seeing her. And the mob on the street would be after her like hounds on a fox scent. Suddenly Elizabeth saw a cab turn the corner on Madison and make its way toward her. She raced into the street, waving wildly.

The boxy, black taxicab moved slowly up Sixty-fifth Street. The driver stared at the white-gowned woman who had just leaped out into the street, but didn't stop. He already had a passenger, and from the looks of him, the fellow was a big tipper. Top hat, evening clothes. He began to swing his cab away from the woman when his passenger tapped him on the shoulder.

"Pick the lady up," George McManus ordered. "I think she's in a hurry."

The cab stopped abruptly and Elizabeth yanked open the door. She leaned in and then pulled back as she discovered the other passenger. George smiled and lightly touched the brim of his hat. "Get in," he said engagingly. "There's room for one more."

Elizabeth hesitated, still clutching the door handle, uncertain which way to turn. Down the street a thick, heavily-accented voice bellowed, "Dere she is!" followed in rapid succession by other voices shouting, "That's Lizzie Wainwright!" "Are you sure?" "Is Bobby with her?" The crowd began pressing against the wooden police barricades, straining to get a better look.

Elizabeth made up her mind. She leaped into the cab and slammed the door shut. "Get me out of here," she commanded.

Some of the crowd had already slipped past the barricades and were running toward the cab. The driver gunned the engine and pounded on the car's horn, but more and more people began moving toward the cab, blocking any hasty exit. The cab driver moved his black Ford slowly, trying to avoid hitting anyone. To Elizabeth it seemed to be taking forever to reach the corner.

"Faster. Go faster," she said in exasperation, pounding her fist on the overstuffed back seat of the car as the cab finally neared the corner.

The cab braked suddenly and the driver turned to glare at his female passenger. "Look lady," he said gruffly, "it wasn't my idea to pick you up and I ain't gonna run nobody down just 'cause they're in your way." Without waiting for a response he turned back and began moving the car again, muttering under his breath. He resumed pummeling the car horn.

Elizabeth wanted to cry out that she didn't care how many people the cab ran over but she held her tongue, fearful that that would cause the driver to go even slower. The car leisurely turned onto Fifth Avenue and Elizabeth stared out in horror. Bobby Cooper, a glass of champagne in his hand, was standing at the gate of the mansion with his best man. They were looking at the crowd and laughing when Cooper suddenly saw Elizabeth in the cab. The smile left his thin, sophisticated face. "Hey," he shouted, poking his best man, "that's my wife. I mean, that's . . . Elizabeth wait! Where are you going?" He began running toward the taxi, the glass still in his hand.

"He's going to catch me," Elizabeth cried, looking at her fellow passenger for the first time. The man had a bemused grin on his face that would have infuriated Elizabeth at any other time. But today she was too agitated to notice.

"Can't you make him go faster?" she pleaded.

George tapped the driver on the shoulder. "There's fifty in it for you if you shake this crowd."

"You got it," the driver said, suddenly wide-eyed in the mirror. He shifted into second gear and deliberately bumped two pedestrians out of the way. The cab began to pick up speed as people frantically leaped out of its path.

George peeked out the back window. Cooper was now nearly on them, close enough so George could hear him yell to the crowd, "Stop that cab. I'll give ten dollars to anyone who stops that cab." A dozen men took up the chase, running as fast as they could.

The car was making better progress, darting in and out of traffic. But as it reached Sixty-third Street Cooper and two other young men were still in close pursuit. Elizabeth jumped as she noticed George's head alongside hers peeking out of the back window of the taxi.

"Get down," she hissed, pushing George's face into the seat. "I don't want them to think I'm running away with someone."

George obeyed. He had little choice, for Elizabeth held his head down as she continued to stare out the back window. Not that he had any complaints. Being slumped down in his seat may not have been terribly comfortable but it certainly offered a more than satisfactory view. Elizabeth's breasts lay tantalizingly before him. He took a long look before turning his attention to the girl's face. It was a gambler's habit. George made his living by reading what was in people's eyes. And Elizabeth's eyes were unusually expressive. George had expected to find fear and panic in them, but this girl was enjoying every moment of her escape. Her eyes flashed.

The cab suddenly turned right onto Fifty-seventh Street, throwing Elizabeth into George McManus's lap. She laughed, an easy laugh that was so infectious the gambler soon found himself joining in. The laugh was like the woman—free, unrestrained, and full of life.

George's arms held her briefly as she struggled to get back to her side of the cab. She was surprised at his strength. She had become accustomed to associating evening clothes with softness in men. But there was nothing weak about this man. His chiseled face and black eyes studied her and Elizabeth caught herself staring back at George. She quickly turned around to look out the back window again.

Incredibly, Cooper was right behind them, running for all he was worth. As the cab slowed to avoid a truck, he leaped to the runningboard on Elizabeth's side with one last tremendous heave.

"What . . . what in heaven's name . . . are you doing?" Cooper wheezed, fighting for breath, his fingers hooked like claws on the car's window sill. "Where do you . . . think you're going . . . with that son of a . . . bitch?" He gasped out, looking at George. "We're going to . . . get married."

"Don't wait for me, I've got other plans," Elizabeth shouted at him as he clung desperately to the door. The cab picked up speed and Cooper's hair streamed in the wind. Elizabeth made a fist and began to bang on his fingers, trying to break his grip.

Cooper shrieked, clawing at Elizabeth with one hand while she pounded on the fingers of his other hand. "Stop that, you

40

crazy bitch. You're going to kill me," he cried. "Help . . . police . . . help!"

George called to the driver to stop and the cab pulled to the
curb, over Elizabeth's protests.

"What are you doing?" she shouted at George. "I don't
want to go back with him."

"Well, that's much better," Cooper finally said when the car
came to a stop. He ran his hand through his hair and pushed
his face through the car window. "Now we can talk like civilized men and women."

A moment later he was sitting dazed on the pavement,
blood streaming from his nose, thinking that he had never
even seen George's fist coming at him. The cab pulled away
and he watched it disappear in traffic.

Blocks away, Elizabeth leaned back and relaxed, her left
shoulder lightly touching the stranger's right arm. He smiled.
It was an easy, kind smile, she thought. She leaned a bit
closer.

"You have awfully persistent friends," George said, breaking the silence.

"You should see my enemies," she replied, straightening
her gown.

George caught their reflection in the cab's rear-view mirror.
"We look like the couple on top of a wedding cake."

Elizabeth laughed softly and George tentatively placed his
right arm around her. "You do this often?" he asked.

"What?"

"Bolt out of your own wedding?"

"Every once in a while." She leaned back against his arm.
"Keeps the boys on their toes."

"Someday they're going to get even with you."

"I'm not worried." She smiled at McManus. "I'll always
find someone to rescue me."

"I bet you will," George agreed. "I just bet you will."

"We're here, mac," the cab driver interrupted. He stopped
the car in front of an inconspicuous brown building with a
green shamrock on its front window. Elizabeth recognized
the place as the notorious El Fay Club. George pulled out a
wad of bills, peeled off a fifty, and handed it to the driver.

41

"Take the lady wherever she wants to go," he said, then turned to Elizabeth. "I'd ask you in but I'm here on business."

"Oh, I'm busy anyway," she said. "I have to start thinking up some great excuses." The cab ride had ended too soon for her, but she had no intention of admitting it to him.

George opened the car door on his side. He put one foot out on the curb, then turned back.

"I almost forgot," he said, snapping his fingers. He reached out and grabbed Elizabeth, holding her close in his arms.

"It's bad luck not to kiss the bride." He pulled her closer and placed his lips on hers.

Neither pulled away until the cars backed up behind the cab began honking their horns. "Hey, c'mon, mac," the driver said. "The natives is getting restless."

George never took his eyes off Elizabeth's face. He kissed her once more, this time tenderly on the forehead. "We'll meet again," he promised, then he hopped out of the cab.

Elizabeth sat stunned, watching the stranger walk into the El Fay Club. She could still feel his lips on hers, still smell his scent.

"Where to, lady?" the driver asked, putting the car in gear. Around them, the horns honked more insistently. People on the street began to stop and stare at the cab and the beautiful woman inside. But she didn't answer. She only sat thinking with a smile on her face.

"Hey lady, if you don't tell me where ya want to go we're both gonna get arrested." The cabbie pointed to a beefy policeman strolling purposefully toward the cab. "You'd sure make a hit in the slammer wearing that get-up."

"Sands Point," she finally said, looking around in embarrassment.

As the cab sped down the street, Elizabeth suddenly realized she didn't even know the man's name. We have to go back, she thought briefly, but then relaxed in the seat. There was no hurry, she decided. They would find each other again. New York wasn't that big a town.

5

THE BIG ENGINES of the *Fatima* sputtered and coughed like an old man rising from sleep. As the cabin cruiser bumped gently against the dock Alfie Beachum sat, his feet dangling over her deck, staring at the lights of Queens across the East River. He was bored. They'd been waiting for hours and nothing had happened. Maybe tonight's run had been called off, he mused, since there wasn't much night left. With nothing else to do he had checked the boat repeatedly, running the engines to make sure that everything was perfect. She was a beautiful craft—forty-five feet long, sleek steel hull, mahogany deck and trim, and capable of thirty-five knots in a pinch with a good load. Beachum hopped down to the *Fatima's* wheelhouse and killed the engines. He stood at the controls, idly caressing the wooden wheel with his big grimy hands, then wiping the grease away with the sleeve of his thick sweater. Behind him on the dock he heard Licata muttering to himself. Beachum turned to see the other man leaning against a piling, about to light a cigarette.

"Hey, Licata, you nuts? Douse that match! There's enough gas fumes trapped in here to put half of East Harlem in Jersey!"

Tony Licata glanced at Beachum and, with disdain, threw both match and cigarette into the oily water. Where did Dwyer get punks like Beachum? Licata muttered to himself; a greasy no-necked slob with dirt under his fingernails and three days of stubble on his chin. You had to watch Beachum constantly to make sure he wasn't drinking up the boss's booze before he even got it ashore. If Beachum wasn't a crack marine mechanic . . . And where the hell was Dwyer, anyway? Under his curly black hair Licata's pretty-boy face was tense. He hated being kept in the dark, hated waiting. He worried a loose thread on his dusty jacket, pulled the brim of his newsboy cap lower. He still didn't understand why Dwyer would make a run so late at night, even if there was something special about this load. It was already after three, only a couple of hours before dawn.

A beam of light chopped through the darkness in the marine garage. It was followed by the sound of a car pulling up at the head of the dock. Licata trotted toward the car, a long Packard limousine. Before he could reach it a chauffeur in livery jumped out and pulled open the back door. A tall, thin, dignified man in a well-cut pearl-gray suit and gray derby stepped out. Even in the dim light Licata could see the big diamond stickpin in the man's tie. William Vincent Dwyer surveyed Licata and the *Fatima* in one quick glance.

"If everything is set I think we should be off, Tony," Dwyer said. He beckoned to a figure in the back seat of the limousine. A bookish little man with a prominent adam's apple and pop eyes behind rimless glasses climbed out. Licata recognized him as Otto Berman, a recent immigrant from Brooklyn. Berman was Dwyer's private handicapper and financial adviser, an innocuous little man who always had Dwyer's ear and followed him like a shadow. Berman carried a wicker basket. George McManus stepped out behind him.

Licata looked puzzled as he walked down the dock beside Dwyer, the others following them. "I knew you were coming, Big Bill, but you didn't say anything about passengers. Who's the lug in the monkey suit with Otto?"

"I pay you to run my boats, not make small talk," Dwyer spoke precisely, with authority, making clear to Licata that he was asking too many questions. Dwyer carried himself proudly as they walked down the dock, a man of refinement from his precisely trimmed dark-blond hair to his carefully manicured fingernails. He could have been a banker instead of a bootlegger, except for his eyes. They were too kind.

When all four men had boarded, Licata untied the *Fatima*'s lines. Beachum started the engines with a roar and a cloud of smoke, then smoothly eased the cruiser into the East River. Dwyer relaxed on a padded seat that ran around the rear deck behind the wheelhouse. Berman sat stiffly next to him, while George sat directly across, watching the pair closely. The boat picked up speed and slipped quickly past the lights on both shores. Licata stood next to Beachum at the controls, trying to hear anything the other men might say. Listening was one of the things Licata did best, particularly when it could be profitable.

44

"Otto, how about the wine now," Dwyer said loudly, assuming Licata was listening in. "You know," he continued, "I'm glad now that my doctor advised a little wine for my blood pressure. I never acquired much of a taste for alcohol. I've seen too many good men destroyed by the craving. But a little wine, now that I'm pushing fifty, is becoming a rare pleasure."

Up front, Licata sneered to himself. "The boss is getting to be a regular Fifth Avenue swell, ain't he," he muttered to Beachum. "A guy would never know he started out pinching apples on Eighth Street."

"Just watch out for cops and sandbars, willya?" Beachum growled.

Muttering to himself, Licata stepped out of the wheelhouse and walked to the bow. Meanwhile, Berman had extracted a bottle of wine from the basket, uncorked it, and poured a half-glass for Dwyer, all his doctor allowed at one time. Dwyer rolled the wine around the glass thoughtfully, looking over at George for the first time. "How about it, McManus? Like some wine?"

"Could we cut the small talk," George said, shaking his head. "What's next? Ladyfingers and little sandwiches with the crust cut off? Let's talk business, Dwyer."

"Patience. I don't like to rush into things, especially with people I don't know. And especially with gamblers I don't know. That's why I asked you to take this little boat ride. You can learn a lot of things about people at sea, even on a short cruise."

George ran his fingers through his hair. The cool breeze helped ease his impatience. "You know, Dwyer, I've been dancing you around like a groom with a reluctant bride on his wedding night. What is it, six hours now I've been talking and you've been listening? A man could get very tired of this. If you had a wall out here I'd bang my head against it for relief."

Despite himself, Dwyer smiled, but he still wasn't ready to say yes or no. It had started at. the El Fay and continued through two meals and stops at three more speaks. George would make a proposal, Dwyer would consult with Otto Berman in whispers, then come back with more questions. Their only real point of agreement was that they were both fond of

45

corned beef and cabbage. Both men realized they were playing a sort of stylized game, matching wits. But Dwyer held
the aces here. He hadn't become the biggest rumrunner in
America by making snap judgements, even though he gam-
bled that way.

"I don't get it," George began again. "I'm offering you a
million-dollar deal and you treat me like I had the plague.
You got something against money?"

Dwyer gave him a queer look, wondering how much
George really knew about him. He glanced over at Otto Berman, who sat inscrutable behind his thick glasses.

"It's true, I could use some money. Luck hasn't been shining my way much lately. The way Otto here has been picking
them for me, I'm down almost a million on the nags in the last
two months." For a moment Dwyer lost his usual calm expression and looked uncharacteristically sour.

A tug huffing upriver bounced the *Fatima* lightly in its
wake. George saw Berman grab the railing in mild panic, then
hang his head as the waves of water subsided but the waves
of remorse grew. He pulled his straw skimmer down on his
head.

"That's one of the things I like about Otto," Dwyer said
after a few minutes of silence. "Even when he throws a monkey wrench into the works he doesn't make any excuses."

"It's just a bad streak, boss," Berman blurted out. "We had
them before. I'll getcha some more winners."

"You want to bet?" Dwyer shot back, and Berman smiled.
It was Dwyer's little joke.

But George had found out a great deal about Dwyer in the
four days since going to Tammany Hall, and he knew the
losses went a lot deeper than the bundle lost on the ponies.
Dwyer's horse farm in New Jersey wasn't burning up the racing world either. The horses he bred looked great running
wild in the meadows at the farm. But at the track they ran like
they were taking a rest cure. And there was the quarter-mil-
lion Dwyer had sunk into Earl Carroll's Broadway extravaganza. The critics said it could be smelled in Philly. People
said Dwyer had laughed it off; he laughed everything off. Let
that skunk Rothstein take a hundred grand off him and Dwyer,
all smiles, was the first to pop for a round of drinks afterward.

Dollar bills were just markers, Dwyer liked to tell his friends, to measure whether you were winning or losing. Only the game counted, the next bet, taking a chance.

The *Fatima* rumbled along steadily, throbbing beneath their feet like some living thing. Dwyer finished the wine with a gulp and tossed the glass into the basket. "Of course, Otto's right, McManus. My losing streak has to end soon. Did you know that Nate Raymond lost fifty-eight straight games at blackjack in Miami last year? On the way out of the hotel with eleven bucks in his pocket he stumbled onto a crap game and made thirteen passes in a row. That's the way luck is. You can never see it coming—or going."

"The hell with luck. Let's get down to cases here, Dwyer. I know you're broke, you know you're broke, everybody over the age of five in New York City knows you're broke, because you owe everybody. And I know what you're doing out here in this canoe tonight."

Otto's jaw dropped with an audible click. He forgot to close his mouth as he stared at McManus. Dwyer put a finger under Otto's jaw and pushed his mouth shut, then turned to George. "Go on, I'm listening."

"The word is you've got a load of first-class hooch sitting on some tub, and you're so hard up you're going to get it yourself because you can't afford any screw-ups. That about cover it?"

"Where do you steal your information?" Dwyer tried to look nonplussed.

"I notice you're not denying it. So, how about it, do you want to talk business? You've got nothing to lose, Dwyer. Goddammit, I tell you, this game is sure-fire with the right protection." George viciously banged the railing of the boat for emphasis and Otto jumped.

"Maybe that's what bothers me, McManus," Dwyer said after a moment's thought. "You know as well as I do, there are no sure things."

George shook his head in exasperation. "I've made my pitch, Dwyer. Talk it over with your boy here. I'll go up front and leave you alone."

George carefully made his way to the wheelhouse as the *Fatima* raced through the Narrows and toward the Atlantic Ocean. He stood between Licata and Beachum, looking at the

47

black water, thinking it was so dark he couldn't tell where the sea ended and the sky began.

Licata pulled a map and a sheet of paper from his coat pocket. Turning on a tiny light he studied the figures on the paper and the map, then passed them over to Beachum. Beachum checked their position, squinting to see Ambrose lightship nearby and the lights of Brooklyn behind them. He turned the boat due east.

"I make it about eleven miles," he said quietly. "About twenty minutes."

George braced himself as Beachum hit the throttle and the boat leaped toward Rum Row, the haven for bootleggers just over the U.S. three-mile coastal limit. A sense of unreality engulfed George as the boat plunged deeper into the darkness, the twin motors wailing. He looked up and saw hundreds of stars he had never seen before, stars that were always blotted out by the hard city lights. There was no moon. Bootleggers liked to say that the rumrunning business was a cinch. The only thing to remember was when the moon was out they were in, and when the moon was in they were out.

Snatches of music drifted over the water from the open-air restaurants of Coney Island. A mournful trumpet wailed the "Limehouse Blues." Beachum hummed quietly, under his breath, slouching over the wheel. Suddenly George felt both men tense, watching the lights of a boat lumbering in the distance.

"Wrong shape," Beachum finally said quietly. "Just a fishing boat."

"What is it?" George whispered, not sure why he was whispering.

"This is where we earn our dough," Licata cut in, looking out at the sea intently. "The Coast Guard is all over these waters."

"But they can't touch us," McManus said. "We're not carrying any booze."

"We're heading for a booze gold mine, buddy. The Feds would love to follow us to the Two-sixty-six." Licata gave him the kind of look people usually reserve for idiots. George started to say something, then decided against it. But suddenly it seemed as if there were hundreds of boats and ships

48

in the water, lights blinking and winking everywhere. And every distant noise sounded like a patrol boat's rumble. For long minutes no one spoke. Once George looked back at Dwyer, but he was now watching the sea, too.

Beachum finally broke the silence. "There she is, all right." He steered for a small bump in the distance that looked even darker than the surrounding water. Four times a month Dwyer's crews met the 266 like this. On each trip the converted submarine chaser delivered up to 4,000 cases of liquor from the island of St. Kitts in the Caribbean, where Dwyer's agents paid about $10 a case. In New York's 20,000 speakeasies a case brought $75 or more. Dwyer's liquor, known for its high quality, was much in demand.

The *Fatima* glided to the larger ship's side with a gentle bump. The 266 remained silent, as though abandoned, not a light showing. Without warning a searchlight clicked on somewhere on the ship's bridge and swept the *Fatima*. The light stopped on Licata.

"Ahoy, supercargo, good to see you again," came a gruff voice from the bridge, amplified by a megaphone. In a moment lights blazed all over the ship and crewmen appeared at the railing, peering down. A narrow metal stairway was lowered and Licata, Berman, Dwyer, and McManus clambered up.

The moment Dwyer set foot on the deck an immense pair of arms engulfed him and swept him off his feet.

"Big Bill, darlin', what a joy to see you agin," roared a burly giant of a man in a blue uniform. Francis Augustus O'Brien crushed Dwyer to his chest and planted a wet kiss in the middle of his forehead. A wide smile appeared through his full beard.

"Frankie, you're killing me, put me down," Dwyer laughed, struggling feebly. O'Brien held Dwyer at arm's length and looked him up and down.

"Bless me, but you're looking elegant for an old bootlegger. Why that suit alone must of cost three cases of your best. But tell me, my friend, what are ya doin' ridin' around in little boats in the midst of the night with the coppers patrolling like ticks lookin' for an old hound?"

"You know you old seadogs have to be watched closely or

49

you'll revert to piracy," Dwyer said with a smile, taking O'Brien's arm. They walked toward the stern and the cargo hatch where Licata already was directing the unloading. A dozen sailors bustled about with winches, nets, and cables.

"But I really came to watch over the special cargo you're carrying," Dwyer said, glancing back at George.

O'Brien stroked his luxurious beard, a mark that he was perplexed. "What's in those cases, anyway, Billy? In St. K. your man Antoine said to treat them gently as sleeping babes."

Dwyer watched as the first of the cases—marked "English bone china"—were carefully lifted from the hold in a net and lowered to the *Fatima*.

"It's wine, Frankie, rare fine wine for some very fine people who want more than hooch and will pay for it." Dwyer watched the men straining to clear more cases over the rail of the ship. "One bottle of that wine is worth a case of the other stuff you're carrying. I wish I could tell you how many people I had to pay off to get that stuff out of some of the best cellars in France. But it'll be worth it."

"Careful with that or I'll have your neck," Licata bellowed as a net caught on a rail and several cases nearly tumbled into the sea. Dwyer walked over and asked Licata whether it was safe to take the whole 350 cases at once.

Licata wordlessly pointed to the horizon, where the first pinkish-blue hue of morning was visible. Dwyer nodded and stood back.

The *Fatima* was soon loaded and ready to leave. Dwyer slipped a bulky envelope to O'Brien, then climbed off the 266. McManus and Berman followed. The *Fatima* was now heavily burdened with lashed-down crates covered by tarpaulins. Beachum had the engines going already and quickly pulled away from the larger ship. The motors growled deeply now as the *Fatima* ran low in the water. Behind them the lights of the 266 abruptly went off and she was soon lost in the gloom. The air was cooler now, with occasional wisps of mist. No one spoke, but George saw Dwyer and Licata glance nervously at the graying horizon. He realized that they were in trouble, that the higher the sun rose the more vulnerable they were to Coast Guard detection. Perfect, George thought. In the distance nearer shore a flock of gulls riding the dark waves slowly wakened, stretched, and dug at their feathers. A few rose awkwardly into the air.

After long, tense minutes, Dwyer stirred. "How long before we're in the harbor?"

"About fifteen minutes," Licata said, half turning to look at Dwyer. "Should be before the sun gets too much over the horizon, boss."

"Damn." Beachum was squinting into the distance. He pointed to a set of red and green lights moving quickly far to the west. "That doesn't look good." All five men stared through the gloom, watched the lights turn and make for the *Fatima*.

"It's the Coast Guard, all right," Beachum said. "I don't know if we can outrun her with this load, Mr. Dwyer. Should I head her out to sea?" His hands gripped the wheel tightly but his voice was calm—he'd been the quarry before.

Dwyer looked at the men around him. Even in the dimness Dwyer could see that Berman was pale, his adam's apple bobbing like a canoe in a hurricane, eyes glued on the lights now rushing toward them. He looked at George confidently, unruffled.

"We gotta dump the booze, boss, or they'll run us down sure," Licata said, pounding one fist into the other in anger. "A whole night's work for nothing."

"No, we won't throw the wine away," Dwyer said. He took a deep breath. "But I don't want to take a chance on them firing at us if we try to run. They might damage the bottles."

"And us, too," Berman said quietly.

"And us," Dwyer agreed. "So head for them, slowly, Mr. Beachum."

Licata opened his mouth to argue, but Beachum grabbed his arm and hissed a warning. Beachum spun the wheel, aiming for the searchlight that now reached for them from the cutter. Berman only muttered under his breath as the gap between the boats narrowed quickly. George could make out several sailors standing by a deck gun, cranking it in the direction of the *Fatima*. The American flag snapped crisply on the cutter's mast as it moved to cross the smaller boat's bow.

"Kill the engines now, Mr. Beachum," Dwyer said calmly.

The *Fatima* slowed and finally stopped, wallowing in the shallow Atlantic troughs. The cutter slowly approached, a beefy blond officer leaning over the rail directing the searchlight. Other sailors with rifles lined the rail. The light played on the tarpaulins and then came to rest on Dwyer from a hundred feet away. Then George saw Dwyer's face turn white as he looked at the officer. Dwyer sagged, then sat heavily on a crate of wine, looking utterly dejected. The others stared at Dwyer as if he were their last hope, but he turned to George hopelessly.

"It seems we have no deal after all, McManus. I'm going to lose the load. I own most of these Coast Guard skippers out of New York." He threw up his hands helplessly. "But I've never seen that one before. Someone's thrown me a curve."

But George grabbed Beachum and shook him to get his attention. "You got any fishing gear on board?" Beachum looked at George as if he were mad, but finally nodded.

"Then get it up on the deck and scatter it around," McManus said, giving Beachum a shove. "Quickly."

The others stared at him with uncomprehending eyes. Otto Berman was whimpering quietly at the thought of going to prison. Beachum pulled three rods, a net, and a metal box full of lures from a tool box and threw the rods around. He opened the tackle box and scattered some lures on deck, then looked up in confusion. The Coast Guard cutter loomed over them now like a white wall. Everyone froze as the blond officer played the light around the *Fatima* until it came to rest on McManus. For a brief moment it seemed to Dwyer that a flicker of recognition came over the officer's face. Then George stood, doffed his hat, and performed an elaborate bow. The searchlight clicked off.

"Nothing here, coxswain," the officer called above them. "Just a party boat with some big fish." The cutter's engine began to throb and it slowly turned away.

Beachum and Licata stared at the cutter's wake for a few moments, then began pounding George on the back with glee. Otto Berman lurched to the boat's side and vomited into the sea. Dwyer never took his eyes off George.

"You set that up," he finally blurted out. "But how did you know where?"

"Big Bill Dwyer doesn't have any secrets," George replied, sitting next to him. "I just couldn't take a chance on anything happening to your booze. Not when I needed your money. So I invested my last few dollars in insurance."

"I should arrange to have you visit the bottom of the sea for that trick," Dwyer said without conviction.

"And bump off your business partner?"

"You that sure of yourself, McManus?" It wasn't really a question.

"Let's just say I'm learning how things are done. You know, if I'd had another five hundred that Coast Guard lieutenant would have delivered the booze for you."

George laughed but Dwyer didn't. "Well, let's get this boat moving again," said McManus. "It wouldn't be too wise to cruise up the East River in broad daylight with enough booze to float the Bronx. People might talk." He turned and went into the wheelhouse.

Otto Berman sat down, wiping his pale face with a handkerchief.

"You heard?" Dwyer said.

"I heard. That's one smart cookie. He's takin' over already."

Dwyer took the bottle of wine out of the wicker basket and poured a glassful for the little man. Berman downed it in one gulp and some of the color came back into his face. The boat's motors coughed, caught and the *Fatima* was on its way again.

"I've made up my mind, Otto. I'm going to give McManus the money, throw in with him," Dwyer finally said. He watched as the sun tinted the stray clouds in the east blood red. The sea smelled sweet, the air fresh.

"After all, if I'm going to gamble, I might as well own the house," he went on, sounding as if he was trying to convince himself.

"I think he's okay," Otto added, nodding his approval. "McManus is hungry. I don't think he'll steer you wrong."

"You want to bet?" Dwyer said and Berman smiled. But he didn't see the look on Dwyer's face.

6

THE SIGN above the corset shop on Forty-sixth Street read "PARADISE REHEARSAL CLUB—BALLET, TAP, AND BALLROOM DANCE LESSONS FOR REFINED YOUNG LADIES—ONE FLIGHT UP." George McManus looked up at the sign and checked the ad he had torn out of that morning's *American*. This, as the man said, is the place. He yawned to himself. It was four in the afternoon but he had just gotten up and he could almost feel the bags sagging under his eyes. It had been a long night. The hours of twisting Dwyer's arm, the boat. That had almost drained him, and scared him badly. But it had worked, dammit! It had worked. And when they went to Harlem later there wasn't enough booze to quench the fire of elation in him. Though that high yellow had tried. He couldn't even remember who had put him to bed.

Looking at his reflection in the corset shop window George thought he looked pretty swell, though, for someone whose head had been several sizes larger only a few hours before. He liked the sensual feel of the well-cut blue suit he wore, the snow-white silk shirt, and the fedora at just the right angle over one eye. Jaunty. There had been no time for a bath so he had slapped on extra bay rum water and smelled, he thought, very proper indeed.

George climbed the stairs quickly, carefully avoiding brushing the dingy gray walls. At the landing he pulled open the door and walked into a large gymlike room. The blond wood of the floor and the white walls seemed to shimmer in the strong afternoon sunlight pouring through the big windows along the far wall. Across the room, a dozen little girls in garish make-up and flouncy white costumes tap-danced in a ragged line in front of a pretty but tired-looking red-haired young woman in shorts. "Tea for Two" rasped out of an ancient Victrola on a chair. A telephone hung on the wall to his right, phone numbers, scribbled messages, and smudges covering the wall around it. Beyond the telephone a number of women sat in straight-backed chairs, nudging each other and clucking but never taking their eyes off the children.

A dark-haired, beefy woman in a tight blue dress got off her chair and walked quickly toward the children, calling, "Miss Flynn, yoo-hoo, Miss Flynn! Can't you please put Emma on the end of the line? That poor child next to her is confusing my Emma terribly."

"Ah, siddown, Bessie, how many times are you going to butt into this lesson?" wheezed a rail-thin woman in pink, rolling her eyes in a gesture of exasperation. "Can you believe it? 'My Emma this, my Emma that.' She's a nut case!"

The woman in blue looked at the skinny woman for a moment and sniffed, then went back to red-haired Miss Flynn. After a few words the heavy woman grabbed one child's hand and dragged her to the end of the chorus line. The children stood open-mouthed, scuffing their tap shoes on the floor. Miss Flynn put her hands on her hips, then grabbed the little girl's hand and put her back in the center of the line.

"Who's paying for this lesson, anyway?" blue-dress shouted over the tinny music.

"I am the teacher here, Mrs. Birdstone. You pay me. I teach. You sit over there and watch. Please?" Miss Flynn's hands were back on her hips. She spoke with amazing self-control, George thought, considering the color was rising in her face like lava in a volcano. She took the older woman's arm and half pushed her toward the chairs as the children giggled.

Miss Flynn turned back to the students just as "Tea for Two" was running down into a prolonged groan. She walked to the Victrola and gave it a few vicious cranks. Then she pulled little Emma out of the center of the line and led her to one end. Miss Flynn looked resignedly over her shoulder to see the triumphant smile on Mrs. Birdstone's face.

"All right, girls," said Miss Flynn. "From the top now— one, two. . . ." Ruffles bounced, matchstick legs blurred, arms pumped, and metal taps scraped the floor in a rough rhythm as the tiny chorus line puffed from one side of the big room to the other like marionettes with a madman pulling the strings. On the end of the line little Emma Birdstone danced desperately, always a step behind, trying to watch the feet of the child next to her, her chubby little face sweating bullets.

"Oh, Miss Flynn," came the familiar grating voice behind her. Mrs. Birdstone bobbed out of her chair, nibbling on her lower lip in frustration, her hands waving a halt to the proceedings. "You don't suppose her shoes are too tight?" she said loudly over the music. "Something is definitely wrong, and as Emma's teacher I demand that you do something. Why, you're ruining that child."

"Yes, Mrs. Birdstone, something is very definitely wrong," replied Miss Flynn. It was Vesuvius time, George decided, leaning against the wall and watching with interest. The red-head turned back to the children and motioned for Emma to come over. She took the child's hand and put it in her mother's. Then she leaned over and said, very distinctly, through clenched teeth: "Dear, will you please get your mother out of here, before I kill the bitch."

The little girl giggled and led her mother off as Mrs. Birdstone, her face like stone, swelled in indignation until George was sure she would explode out of her dress. The woman looked down and saw her daughter gently wave to Miss Flynn. She half dragged the child through the door as she swept past George, almost knocking him over.

Except for the rasping of the Victrola there wasn't a sound in the room. Then the thin woman in pink rushed out of her chair and took Marie's hand.

"Marie, you were marvelous." She laughed. "I've been wanting to tell that woman off for weeks myself." The other women clapped and nodded agreement to each other as their daughters flopped to the floor, vacant-eyed.

Miss Flynn managed a thin smile. She stalked to the record player across the room, cranked it again, and started "Tea for Two" over. She told the children to keep practicing their routine.

"Remember, it's only a week to go before the recital," she warned as they got back in line.

Then she turned quickly and walked into a small office with frosted glass windows, closing the door behind her. George followed. When he looked in the door she was pouring liquor into a glass from a dark bottle.

"Excuse me," he said, "but I don't think you noticed me in all the commotion. If your recital is as exciting as the rehearsal, I wish you'd send me a ticket." George smiled but she didn't.

She asked him to sit down and offered him some of what was in the bottle. As she got another glass he looked her over appreciatively. She had fine legs, nice curves, a rather long and angular but pleasing face with a large mouth and blue eyes. Her face was still tinged red, but only a little of it was make-up. He liked her luxurious shoulder-length hair, un-usual in the rage for bobbed hair. He was pleasantly aware that she inspected him just as frankly as she sat behind the desk. Coquettes bored George. Outside the office the chil-dren's shoes tapped rhythmically as the crooner sang: *"Pic-ture you, upon my knee . . ."*

"You don't look like the type who needs dancing lessons, Mr. uh . . ."

"McManus. George McManus. And I'm very light on my feet already."

"Pleased to meet you. So what can I do for you?"

"I'm answering your ad in the *American,* to sublet rooms," he said, taking his fedora off and laying it on the desk. "I and some associates have sort of a fraternal organization, and we're looking for a regular place to meet. A clubhouse. You understand?"

"Of course. I was so flustered by Mrs. Birdstone that I forgot about the advertisement. That old battleax." She flushed red again. "Come on, I'll show you the rooms."

They walked back out on the dance floor, where Miss Flynn called more instructions to the children: "No, Carla, heel, crossover, heel-toe. Now keep trying that. That's it, Margie, very good." But she secretly grimaced to George.

Then she led him to a short stairway. The women in their chairs nudged each other as they followed them with their eyes. George could smell Miss Flynn's perfume as they climbed the stairs. Perfume and sweat. Upstairs they walked down a narrow corridor with small cubicles, dark now, on either side. At the end of the corridor she opened a large door and clicked on a light. The room was about eighty feet long, maybe sixty wide, with high ceilings and no windows. At the other end was another door. On the dusty blue-painted walls were posters advertising old Broadway shows and vaudeville acts. The floor was bare wood, the only furniture a few old wooden chairs.

"It's not exactly the Taj Mahal right now," she said, looking around, "but it could be fixed up nice." She walked across the room to the other door and clicked on the light in the next room. It was about a quarter the size of the first, with windows at the rear. Through the grimy glass George could see a fire escape.

"Planning a quick getaway?" she said, following his gaze.

"No, no, nothing like that. You know, I think this place will do fine. The only thing, we wouldn't want to interrupt your dance classes. What time do you close at night?"

"The last class ends by eight every night." There was a note of suspicion in her voice. "Let's be frank, Mr. McManus," she said as she clicked off the light in the smaller room. "Are you sure what you are planning is kosher?"

"What does a pretty red-haired Irish lass know about kosher?" laughed George, touching the small gold crucifix she wore on a chain around her neck.

She held the crucifix in her fist. It was silent downstairs for a moment as "Tea for Two" ran its course. Then the song and the tapping began again, drifting up the stairs, down the corridor, and through the door like a distant complaint. She walked around the room looking at the old show posters, tracing a mustache in the dust covering John Barrymore's face on an old *Hamlet* poster.

"I used to be a hoofer, a Ziegfeld girl in fact. My best friend was this Jewish girl. It's funny, but she gave me this cross."

"You sure have the legs to be with Ziegfeld," George said appreciatively. He couldn't take his eyes off her. "Why did you quit?"

"Blame Horace Greeley," she said with a smile, walking back to him. "You know, he said 'Go West.' So my friend and me bought this place a couple blocks west of the Follies. We were doing pretty good, too, until she got married last year. She had the connections, I guess. Since she left there haven't been many acts or shows rehearsing here. I'm down to giving the little darlings tap lessons." She danced a few steps in front of George and then bowed low.

He walked up to her, took one hand, and slipped an arm around her waist. "Maybe I could use some dance lessons, after all, Miss Flynn." He pulled her close and they began to move around the floor. At first she was stiff, surprised, then relaxed against him, moving easily to the music. *"We could raise a famileee—a boy for you, a girl for me. Can't you see . . ."* The words floated through the room as he swirled her around. She was very close to George now and he could smell her fragrant hair, study her pink ear. The music stopped.

"Thank you, Mr. McManus." She pulled away quickly, without looking at him. Her face was flushed again. "But I don't think you'll need very many lessons. You pick up things very quickly." She said it with a smile and this time she looked at him. "I really have to get back to my students, though. Maybe we'd better discuss terms?"

George looked at her wistfully and finally sighed. "Okay, how about a thousand dollars a month for the rooms, with six months in advance? But no questions." She stared at him, then nodded quickly. He pulled a wad of bills from his pocket, counted out the money, and laid the cash in the palm of her hand. When she had it all she closed her fist tightly. They both knew it was ten times what the rooms were worth.

"You're not asking so many questions now, Miss Flynn," he said lightly. "Money got your tongue?"

"You can call me Marie. And what's wrong with money, Mr. McManus?"

"You can call me George, and the answer is nothing."

She looked up into his eyes for a moment.

"Yes, well, I'd better get back downstairs," she finally said, "before I lose the rest of my pupils."

She flicked off the light and they walked down without speaking. The children had stopped dancing and were sitting on the floor again. Their mothers didn't look happy. Miss Flynn gave them a big smile and walked to her office. She came out and handed George a key.

"To the door," she explained, walking with him to the landing. For a moment they faced each other. George bent to kiss her. At the last second she turned her face and his lips brushed her warm cheek. But she pressed against him briefly and he could feel her bare leg touch his leg.

"I'm through about eight," she whispered.

George smiled, pulled his fedora lower over his eyes, and pushed through the door, followed by a burst of little-girl giggles.

The sun hovered low above the Hudson River as George reached the sidewalk and strolled west toward Broadway, feeling good. As if released by the lengthening afternoon shadows, thousands of people rushed from shops and buildings. Intent upon a seat on the subway, home, and their little pleasures, they flowed around him like white water around a boulder in rapids. As the day people left, to the cries of newsboys hawking the late afternoon editions, the nocturnal denizens of the area known as the Tenderloin appeared, slowly resuming possession of the streets. Like McManus, they were in no hurry—the high rollers, the well-to-do and culture lovers looking for a laugh or a drink in the theaters, moviehouses, and speakeasies of the Times Square area. And the whores, pimps, poor, and greedy-eyed who hated those with money but could not survive without them. Prohibition was the law of the land, but pleasure was the law of the jaded streets of the Tenderloin. And bootleg liquor and illegal gambling fueled those pleasures as electricity fueled the blizzard of lights that began to glow on marquees, in shops and restaurants, and in a thousand smoky back rooms around Times Square.

He walked past the Republic Theater where the marquee announced that *Abie's Irish Rose* was going into its third boffo season. At the corner of Forty-eighth and Broadway he stopped in front of a newsstand festooned with magazines. Behind the counter piled high with newspapers sat an immense hunched figure. Huge rolls of fat strained the material of his tee-shirt and almost covered the change apron around his enormous waist. In one stubby hand the man held a juicy tomato, in the other a raw onion. He alternately took a bite out of each and the tomato seeds and juice ran down his face.

"How'd the fifth come out at Empire City, Chins?" George asked, thumbing through a *Saturday Evening Post*.

"Bou Chaib aced Cloudland by a tit-length," replied the fat man, setting in motion several of the protuberances for which he was named. "Too bad. I wish to tell ya I took a bath on the pig myself. Hey, but listen, I got a tip from Frenchy Charley on this nag in the sixth tomorrow, King Solomon's Seal. Runs like the wind, Frenchy Charley swears. Want I should put down a hundred for ya?"

George shook his head. "Why don't I just take poison now and save myself the trouble of betting, you big slob. Everybody knows Frenchy Charley's information is about as good as next year's weather report. And wipe your puss, willya!" George grimaced in disgust as the fat man swiped at his mouth with the back of his hand.

"Anyway, never mind that stuff now," George said. He looked around to be sure no one was close by. "Listen, I want you to put out the word. I need some of your friends with small brains and small mouths, about a dozen of them, for some business for a few nights. You tell them to be there tomorrow night at nine." George scribbled the address of the Paradise Rehearsal Club on the corner of a magazine, tore it off, and handed it to Chins. "Can you handle that?"

The other man's eyes became thin slits as he leaned conspiratorially close, breathing heavily into McManus's face. "Sure, Georgie, everybody knows you're all right. I'll get the boys there and even come myself. But what's the scam? You can tell me. Chins knows how to keep his mouth shut."

"If you could keep your mouth shut you wouldn't look like a small mountain." George jerked away to avoid the other man's foul breath. "And here's two bits—buy some mints or mouthwash. You keep eating those onions and you'll set this shack on fire." He flipped Chins a coin and walked away. Behind him the newsstand quivered as the fat man looked at the coin and guffawed.

George continued up Broadway, looking disinterestedly into the bright shop windows, hunting for someone. The traffic roared past, horns honking at the crowd overflowing the curbs into the streets. Every few yards music seemed to come out of a different bar or theater, melding into a whirlpool of noise with the shouts of hucksters, the laughter of strollers, cop's whistles and squealing tires.

Three blocks up Broadway George spotted Izzy the Stub admiring a sport coat in the dusty window of Nussbaum's Clothiers to Gentlemen. Nussbaum's wasn't the classiest joint on the street, but his clothes had a certain loud panache that people like Izzy the Stub found irresistible. There wasn't an outfit in his shop that wouldn't drive a chameleon to suicide.

Rumor had it that Ty Cobb, who was very fond of shocking-pink socks, had once entered Nussbaum's and fingered a pair of argyles, although he didn't buy them. Nussbaum actually had an autographed picture of the hard-hitting Georgia Peach pasted on the cash register, but certain disbelievers said the signature looked suspiciously like Nussbaum's own. Nussbaum had recently unveiled his fall line and Izzy the Stub now stood admiring a garish double-breasted plaid number with shoulders like Himalayan foothills. George noticed that Izzy the Stub was still wearing the tie with the Hawaiian dancing girl that had figured so prominently in George's dreams the other night. Izzy was a good-looking, stocky man of around thirty with large, knowing eyes that didn't miss much. He sported a thin mustache that he hoped made him look like a dead ringer for John Gilbert. It didn't.

Izzy made a living scalping tickets to theaters and sporting events all over town. That's how he got his nickname. But he had been Izzy the Stub so long that no one could even remember his real name. While he could dig up tickets for practically anything, Izzy's real love was the opera, since he felt he was dealing with a high-class crowd. For a large-enough fee, George had heard, Izzy the Stub could get you seats right in the orchestra pit. As for himself, Izzy never missed a performance of *Carmen* at the Metropolitan. He felt it was absolutely the best opera for looking up singers' dresses.

Nussbaum, a balding gnome of a man with spectacles always about to hurl off his nose, was fingering the lines of the sport coat and making little noises barely audible to Izzy on the other side of the store window. As George watched from a few feet away they dickered silently through the glass. Nussbaum held up various numbers of fingers and Izzy the Stub cocked his head to study the offending garment again, finally shrugging his shoulders and shaking his head no. Nussbaum crinkled his nose, puffed out his cheeks, rolled his eyes, tore at his hair, grinned, frowned, wrung his hands in elaborate pantomime. Only let Izzy the Stub take this atrocity off my hands, the man prayed.

"You'd better buy the godforsaken thing before the old man has a heart attack," George spoke up. Izzy turned to look at him with a smile.

"It's just a game we play, Georgie. I jew him down, he tries to con me it's a Paris original." He looked back at the coat. "It ain't no fun if you don't play the game."

Behind the glass, Nussbaum was now giving George a dirty look, afraid that he'd distract Izzy from buying the coat. "I'm looking for Broderick," George finally said. "The mick been around?"

Izzy shrugged. "We're not exactly brothers, I should know where that son of a bitch is. What do you think, Georgie? This *shmatte* worth seventeen dollars?"

Now both men studied the coat gravely, and a gleam of hope came into Nussbaum's eyes. He started draping ties over the coat's shoulders, straightened the seams, shoved a yellow handkerchief into the breast pocket and fluffed it.

"I hear you got some hot stuff cooking," Izzy the Stub said after a minute. "A deal with Big Bill Dwyer, yet. A casino. Maybe I should try the coat on, what do you say?"

"What fool told you that?" George was surprised.

"Not such a fool, Georgie. One of Dwyer's boys. Say, maybe you could throw a little business my way? After all, it was Izzy who told you about those rookie cops, if you will please to remember."

"Maybe I could use you." George looked from the coat to the other man. "Tell me something. How'd you hear that the mayor was going to transfer all the veteran cops out of the Tenderloin anyway? I never even got a whiff."

Izzy chuckled. "Did you ever meet the mayor's brother? He is the biggest shmo east of Jersey but he loves Babe Ruth more than his own wife. In fact, a lot more than his own wife. I get him six beauties in a box behind first base so he could take out his five kiddies—each one uglier than the next, by the way. In return, he gives me everything but his shoe size."

Nussbaum tapped on the glass, pulling their eyes back to the coat, then froze in mid-grimace looking past George's shoulder. The old man trotted to the back of the shop and busied himself with shirts.

63

Puzzled, George turned around to find a New York Police Department badge, Number 869, floating in front of his eyes. Attached to the badge was a blue uniform containing a hefty six-footer with blue eyes, veined red nose, and skin that had been plowed by pox many years before. Detective Sergeant John Broderick laid his nightstick next to George's left ear and looked down into his eyes. The nightstick tickled and George tried not to squirm.

"I'm walking out of a candy store on Forty-sixth a leetle bit ago when who should I see but me good friend and countryman George McManus coming out of a dancing school." Broderick's words rumbled out from deep in his vast chest like heavy trucks leaving a tunnel. "Sure now, I know that the only dancing this fine figure of a fellow does is when he is doling out aces and spades. So I decide to follow for a bit."

Over Broderick's shoulder George could see the evening crowds hurrying by, pretending not to notice the cop pressing him against the window glass. Izzy the Stub was slowly edging away, too. So far George hadn't had a chance to speak, couldn't speak with Broderick leaning so heavily on him. The cop had red hairs sticking out of his nose, George noticed.

"Johnny," he managed to groan, "just the man . . . I wanted to see."

"Hush now, Mr. McManus, the law is talking here," Broderick said, pressing his bulk even closer. "Have ya no respect for the law?"

"Sure, sure, but listen—"

"Then what should I see but this same dolled-up mick jawing very suspiciously with the fat man selling newspapers—and this little sheeny Izzy the Stub. A very bad element they are, too. So why don't you tell me what mischief you be cooking up now? And be quick about it or I'll run you in for loitering. And people sometimes have nasty accidents in jailhouses."

Broderick backed off slightly and George caught his breath, thinking how much he hated cops, Broderick in particular. Broderick was different, however. He hated everyone, including other cops. The big Irishman was as tough and corrupt as they came, owning a piece of the action in half the speaks and poker games in the Tenderloin. It was Broderick's fists that had made the Tenderloin tender, people sometimes joked on Broadway—when Broderick wasn't around. George wasn't afraid of scuffling with any man, but Broderick, his brutality backed by the law, was almost beyond touch. He knew where the skeletons were buried, having buried many of them himself.

"Johnny, I have something to offer you that will delight your old bull heart," George said lightly, carefully pushing Broderick back and straightening his suit. "But let's go somewhere a little more private, huh? And I'll tell you all about how I want you to arrest me."

Broderick looked puzzled, but interested, as he twirled his nightstick. George took his arm and led him away. Nussbaum saw them leave and trotted to the window. He tapped to try to get Izzy the Stub's attention.

But Izzy didn't hear him as he watched the other two men walk down the street, their heads close together.

7

THE FIRST RAID on the Paradise Rehearsal Club was a calm affair. It was about ten o'clock on a Wednesday night that Sergeant John Broderick led the first contingent of shiny-faced young cops up the dingy stairway, across the dance floor, and up the steps to the big wooden door. Outside, in front of the corset shop, a half-dozen young cops stood guard, as did an equal number in the alley. They were a handsome lot, these young officers. Every badge carefully polished, every shoe shined, every pair of pants creased. Even their guns shone in their spanking new holsters. Three weeks out of the police academy, these men were pleased and proud to be taking part in such an exciting venture, instead of walking a beat in Brooklyn or the Bronx with the rest of the rookies.

The two lookouts at the door on the landing were surprisingly docile as the cops swooped in. In fact, the lookouts were asleep, propped against the wall. When told they were under arrest the two just yawned. Rookie Patrolman Melvin Farkas was surprised at how smoothly the operation was going, and said so in whispers to his friend, rookie Patrolman Vito Marconi. Both men nervously fingered the safety catches on their chunky black Thompson submachine guns. But they were reassured by the stern visage of Detective Sergeant Broderick. All the rookies admired Broderick greatly, both for his reputation as a tough cop and the rumors that he had amassed savings of over $100,000 in his ten years on the force. On a salary that never exceeded $3,200 a year.

"All right, make matchsticks out of it," Broderick ordered gruffly, pointing to the big door at the end of the corridor. Two young cops carrying axes quickly went to work, sinking the blades deep into the wood and tearing out great jagged splinters. In a few moments the lock was torn away and half a dozen officers barreled into the room, guns at the ready. Broderick followed at a saunter.

"Against the wall, ya bums!" he bellowed. "Move!"

George McManus nodded to the men at his and the three other tables. They all rose and walked to the wall without a word, most of them looking somewhat puzzled. One man lagged behind the others because he had trouble getting out of his chair—an incredibly fat man in a tee-shirt covered with red-orange stains. As they were being frisked Broderick came up behind George.

"Ya did a right nice job with this place," he whispered, patting George's pockets. "Cleaned it up real pretty."

"It's in my inner coat pocket," George answered in a whisper. "And did you have to wreck the door? It wasn't locked."

Broderick found the envelope, slipping it carefully out of George's pocket and into the blouse of his uniform.

"I always break down the door. It's a matter of pride," Broderick whispered back. Then he whacked George across the shoulders with the barrel of his shotgun, bellowing, "I'll take no lip from you, lad."

Broderick walked into the middle of the room and began kicking over the tables covered with cards and poker chips. Satisfied, he ordered his men to take the prisoners downstairs and load them into the Black Marias.

"But sergeant," Melvin Farkas said hesitantly, "how can

we arrest these guys? There's no booze or money here. They weren't playing for money."

Broderick glared at Farkas for a long minute. "Well," he finally said, "they would have if they had any."

At the police station attorney Joseph Rosenbach was already remonstrating with the harried desk sergeant when George walked in the door.

Rosenbach was a short, slight man with a head far too large for his body, as though all his life force were crammed into his brain. People said he had looked like an old man by the time he was ten years old. But he was one of the top lawyers in the city. Many a bootlegger, including Big Bill Dwyer, was still in business because Rosenbach could outthink or outshout any district attorney. He was the man to see, George had heard, when you were guilty. Now his pipestem-thin arms waved wildly in the air.

"Where's your evidence?" Rosenbach shouted. "Where's your crime? You cannot hold these gentlemen for a minute on this flimsy basis. . . . The Manhattan district attorney will hear of this. . . . I'll have you all pounding beats in Canarsie." Rosenbach's large head bobbed wildly on his thin body as he screamed at the pitch of a factory whistle.

George and most of the others were back out on the street free when the last Black Maria pulled up carrying Chins Hamner and several other men. A second van had had to be sent for them—Chins had broken the axle of the first as he jumped aboard. They all headed for a nearby bar and ordered near beer while George called Dwyer and told him the night had been a success. Dwyer sounded pleased.

The second raid on the Paradise Rehearsal Club was as exciting as a week's vacation in Hoboken. There had been some reluctance on the part of the precinct brass to allow another raid. But Broderick argued strongly that he knew something was going on, and it wasn't dancing lessons. He finally won out when he hinted that he might blow the whistle on the officer's slush fund, reluctantly donated by local merchants, if he did not get his way. But the skepticism of the brass had even filtered down to the rookies. This time Officers Melvin Farkas and Vito Marconi left their submachine guns in the stationhouse. But they had their revolvers handy when they ran past the organ grinder and his monkey and up the dingy stairway next to the corset shop. At the top of the stairs the same two lookouts sat sleeping—this time on chairs. And when the cops finally reached the new wooden door at the end of the corridor there was little of the anticipation that had accompanied the last affair. Broderick, however, still looked stern and resolute.

"Chop the beauty down!" he ordered again. He hooked his thumbs in his holster belt, in front of the two pearl-handled revolvers his wife had given him for his birthday the day before. Again the splinters flew. The club had been fixed up considerably since the last raid, with a new coat of red paint and portraits of graceful patrician-looking thoroughbreds on the walls. As the cops broke through the door Melvin Farkas also admired the ornate new crystal chandeliers that had replaced the old bare lightbulbs. As George McManus and his associates calmly put down their cards, rose, and lined up against the wall, the chandeliers tinkled merrily.

"Again with the door?" George hissed through his teeth as Broderick frisked him. "You dumb mick—it wasn't locked this time either! I'm telling you, I'm taking the damage out of your cut!" Broderick only looked at George with disdain before again kicking over the tables and chairs.

At the stationhouse Rosenbach was in rare form, bobbing, weaving, gesticulating. He shoved George in front of the unhappy-looking middle-aged Irish desk sergeant.

"This man," Rosenbach shouted, "rotted in the trenches of Flanders and Verdun, braved shot and shell, to defend the very liberty that you now deprive him of over an innocent game of cards. . . . This is a travesty of justice that I will not let go unpunished. . . . Harassment, that's all it is, pure and simple. . . . Grave consequences. . . . Law suits. . . ."

Very nice, thought George, who had spent most of the Great War over table number 3 at a certain Times Square pool hall.

Sitting on a bench, his flab shaking as he giggled over Rosenbach's oration, Chins pulled two huge onions out of his jacket pocket and sliced them in half with a penknife. The pungent odor wafted through the stationhouse as Chins chomped happily. Slowly all eyes began to water. Finally, with tears rolling down his cheeks, the desk sergeant interrupted Rosenbach and told him his clients were free to go, that no crime had been committed, and this was all a mistake. And please get the fat slob and his onions out. At the bar George called Dwyer again. He had to explain why he was laughing and crying at the same time.

The third raid on the Paradise Rehearsal Club was talked about for years. Actually, the raid was a mistake. George had scheduled it for Saturday night but, in the confusion of the stationhouse, Broderick thought George said Friday.

Assistant Police Commissioner Robert McGuire had listened intently on Thursday as Broderick tried to explain away the two abortive raids and his request for a third. The evening before, McGuire had stood before Mayor Hylan at City Hall and listened equally intently as the mayor showed him a clipping from the *New York World* and demanded an explanation. The brief clipping reported that police had raided a dancing school on West Forty-sixth Street, arrested seventeen people, and then freed them immediately for lack of evidence. It went on to say that an organ grinder's monkey had been brutally crushed under the heel of a New York City police officer taking part in the raid. There was no mention of the first raid.

So Broderick explained. And McGuire grew increasingly skeptical, the wrinkles over his eyes growing more pronounced the more he frowned. There had to be something going on at the Paradise Rehearsal Club, Broderick argued. He would stake his reputation on it. The burly sergeant spoke darkly of gambling and illegal liquor, rumors that women were being used for immoral purposes, stories of a dope den. McGuire was unimpressed, pointing out that nothing had been found of an illegal nature in the previous raids. Broderick took a deep breath, leaned low over McGuire's ornate desk, and looked him hard in the eyes. It was time for his hole card.

"And what about the children?" Broderick said quietly.

"Children?" McGuire sat up.

"One of my canaries said they were recruiting children from the dancing school for, well . . ." Broderick looked away, gasped, as if he were choked up and couldn't continue.

69

"Children," McGuire said dumbly, thinking of his own little brood of nine safely tucked into their beds at home, Martha crooning lullabies to them. And think of the headlines.

"By God, Broderick, you go into that place and tear it apart good! They can't get away with that! Children, for God's sake!"

Officers Farkas and Marconi didn't even have their guns drawn this time. The organ grinder was gone, they noticed, as they climbed the stairs behind Broderick. From somewhere upstairs they could hear music, though. "Tea for Two," Farkas thought, humming.

"All right, boys, let's get them this time before they can abscond with the evidence!" Broderick shouted on the landing. Pulling out his pearl-handled pistols he led the rush through the door.

There were no lookouts on the door this time, just two little girls in party dresses and dimples sitting behind a small table with a cigar box in front of them.

"Tickets please, mister," one of the little girls said.

Broderick wasn't listening. In the dimness he barely had time to make out the rows of seated men, women, and children, arranged around a low, brightly lit stage, before the officers dashing in behind him pushed him into the lap of a large and very surprised woman. She leaped up screeching. Broderick caught a quick glimpse of children tap dancing on the stage before he hit the floor and both pearl-handled revolvers went off. Officer Melvin Farkas felt a sharp sting in his left leg, and warmth trickling into his shoe.

"I'm shot," he screamed in the darkness. "I'm bleeding." Flailing about, running blindly, stumbling over feet and chairs, he found himself on the stage. The children, though confused by the noise, continued to dance.

"Down in front," a man shouted at Farkas from the second row. Other people were twisting in their seats to see what was happening at the door, where Broderick, dazed and still on the floor, was blowing his shrill whistle.

"Reinforcements," Broderick gasped as Officer Vito Marconi bent over him. "More men. Arrest everybody."

The stationhouse, three blocks away, virtually erupted blue-uniformed bodies as the riot call came in. On foot, in

70

cars and vans, on motorcycles and on horseback, police converged on the club, followed by hundreds of the curious. Meanwhile the cops already in the club were rushing about trying to arrest everyone. Children began to cry, women shrieked, and men demanded to know what was going on. Marie Flynn was fighting her way to the light switches when a big cop grabbed her about the waist and, liking what he had found, held on for some exploration.

"Honey, you make being a cop a pleasure," he growled as he grabbed between her legs. Marie spun around in his arms and poked a finger in his right eye. With a curse she shoved the policeman through a paper partition. He found himself on the floor looking up at a half-dozen puzzled children in glittering devil's outfits, complete with pitchforks.

"You cossack," Marie shouted at the cop, and planted a dainty shoe in his ribs. Watching her teacher, one of the children calmly bopped the policeman on the head with her pitchfork. The other children began to whimper.

Broderick finally found himself back on his feet. He managed to stumble down the stairs and into the street, where he was met by dozens of officers and onlookers milling about.

"Get up there," he shouted hysterically, pushing more cops up the stairs. "It's a riot, a cop's been shot. Tear gas, give me a tear gas gun."

Two officers rushed up with the stubby gas guns at the ready, and fired two pellets into the windows of the club. More shouting could be heard through the broken windows. On the street, traffic had halted and dozens of car horns were honking, onlookers were shouting, police were rushing to and fro. A new roar went up as a police horse, hit by a stone, went berserk, bucking and rearing. Over all the noise the words floated down clearly: *Picture you upon my knee, just tea for two and two for tea . . . Can't you see how happy we will be.*"

Marie, weeping from the tear gas, tried to shout over the hysteria, but no one listened as dim forms thrashed around the dark room. Finally she rushed upstairs and down the corridor and slammed the door behind her. George McManus, alone in the room under the tinkling chandeliers, looked up from his game of solitaire.

71

"Your talent recital must be going great, Marie, judging from all that noise downstairs."

"George, you rat, what have you gotten me into?" And she burst out laughing, rushing into his arms.

Behind her, the blade of an ax tore through the door.

8

THE COURTROOM was a forest of dark wood pillars and benches. Cool marble floors reflected the watery morning light from the high windows that overlooked City Hall across the park. William Marcy Tweed, commonly known as Boss to his friends and enemies, had pocketed millions in the building of this courthouse that had come to bear his name. But, thought George McManus, looking around from his vantage point behind the plaintiff's table, the massive pile would stand forever. Sometimes the right things are done for the wrong reasons.

George's gaze lighted on a stocky figure in the back of the courtroom. Big Bill Dwyer sat as calm and respectable as a church deacon on Sunday, the ever-present Otto Berman whispering into his ear like a visible conscience. George nodded but Dwyer looked back without expression, reserving his decision. There are no sure things, Dwyer had said.

But here it was, a sure thing. A little play in one act being spieled out before them. George knew all the lines, knew when the bad guys would triumph. The tiny but titanic Joseph Rosenbach was giving the performance of his lifetime. He thundered, raved, flapped his arms, dropped his voice to a dramatic stage whisper, then was off to a crescendo again. The little man paced up and down in front of the judge and the empty jury box like a persecuted saint, eternally denied his rights, battling for justice for the downtrodden. It was a marvelous display of the lawyer's art, and even the fuzz-on-the-cheek opposition, one city attorney Timothy Conlon, was visible awed.

72

"Has there been any evidence presented that my clients did wrong? No!" shouted Rosenbach, answering his own question with a dismissing wave of the hand.

"Have there been any complaints lodged by citizens against my clients? No!" He turned quickly in front of the empty jury box and paced back in the other direction, his thin, sharp face alive with his intensity.

On George's right, Marie Flynn sat on the edge of her wooden chair, her eyes following every gesture that the attorney made. As he shouted "no," George watched her nod in agreement, her face a picture of approval, outraged herself.

"Is it illegal in this great country of ours for friends to get together for a few hands of cards? Should they be treated like Bolsheviks?"

Before Rosenbach could get out the "no" the young city attorney was on his feet, sputtering. "I object, your honor. The city never accused Mr. McManus or Miss Flynn of being Bolsheviks."

"But you treat them like it, you and the police," Rosenbach hissed, planting himself in front of the tall, ruddy Conlon and glaring up at him. "Midnight raids, shooting at children. Is this why we fled the oppression of Europe?" Rosenbach brought his liver-spotted fist down on the table in front of Conlon with a bang and the young man started.

The rap of the gavel came between the two men and every eye in the court shifted to the judge—stout, distinguished, with the white hair of wisdom. John O'Reilly sat on his bench as the Greeks thought Zeus sat on high, quiet most of the time but always ready to hurl a thunderbolt. "That will be enough of that," the judge was saying, and George was glad that Tammany had chosen him to oversee this case. With his blue eyes, swirling black robe, magisterial appearance, and tough reputation, he was worth a $20,000 bribe any day of the week.

"The facts are clear," Rosenbach began again, giving Conlon a look of disdain. "The New York City Police Department has denied my clients their civil rights. Not once, not twice, but on three separate occasions they stormed their property, ripped it apart, and finally arrested them and a great number of totally innocent women and children—children!—as if they were common criminals. This must be stopped. It will

73

be stopped! The police must be prevented from ever again entering the Paradise Rehearsal Club. I demand you issue an injunction against the police department, your honor, enjoining such future raids."

Conlon was on his feet again. "But your honor, prohibiting the police from ever entering this club is an invitation to commit mayhem—a license to steal, if you will."

Of course it is, thought George, sitting forward on his chair. Of course it is. Didn't the fools realize that was why they were there? He looked from one face to another—the attorneys belligerent; the judge unruffled, blank-faced on the bench; the clerk taking dictation with her thoughts a thousand miles away; the court bailiffs half-asleep, trying to stifle yawns. It was a game; keep a straight face with a full house and try to sweeten the pot until the suckers lost everything and didn't even know it. A license to steal. The judge was waving both lawyers down now, asking to hear more testimony, talking about law, precedents, as if, George thought, the law had anything to do with what was happening in this somber room. The words floated by him but meant nothing, just minor irritants on this stage where George moved the pieces, pulled the strings. He was in charge here, and he liked the feeling. He glanced over his shoulder again at Bill Dwyer. Was that a smile on his face?

Now there was the shuffling of heavy shoes, a stir in the court as a dozen or so young policemen trooped down the aisle single file and then sat stiffly in one row, shoulders right against each other as if for moral support. Next to them, Detective Sergeant John Broderick, his thinning red hair pasted slickly over his scalp, sat unconcerned, relaxed, his red neck bulging over the tight choke collar. Broderick's watery blue eyes found George, and for a moment they stared at each other. Then Broderick looked away as one of the rookie cops was called to the stand.

Officer Vito Marconi's eyes darted all over the room as he was sworn in. Rosenbach stalked the floor before the cop and began spinning off questions in rapid order. Yes, Marconi testified, his pale boyish face reddening, he had been in on the raids at the Paradise Rehearsal Club. No, he hadn't seen any real gambling or money on the tables. No, there were no laws obviously being broken. Big, dark circles of perspiration began to grow under the cop's arms as he told of the night of the third raid, of the dark, the lights, the gun shots, the tear gas, and arresting seven little girls in devil suits. Yes, he was sure, devil suits. No, he did not think they were evil, he told Rosenbach, and the few spectators in the court laughed until the gavel sounded. Then Rosenbach let Marconi go.

One by one the other rookie officers followed. Rosenbach made each of them tell what they had done in the raids, and all admitted they had found nothing wrong. And when Rosenbach was done with each man he would offer the witness to city attorney Conlon, who would simply shake his head in resignation and scribble even faster on his smudged legal pad.

"Those boys," Marie whispered to George with genuine sympathy as the last of the rookie officers left the stand, "don't they understand?" She looked over to where they were sitting, bewildered, wondering how they had gotten into this mess right out of the police academy. Each looked straight ahead now, avoiding the others' eyes.

George turned to Marie, wondering how much this woman really knew. She was a last-minute addition to their lawsuit and Dwyer hadn't liked it. Rosenbach thought she would be the perfect injured party. George had agreed with Rosenbach. But Marie had been very quiet through the trial, as if she were adding two and two but it kept coming up five.

"Don't worry. about them, toots," he told her quietly. "They'll learn fast enough and then they'll have their hands out like the rest of New York's finest."

She turned her blue eyes back to him with a look of unblinking innocence. "Do you think everybody's crooked?"

He squeezed her knee under the plaintiff's table, wondering how Marie could sometimes sound so incredibly naive and yet know how to do things to him when they were alone that gave him goosebumps for a week. "I *know* everybody's crooked," he finally told her with a little smile. "Or else they're just waiting to be asked." She never blinked an eye.

Rosenbach's nasal voice cut between them as he asked that another witness be called to the stand—Detective Sergeant John Broderick. The big man's heavy police shoes thumped down the aisle until he stood before the witness chair, right hand already up, waiting for the bored clerk to swear him in. Finally Broderick sat and the chair creaked under his weight. He belched, shifted his holster around between his legs for comfort, ran a thick finger inside his tight collar to loosen it, then settled back to wait for Rosenbach's first question. The lawyer studied Broderick from his seat for a moment, then turned to give George McManus a barely perceptible wink that George thought made him look like some crazed leprechaun in a three-piece suit.

Broderick fought off the urge to scratch his genitals as Rosenbach established his name, occupation, and that he had led the raids on the Paradise Rehearsal Club. Had you and Mr. McManus met before the raids? Rosenbach asked.

"I picked him up a couple, three times," the big cop answered, shifting around in his chair. "Strictly small potatoes. Craps, nickel-dime games, like that."

"Are you friendly with Mr. McManus?" Rosenbach went on.

"That mick sonuvabitch? I wouldn't piss on him if he were on fire," Broderick said with irritation, thinking, this little Barrymore act is going to cost you extra, Georgie boy. Several women in the courtroom blushed and murmured disapproval at the language, and Judge O'Reilly turned a stern Irish eye on the policeman.

"You'll keep a civil tongue in your mouth in my court, officer," he warned, and Broderick nodded, then pulled out a broad white handkerchief, honked into it, and settled back.

"So you don't like George McManus," Rosenbach went on. "Is that why you continued these harassing raids on him and his friends? Were you using the police department for some personal vendetta?"

"Nah, I heard there was a crime going on, that they were gambling." Broderick studied his nails, belched again, louder. "I mean, that's my job, to stop crime in the Tenderloin. I don't let any beggar get away with anything on my beat."

"And did you find any heinous crimes being committed?" The sarcasm in Rosenbach's high voice was heavy enough to sink a battleship.

76

"Well, I'll tell ya, that little shitpile McManus is getting smarter, because I didn't find anything. But I knew something was going on up there all right because I got it from two different snitches."

Judge O'Reilly was getting red-faced. "Any more profanity, sergeant, and I'll charge you with contempt of court."

"Sorry, your honor, but you'll have to understand, this George McManus here has been up to no good since he was whelped in Hell's Kitchen. I know him and his type. They're all just thieving bastards down deep, your honor. I'm as good an Irishman as you, judge, but little rats like McManus there are never going to amount to more than a bucket of spit."

Rosenbach was shouting, the gavel was banging, and from the defense table there came a low moan as lawyer Conlon tried to rub away his growing headache. But Broderick was enjoying himself too much to stop.

"I knew they were up to no good all right in that Paradise joint, your honor. This McManus and his little bastard partners in crime were scurrying all over Broadway making deals and whispering in corners and getting their little kike and dago buddies—"

"That's fifty dollars—no, a hundred dollars for contempt," cried Judge O'Reilly, finally shouting down Broderick. "Control yourself, man."

"What more can I say judge?" Rosenbach cut in, virtually dancing across the floor. "The city has no case here, no defense of these raids. They were totally uncalled-for and unjustified. The whim of one police officer who just didn't like Mr. McManus."

It was getting to be too much for George. He sank his teeth into his lip to keep from smiling, until he tasted blood. There was a murmur of amazement coming from the smattering of people in the courtroom. Marie looked around the room and then back to George. She started to say something but he squeezed her thigh tightly and hissed through clenched teeth: "Not now, don't say a thing now. I'll explain it all to you later."

On the stand Judge O'Reilly was wondering if things weren't getting a little out of hand himself. He searched the faces of the people in court and was relieved to find there were no reporters. After all, O'Reilly had a reputation for toughness to uphold. He had sentenced so many people to the electric chair that he was known as the frying judge. God-dammit, O'Reilly thought, taking a bribe was one thing, but not when it interfered with the decorum, the majesty, of the law. The thing now was to get this case over with, he decided. Get them out of here as fast as possible, and then go fishing. He looked up as a thin man, but with a marked pot belly, wearing a blue suit and carrying a briefcase, slipped into the courtroom and took a seat in the back at the other end of the row from Big Bill Dwyer. The thin man had a harelip, badly covered by a sparse mustache. It's about time that jerk showed up, thought O'Reilly, watching the new arrival carefully dust off his hat and place it on the bench next to him. What my sister sees in Seamus Ryan . . . The judge shook his head.

Judge O'Reilly shifted his gaze from the man in blue to city attorney Conlon, who was still scribbling at breakneck speed on a yellow pad.

"Do you have any questions for this witness, counselor?"

Conlon looked up at Broderick, who was now slouched so far down in the witness chair his butt was in danger of slip-ping off the seat entirely. Conlon shook his head sadly and went back to scribbling. Broderick rose heavily, turned the holster back to his side, then shambled back to his seat.

"How about you, Mr. Rosenbach?" O'Reilly asked. "It's getting near the lunch recess, but do you want to put anyone else on the stand?"

"One more witness, your honor." Rosenbach rose from his chair. "Mr. George McManus. And then I think this case will be easily disposed of."

With a smile to Marie, George rose and walked to the wit-ness stand. It really was like a play, he thought, as he was sworn in. And now here he was the star on center stage. Things were going so well even Dwyer in the last row looked almost happy, though that Otto Berman never stopped work-ing Bill's ear. A queer little bird, George thought. Berman always looked as though he had just messed his pants. George took a deep whiff of the red carnation in his lapel and settled back as Rosenbach planted himself in front of the judge's bench.

"I'm just going to ask you a couple of questions, Mr. Mc-Manus," Rosenbach said, stalking in front of him. "Have you ever taken part in any illegal activity at the Paradise Rehearsal Club?"

"Absolutely not," George responded. Not yet, that is, he thought.

"What were you doing on the premises when you were raided the first time?" Rosenbach continued.

"My friends and I were playing cards, for matchstick stakes."

"And the second time you were raided?"

"The same thing. And I was doing very well, I might add. I won practically every match in the house."

"And what were you doing when the police broke in for the third time, Mr. McManus?" Rosenbach said matter-of-factly.

"I was alone, waiting for someone."

"And who was that?"

"I was waiting for Miss Flynn there. We had a date."

"And once again, Mr. McManus, you were not engaged in anything illegal?"

"As God is my witness," said George, hoping he looked even slightly pious.

Rosenbach turned, half bowed to Conlon, and trotted back to his chair. The young city attorney rose, polishing his glasses with a large blue handerchief. He squinted at George, then put his glasses back on and leaned on the railing of the witness stand, staring at him, trying to mesmerize.

Judge O'Reilly watched the face of Seamus Ryan, calmly asleep in the last row. With each measured breath his mustache rippled ever so slightly. The man in blue turned in his seat and found a more comfortable position. His coat fell open and his pot belly protruded over the waistband of his pants, straining the shirt buttons. His fly was open, the judge noted with embarrassment. And that's what my sister wants to marry? he mused. No, decided Judge O'Reilly, he'd be doing his sister a favor getting this Ryan out of her life.

"What do you do for a living, Mr. McManus?" Conlon began suddenly.

"Well, a little of this, a little of that. Times are tough, counselor."

79

"Detective Sergeant Broderick characterized you as a gambler. Would you agree with that, Mr. McManus?"

"Well, I've been known to pick up a card now and then, maybe even bet on the odd horse."

Conlon stared at George, then began to pace to and fro in front of him. "Isn't it true that you planned to use those rooms at the Paradise Rehearsal Club for illegal high-stakes card games?"

"Nope," George replied calmly.

"And weren't you also planning to open a speakeasy in those rooms?"

"Wrong again."

"So you still maintain, as you told the police, that you rented those rooms for a social club for your riff-raff friends? Do you expect anyone to believe such a cock-and-bull story?"

"What do you mean, riff-raff?" George sat forward.

Conlon rushed to his table and picked up a sheaf of papers, thumbing through them quickly. "Petty larceny, bookmaking, attempted bribery, breaking and entering, numerous Volstead Act violations, gambling arrests, loitering, assault. The friends arrested with you have very distinguished records."

George stared at Conlon. "I know a lot of lawyers who have worse records."

"Why don't you tell the truth, McManus?" Conlon answered. "What are you up to?"

Riff-raff. All his life he'd seen people like this, George thought—little men with a few dollars in the bank, a new sewing machine for the wife and a little bit of power. Sanctimonious little minds that spawned sanctimonious little rules. Bankers, lawyers, bureaucrats, cops, businessmen with minds as narrow as their girths were wide. Riff-raff? This silly bastard couldn't shine Bill Dwyer's shoes. Why any con man on Broadway could pick him clean and have him say thank you.

My God, George muttered to himself, the urge to tell all was overwhelming. And Dwyer? What would he say? Could George risk everything like this? His hands balled into fists of frustration. Riff-raff, the little bastard had called them. No, no, Dwyer would probably keel over right before his eyes, watching the $750,000 he'd already shelled out for bribes, front money, booze, fixing up the club, slip through his fingers.

But, Jesus God, he wanted to do it, to tell this strutting little dope before him the truth. Lay it all out like a road map and see if he could even understand, comprehend. Look at him, in his practical twenty-nine-dollar suit that's a little long in the cuffs and a little short on sleeves. And then George began to slowly realize it wasn't just this Conlon anymore. It was the gamble, too. Of course. He was playing poker again and all their plans, their money, were on the table before him. The expression on George's face hadn't changed but his hands were suddenly wet.

"Well, speak up," Conlon insisted.

"I surrender, counselor," George finally said with a smile, throwing up his hands. "You're just too good for me to fight anymore. You've beaten me down.

"The plain truth is that us riff-raff are going to open a million-dollar casino in Times Square. We're going to invite the Roosevelts and the Belmonts and the Rockefellers and everybody else on the Social Register and then we're all going to get on our knees and shoot craps for a fortune on every roll, maybe play a little friendly roulette at a thousand bucks a throw. And then we'll snake-dance over to Broadway in our minks and tuxedoes and pinch apples from a pushcart just for the heck of it.

"You know how us riff-raff like to roll around in the dirt with rich folks. Does that satisfy you, counselor? And believe me, it's a load off my conscience to finally tell the truth."

Conlon stared at George for a moment, dumbfounded. In the back of the room, Dwyer's face had turned fish-belly white and Otto Berman's jaw was hanging open again. Marie's eyes were closed tight. Rosenbach had been resting his head on his hands as George spoke, and when he finished the old lawyer's elbows slipped off the edge of the table and his nose crashed into the wood. For about ten seconds that was the only sound in the room. Dwyer and Rosenbach held their breath. The spell was broken by a sudden snore from the sleeping Seamus Ryan.

"Very funny, Mr. McManus," Conlon finally said in disgust. "You should have been a comedian. No more questions."

The judge gave George a very peculiar look, as if McManus had whizzed something by him very fast and he had only

81

glimpsed it out of the corner of one eye. Something had certainly changed. O'Reilly watched a well-dressed man in back loosening his collar, color slowly coming back into his face, while beside him a small man half gagged. And what was the matter with Rosenbach? the judge wondered. The lawyer was positively glassy-eyed.

"It would appear that you have bearded the lion in his den, Mr. McManus," O'Reilly mused. "You may step down and resume your seat."

The judge cleared his throat before beginning again in a droning voice. "It appears to the court that Mr. McManus and Miss Flynn certainly seem to have legitimate cause for seeking an injunction to keep the police out of their place of business. There seems no doubt the police have hounded this man, for whatever reason. I think even you'll agree, Mr. Conlon, that we can't allow the police to run roughshod over any citizens, even if they play cards and have . . . unusual . . . friends."

"But . . ." Conlon interrupted, jumping up. Then he sat down, unable to think of any specific objections.

"A point well taken, Mr. Conlon," the judge continued. "Still, prohibiting the police in advance from entering a building, any building, is serious business. So serious, Mr. Rosenbach, that I'm afraid I must deny your request for a permanent injunction."

The judge was not finished. "However, the evidence against the police department's actions is so strong that I've decided not to dismiss this case either." O'Reilly looked out at Seamus Ryan, sprawled on a pew, hat over his eyes.

"I am appointing attorney Seamus Ryan as a friend of the court. Mr. Ryan will look into this matter further. He will interview more witnesses, hold his own hearings, investigate the finer points of the law, then report back to me as quickly as possible."

O'Reilly paused. "But, until Mr. Ryan gives his final report, I am granting complainant a temporary injunction barring all members of the New York City police force from entering the Paradise Rehearsal Club."

The judge rapped his gavel. "Court is adjourned."

"I've got to know," pleaded Marie, pulling on George's arm. "You weren't lying about the Rockefellers, the casino, were you?"

George closed his eyes. The warm sun felt good on his face as they stood together on the courthouse steps. He smiled as the woman beside him pleaded into his ear now, promising secret pleasures if he would only tell her the truth. He took a deep breath and smelled the dusty trees, the grass around City Hall, the exhaust fumes spewing from the cars that rattled by, Marie's odor. When he opened his eyes Joe Rosenbach was trotting up, his hand out.

"You really threw me a curve there, McManus. You must be crazy." But as he shook the taller man's hand the lawyer looked up at his face with grudging admiration.

"You got balls like grapefruits, kid. Pardon my French, miss," he said to Marie.

Suddenly Dwyer was with them, the ever-present Otto Berman a few steps behind. Dwyer studied McManus for a moment and George met his eye.

"Why?" Dwyer said. "Why did you take that chance? And what went wrong? What's this temporary injunction business?"

McManus touched Dwyer's arm. "The temporary injunction was Rosenbach's idea. He figured this Conlon and the city would appeal a permanent injunction. Something like that could even make headlines. And if they did appeal, we might get stuck with an honest judge. Or one even greedier than O'Reilly."

Rosenbach rubbed his hands together. "But you don't appeal a temporary injunction. You just wait till the hearings are over."

Dwyer shook his head. "I still don't get it. What good is a temporary casino? As soon as this Ryan reports back we've had it."

"If Ryan ever reports back," said George. "This is a complicated case, Bill. Witnesses all over the world. In fact, Ryan's leaving Saturday on the *Leviathan* to go find a witness in Paris."

"And after that?"

"I understand there's a witness in Vienna Ryan is dying to see. He'll be gone for years."

"But what if Conlon catches on?"

"He won't," Rosenbach said. "And even if he did, by that time young Conlon will be looking for a job. Walker will take care of that as soon as he's elected mayor."

A growing look of understanding came over Dwyer's face. "Then we're home free. The casino opens Saturday night."

"So I was right," whispered Marie, taking George's arm. "You weren't lying."

"No, he wasn't lying," Dwyer assured her. "But tell me why you got up there and told them all about our plans. You were taking a helluva chance. What if they'd believed you, McManus?"

George looked at the others, then came back to Dwyer. "I'm surprised you'd ask, Bill. You've pulled some scams in your day. You should know that the one thing an honest, upright citizen almost never believes is the truth."

9

THE DAY had been hot, sultry. But with the evening came a sweet and persistent breeze that swept away the heat and invited deep breaths. Refreshed by the wind, people seemed excited, anticipatory. They left their parlors and kitchens by the millions until the streets were full and alive with noise. Children shrieked with joy as they raced around stoops; neighbors found excuses to chat for the first time in days; and old enemies hefted pints of near beer.

The mood found its way up to George McManus's suite at the Park Central. He was humming "Vagabond Lover" as he pushed the final studs into his white silk dress shirt, pulled on his black evening jacket, shot his cuffs, and carefully put a red carnation into the buttonhole of his lapel. He took two military brushes off his dresser and swept his coal black hair back one last time. Finally he straightened his bow tie with a tug and winked at himself in the mirror.

After all the planning, the manipulating, the greasing of the right palms, tonight was the payoff—the opening night of the Paradise Rehearsal Club. Early that morning George had watched the *Leviathan* set sail for Southampton with a very happy Seamus Ryan aboard. McManus had provided Ryan with a willing brunette to share the crossing and the attorney was in his cabin investigating the finer points of a few natural laws as McManus watched the ship pull away from the pier.

It was nearly 9 P.M. when George's cab pulled up in front of the club. McManus tipped the cabbie a twenty and climbed out of the car as the driver studied the bill to be sure it was real. McManus took a deep breath and raced up the stairs two at a time. At the landing he pulled open the door and stepped onto the large dance floor. The room was dimly lit but George could see his reflection in the highly polished wood.

The upstairs door to the club had been replaced since the last raid by a heavy, thick, refrigerator-type door like those found on meat lockers. People who ran speakeasies appreciated the extra few minutes it took police to cut through such a door. While the club had no worries about police raids, George knew the big door gave that illusion of illegality that was so necessary to the success of any Manhattan night spot.

McManus gave the buzzer three short rings and stood back as an eye appeared at the peephole cut into the center of the door. It opened slowly and George was admitted by Izzy the Stub. Izzy had forgone his usual garish wardrobe and was wearing a black tuxedo. But he had been unable to resist some splashes of color. The red carnation in his lapel matched his bright red bow tie and a pair of equally bright red spats which covered a pair of two-tone black and white wing tips.

"You look like some kind of snazzy barber pole," George said, looking the other man over.

"You mean this ain't classy enough, boss?" Izzy looked down at his clothes. "Nussbaum promised eyes would fall from people's heads if I wore this."

"You'll do, Izzy. Everything ready?"

"Hey, the joint is perfect. As your official manager I have taken care of every detail to perfection. I tell you, the marks are going to think they have died and gone to heaven when they walk in here. The booze is ready, the band is hot, but my hands are a little cold, to tell the truth."

George smiled as he left the other man at the door. The place *was* dazzling. The three huge crystal chandeliers cast a soft glow throughout the room. Plush red carpeting and red silk wallpaper covered the floors and walls. Mirrors covered the entire twelve-foot-high ceiling.

On one side of the room sat two fourteen-foot-long crap tables of burnished mahogany covered with green felt. The roulette table was also green felt and mahogany, with a betting layout of black, red, and green velvet. Dark-brown, high-backed oak and leather chairs were arranged around the table. The wheel itself was silver-plated. As George approached the roulette game, a slight, tuxedoed, middle-aged man with a long, thin, rodent-like face was busy polishing the wheel.

"How's it play, Rats?" George ran his hand across the velvet slowly.

"Like a dream, Mr. McManus." Rats Wolnik spun the wheel. "See that. Perfect balance." He dropped a shiny steel ball into the spinning wheel.

"What you got here, Mr. McManus, is the only honest wheel in the East. You're gonna put every roadhouse in Jersey out of business in two weeks."

George straightened Rats's black bow tie, then walked to the casino bar. In the corner a pasty-faced young man played the opening bars to "Wang Wang Blues" on his saxophone. The rest of the five-piece combo sat behind the bar sampling Bill Dwyer's liquor.

George ordered a straight scotch from the heavy-set bartender and drank it slowly, his elbows on the bar, as he looked at his place one more time. His place. He liked the sound of it. Of course, it was Bill Dwyer's club as much as it was his. But George would be running it.

Izzy the Stub walked up, a slight look of worry on his face.

"So where are the marks? It's almost ten o'clock and you could drive a Duesenberg across the room without touching anybody."

"I wish you'd quit calling them marks, Izzy. Patrons, maybe —or customers. They're coming here to gamble and have a good time, not to have their watches heisted."

"Sorry, boss. But where is everybody? I'm getting jumpy."

"They're coming," George assured him. "Meanwhile, where are your shills?"

"I told them ten-fifteen, right after their play ends. But you know how it is. These actors get a couple of curtain calls and a few bravos and the hams got to stay at the Astor until the last seat is empty."

George looked at the clock, then back at Izzy the Stub. "What play are they in?"

"A laugher called *Main Line*. High-society comedy, you know the kind. The shills will probably look classier than the marks—I mean customers."

George smiled.

"But what do you need them for, boss? Seems like a waste of money to pay people to play craps for you."

George put down his empty scotch and glanced at the clock, wondering if it could be broken. Where *was* everybody?

"I'll tell you, Izzy. You ever go to a party and you're the first one there?" McManus explained. "Everybody sits around sucking his thumb and trying to look like they're having a good time. The shills will get things rolling right away. Got it?"

Izzy nodded and trotted off to check the waiters. McManus had the bartender pour him another scotch. As he was finishing it the buzzer sounded. His heart jumped but quickly calmed as he watched Izzy admit Marie Flynn. Marie's face was flushed with excitement. Her low-cut fringed red gown matched the hue of her face and hair. It was definitely the proper get-up for her new job as the club's hostess, George decided. It matched the wallpaper perfectly.

Izzy whistled as Marie walked past him. He grabbed her hand, executed a courtly bow, and kissed Marie's knuckles as George approached. But Marie was too busy looking around the casino, amazed by the changes in the room, to notice them.

"What do you think, toots?"

"I never thought this place could look this good, Georgie."

"If you like this part," Izzy interrupted, "you should see the money room. Wall-to-wall green."

"Come on, gorgeous," George said, "I'll give you the grand

87

tour." He grabbed Marie's hand away from Izzy, who was still savoring the knuckles.

The money room door was thick, dull steel with a small peephole cut out in the center. George tried the handle and was annoyed when the door opened. It was supposed to be locked. Inside, Otto Berman sat in his shirt sleeves, happily counting money, neat stacks of tens, twenties, fifties, and hundreds around him. Front money provided by Dwyer. Berman didn't seem to notice Marie's and McManus's entrance. He jumped when George spoke.

"How many times do I have to tell you to keep this door locked, Otto? And don't let anyone in except Izzy, me, and Bill," George warned.

Berman nodded absently without taking his eyes or his hands off the money.

Marie's eyes glazed over as she watched Berman's fingers run through the money. She picked up a packet of twenties and rubbed her thumb across the side of the bills. The soft, green paper had almost a sensual feel. She sighed, then put the money back on the table, but George grabbed the packet and tossed it back to her.

"Gambling money. It'll give you something to do before the big crowds get here."

"There must be two thousand dollars here," she purred, then hugged McManus and kissed him on the mouth. "I just love generous men."

McManus pulled her closer. "Not as much as I love generous women."

He kissed the hollow of her throat. Marie's face and neck reddened, her head fell back as George's mouth touched hers. Then he stopped abruptly and kissed her one last time, softly, on the forehead.

"We'll continue this later," he said, pulling Marie out of the money room. The redhead hurriedly straightened her gown and tried deep breathing to take the high flush out of her cheeks.

By now the band was playing a hot jazz number. It sounded like "I'm Forever Blowing Bubbles," George thought, but none of the musicians came close enough to the melody to really tell. George left Marie at the roulette table and began a final review of his troops. He straightened the already-straight ties of the eight immaculate, red-coated waiters. He flicked several nonexistent pieces of lint off the jackets of the bartender, Rats, the other croupiers, and Izzy the Stub. He adjusted the chairs of the dozen small tables near the band. He personally carried cash from the money room to the crap and roulette tables. And every few seconds McManus would glance furtively at the clock above the money room door.

The clock seemed to have a life of its own, and a slow-moving life at that. The hands barely budged. The invitations had said 10 P.M.—only a few moments away. But each minute seemed an eternity. Could something still go wrong? The place had to be jammed the first night, he knew. Crowds bred crowds.

George glanced about the club. The band had stopped playing. George's tension was contagious. Everyone felt it—waiters, croupiers, musicians. They all stared at the big door. Suddenly the silence was broken by the door buzzer's loud "Braaaaa." McManus joined the others in a collective sigh of relief, then rushed toward the door.

"Slow down," he whispered to himself. But he ignored his own advice and reached the door just as Izzy the Stub admitted eight couples in evening clothes.

"Welcome, welcome to the Paradise Rehearsal Club," George half shouted in relief, hovering around the newcomers.

"Uh, boss . . ." Izzy started to say.

George grabbed the hand of a distinguished-looking man with a goatee and shook it.

"McManus is the name. George McManus. This is my place and I want you to feel at home here. If you need anything—liquor, credit—just ask for me or my assistant, here."

"Boss, these are . . ." Izzy began again, but George cut him off.

"A pleasure to have you at the Paradise Rehearsal Club," George told a buxom woman in a heavy gray gown with a tiara in her hair. He bowed and began to lead them toward the gaming tables, clicking his fingers for a waiter with champagne, when Izzy pulled him aside.

"Boss, those aren't the marks. They're the shills."

George shook his head and looked at the newly arrived couples. And as they laughed he could suddenly see the theatrical make-up, the phony jewelry.

"Jesus, they *do* look better than rich people," George muttered.

"Have another drink, boss. Calm down. I'll take care of everything out here," Izzy assured him.

George wandered back to the bar, where Marie was sipping a cocktail.

"I'm afraid to look at the clock again, Marie. What time is it now?"

"It's time to take it easy, honey. You're starting to look like a nervous wreck." She straightened his lapel, fluffed his red carnation. There was an odd gleam in her eye. "Anything I can do to help?"

"Hell, yes." And he grabbed her hand and half dragged Marie to the money room door.

"Get out for a few minutes, Berman," he told Otto when the little man opened up to his knock. With a lingering look at his beloved piles of money Otto shuffled out of the room and George slammed the door behind him.

"There's only one way I know to make sure that people will show up soon. And that's to be doing something else where you don't want to be interrupted."

He sat in a big leather chair in the corner and pulled Marie onto his lap. His hands reached for her hips as she looked at him, surprised. Then she kissed his eyes, his nose, his mouth as George ran his hand up her back, unzipping the flimsy gown. She shuddered as his lips brushed her breasts, then shifted in the chair to straddle George. His hands pushed her dress up her thighs, around her waist, the fingers groping under her silky underthings, finding their target. She was ready, grinding her hips into him. Marie moaned into his ear, her tongue busy, probing, her hair over his face.

"Let me undress," she whispered as his hands moved under her, roughly pulling her panties aside. "You'll muss me up. This dress cost a small fortune."

"I'll have a small fortune," he mumbled from between her breasts. "I'll buy you another."

And then he was inside her and she didn't care about the

dress anymore as they moaned and groaned together. His hands dug into her soft buttocks under the gown, raising and lowering her to their rhythm.

"This is the only way," George gasped. "The only way."

"Oh yes!" she cried.

"Braaaa," came the distant buzz from the front door. And then two more times: "Braaaa, braaaa."

"I told you," George screamed, heaving her up and down, frantically biting her nipples.

And now the faraway buzzer wouldn't stop and George could hear voices, shouts, laughter from the casino. Someone was pounding on the door, telling them to hurry.

"Goddammit, I'm trying," he shouted. Marie stood up shakily, rearranging her clothes, as he buttoned up, ran his hands through his hair. She pulled a handkerchief from her purse and wiped away the lipstick smudges on George's face.

He kissed her very quickly on the cheek and then pulled the door open. Otto Berman looked at them suspiciously as George slipped by and into the casino.

People were everywhere, crowded around the crap tables, the roulette game, and the bar, spilling onto the small dance floor.

They were rushing in so fast that George was pushed back against the money room door. He didn't try to greet guests but instead just watched the action, growing more excited at the sights and sounds. People were laughing, dancing, cursing. The band wailed "The Black Bottom." Fists with bunches of twenty-, fifty- and hundred-dollar bills waved in the air. George could see one of the crap tables from his vantage point, money scattered over the green felt. With every roll of the dice the club had to be winning over $5,000. And the dice were rolling awfully fast. As soon as they hit the table, another player would pick them up and throw. The action was more sedate at the roulette game. It always was. But the bets were larger. George stood transfixed as he watched one old dowager lose $30,000 on one spin of the wheel.

For a half hour, an hour, it seemed to George as if he barely moved. He was transfixed by the crowd, the noise, the smell, the money. And even more customers surged in until it seemed the club had to burst like an overripe watermelon. He watched Izzy the Stub, the waiters, Marie dash around the room, taking orders, soothing ruffled feathers, greeting newcomers. Finally he began to walk around himself, shaking hands, getting whacked on the back by happy friends, introducing himself to strangers. And always the noise, the glint of the lights off jewelry, the money flowing, crashing, streaming in torrents. He seemed to dance through the room, seeing everything and feeling nothing but a wonderful numbness.

It was then that George spotted her, and pulled up with a start. He couldn't see the woman's face, just the back of her head. But the auburn hair was right. So was the figure. He was certain the green-gowned woman bending over the far end of the second crap table was the one he had rescued from that Fifth Avenue wedding. Why you randy bastard, he told himself, you just got through banging Marie. But suddenly he remembered everything about the girl. Especially the laugh and those gray-green eyes. And he was surprised that she was still so vivid in his memory.

George pushed through the crowd. He put his hand on the woman's shoulder and gently spun her around.

"How've you be—" He stopped abruptly. It wasn't her, not by a long shot. This one was nearly forty with dark eyes and a pinched face. Not unattractive but nothing like the girl in the wedding dress.

"I'm sorry," George said, trying to hide his disappointment. "I thought you were someone else."

"I wish I was," the woman said pleasantly. "Mr. McManus, isn't it? My friends and I were just talking about what a wonderful place this is." The others with her nodded.

"But next time," the woman continued, "we're going to bring less money. I could have toured Europe for what I've lost tonight."

McManus laughed and leaned toward the woman. "I don't do this for all my customers," he said in a conspiratorial tone, "but if you want to cut your losses, bet against the shooter. Every time."

"Every time?" She put her right hand on George's forearm almost intimately.

George nodded and covered her hand with his.

"Can't lose?" she asked.

92

"No promises," he smiled, "but you will do better."

The woman now seemed more interested in him than in craps, but McManus had no time to pursue. Izzy the Stub tapped McManus on the shoulder.

"Rothstein's here, boss. And he's brought some awful shady-looking guys with him."

"How shady?"

"Their coats are bulging," Izzy whispered, "and one guy's wearing one of those suits you get when you graduate from Sing Sing."

McManus excused himself, then pushed his way through the crowd and met Rothstein and his entourage at the door. Arnold Rothstein was elegant in a black silk tuxedo and ruffled white satin shirt. But, thought George, that may only have been in contrast to his bodyguards. Rothstein's favorite gunsel, matinee-idol-handsome Legs Diamond, was stuffed into a blue pin-stripe suit two sizes too small for him.

The other bodyguard McManus knew by rumor only. Lean, pockmarked Owney Madden had spend the last thirteen years in prison. A minor matter: he'd killed five men. He would have gotten the chair, George had heard, but Madden was only fifteen years old at the time. No wonder, George thought, Rothstein never got robbed.

McManus nodded at Rothstein and studied the slim, green-eyed blonde who was hanging on Rothstein's arm and giggling to herself. Rothstein glanced around the crowded room. "You've come up in the world, Georgie. Last time I saw you I left you without a nickel for the subway."

"Spare change, Arnie. Hardly worth mentioning. I'll win more in ten minutes in my club than I lost that whole night."

"Don't spend your money just yet," Rothstein warned. "I'm feeling lucky tonight, Irish. I might just clean you out again."

"You're welcome to try, Arnie. You're welcome to try."

Rothstein led the blonde, still giggling, to the roulette table. McManus followed and politely cleared a space at the table for them. George was a bit surprised at Rothstein's choice of game. The racketeer's prowess at craps was legendary. Rothstein could make the dice change spots, people said. McManus once had seen Rothstein beat a Chicago hood for $500,000, using the hood's own bones.

McManus watched intently as Rothstein placed a small bet on the red. You're not going to wipe me out that way, George thought. Rothstein lost the first bet and placed another $50 on the red. He lost that as well. McManus stayed for a few more minutes but soon grew restless. Rothstein won a few, lost a few. Nobody was getting hurt. Some high roller, McManus thought—he must be down all of $200.

"I figured how you're gonna make a killing, Arnie," McManus finally said. "You're going to bore me to death."

"Have patience, Georgie, you'll be losing soon enough."

But McManus was no longer interested. He moved around the room again, then knocked on the money room door. A flushed Otto Berman opened it.

"How we doing, Otto?"

"It's incredible. They're losing it so fast you'd think it was counterfeit. But it's real," he quickly added. "I haven't found one phony all night."

McManus pulled a bottle of scotch from a rolltop desk next to the fire escape. He poured two drinks, downing his almost as soon as the liquid hit the glass. He pushed the other toward Otto. Berman pushed a ledger filled with figures toward George.

"That's our winnings for the first three hours, compiled every half hour, table by table," the bookkeeper said proudly.

McManus read the figures quickly, then read them again more slowly. He knew they were doing well, but not this well. He poured another drink, then handed the bottle to Berman. George continued to stare at the numbers, a dreamy, faraway look in his eyes. He was shaken out of his reverie when someone banged on the door. Berman let in a very nervous Rats Wolnik. The croupier grabbed McManus by the shoulders and shook him, spilling what was left of his drink.

"We got trouble, boss. Big trouble. He's got a system. I don't know how he's doing it, but he's beat us for close to five hundred thousand already." Wolnik spoke quickly, his nose twitching. He literally pulled McManus out of the room and toward the roulette table.

"You gotta stop him."

"Who . . . ?" McManus began. But he could tell the source of the problem before they were halfway there. Arnold Rothstein's eyes mocked him from across the room as he sat behind a big stack of bills.

George pulled Rats to a sudden stop. "How the hell did Rothstein win so much money so fast? I was just there. He was betting nothing. And losing."

Wolnik gulped. He was sweating profusely, his eyes bulging. He'd been a croupier before and knew bosses usually blamed the dealer for a big loss.

"He kept betting pennies for a few minutes after you left. Then all of a sudden he turns to that *shikse* with him and says, 'Well, I think I've got it now,' and out comes the bankroll," Wolnik explained nervously. "He starts betting a thousand, then five thousand, then ten thousand on every spin. Now he's up five hundred grand."

McManus approached the roulette table, trying to force a smile, but it wasn't working. If I had to lose, George thought, why the hell did it have to be to Rothstein?

"Your boy says I can't play anymore," Rothstein said evenly. "Is that the kind of two-bit joint you're running? You can only bet as long as you lose?"

McManus stared at the pile of money in front of Rothstein, feeling a little sick as he remembered the last time Rothstein had cleaned him out. Three dozen people crowded around the table and watched George. Finally he turned to his croupier.

"No limit. Let him bet as much as he wants."

Rothstein put half his stack of bills on the black. The blonde counted out loud five stacks of $50,000 each. Rothstein placed one stack each on black number 15, black number 20, black number 28, red number 18, and red number 36.

Rats blanched. The blonde giggled. The other bettors at the table gasped. George McManus's face registered no emotion whatsoever. But he felt a sudden sharp pain in the pit of his stomach. Now he knew why Rothstein was playing roulette instead of craps. In craps, Rothstein would only be playing against the other players. But in roulette he was playing against the house—against George. Only in roulette could Rothstein hurt McManus. If Rothstein hit black, George calculated, they'd break even. But if he hit one of his red numbers, Rothstein's profit would be $1,300,000. If he hit one of his black numbers, Rothstein would beat the club for nearly two million.

Wolnik picked up the steel ball. "Place your bets, ladies and gentlemen. Place your bets," he managed to croak.

The others at the table stared from McManus to Rothstein looking for some sign—a loss of nerve, a glint of sweat—some hint who might prevail. But both faces were now blank. Tentatively, the other gamblers pushed their money alongside Rothstein's. Go with the hot hand, they all decided. Let the streak last one more spin.

The croupier grabbed the wheel and spun hard, then dropped the ball. Wolnik closed his eyes.

Rothstein was intensely drumming his fingers on the table as the ball rolled in—and then out—of one of his numbers. McManus thought he saw a flicker of anger in Rothstein's eyes.

The wheel began to slow, the ball bouncing from number to number, color to color. The ball now started its final tour of the wheel, rolling past red 18, red 36, black 15, black 20. McManus was almost home free. Only one number to go. The ball hadn't the momentum to reach Rothstein's other numbers again.

The ball clicked and slid toward Rothstein's final number, black 28, slowing perceptibly every millimeter of the way. McManus stared, mesmerized, as the ball stopped its forward motion, spinning gaily on its axis on the metal border between Rothstein's last number and green zero. Rothstein ceased drumming his fingers.

For what had to be an eternity the ball continued to spin, then stopped, still hovering between the two slots. Keep going, move on, George whispered softly. He could see his face distorted in the shiny ball. Then, as if the ball had heard him, it nestled safely into the green slot.

The other gamblers muttered and groaned. The blonde had stopped giggling. Rothstein said nothing. McManus pulled in the money with a wooden rake and looked across the table at the beaten Rothstein.

"That's the trouble with you, Arnie. You're just too greedy. You never know when to quit."

Rothstein's ears turned slightly pink. "Where have I heard

that before?" he said, trying to sound light, then stood up to leave. "Next time, Georgie." He took the blonde's arm and walked coolly out of the casino.

Rats Wolnik handed the steel ball to McManus.

"Take over for a minute, okay, boss? All of a sudden I gotta go to the bathroom."

McManus laughed as he set the roulette wheel in motion.

Through the night the fever grew. Money—fifty-, hundred-, thousand-dollar bills—moved and danced, in fists, on tables, back and forth, in a blur of green and flesh. Shouts, groans, shrieks, the jazz band cranking up until the notes virtually danced in the air and bulled their way through the cigarette smoke. Sometimes it seemed to George that it was almost impossible to breathe, to see, to think.

Then, as suddenly as it began, it ended. The early morning light began creeping through the casino's open door and the patrons began to slip away. The musicians undid their ties, put away their instruments, and lit up cigarettes, exhausted. The weary waiters took advantage of their first opportunity to sit down.

Only a few big losers remained around the roulette and crap tables, desperately trying to get even for the night. Soon even they were gone as McManus closed down the games and gently invited the survivors back again. Then he dismissed the waiters, the shills, and the rest of his staff, sending Marie and Izzy into the money room to help count the night's profits.

McManus looked around the empty casino. Wisps of smoke still hung in the air. Ashes and butts were scattered all over the new red carpet. George could still smell the aromas of bay rum and sachet, clashing with the stench of alcohol and sweat. Behind the bar, nearly every bottle was now empty. They had expected the supply to last two weeks.

McManus felt a strange reluctance to join the others in the money room. It was really a reluctance to end the night, he knew, to leave this room. He had never felt so at home before. He belonged here. McManus yawned and stretched. He had been up since dawn. Fatigue was beginning to hit him. He gathered the cash remaining on the gaming tables and stuffed it in his pockets. Finally he walked into the back room.

Money was stacked and scattered everywhere—on tables, chairs, the floor, the desk, even the windowsills. Izzy the Stub and Marie sat around the table with Otto Berman counting, looks of disbelief on all their faces.

McManus pulled the cash out of his pockets and threw it on the pile on the table. Berman grabbed it and quickly began counting that, too.

Finally the bookkeeper grinned. "This puts us over. By seven thousand three hundred."

"I don't believe it," Marie said slowly, then rose and kissed McManus. "You won a million dollars in one night."

McManus sat down hard in a chair next to the door. He was stunned, speechless. A million bucks. They must have counted wrong. He looked at Berman, but the bookkeeper just kept nodding up and down, up and down, grinning like a halfwit. The count was right. A million bucks. A smile slowly began spreading on his face.

"I never saw anything like it," Izzy the Stub said in amazement. "They were crazy out there, throwing it away with both hands. You know we even had cowboys up here to-night?"

"They weren't cowboys, they were oilmen. From Texas," explained Marie. "They said they were friends of Bill Dwyer and came up to New York in a private train. Can you believe it?"

"A million dollars," George whispered reverentially.

"And you know, I think I saw Eddie Cantor," said Izzy. "He was dragging a dame that had more fur on her back than they got in the Bronx Zoo."

"A million bucks," George said louder.

"A million seven thousand and three hundred bucks, to be exact," corrected Berman, going over his figures on the adding machine for the fifth time.

George whooped, leaped out of his chair, grabbed Marie's arm, and began dancing her around the room. Then he grabbed Izzy's arm and all three whirled around. George whooped again and threw a packet of bills in the air, and as the money fell, the others joined in, throwing handfuls at each other.

"Hey, hey, you crazy? That's money you're playing with," Berman scolded, looking over his wire-rimmed glasses.

But Marie suddenly grabbed the skinny bookkeeper and pulled him to his feet. She jammed a handful of bills down the front of his pants and whirled him around the room over his protests until they were all bouncing around like children, laughing and throwing money.

Outside, Big Bill Dwyer came up the stairs, down the hall, and into the casino, looking for McManus. He glanced around the empty club, then heard the noise coming from the money room. But when he got to the door he could barely see McManus or anyone else. All he could see was thousands of green bills, floating gently through the air like a spring rain.

10

WITHIN HOURS the word was passed from Wall Street to Fifth Avenue to East Hampton, then to Newport and Saratoga and all the summer watering spots of the rich. A new club had opened in the middle of Manhattan, a high-toned casino that offered free booze, hot jazz, and on-the-level action until dawn and beyond. A club that knew how to treat people with money.

And so they came. Their limousines—long, sleek touring cars crawling with chrome—hogged the curbs for blocks around. The second-night crowd jammed into the Paradise Rehearsal Club and gaily topped the losses of the first-nighters. The third-nighters did even better. They were undaunted by the knowledge that there were so few winners among them. Manhattan had a new toy and no one was willing to miss the chance to play with it.

It was not until the third week that the passion subsided to mere madness. But even then the casino was usually packed. The take slowed to $100,000 a night. It rarely dipped below. By the third night George McManus was well-to-do. By the sixth night he was rich. By the tenth he had stopped counting.

The money was flooding in so quickly George was running out of places to put it. The safe in the club office groaned from its burden, and many nights he could hardly swing the door shut, even after Big Bill Dwyer left with his lion's share.

Now that he had money, George reasoned, he had to buy things. He had moved from his suite at the Park Central to the penthouse. Because he was usually at the club Marie Flynn had volunteered to decorate his apartment for him, and he was jolted late one morning to awaken to a placid fifteenth-century madonna and Christ child staring benevolently at his rumpled silk pajamas. It's culture, Marie had explained. And gradually she filled the entire penthouse with expensive relics. Botticelli saints stared at him as he bathed. A doleful Rembrandt portrait watched darkly as George fried eggs in the kitchen. A magnificent hammered-silver Augsburg suit of armor greeted George at the front door and held his hat. He threw his loose change into a priceless thirteen-hundred-year-old Greek amphora vase.

George could deny Marie nothing. It seemed only natural that she would spend most days in bed next to him in the darkened bedroom, after they left the club at dawn. They were easy together. She was sensual, comforting when he needed it, never asked questions, and the club's patrons liked her quick banter. Little was ever said between George and Marie, but often he would slip Izzy the Stub a fistful of money to buy her some new diamond or gold trinket. Like a child with new toys, Marie would try to wear as many of her jewels as possible until sometimes she could barely lift her arms.

He had bought a car, too. Or rather Marie had bought it for him. A trim red Reo roadster with black leather interior and a horn that could put a locomotive's hoot to shame. But George rarely drove the car, leaving it to Marie or Izzy the Stub or Rats Wolnik. George preferred cabs because they gave him a few free minutes to sit back and think. And there was much to think about. He liked having money enough not to have to worry about it. Somehow he always knew it would be like this, but now that it was reality it was even better than he had expected. All the clichés about having money were true. People *did* treat you differently. Men who had owed him money for years suddenly started to pay up to stay on his good side.

Friends from Hell's Kitchen began finding their way up the stairs to the Paradise Rehearsal Club, and George would never send them away empty-handed.

Businessmen who once only sought him out for poker games were now inviting him to their homes, introducing him to wives and daughters. Brokers asked his advice about stock. Everybody wanted him to invest in something or other. Even the boys at Tammany looked at George in a different light, as if he were a brilliant new planet they had just discovered in the heavens.

And of course, the women. Married, single, pretty, homely, heiresses and dress-shop girls. When they were introduced to George they batted their lashes so hard he wondered that their eyes weren't black and blue.

Through it all George McManus moved as if in a wonderful, crazy dream. The nights at the Paradise Rehearsal Club ran together in a swirl of faces, shouts, money—like sparkling waves scrabbling back out to sea even as new ones came into shore.

In the mornings, after a night at the club and an early breakfast, George would lie awake for a few minutes in his cool bed. Next to him Marie would already be asleep, clutching her favorite new ruby necklace in her hand. Once George had tried to remove the necklace but she had tossed and turned in her sleep until he gave up. Then she had settled back, reassured, the necklace clamped tightly in one fist.

He would lie with his hands behind his head, looking around the handsome room, weary but contented. The last thing he would see as the dim light crept around the heavy curtains was the smiling Botticelli madonna, satisfied with her divine inner secret. Then he would sleep.

11

SHE HUMMED "It Had to Be You" off-key and loud as she skipped about the cavernous bedroom, flitting from the closet jammed with dresses back to the mirrored table covered with

101

bottles and jars and pins. For the first time in weeks Elizabeth Wainwright was really happy, excited. Her exile was officially ending. Now she knew how Robinson Crusoe felt when he saw that startling, naked footprint in the sand. She was not going to be alone anymore. She was going out tonight; out, *out, o-u-t.* Elizabeth pushed an ivory pin into her auburn hair and stuck her tongue out at the face that looked back from the mirror.

"Christ, if I'd known I was going to cause all this trouble I'd have married the poor jerk," she muttered.

But no, she told herself. No, I wouldn't have. She went to the big windows overlooking Long Island Sound and watched the surf splash at the bottom of the shallow cliff. Whatever hell her father had made of her life these past two months, it had been worth it. She was still single and free and ready to go out on the town for the first time since the aborted wedding.

Elizabeth would never forget the look on her father's face when he finally found her in the library of the Sands Point estate. She was soaking her feet, her wedding gown pulled up to her thighs, when he rushed in. He looked like a beet that was about to explode—dark purple with white splotches on forehead and cheeks. He puffed and sputtered so much she barely understood him. Horace Wainwright had been so angry he had actually drooled. But the punishment had been clear enough. She was to stay at Sands Point until the scandal had blown over. She could have fought—normally would have— but for the first time she was actually afraid that her father might have a stroke. No one could stay as purple for as long as he did without bursting something. So she had only nodded and gone back to soaking her feet as her father stormed out. He slammed the double doors so hard a stuffed boar's head fell off the wall over the mantel and landed, grinning, on an easy chair.

In truth, it had been a pleasant enough exile. For a while. She spent long, lazy hours in the vast garden, walking on the beach, sailing the handy little catboat her parents had given her when she was ten. She read, dreamed, swam, rode horses. For weeks she didn't even call her friends, although they were burning up the telephone wires trying to get through to

102

her. She could imagine the furor she had left behind on her wedding day. High society was a harsh taskmaster, and she guessed that New York's Four Hundred had already made up at least twice that many lies—studiously ignoring the simple truth that she just didn't want to get married.

One day Elizabeth had even overheard the upstairs maid telling the downstairs maid that she had heard the Van Rynds' chef say that Letitia Van Rynd had heard that Elizabeth had been packed off to Brazil where she was soon expected to give birth to highly illegitimate twins. The maids had giggled. So had Elizabeth.

Dinners, of course, were a little comedy unto themselves, when her father and mother came out from the city. Horace Wainwright would maintain a stony silence at his end of the enormous dining table, broken only by the smacking of his lips when he chewed—a habit which he sometimes used as a weapon to drive strong men mad. Flora Wainwright would babble nervously at the other end of the table about her sister Isobel's trip up the Nile to the Third Cataract and how a camel actually had the gall to spit at Isobel while she was poking it with a pointed stick. Flora Wainwright was a fluttering, diaphanous, lacy wisp of a woman whom everyone simply loved and almost totally ignored. She was, her husband often said with resigned awe, lighter than air.

Finally, one evening as her father smacked, her mother babbled, and the maids padded soundlessly about removing dishes and refilling wine and water glasses, Elizabeth decided to say something.

"Father, don't you think I've been punished enough?"

Wainwright looked at his daughter as if she had burst out laughing hysterically during a high mass.

"I'm sure that's not for me to say, Elizabeth. You have only caused me immense embarrassment and tremendous expense." He drained his wine glass and smacked his lips, satisfied that he had not been the first one to break the silence. "Perhaps you should ask your mother, since you happen to have broken her heart by your little escapade."

Elizabeth looked to the other end of the table, where her mother was intently tracing the garland pattern on a spoon with her finger.

103

"Mother, don't you think this has gone far enough? Father says I must ask your forgiveness to get out of prison."

Flora Wainwright looked up, surprised, and the spoon clattered to the floor where a maid rushed to retrieve it. A lock of hair fell over Flora's eyes and she pushed it away absently.

"What, darling? Did you say something?"

"I'm going batty, Mother, rattling around this big house. If I have to stay out here much longer by myself without seeing anyone I'm going to wrap myself up like a mummy, lie down on my bed and die." Elizabeth crossed her arms over her chest and rolled her eyes grandly for dramatic effect.

"Don't do that, dear, you'll ruin your vision. And wouldn't it be interesting to have a mummy," Flora mused. "Isobel has such marvelous stories. So ancient and wrinkled. The mummies and tombs and things, I mean, not Isobel."

Wainwright coughed. "Shall we take a stroll in the garden, Mother? It's such a warm night." He rose, smacked his lips on Elizabeth's forehead without actually touching flesh, and then helped his wife out of her chair as Dawkins, the butler, rushed to open the French doors to the garden. "I think you'd better stay put for a while longer until you see the error of your ways, Elizabeth," Wainwright said over his shoulder. "I'm very worried about your wild attitude."

As they strolled through the French doors Elizabeth heard her mother say: "Oh, no, dear. Isobel says the altitude isn't at all bad. In fact, Egypt is quite low. . . ."

But that was only the first skirmish in what became a war. One particularly long night she tried sneaking out of the house, only to find her father had turned it into a very posh prison. As soon as she left the house a large black dog came at her, barking and snarling and causing such a racket that the servants rushed out with rakes and rolling pins and the butler called the police. A young policeman had to climb up the tree Elizabeth had taken refuge in and help her down, during which he gave her a pinch that left her black and blue for six days.

For several nights thereafter Elizabeth watched the dog through her window as it roamed the grounds, happily leaving the essence of its presence on every tree and bush. One of the maids told her it was a champion Doberman pinscher named

Nebuchadnezzar's Night Song. Trust her father not to get a plain old watchdog. She tried befriending Nebuchadnezzar with raw meat, and it seemed to work.

Then one night, as the dog greedily gulped the pile of meat she put out for him, Elizabeth made a break for the front gate and freedom. But once Nebuchadnezzar finished the meat he decided to have Elizabeth for dessert. When the policeman pinched her this time, she bit his ear until it bled. They both nearly fell out of the tree.

Well, if she couldn't get out of the house, Elizabeth decided to escalate the war from within. On a Friday afternoon, when her parents were due for dinner that evening, she ordered a complete banquet for a hundred people sent out to the estate from Delmonico's restaurant, along with a dozen waiters. When Horace and Flora Wainwright walked into the dining room it was a sea of candlelight, fresh white linen, liveried waiters, shining silver, handsome flower arrangements, and empty chairs. And at the table in the very center of the room sat Elizabeth, in her wedding gown, sipping wine.

"How marvelous, beautiful," whispered Flora. "You did such a wonderful job with the arrangements, Elizabeth. But I didn't know we were having people to dinner."

Wainwright refused to pay the bill. Delmonico's refused to clean up the mess. The waiters left. One hundred seven-course prime rib dinners sat on the tables in the summer heat as Wainwright ordered the dining room doors locked. For days strange and then alarming smells wafted through the house. Flora Wainwright took to waving a perfumed handkerchief under her nose wherever she went, and the maids spent a great deal of time dusting at the other end of the house. Elizabeth fled outdoors to the beach at the base of the cliff. Nebuchadnezzar whimpered a great deal in his kennel. Only Horace Wainwright refused to acknowledge that his home smelled like a ripe garbage dump in a July heat wave.

On a Sunday afternoon Elizabeth found him sitting stolidly in the library in a scarlet smoking jacket. He appeared to be deep in a volume of Shakespeare, but Elizabeth noticed that he was taking short, puffy breaths through his mouth to avoid the smell.

"Dawkins says something is making strange noises in the

dining room," she said, flopping onto a leather Chesterfield couch opposite him. "But he doesn't know whether it's animal, vegetable, mineral, or the jelly mold in the shape of Alaska."

"And what do you think we should do about it, young lady?" He looked up at her over his book.

"I think we may have to shoot it, Father. I'll flip you for first crack."

He fought to keep a straight face as Elizabeth laughed. She rose and came over to him, tossed the book on the floor, and sat on her father's lap. Still his face was stern.

"I'm sorry, you know. For the wedding—and the dining room. I'll apologize, if that's what you want." She touched his chin softly. "Father?"

Wainwright clucked several times, like a frustrated mother hen sitting over a brood of hard-boiled eggs. "We've spoiled you rotten, Elizabeth."

"Of course you have, you old dear. And I love you for it." She planted a big kiss on his forehead.

"You're stubborn, willful, unreliable, unpredictable. . . ." More clucks.

"You forgot a disgrace to the family, Father."

"Yes, that too, daughter." He looked up at her. "But you're a woman now, aren't you? I can't just send you to your room anymore. You'd probably burn it and the whole house down." This time they both laughed.

"I kept my bargain, Father. I've stayed on Long Island for two months now. Won't you let me go back to the real world?"

Wainwright snorted. "It was only Nebuchadnezzar that kept you from running away!"

"I would have come back the next morning if that damn hound hadn't chased me up a tree. I was only going to go into the village, not Manhattan."

There were many things Wainwright wanted to say as he studied his beautiful daughter. He wanted to tell her that he was actually proud of her fierce spirit. He had never liked her spineless fiancé anyway, although it had been a pip of a business match. He wanted to tell her he envied her her freedom and that spark of inner fire that made all eyes turn to her when she entered a room. He wanted to warn her about the real

106

world, as she called it; about the mean people and small minds she would eventually encounter, about those who would always try to tear her down given a chance.

He wanted to tell her about people who would always hate her just for being herself and for being a rich man's daughter. Sometimes he thought he would like to cover her in glass, so the world could admire her beauty but never sully it with grasping fingers or harsh words.

Yet he couldn't say any of these things to her, he knew. Not now anyway, not yet. Now she was too alive, too open, too ripe to the world to be burdened with these worries. In truth, she was not quite a woman yet, but no longer a child. He knew that she would ultimately have to learn all those lessons herself, no matter the cost. And that realization saddened him.

"All right," he finally blurted out, "go put on your prettiest frock and call some of your scabrous friends and go into the city and raise hell if you like."

Elizabeth squealed, kissed his forehead, and leaped up. "I'll be good, Father."

"I doubt it, child," he called as she took the hall stairs two at a time.

"And tell Dawkins to fetch my Remington and load it. We're going to open up that dining room."

12

THE DICE whirred and clicked and danced across the green felt like insects locked in a mad, darting mating ritual. They hit the far wall, bounced back crazily, and settled to the table with a last quiver, eight black dots staring up like sightless eyes. And around the table a dozen people sighed or laughed or cursed or smiled or clenched their fists in anger, driven by the little white cubes which somehow held the players in a tighter grip than they could ever hold the dice.

For the five hundredth time that night the stickman's rake swished across the brilliant green, distributing money to the winners, scooping up the house's winnings, sing-songing

"Place your bets" as the players stirred, poured more bills on the table, and excitedly fought for a little elbow room. A thick-set young man picked up the dice, whispered to them, shook them, breathed on them, caressed them, and sent them flying across the felt again.

Elizabeth loved the dice. She loved the feel of the dice in her fingers, the speed of the game, the movement. Blink an eye and you miss the play. Hesitate and you miss your turn. It moved the way she wanted her life to move, as fast as a Keystone Kops chase in one of those Mack Sennett comedies. She couldn't keep her eyes off the dice, couldn't get their rattle out of her ears.

She liked the excitement, the energy of the gamblers around her, too. They made her feel alive again after her months on ice. They were shouting now as the young man picked up the dice again and looked around to see who was betting that he would shoot his point, and who was betting against him.

His name was Harvey Beltaire. He had a broad face, heavy brows that nearly formed a solid picket fence of fuzz over his eyes and nose, wavy hair, a sheepish grin, a short-armed, chunky body, and a father who built airplane and automobile engines. His father had made Harvey a vice-president of his company, even though he admitted his son didn't know a cylinder head from a cauliflower. Harvey liked to introduce himself to people he met as the Veep, and when drunk enjoyed honking girls' breasts and shouting "veep-veep, veep-veep" for hours at a time.

Except for that, Elizabeth rather liked Harvey Beltaire. He was sweet in a boyish way, she thought, as he turned to her and winked. And whenever she needed an escort to take her out on the town, Harvey was more than available. That's Harv, she thought, as she blew on the dice that he held out. Everybody's safe date. And at least he was one son of wealth that her father didn't want Elizabeth to marry. Harvey had once honked Horace Wainwright's nose at one of those faddish new cocktail parties and then ran out screaming with laughter to fall into the pool.

The others around the table were shouting at Harvey to shoot and he leaned way back, flung his arm out, and flicked the dice away. Seven. Harvey moaned as he studied the dice and realized he had crapped out.

"I'm the shooter now," cried Elizabeth, pushing Harvey aside with her hip and grabbing the dice. "Give me some money."

He dropped a crumpled handful of bills on the table and watched Elizabeth as she swept a lock of hair out of her eyes. As the other players put their bets down, she intently rubbed the cool dice between her palms. She raised her right hand, the dice within her fist, and quickly sent them skittering across the table.

"Eleven for the lady," sing-songed the stickman. "She's a winnah."

"Let it ride," said Elizabeth quickly as the croupier began to shovel her winnings toward her. He shrugged, pulled the bills back to the center of the table. The players around her murmured, fingering their cash, wondering whether to go with her or against her. She rubbed the dice between her palms again and let them fly.

"Seven, another winnah," called the stickman, and now the other men and women around the table stared at Elizabeth. She flushed, realized she was almost panting. But she wouldn't look at the faces around her; she focused only on the cubes in her hand. They were wet now, from her perspiration.

"Ride again," she almost shouted.

This time she heaved the dice hard against the pit wall and they spun back crazily to stop in front of her.

"Another seven," called the surprised stickman. "We got a natural here, ladies and gentlemen. One more time, miss?"

Elizabeth shrieked and kissed Harvey on the nose. People from all over the room were beginning to converge on the crap table, drawn by the commotion. They pressed in close behind her until she could feel the heat of their bodies on her bare back, smell the perfume and liquor odors. Someone puffed cigar smoke in her face but Elizabeth didn't care. Now she realized how much her months away from the city, the nightlife, the excitement had really cost. She wanted to make up for it all in a night, in one throw of the dice. She took the glass of scotch from Harvey's hand and drank it in a gulp, not even feeling it go down her throat but relishing the heat that spread within her and brought tears to her eyes. She thought about pinching herself hard to see if even the sensation of pain felt good right now. Then she laughed at her nonsense and picked up the dice again, to the cheers of the mob around her.

She looked at the pile of bills the stickman had pushed before her. With the back of her hand she swept the money to the center of the table. Harvey Beltaire was saying something into her ear but she ignored him, shook the dice again, threw.

"An eight, the lady's point is eight," called the stickman, sounding almost relieved as the crowd moaned. He looked at his boss, Izzy the Stub, standing beside him in a red tuxedo with yellow piping. Izzy was watching Elizabeth intently.

Her luck had backed off a little, Elizabeth knew. Every time she had rolled a seven or eleven she had doubled her money. But now she had to make her point—roll an eight—to win again. And if she rolled another seven she not only lost but she had to pass those lovely, hot dice to someone else.

"Let's take the money and get out of here, Lizzie." Harvey was talking to her again. "Let's go dancing, maybe find a speak."

"Leave? Now? Not on your life," she said incredulously, as if he had just suggested they leap off the Woolworth Building together.

"I'm winning, Harvey. And I'm having a ball. You couldn't *drag* me out of this club." She turned back to the stickman. "One more time. Everything."

Money was flying all over the table now as the well-dressed players jostled each other to place bets. She picked up the dice lightly this time, with the tips of her fingers. She touched them to Harvey Beltaire's lips and he kissed the dice, feeling foolish. She threw them away quickly. A five. More money flooded onto the table as she threw again. A three. Again and again she let the money ride and tumbled the dice across the felt. Boxcars. Then ten the hard way—two fives. Nine, four, ten again. Snake eyes. She laughed gleefully as the crowd cheered every throw of the dice and piled yet more money on the table, as many betting with her as against her. Three. Six. Five. Twelve again. And then as quickly as it had started it was over.

110

Seven black dots turned up on the face of the dice far across the table from her. The crowd sighed like a punctured tire and was drifting away before Elizabeth even realized she had lost.

"They don't even hang around long enough for the dust to settle, do they?" she finally said with a laugh, looking around.

Harvey smiled. "Losers aren't the most popular people at a casino, Lizzie."

"Who's a loser?" she demanded, her eyes going back to the dice. "I haven't even started yet."

Elizabeth watched as a fat woman in upswept hair, wearing a handsome gold necklace, picked the dice up in her stubby fingers and gingerly threw them across the table.

Harvey was pulling her away from the table when she turned to him.

"Give me some more money," she ordered.

"Huh?"

"Money, Harvey. Cash. I want to play craps again."

"I'm sorry, Lizzie. I thought you understood. I'm tapped out."

She looked at him, unbelieving. "Your father's got seventeen million. You're not going to tell me you left it in your other pants, are you?"

"He cut my allowance while you were in exile, Lizzie. I'm down to a thousand a month." Sadly, he looked to where the stickman was neatly piling up his money.

"And there goes August, September, and the first week of October."

Reluctantly, Elizabeth looked away from the dice. She smoothed his lapels. "I'm sorry. I didn't mean to be such a pig. Have you got enough to buy a couple of drinks?"

"Not even a cup of coffee."

"Well, I'm not going home," Elizabeth vowed. "Not yet. Not tonight. I've got to kick up my heels some more before I see Long Island again, or I'll bust."

"But I'm flat broke," he whined.

"Oh, shut up, Harvey, dear, and give a scheming woman a moment to think." Elizabeth looked around the crowded casino for a familiar face. She didn't recognize anyone. It must be some sort of perverse rule of nature, she thought. If your

111

pocketbook is stuffed, then people you haven't seen in years suddenly pop out of every doorway and repay long-forgotten debts. But if you *need* the money, you can starve to death before you can dig up a dime.

So how do you get money when you really need it? she pondered. As she studied the faces in the handsome, smoky room she realized, with a start, that it was the first time in her life that she could ever remember being without all the money she could want. It was an interesting feeling. Elizabeth had always assumed as a child that money was just there, like flowers in the spring or snow in winter. She had had a vague awareness that not everybody had as much as her father, of course, like the servants.

Once, when Elizabeth was eight, she had had the temerity to ask her father why the servants didn't have lots of money, too.

"They spent theirs on candy," he replied blithely.

She had nodded, thinking that a very logical explanation. After all, that's what she would spend her money on if she had lots of it.

Later, when she learned about capitalism, communism, the rich, the poor, social protest, reform movements, unions, Elizabeth would argue with her father. Why did the few rich have so much, while so many people had so little? she complained one evening at dinner when she was home on vacation from finishing school.

"Because that's how God intended it," Horace Wainwright had replied.

"That's absurd. It's just not right to have so much money," she had said angrily.

"Then, my dear child," Wainwright had answered, smacking his lips, "why don't you be the first to give away everything you have?"

She never brought up the subject again.

"Can you cry?"

"What?" said Harvey Beltaire.

"Can you cry?"

"I didn't lose enough to cry over, Lizzie. I mean, Dad will pop a gasket when I tell him I'm broke again. But he always coughs up a few hundred eventually for the old Veep."

112

"Forget it, Harvey. I'll do it myself."

"Do what? What are you talking about, Lizzie?"

"Just watch."

She pulled him to one corner of the casino, near the small band playing lazily. She smiled at him and then, as he studied her face, the smile disappeared. Her face lengthened, turned sad. The brows began to quiver, her chin to shake. As she concentrated her cheeks reddened, then her eyes became watery. And slowly two beautiful tears welled up, broke through her lashes, and departed on their tender journey down her cheeks. She looked so sad that Harvey was alarmed.

"What is it, Lizzie? Are you all right?" he pleaded. "I'll get some more money somehow. Please stop bawling."

But suddenly the smile was back on her face. She dabbed at the two tears with a finger.

"That's absolutely amazing," he breathed.

She laughed again. "You ain't seen nothing yet, kiddo. I'm going to get our money back. You just keep your mouth shut, look sad, and let me do the talking, okay?"

"You're nuts, Liz. But I'm right behind you," he agreed.

She mussed her hair slightly, pinched her cheeks to redden them, and took his arm. Once again her face became sad, her eyes watery, her chin quivering. "Now I'm ready," she said.

"What about the tears?"

"Not yet. That's my ultimate weapon," she explained.

"Absolutely amazing," he said again, looking at her with admiration.

She pulled him toward one of the croupiers. They exchanged a few words, then the croupier led them to Izzy the Stub. Izzy quickly took them into a small office adjacent to the money room, closed the door behind them, then sat on a corner of the desk.

He recognized her from the crap table. Not bad, not bad at all, he mused, looking her up and down. But what's she doing with him? he wondered, eyeing Beltaire, who was pudgy and slightly shorter than Elizabeth. Izzy thought he had seen him in the club before.

"Now what gives, lady?"

Elizabeth was studying Izzy at the same time. She tried not to stare at the awful red tuxedo. A good strong face but no

113

taste. And he looked as sharp as a fresh rebuke. This was going to take some doing, she knew.

"We . . . we've lost all our money," she stammered out, clutching Beltaire's arm tightly and trying to look shamefaced. "Every penny we had . . . our wedding money." She worked on her quivering chin a little more. "I guess we went a little crazy." A small sob caught in her throat. "But we just got married yesterday, in Albany. We only stopped in New York for one night. We were on our way to Indiana. And now . . . and now . . ." She unleashed another sob. "All the money for the store Harvey was going to open in Muncie is gone." She leaned close to Beltaire and saw that his eyes never left the floor. Good.

"What a shame," Izzy said in a monotone, studying his fingernails. "A crying shame if ever I saw one."

Elizabeth worked on her chin some more and batted her lashes a few times as if fighting back the waterworks.

"I know this is mad . . . you'll laugh in our faces," she sobbed, her whole body trembling slightly. Nice touch, she told herself. "But our lives . . . our whole future could depend on this. Please, just the money we came in with . . . only a few hundred dollars. It would mean so much to us. . . . We didn't realize how much we were losing. If you could give it back. . . ."

Izzy sighed, looking at the girl. What a waste, he thought. Beautiful, eyes as big and green as Central Park in the spring, and she could act better than that babe in *The Perils of Pauline*.

"Let me get this straight, honey. You lost a bundle and now you want I should give it back?"

"Only two thousand dollars," Elizabeth said in a near whisper.

"Twenty-five hundred," Harvey blurted out. He quickly dropped his eyes back to the floor as Elizabeth pinched him hard. "Ow," he muttered.

"So the shopkeeper talks after all," Izzy said matter-of-factly.

"Just a thousand. Even if you could give us that we'd be so grateful," Elizabeth murmured. "A thousand dollars is a fortune to little people like us."

114

"Oh, I can see that, lady. I can see how you watch your pennies. That sexy little *shmatte* you're wearing is from Gimbel's bargain basement, I suppose?"

"We'd bless your name in church every Sunday," Elizabeth tried again. "Isn't that worth something to you?"

Izzy was enjoying himself. She was easy to look at and didn't give up. "My name is Isadore Abraham Goldfinkle. So dropping my name in church probably is not going to do either of us much good since we play for different dealers. Now, you can tell me how you'll name your first kid after me."

It was time to pull out all the stops, Elizabeth realized. This man didn't believe a word they were saying, but maybe he couldn't stand to see a woman cry. She dug her long nails into the palm of one hand.

"Now you're laughing at us because we don't know the ways of the big city," she sobbed, big tears rolling down her face. Oh brother, she thought.

"Lady, I'm not going to give you your *gelt* back for two reasons. First of all, this is not a bank, it is a gambling joint. See, it works like this: You come in here and bet your money. And if you lose you go home lighthearted but broke. We don't give anything back."

He looked at Harvey and grinned amiably. "And the second reason is that I just don't believe you. I know I've seen this palooka in here before throwing around his money. If he's a shopkeeper from Indiana then I'm the Pope's rabbi."

He turned to Elizabeth. "And you sure don't look like any dumpy shopkeeper's wife."

Her greed was beginning to turn to indignation. Elizabeth was used to getting what she wanted, when she wanted it. And now, she thought, this crook in his red clown suit is looking right through me and calling me a liar. Even if she *was* lying, Elizabeth didn't like it one bit. What would her father do in a situation like this? she wondered. Of course!

Harvey leaned over and whispered in her ear. "We're beat. Let's get out of here, Lizzie."

She ignored him. Elizabeth wiped away the tears, slowed the sobs, blew her nose into the silk handkerchief she took from Beltaire's breast pocket.

"Maybe we could make a deal, Mr. Goldberg," she said slowly, looking him in the eye.

"Goldfinkle," he corrected her. "And I sincerely doubt it."

Careful now, she told herself. She blew her nose again.

"Well, Mr. Goldfinkle. If you gave us some of our money back we'd be so grateful. I'm sure we would sort of reward you—for your good deed."

"Lady, you're a pip," Izzy laughed. "You want me to steal you some money and then you'll pay me for stealing out of what I give you? What a mind."

She had a feeling this wasn't exactly the way her father made deals.

"What's so funny?"

"Lady, you slay me." Izzy pulled out his own handkerchief and wiped his eyes. "If I'm going to steal money, I'm sure not giving most of it to Cinderella and Prince Charming. Whatever I steal, I keep."

No one noticed the door to the money room opening, or the man standing in the doorway.

"What's this about stealing?" Big Bill Dwyer said quietly.

Izzy leaped off the desk and whirled to face the other man. "Nobody is stealing anything, Mr. Dwyer. I just mean that if I was going to put my hand in the till, I wouldn't give it to anybody else. I'd keep it. See?"

"Not really," Dwyer said, looking to Elizabeth.

"I was only talking, see? I sure would never steal anything from you, Mr. Dwyer."

"Then who would you steal from?" Dwyer asked softly, turning his eyes back to Izzy.

"Nobody, boss, nobody." He was nervous now. Sweat popped up on his brow.

"Who are these people?" Dwyer pointed to Elizabeth and Harvey.

"They claim that just got married and wandered in here and lost all their dough before they knew what hit them. And now they want it back. I told them to get lost."

Elizabeth stared at Dwyer. He looked so refined, so gentle, so impeccable in his finely tailored suit. His eyes were soft, understanding. His face calm, fatherly, and untroubled. In short, she felt, here was a man she could lie to.

Her tears, which had almost stopped, began to flow again. Her chin resumed quivering. She forced her eyes down, trying to look helpless and vulnerable. She was having a hard time not laughing out loud.

"How much money did you lose, child?" Dwyer asked.

"A thousand," said Izzy.

"Two thousand," said Harvey.

"You know, you shouldn't gamble if you can't afford to lose," Dwyer explained kindly. "I've ignored that lesson many times and regretted it just as often."

Elizabeth bit her lip until it hurt to keep the smirk off her face.

"We lost our heads. But I swear, we'll take our money and never come back." She bobbed her head. "We've truly learned our lesson."

"Give them the two grand, Izzy," Dwyer ordered.

"Boss, this is just some kind of flim-flam."

"Give it to them," Dwyer said again.

"I don't believe it," Harvey muttered under his breath. She kicked his leg. Her sobs were of laughter now, her shoulders heaved as she tried to stifle her glee. She fought to keep a straight face.

Izzy went into the money room and returned with a handful of cash. With a scowl he handed it to Elizabeth.

"Do they have to count it?" Dwyer asked.

Reluctantly, Izzy pulled some more bills out of his pocket and handed them to her. "I tell you, boss, they're goniffs."

"You can't always take, Izzy," Dwyer said as the door to the casino opened and the noise of the players poured in. "Sometimes in life you have to give."

"But this isn't one of those times," said George McManus from the door, staring at Elizabeth's profile.

13

"DID YOU have to throw him down the stairs?"

"Who?"

"Harvey. You shouldn't have thrown him down the stairs."

"Who's Harvey?"

"Just . . . a friend."

"You're beautiful. Even more than I remembered."

"He said you nearly broke his arm, do you know that?"

"Who?"

"Harvey, dammit. The boy you threw down the stairs."

"What did you want me to do, kiss him on each cheek and give him a medal? He tried to steal my money."

"Well, so did I."

"If you like, we can go back and I'll throw you down the stairs, too."

"No thanks."

"Can I touch your hair?"

"No."

"It's so fine. Like silky spider webs."

"I don't like to be touched."

"You were made to be touched."

"Look, will you tell me what we're doing in a carriage riding around Central Park? This horse smells."

"I'm trying to decide whether to have you arrested."

"That's a laugh. You? A mobster who runs a gambling casino? You're going to turn *me* in?"

"Would it surprise you if I told you my business is legal?"

"Would it surprise you if the horse began to recite *Hamlet*?"

"I want to kiss you."

"I'd rather eat worms."

"Then why don't you jump out and call for help? Why do you keep looking at me out of the corner of your eye?"

"Curiosity."

"What?"

"Well, I've never been kidnapped before. It's . . . exciting."

"Your skin is so soft. And your nose."

"It's soft?"

"It's perfect."

"Do you pack a rod?"

"Huh?"

"What kind of mobster are you, anyway? Do you carry a gun?"

"Oh. No, I told you, I'm a legit businessman."

"Then what's that bulge under your coat?"

"That's my heart beating like crazy because I'm with you."

"Good God. You'll have to do better than that."

"How's this?"

"Uh . . . I wish you wouldn't. It tickles . . . I've always had sensitive . . . ears."

"They're perfect. Beautiful. As if Cartier made them out of mother of pearl."

"Good . . . God. Please stop."

"Why?"

"What about the driver?"

"He's practically deaf. You have a lovely neck."

"But what if he looks?"

"He's almost blind, too."

"Oh, my . . . oh, don't stop that."

"I promise I won't."

"But if he's deaf and blind . . . who's driving the carriage?"

"The horse."

"The horse?"

"What's your name?"

"Oh, God. You're making love to me and I don't even . . . know your name. I'm not this kind of girl."

"Yes you are."

"This is crazy . . . That feels so . . . Oh dear. Oh my. Tighter. Hold me. Tighter. Oh yes. . . ."

"It's George."

"George . . . like the king of England. George, darling. . . ."

"You still haven't told me."

"What, George darling? Anything. . . . Oh God, more . . . please."

"I'm crazy about you."

"Elizabeth."

"I'm crazy about you, Elizabeth."

In the cool of early morning the carriage took them back to his hotel. They held each other close, Elizabeth's head on his shoulder, her eyes closed, as they rode the elevator to the top

119

floor. But when they were finally alone she came alive, assaulting him, devouring him. Her legs crushed his waist until George cried out, half in pain and half in pleasure.

She bit, kissed, probed every part of him, drawing him into her endlessly. And he responded as he never had with another woman, rising to her passion until her eyes were wild, her thighs quivered, and her breath came in raw gasps. They touched each other everywhere with tongues, fingers, lips. And still she begged for more, pulling him to her breasts, between her legs, to her lips. He touched her face, her hair, caressed her endlessly. And when he exploded into her she still kept moving, moaning, pulling him farther and farther from the room with four walls into a world of endless expanses and limitless joys.

They were so wrapped up in each other that it was not for hours, as stray shafts of sunlight began to touch their sweated bodies, that he sensed they were not alone. He quickly looked around, startled. Standing in the bedroom doorway was a woman in red, watching them. Marie.

For a moment George followed her with his eyes as Elizabeth sighed, crooned to him, pulled him ever closer, not even aware that Marie was there. He didn't know what to expect—shouts, a violent scene, tears. But Marie silently moved to the side of the bed, stopped in the shadows, waited as if trying to make a decision. Even as Elizabeth pulled his mouth down to her lips he felt Marie reach out and take a lock of his hair, gently curling it around her finger.

A bittersweet wave of emotion swept over George, surprising him and bringing tears to his eyes for the first time in years. Tears he could not understand. Tears of love, confusion, vulnerability. Elizabeth moaned, nibbled his throat, slowly ran her finger the length of his backbone until he trembled in ecstasy.

Out of the corner of his eye he watched Marie lift the ruby necklace he had given her off the bedtable and carefully fasten it around her neck. As he climaxed again—blissful, confused, hurtling into Elizabeth—Marie bent, gently put her lips to his shoulder, then walked out. He barely heard the click of the door.

14

Mayor Jimmy Walker.

Mayor James Walker.

Mayor James J. Walker, Jr.

He crossed out the top two and settled on the third. It would look so much classier on his stationery. The next mayor of New York was in his state senate district office for what he expected would be the last time. In four days he'd have the Democratic nomination for mayor. Then he could stop playing conscientious, sober, young public servant and get back to some serious drinking.

This election had been harder than the others, Walker mused, sitting back in his swivel chair and crossing his feet on the desk. He enjoyed the campaigning but the Tammany boys were driving him batty. They wouldn't let him drink, wouldn't let him go near a speak, made sure he was home in bed with his wife every night by nine. His girlfriend was no happier about it than he was. But Tammany said it was essential. And so he went along.

His private phone rang but Walker hesitated before answering it. Probably some disgruntled chronic bitcher, irked because his garbage wasn't picked up on time. He wondered how these cranks always seemed to get his unlisted number. The phone rang fifteen times. He was tired of listening to complaints, he decided. The phone rang twice more and stopped. That's all anyone ever called about. He never once had a constituent ring up and tell him what a great job he was doing. The phone started to ring again. He finally picked it up with a sigh.

"Walker?"

"Yes."

"Don't you answer your phone anymore?"

"Who is this?" The voice sounded familiar.

"Are you alone?" demanded the caller. "Is anyone listening on the line?"

"This is my private line. Who the hell is this anyway?"

121

"Horace Wainwright. I'm sure you remember me." There was sarcasm in his voice. And something more.

"Of course, of course, Wainwright. You're one of our most loyal—"

"Turn off the fertilizer, Walker. I've got bad news."

Walker said nothing.

"You .. we're in big trouble," Wainwright continued. "Hearst knows about my campaign contribution and he's going to spring it in a special issue of the *American* just in time to throw the election to Hylan."

"Is that all?" Walker took his feet off the desk. "Old Willie Randolph does this every election. He calls me a crook. I deny it. And the voters ignore us both."

"They won't ignore it this time. I hear Hearst even has a photograph of me dumping that money on your desk."

"That's impossible."

"Maybe it's a doctored picture. I don't know, but my source saw it. He also saw the article Hearst cooked up. I come out looking like the devil incarnate and you look ten times worse. That paper reaches the streets and you're dead. We're dead. You've got to stop it."

"Stop a newspaper? How?"

"I don't care. Bribe people. Murder people. But stop that newspaper from coming out." Wainwright was puffing angrily.

Walker paused. "Take it easy. I know you're upset, but they can't hurt us that bad. We'll just deny everything, say the pictures are doctored, throw some mud on Hylan. It always works."

"You won't have time. I told you, Hearst isn't pulling the switch until the last possible moment. Too late to fight back."

Walker scratched his head and stared at the black phone. He was surprised by Wainwright's fear. Most voters thought all politicians were crooks, anyway. The exposé might hurt but the last straw poll had him so far in front it seemed he couldn't lose no matter what. He could imagine Hearst, a lock of thinning hair falling over his forehead and his pudgy cheeks puffing in and out in concentration, coming up with something like this. Hearst hated Tammany like Cain hated Abel, with an intensity born of jealousy. Tammany had denied

Hearst the mayor's office and then the governor's chair. Worse, in doing so Tammany had thwarted his consuming ambition to be President. So Hearst used his papers, particularly the *New York American,* to bloody Tammany whenever he could—like getting dull John Hylan elected a Democratic mayor on an anti-Tammany platform. No wonder Wainwright is worried, Walker thought. Hearst is against the traction interests. If his puppet Hylan is reelected there won't be another foot of subway track built in New York City for four more years.

Walker wondered if Hearst was on the telephone at this very minute, chuckling behind his ornate marble desk in his antique-filled apartment on Riverside Drive, while droves of employees scurried about doing the great man's bidding. How ironic, Walker thought. Hearst would have made a terrific Tammany boss.

"Look," he said soothingly into the phone, "maybe it's not as bad as you think."

"No, it's worse," barked Wainwright. "I didn't tell you all of it. Do you know a chorus girl named Rosie Garrett?"

Walker swallowed hard.

"I thought you might. Your gal Rosie is going to tell all in Hearst's *American,* complete with photographs of your man-handling her in the back seat of a car in Albany."

Walker groaned. He remembered when the picture had been taken, on a hot summer night two years ago. At first he had thought the flashing light had been part of an unusually intense orgasm. Until Rosie showed him the negatives. He thought she had destroyed them when he made his final payment. He wondered how long Hearst had had the pictures.

"Now," Wainwright demanded, "what are you going to do to stop that newspaper?"

"I'll think of something," Walker said without certainty.

Wainwright hung up without saying good-bye. Walker sat back in his chair for a moment. Then he reached for the telephone again and started dialing, quickly.

15

EMPIRE CITY RACETRACK sat on a low rise within spitting distance of the homes of the solid, stalwart burghers of Yonkers, New York. On occasion, some of Yonkers' better citizens would make use of this proximity to do some literal spitting. Empire City, complained those righteous elements who preferred to keep their money safely in a sock stuffed inside a mattress, was a smelly, noisy blight which attracted the worst elements of the Gomorrah just a few miles down the Hudson River.

It was to Empire City that Elizabeth was bound as she wheeled the red two-seater away from the curb of the Park Central Hotel. Beside her, George McManus slept slouched against the door, fedora over his eyes. She glanced at him occasionally as she drove but he never stirred. Only his chest rose and fell rhythmically. One hand lay against her leg. He had fallen asleep the moment the door had closed behind him.

Not very flattering, she thought, to have a man doze off the moment he's alone with you. But she knew he was exhausted. Except for the hours with Elizabeth he spent virtually every waking moment at the club, as if it would all collapse if he were not there to personally hold it up.

She wheeled the car easily through the heavy afternoon traffic, darting around trucks and buses until she was driving up the West Side paralleling the Hudson. How long had it been? Six days? No, a week. Only a week since she had known this man beside her. And already everything was different in her life. In that week she had barely been home and hadn't seen her father at all, only grabbing some clothes and leaving a hurried note to say she was all right and not to worry. Was he pacing up and down in his study right now worrying about his errant daughter? Or was Horace Wainwright consumed by one of the business deals that wiped everything else out of his mind for days at a time? Either way, she realized, it didn't matter. As long as she was with George McManus, it was enough.

A boxy black Ford cut sharply into the lane in front of her and she braked quickly. George stirred, stretched, awakened by the car's sudden motion. He threw his hat into the boot behind the seats and ran his hands through his hair.

"What's that?" he squinted. "That bright light."

"The sun," she told him.

"Jesus, I've been crawling around at night so long I forgot what it looked like."

He rubbed the sleep from his eyes, then turned to her.

"And who are you?" he demanded.

"Funny," Elizabeth said.

"Wait. That voice. I recognize the voice. And the nose. It's coming back to me now." He snapped his fingers, feigning concentration. "Eudora? Ella? Eliza?"

"Rumpelstiltskin."

"You're even more beautiful in the daylight, Rumpelstiltskin. Did you know that?" He touched her ear, ran his finger down her neck to the knot in the blue silk scarf that waved in the breeze. Then he leaned over and gently kissed her throat. The car swerved across the lane.

"You're going to get us both killed that way," she warned.

"What a way to go," he whispered. "But all right." He sat back in the seat. "Get me to the track by the third race or it's no more free love for you, toots."

"You mean you're going to make me pay?"

"Ain't I worth it?"

"Yes."

He took a cigarette from his jacket pocket, cupped the match as he lit up. He watched the trees, the shimmering river, content not to speak as Elizabeth drove. There would sometimes be these silences between them now, when neither felt it necessary to speak. They would just glance at each other and somehow know the other was happy.

It had all been so easy, so right. Somehow they had fit together like the pieces of a jigsaw puzzle. The pieces were jagged, totally different from each other, crazily shaped. And yet they fit each other in some kind of master plan that amazed him.

Languorously, knowing there was no hurry, George and Elizabeth had discovered each other, drawn each other out, on the long afternoons before he went to the club. He found the tiny mole high on her thigh. While he slept she would trace the scar on his forehead for hours. In wonderment he would run his hands over the pleasing curve of her buttocks, as if savoring the classic lines of a fine sculpture. She pressed his hands to her face and explored his strong fingers as if they were a new invention. He found out she flew a biplane, went to schools in Switzerland and Paris, had an affair at eighteen with a Bourbon cousin only once removed from the deposed French throne.

George told her about Hell's Kitchen, stealing coal in the winter and ice in the summer. About sleazy workmen's bars with sawdust and sweat and vomit on the floor. About alleys and tenements and poolrooms and poker. Using coins on the bedsheets he explained massé shots, three-bankers, how to break leaving the other player behind the eight ball. He showed her how to deal from the bottom of a deck.

She remembered nannies. He remembered street gangs. She saw the Vice-President of the United States at a coming-out party in Newport when she was sixteen. When he was sixteen he saw a jealous husband slash a neighbor's throat in a dim hallway. As they talked, each marveled at how far they had come to find each other, and how none of those other things mattered anymore. Then they would turn to each other, losing themselves for hours in a tangle of arms, legs, hair, sheets, blankets, pillows, cries, whispers. And when it was all over they would lie back drained, not touching, until they slowly began to talk again, probing each other's lives.

Late in the evenings she would watch him dress before the mirror to go to the Paradise Rehearsal Club. Sometimes she would hide a shirt stud or a shoe and laughingly threaten not to return it to keep him at home. She would always give it back, though, and then send George off with a quick kiss. Only when he was gone would she finally eat or sleep, as if the moments with him were too precious to waste on unimportant functions.

Some things they did not tell each other. Elizabeth didn't talk about her family much, other than to laugh about its wealth. She wanted George to herself, didn't want to share him with the inevitable friends and relatives. Not yet, anyway. And she knew there was almost no chance Horace Wain-wright would approve of George McManus. A wealthy Protestant pillar of the community and a hustling Irish Catholic gambler. No, she knew, there could never be any love between these two men. Better to wait, put things off, keep George as hers alone.

And he never mentioned Marie Flynn's presence that night in the bedroom while they made love. Sometimes, when he thought about it, he could hardly believe it had happened. Marie stayed on at the club as hostess and she seemed as happy and raucous as ever. Now she was insulting the customers until they squirmed with delight. But she never spoke more than a few flip words to George, never touched him, never talked about going home with him anymore in the weary, boozy, smoky half-daylight when the last gamblers left the club.

He often asked Elizabeth to go to the club with him, and was surprised when she refused. He had told her about the Paradise Rehearsal Club, of course. How they had bought the right people and fooled the others to get the club going. George loved the story. He told her about Big Bill Dwyer and Izzy the Stub and Rats Wolnik and even Marie Flynn. He told her about the raids and his day in court. He told Elizabeth how he felt about cards, gambling, taking the ultimate risk. He told her about the excitement of watching all that money changing hands, of outsmarting so many people, of laughing in the face of convention, of beating the odds.

When he talked about gambling and the club, she saw the same shining, excited look in his eyes that he had when they made love. And that's why she stayed away. Because she did not want to share him with the Paradise Rehearsal Club, did not want to compete with the casino and its glamour. He talked about the club as if it were a mistress, she realized. And having two mistresses in the same place could only diminish both. Elizabeth was only slightly surprised to find she was thinking of herself as a mistress.

Somewhere down deep, too, so deep she never really brought it to the surface to examine, she was afraid of the club. Afraid that, maybe, he loved that mistress more. Give it time, she told herself. Give it time.

But Elizabeth had been proud when he told her he wanted to take her to the racetrack to show her off. Had the other men in her life—boys, really—said they wanted to show her off, Elizabeth would have laughed in their faces. Was she a prize sheep or pet pig to be paraded around? She would have torn them to pieces, humiliated them, reduced them to tears. She had done that, sometimes, just when she felt wicked. It wasn't hard with most men, she knew. Destroy their vanity and you destroy them.

For George McManus, though, she primped and checked her make-up and her hair endlessly as she dressed for the track. Now it was important to her that people she didn't even know approve of her. Important because it would tie him to her even more. And she even drove the car while he slept. How the mighty have fallen, she thought with a smile.

George flipped the stub of his cigarette out of the car and patted his pockets looking for another smoke. Suddenly he realized that something was missing.

"Goddamn. I left my billfold at the hotel." He searched through his pockets again.

"The last of the big-time spenders doesn't have a dime?" Elizabeth mocked.

"You have any money, toots?"

"You forget, you haven't let me out of your sight for days. All I've got is my emergency mad money. A ten-dollar bill."

"Not much." He turned and touched her throat again. "But I'm feeling lucky. Hand it over, lady."

Elizabeth steered the car around a curve. "Would you believe it's hidden in my shift? Father taught me years ago that was a safe place. He said no gentleman would ever violate my person. I guess the lesson stuck."

"Well, you keep your eyes glued to the road," George said, "and I'll make a withdrawal from the bank."

The car veered across two lanes this time.

When they pulled into the Empire City lot the crowd was already noisy, impatient for the horses to parade onto the track for the third race. George bought a program and a couple of garishly colored tip sheets to see what the experts liked that day. As usual, the scratch sheets contradicted each other—

each claiming it had the real winners. He tore them into small pieces and tossed them over his shoulder.

"I've got a hunch, Elizabeth. Can you guess which one it is?"

She scanned the program. "Rags to Riches?"

"A natural," George said. "Now let's go see the Dancer."

"Who's the Dancer?"

But George was already dragging her through the crowd to the bookmakers at the rear of the grandstand, where the throngs were thickest.

George stopped before a tall man in a bowler hat who looked, Elizabeth thought, like the world's happiest undertaker. Dancer Hyams was in his fifties, cadaverously thin, with huge, bright eyes, sunken cheeks, and a sharp, hooked nose. He was dressed in black except for a white shirt and spotless white spats. Hyams constantly rubbed his pale hands together and showed a yellow-toothed smile, as if he were measuring everyone for an expensive coffin. When he spotted George the smile grew by eight teeth.

"Bless me, if it isn't my favorite customer," the bookmaker called, ignoring a dozen men clamoring for his attention. "Come to make the Dancer a little richer."

Hyams jumped off his box and came to them, grasping George's hand. "And you've brought a lovely lady. Good. Good. I hope you love her, George, because she'll be a jinx with the ponies."

George introduced them, then said, "Rags to Riches in the third. Give me some numbers."

"Twenty to one. But save your money, Georgie. I hear the plug has bandages to the eyeballs. Sore."

"It's a hunch. Make it fifty to one."

Hyams shrugged. "Ah, Georgie, you should listen when a bookie touts you off a nag. I wouldn't do it for my own brother. But, if that's what you want. . . . How much? Five hundred, a thousand?"

"Ten," George said, looking at Elizabeth.

"Ten thousand?" Hyams whistled.

"Ten dollars."

Hyams touched Elizabeth's arm. "Tell me he's joking now, miss. Ten dollars?"

Elizabeth shrugged.

"If you're short, Georgie, your marker's good with the Dancer."

George shook his head. "Ten dollars. Can you handle that much action?"

"He's possessed. She's bewitched him," Hyams muttered, walking back to his soapbox.

"Have you really bewitched me?" George took her arm and led Elizabeth away from the mob.

She looked at him as they got into a wire-mesh elevator and the operator slid the door closed.

"If I haven't, darling, then I've wasted the last week."

When the elevator stopped, he led her to the front of the grandstand, nodded at a red-nosed attendant, and they went down a few steps to a private box bearing a brass plate marked "G. McManus." They settled in and he looked pleased, as if the plaque were some sort of diploma, certifying that George McManus now belonged with the rest of the blue-blooded swells who were firmly entrenched in the other private boxes around him.

The crowd noises swelled and Elizabeth turned to see the horses parade onto the track, the tiny jockeys perched ridiculously and precariously on their muscled backs. The horses were trotted halfway around the track, then quickly brought back to the starting line where they danced nervously as the starter tried to get them into an even row. Rags to Riches was standing somnolently in the middle of the pack when the starting flag fell. With an incredible burst of speed the colt was five lengths in front by the first turn, running furiously with one loose bandage flapping from its left foreleg. Elizabeth was on her feet cheering with the rest of the crowd, the noise rising from crescendo to crescendo, as Rags to Riches cruised to a two-length victory.

"Not bad," George said calmly.

"Is this the celebrated McManus poker face I've heard so much about?" She sat back down, flushed.

"Let's go get a drink and pick another goddamn winner." He took her hand.

George led Elizabeth from the box through the crowd to the

restaurant overlooking the track on the second floor. Empire City's dining quarters were as exclusive as the best restaurants in the city. Gentlemen were required to wear coats and ties, unescorted ladies were not permitted, and the prices were heftier than the horses running outside the huge picture windows.

A formally dressed maitre d' nodded to George and led them to a prime table overlooking the track. George ordered tea and a waiter in a snow-white jacket quickly deposited a large pot, cups, and saucers, then poured.

"What kind of tea is this?" said Elizabeth. "It's not hot."

George took a sip from his cup. "Delicious."

She sipped. "It's scotch!"

"And good stuff, too."

"But why didn't you just order scotch?"

"Toots, I know you're rich and privileged, but you must have heard of Prohibition. If the Feds catch you serving scotch, you go to jail. So we order tea instead."

"Of course. Prohibition—I think I read about that," she said with a straight face.

"It's nice how even you rich dames keep up with the times. It gives us all so much in common."

She sipped from her cup again. "The tea is growing on me."

"I've never tried getting a girl drunk on tea. Do you think it might help me batter down your defenses?"

"They're already in smoking ruins, Mr. McManus."

They looked at each other for a moment. George took her hands in his, studying them.

"Maybe I love you too much, Elizabeth." He looked into her eyes with mock gravity. "You're interfering with my gambling. It's almost time for the fourth race and we haven't picked a horse yet."

They scanned the program together and decided on a mare called Patent Leather. As the bugle sounded, George ran off to bet everything they had won. He returned to Elizabeth's side in time to see the mare surge to the front at the final turn and pound to the finish a one-length winner. George and Elizabeth were toasting Patent Leather with the tea when someone stopped beside their table.

131

"Another winner, George? The Dancer told me you were hot today." Arnold Rothstein looked quizzically from George to Elizabeth.

George introduced him and Rothstein pulled a chair up to the table.

"The Dancer also told me you were with a real looker, George. He wasn't kidding about that either." Rothstein studied Elizabeth like a government inspector evaluating a piece of prime beef.

"Arnie here is one of my oldest acquaintances," George explained. "We've had a strong mutual distrust for years. Or should I call it mutual dislike?"

"Yes, lovely. Lovely," Rothstein murmured. "But what are you doing with this hard-bitten gorilla?" His laugh was unamused.

Like most people, Elizabeth couldn't take her eyes off Rothstein. There was something sinister and snake-like about the man, she decided. He delicately scratched his cheek with his pinky and the ruby on his finger gleamed like an evil third eye. She imagined him as a scheming court counselor to some foppish medieval king, constantly whispering, whispering in the king's ear, turning his head while plotting his doom. She nearly shivered as she watched him.

"Oh, Mr. McManus is teaching me how to cheat at cards." She managed to sound light.

"How useless. A woman with a sense of humor," Rothstein said dryly.

"What did you come to do me out of?" George broke in.

"As a matter of fact, I did come to talk a little business. Something to our mutual benefit."

"I'm on pins and needles, Arnie."

"It's about the Paradise Rehearsal Club."

"Somehow I knew it would be. I don't have anything else you'd want."

"I'm not taking anything, Georgie. I'm offering. I hear good things about you. You've got a nice little hustle in that club. But I think I could help you make it even better."

"I doubt it." George looked at Elizabeth. She was glancing at Rothstein out of the corners of her eyes.

"For a percentage—a partnership—I could do big things

132

for you." Rothstein rested his chin on one hand. "Money if you need it. Protection for a rainy day. And you could cut loose from Big Bill Dwyer. Be your own man."

"I don't need your dough." George held out his hand, palm up. "And I don't feel any rain."

Rothstein smiled, showing bad teeth. "Some people aren't smart enough to buy an umbrella when the storm clouds start building. They wait to get wet first."

"You can't stand it, can you, Arnie?"

"Pardon me?"

"You can't stand anybody having any action unless you got a piece of it. It threatens you, doesn't it? Makes you feel small."

Rothstein stood up, nodded to Elizabeth.

"You're still small potatoes, George. Still don't know when to quit. I'll give you a little while to think about it. You'll come around. Everybody comes around eventually." Rothstein walked stiffly away from the table.

"What a nice man," Elizabeth said, watching his back. "All the charm of a fly in your soup."

George got up. "Suddenly the air stinks. Let's get out of here. Let's go downstairs with the real people." She took his hand.

Downstairs in the grandstand, as they elbowed their way through the dense crowd, Elizabeth could feel the excitement growing around her. They went to the rail to see the horses and she stared at the men and women milling about, feeling the harnessed, sweaty energy they were exuding. It was almost sensual down here, she decided. Like being at the center of great events or in the bowels of a huge machine that was shaking and roaring and nearly ready to explode.

As they reached the rail the bugler blew the call to the colors. The handsome animals walked by and the crowd pushed forward as if someone had thrown a switch and sent an extra surge of electricity into them. Elizabeth glanced at George as he intently studied the first of the animals to appear. Around them people argued loudly, muttered to themselves, cursed the jockeys, cajoled the jockeys, rushed to place their bets in wild-eyed fear that they would be too late, or just dithered in indecision. George's hand stroked Elizabeth's back absently, his mouth near her ear. She could hear his level breathing.

Elizabeth wondered if he was really thinking of Arnold Rothstein, when someone put a big hand on George's shoulder. George turned and smiled broadly.

"Basher, you broken down son of a bitch, how the hell are you?"

The other man was big and wore an ill-fitting brown suit. When he smiled at Elizabeth she noticed one front tooth was missing. George introduced him as Seamus Mulcahey, "better known as Seamus the Basher, the best street fighter and the worst club fighter south of Fifty-fourth Street."

The Basher was tall, thick in the body, with a broad face that showed the remnants of old beatings. His eyes were small and shrewd, however, and she thought he was not just some burned-out hulk of a boxer. His most noticeable feature was his ears, which were callused and puffy enough to win a blue ribbon in a state-fair cauliflower exhibit. They made his head look as if it had handles.

George looked past him. "Where are the others? Pete the Gyp and the Colonel. Crazy Madeline and Tootie Bones. If you're here, they have to be around."

"Oh, they're here all right, up by the books. We like to hang out and get the last-minute action, ya know. We've missed ya, George." The Basher turned to Elizabeth. "We used to hang out together, in the days before George got himself all high and mighty."

"Not so high and mighty," George said, "that I'd forget a friend. Could you and the others use a little?"

"You know we're tapped out, George. Even when you was around we couldn't pick a winner in a one-horse race. But I don't take handouts." He held up his hands. "Nope, never took no handouts."

George nodded. "The lady's a little dry, Basher. Why don't you do me a favor. Go see Dancer Hyams and tell him I said to give you a yard. Then you might get us a couple of cups of tea and keep the change. Okay?"

When the Basher got back with the tea cups, Elizabeth gulped the scotch down and then sipped some of George's, surprised at how thirsty she was. With the heat and the scotch she began to feel warm—and almost aroused. Again George bet all their winnings. Was the time between races becoming shorter? Or was it just the liquor and her excitement? She deliberately leaned close to him as they waited for the race to begin. She breathed on his neck, in his ear. George looked down at her, surprised. Then he touched her shoulders, her hips, her hair, and she could feel the heat of his fingertips.

The horses lined up in front of them, the near one almost close enough to touch. Elizabeth could see the animal's white-rimmed rolling eye, the foamy sweat on his shoulders where the reins rubbed. Then they were off and George pressed against her, pushing her into the fence as he strained to see.

Down here the roar of the crowd rose higher and higher until the drumming of hooves was drowned out. Elizabeth couldn't hear any one voice, even her own, but thousands of throats crying as one. She couldn't stand still. She couldn't resist the tide. Her hair was in her eyes, her face sweaty, her throat raw as the animals raced past her. Suddenly, she realized, the race was over. The crowd was nearly silent. But she found she didn't want to stop shouting.

"I can't talk," she half-croaked. "My throat is so sore."

"Then don't talk. Just smile." George was beaming. "We're going to get 'em today, Elizabeth. They're never going to forget George McManus today!"

"Did we win?" she asked softly, turning to face him.

"Only about sixty thousand," he said with a laugh. "Where were you?"

"I'm not sure."

"Are you all right?"

She nodded. "I want to go now. I want you to take me back to the hotel."

"Soon," he promised. "Very soon. But first we have to see the Dancer again."

"I don't want the Dancer. I want you."

He shook his head. "It's bad form to quit while you're ahead."

She stood on her toes and roughly nibbled his ear. "Can the Dancer do that?"

"Just one more race." He was half pleading.

She sighed, took his arm. "Let's go see the Dancer."

The bookie's face was as white as his shirt. His hands shook. Those huge eyes darted around looking for trouble in every corner. He found it in the form of George and Elizabeth.

"You'll get your money. Don't worry. I won't stiff you," he hissed as he pushed through the crowd to them.

"I don't want it," George said.

"Tonight. I'll drop it at your hotel. Don't worry. The Dancer always pays. A bookie who doesn't pay doesn't have any friends. You know that."

George glanced at Elizabeth. "I said I don't want it, Dancer."

Hyams looked as if he'd been hit with a large rock. "You don't want the sixty grand?"

"I'm going to give you a chance to get even. We want to put the whole bundle on Saber Dancer in the sixth. Right, honey?"

Elizabeth leered at him. "You know what I want," she said softly.

"I'll give you two to one," Hyams said hurriedly, looking as if he had just leaped off the last bus to purgatory. "Done?"

"Done," George said. "If I win, I'll find you."

"And if you don't," returned the Dancer, "just forget about me. I can't take another streak like you had today."

George practically dragged Elizabeth outside, where they threaded their way through the crowd to the rail. "Do you know what it means if this horse wins, toots?" he whispered, standing behind her.

"It means we can go," she said dreamily. She took his hands and pulled his arms around her waist.

"It means almost two hundred thousand bucks, is what it means."

She moved his hands up until they were just touching her breasts. "Money isn't everything, darling."

George looked around and realized that no one was watching them. In the mob that surrounded them, every eye was on the horses as they daintily walked to the starting line. He could have walked around naked and no one would have noticed. Slowly one finger on each hand began to rub Elizabeth's breasts. She moaned softly as he gently pinched her nipples through the soft dress.

"Hey George, I got something hot." McManus dropped his hands and looked around. Seamus the Basher was directly behind him, whispering into his ear.

"What do you want?" George said.

"The fight tonight in Red Hook—McGraw and Ravelli. I hear McGraw is gonna go down like a cement submarine. No shit."

The Basher's breath was hot on George's neck. Elizabeth was wriggling as George's hands moved on her breasts again. Her hips began to gyrate against him.

George licked his lips. "McGraw is getting ready for the champ. This Ravelli is supposed to be a walkover, to get him tuned up."

"Sure, that's what the mick thinks, too. And that's why he's been training with a beer in one hand and a babe in the other," the Basher muttered. "I tell ya, McGraw thinks road work is dorking some babe in the back seat of his Cadillac. I been talkin' to guys who spar with him. I know!"

"Oh, God," Elizabeth moaned. Her breasts were hot and sweaty, the nipples raw and growing as George pinched them. She moaned again as the horses broke for the first turn, Saber Dancer lost in the pack.

"Where is the fucking thing?" George shouted, craning to see.

"It's a lock, Georgie. Dead certain," the Basher hissed in his ear. "McGraw won't go five, Georgie."

Saber Dancer flashed in and out of a cloud of dust, moving to the leaders. But the favorite was four lengths ahead of the pack and gaining with every stride and the crowd was roaring wildly. Elizabeth took his other hand and began rubbing it over her stomach. She leaned her head back and kissed him hotly on the throat, her teeth nipping the skin.

"Georgie, ya listenin'?" the Basher half-shouted.

"I want you," Elizabeth whispered.

"I hear you," George told both of them, still looking for Saber Dancer.

The crowd was frantic now as the favorite rounded the turn

and headed for the finish. Saber Dancer's jockey whipped his horse viciously and methodically, switching the whip from one hand, to his teeth, to his other hand. George saw the horse respond, prick his ears, lengthen his stride.

"Georgie, waddya say?" the Basher pleaded behind him. "McGraw ought to be worth a few more potatoes."

"Oh, my God," murmured Elizabeth as George moved his hand down her stomach, rubbing steadily.

"Get lost, Basher. Go tell the Dancer I said to give you another hundred."

The other man slipped away as George looked for the horses in the stretch. Saber Dancer was straining, leaping mightily, the jockey swinging the whip heavily as a knight would a mace. But too far, too far, George muttered, as he watched the favorite falter, weaken, but still stagger in front toward the finish.

"We're losing, Elizabeth, we're losing," he moaned, squeezing her breasts even harder in his anguish. She bit his neck again.

And then it happened. A stone, a bird, a shadow—something flashed in front of the favorite's nose. Startled, his head rose, eyes white with fear. Mustering its frightened strength the horse leaped into the air, four white stockings flashing in the sun, and tried to jump whatever it saw. The surprised jockey gracefully flew through the air, over the inner rail, and into a bush heavy with blueberries. Saber Dancer came in second behind the riderless horse. And was declared the winner.

For a moment the crowd was stunned into silence. Then the combined roars of anguish and victory rose. George spun Elizabeth around, hugged her, shouting incoherently. But she knew what she wanted.

"I want you now," she yelled up to him, then took his arm and pulled him. "The car. Let's go to the car."

He caught her urgency. He kissed her. They ran through the crowd with arms around each other, bumping into people, tripping, but not caring, Elizabeth biting his ear as they ran.

When they reached the car Izzy the Stub was waiting for them.

"Big Bill wants you, boss. *Tsuris*."

138

"Oh, oh," said George.

"Oh, hell," said Elizabeth.

16

GEORGE MCMANUS stared at the tips of his fingers forming a steeple in front of his face and tried to pretend he was listening to the others. Jimmy Walker chain-smoked as he paced about the club's office talking in a low voice. Across the room, sitting on a sofa, Dwyer looked moderately grave. Beside him James Hines was wreathed in his customary political-boss cloak of cigar smoke.

Walker sat on the edge of the desk, a cigarette dangling from his lips. He crossed his arms and stared at the others. No one spoke. George was thinking of his hands on Elizabeth at the track, the feel of her. He was thinking of her sipping coffee in her dainty way in the delicatessen across the street. He was wondering why she wouldn't come into the club to wait for him. He was thinking how much he wanted her right now.

"You palookas are about as much help as a case of the crabs," Walker finally complained, breaking the silence.

Dwyer crossed his legs, careful to preserve the crease in his trousers. "I'm not sure just what you want from us, Jimmy."

"About a hundred thousand in cash," Walker said. "And some ideas."

George heard that. "How do we rate the honor of bailing your ass out of hot water?"

Hines got up, leaving his smoke cloud behind. "You owe us, boys," he said matter-of-factly, tapping his ashes into a wastebasket. "We did you a big favor."

"I seem to recall paying a bundle of money for that favor," said Dwyer. "Doesn't that cancel out any debts?"

Hines walked behind the desk and stopped in front of a document on the wall. It was the court injunction giving the club immunity from police raids. George had had it framed and hung.

"If Hearst pulls this little scheme off, he could just get that fool Hylan reelected." He tapped the frame with the wet end of his cigar. "And if that happens, Tammany influence isn't going to be worth a hunk of dried shit. How long do you think this piece of paper is going to keep you in business then?"

Dwyer and McManus looked at each other across the room. George walked over to Hines and wiped the cigar stain off the frame with a handkerchief. Outside he could hear the band warming up as the first gamblers of the evening trickled into the club.

"We had a meeting of political advisers down at Tammany this afternoon on how to deal with this situation," Walker went on. "It was decided that the best way to handle the straying precinct workers was to purchase more loyalty from them than Hearst did. That's where your money comes in.

"But the ticklish part is this special edition of the *American*. For political reasons it was decided that outsiders should handle stopping its publication. Tammany doesn't want to know anything about it. All we need is every paper in the city on our backs. Understand?"

Walker and Hines rose, put on their hats, and went to the door. "Let us know what you come up with," Walker said. "And we'll be expecting the money downtown in the morning."

"Tell me something," George called as they went out the door. "Why us?"

Walker turned and smiled. "Because you're such smart boys."

17

THE CAR RUMBLED across the steel-mesh roadway of the Brooklyn Bridge, under the span's dramatically soaring stone arches. The Brooklyn shore loomed ahead, heavy with gloomy warehouses. On the right the torchlight of the Statue of Liberty twinkled in the distance close by the southern tip of Manhattan. Below, tugboats churned busily through the inky East River as, somewhere, a freighter hooted moodily.

George McManus left the bridge and wheeled through the local streets, finally turning onto Atlantic. It was late, ten o'clock, and most of the shops were closed. But people were still out strolling on the broad avenue to beat the heat.

"I'm going to start calling you Machiavelli McManus," Elizabeth said beside him.

"Who's that?"

"Machiavelli? Oh, he ran a sort of one-man Tammany Hall in Europe a few years ago. But his schemes had nothing on yours."

He glanced at her as he drove. "Are you laughing at me?"

"God, no." She rested her hand on his arm. "I guess I'm sort of stunned. You change so fast. From gambler to Boss Tweed in one easy lesson. Just who are you, George Mc-Manus?"

"Did you ever hear of George Washington Plunkett, Elizabeth?"

She shook her head.

"Well, he wasn't in your crowd. A Tammany ward heeler. He parlayed that into a couple of minor city jobs. Never made more than a couple grand a year. But he retired fat, happy, very rich, and a hero in Hell's Kitchen."

She looked at him quizzically.

"And do you know what old Plunkett said when people asked how he made all that money, and started hinting that maybe he was a crook? He would take them into the garden of his mansion, stand as tall as he could, stick out his chest, and say proudly: 'I seen my opportunities and I took 'em.' "

She smiled. "So this is your opportunity and you're going to take it."

George nodded.

Elizabeth leaned over and rested her head on his shoulder. "William Randolph Hearst is a bad man to cross, George. I've seen him at parties. He walks, talks, eats, and sleeps money and power. You don't want to get caught in the middle—between him and Jimmy Walker."

He looked down at her. "You've met Hearst? Then maybe you know where he's vulnerable."

"He's not," she warned. "With all his newspapers, he can

141

say or do virtually anything he wants. My father says Hearst is more powerful than the President."

George turned off Atlantic and drove through side streets back toward the river. The blocks quickly got shabbier and shabbier, with dim figures watching on the street corners as the roadster went by.

"Why do I feel like I'm being shanghaied?" Elizabeth moved closer to George.

"It's his paper that bothers me," George mused. "There'll be lots of confusion and we can stop it for a while. But eventually some of Hearst's rags are going to hit the streets. I can't stop them all."

"Just who is this bigshot you're trying to protect?" Elizabeth asked. "And what's he to Tammany?"

"For such a cute little nose, you sure stick it in some bad places."

She sat up straight. "Don't patronize me. I won't be treated like a child."

"I'm sorry. But Walker wants this guy's name kept in the dark. Some big political contributor."

She put her head back on George's shoulder. "Well, I hope he gets everything he deserves. Eventually."

They pulled up in front of a sagging old two-story building badly in need of a coat of paint. Even at night Elizabeth was struck by its shabbiness. Peeling fight posters covered the lower windows. To call the Twenty-third Street Athletic Club in Red Hook a dingy old gym was to malign dingy old gyms. Inside, its bare wooden floors were chipped and spattered with old bloodstains. The walls and ceiling looked as if they had been built with driftwood. The malodorous scent of sweat permeated the air, the wooden benches, and everyone who entered the place. It was a popular gag in Brooklyn that the Twenty-third Street gym was so crummy, even sportswriters gave the place some class.

Elizabeth fidgeted uncomfortably in the front-row seat where George left her when he went off to find Dancer Hyams. She felt out of place. She saw only four other women near the ring. One was a fat little dumpling with thinning red hair and a death grip on a large silvery crucifix. Every few minutes the woman would close her eyes, mumble a few words, and cross herself in prayer. Elizabeth guessed she was the mother of the Irish fighter McGraw. The other women looked as if the term floozy had been invented for them.

A hulking red-faced man sat down next to Elizabeth and gave her the eye. His face was puffy under a sweat-stained straw hat. He gripped a huge cigar in his teeth. He took off his coat and rolled up his shirt sleeves to display bulging muscles. When Elizabeth tried to move over, she discovered he was sitting on the edge of her dress.

"Brannigan's the name. Eddie Brannigan." He stuck a big hand in front of her. "I woik the docks."

She shook his hand. "Elizabeth's the name. I woik the cocktail parties."

"Huh?" He looked into her face, then laughed. "Oh, yeah. Funny."

He was about to say something else when George sat down.

"I found the Dancer all right. You can always count on him to be where the action is."

"So you got the money. Let's go out and spend every penny."

George paused. "Well, we can't exactly do that. I bet it on the fight the Basher told me about."

"All of it?"

"No, no. Only half. I want to see how it goes."

"Then we stay," Elizabeth sighed. She tapped the man next to her on the shoulder. "Mr. Brannigan, meet Mr. McManus. He woiks lady luck."

The growing crowd turned noisy as the time for the main bout drew near. It promised to be a bloody one. Half the mob was already chanting "McGraw, McGraw." The other half began picking up "Ravelli, Ravelli" in the same cadence. When she came in Elizabeth had noticed the ticket-taker saying over and over again "Micks to the left, dagos to the right" —perhaps on the theory that if he insulted both nationalities neither would take offense. Now she knew why the customers were being divided. The fight was merely an excuse for an ethnic war.

The shouts became louder as the fighters finally reached the ring. McGraw, in a flashy green robe that labeled him "The Irish Fist," vaulted over the ropes and bounded into the

143

ring first. He grinned broadly and held his hands above his head in the traditional champion's salute. The crowd, the Irish half at least, roared. Ravelli fans contributed a couple of bottles and a sandwich to the ring scenery.

Mike McGraw was handsome, black-haired, and without a mark on his well-muscled body. He was known in the trade as a killer—someone who was merciless when his opponent was hurt. And that was often enough to have made him a contender for the middle-weight crown.

Ravelli, wearing a robe that proclaimed nothing except his threadbare existence, stepped into the ring tentatively as if his feet hurt. He looked more like an elder statesman than a boxer. Prematurely gray hair at his temples and a thin, studious face gave him almost a distinguished appearance, if any man can look distinguished in baggy shorts. But his upper arms desperately needed meat and his ribs protruded. Ravelli's feet definitely did hurt him, Elizabeth decided, as the announcer called their names.

"Congratulations," she said, leaning toward George. "You've got ninety thousand riding on a scarecrow with corns."

"Hey, if he looked like Dempsey I wouldn't have gotten four to one."

McGraw snarled at Ravelli as the referee called the fighters to the center of the ring. To his credit, Ravelli snarled back, provoking hoots of delight and two fistfights in the back of the room. When they went back to their corners George noticed Seamus the Basher sitting directly across the ring. The Basher winked broadly. George winked back.

The crowd hushed as the bell sounded for the first round. The fighters were tentative at first, feeling each other out. Ravelli struck first with a left to McGraw's jaw. The bigger man's hands went up to protect his face and Ravelli shot a hard right to his gut. McGraw doubled over, his surprised gasp audible throughout the gym. Ravelli pursued his advantage, throwing combination after combination at McGraw. But the Irishman had adopted the crab posture. Hunched over, fists covering his face, his only exposed spots were his forearms and knees.

144

McGraw was safe from Ravelli but not from the crowd. Gentlemen on both sides of the ring were booing him as Ravelli danced around, vainly looking for an opening. The crowd had come to see a fight. If the Irishman didn't hand them Ravelli's head, they'd take McGraw's instead. A tomato whizzed past McGraw's ear. A cucumber hit him in the knee. McGraw was getting nervous. He had seen the bullet holes in the walls of the gym, marks of anger over other boxers who failed to perform. McGraw looked to his corner where his white-faced manager was staring worriedly at the crowd. He decided he'd better fight.

McGraw straightened up but Ravelli continued to score with blow after blow. With an enormous effort Ravelli screwed up his arm and suddenly dropped McGraw with a solid right to the chin. The crowd leaped to its feet.

"I don't believe it," Elizabeth shouted.

"I don't either," George shouted.

"Getta you up, I moidah you," Ravelli shouted as McGraw sat on the canvas, his eyes glassy and wild. Ravelli hovered over his opponent, ignoring the cries of his backers and the referee to get to a neutral corner, the bloodlust overwhelming the diplomat.

Finally Ravelli's manager charged into the ring and pulled his fighter back. The fat referee hiked up his pants, dropped to one knee, and began the count. The Irish screamed for McGraw to rise. The Italians joyfully counted with the referee. At the count of eight, the bell rang ending the round.

McGraw staggered to his cornermen. They slapped and sponged him awake, shouting in his ears and holding up fingers he failed to count. On the other side of the ring Ravelli sat down heavily, chest heaving, as his cornermen made gestures involving fists and forearms at the other corner.

Elizabeth looked at George. "Interesting fight."

"Yes," he said absently.

"You're going to visit the Dancer again, aren't you?"

He smiled. "You know me too well. I couldn't sleep tonight if I didn't bet the rest of the bundle."

He kissed her quickly, then trotted up the aisle, squeezing past two dim figures at the top of the stairs. The bookie would

145

be downstairs near the pay phone between rounds, George knew, only a nickel away from his customers. Hyams hung up the phone's earpiece as George came up to him.

"I'm getting very tired of your face today, Georgie. Every time I see it it costs me a lot of money."

Upstairs the crowd became noisy as the second round was about to begin. They heard the bell sound.

"You still owe me ninety thousand," George said.

"This isn't news to me," Hyams shrugged. "You want to put it all on the dago. Correct?"

George nodded.

"The same odds?"

George nodded again.

"Will you listen to some advice?"

"Look me up in ten or twenty years, Dancer. I might need it then. Right now I'm too busy. And there's a pretty girl waiting for me upstairs."

"Listen to the hotshot dish out the applesauce." Hyams' tone was mocking. "Two months ago you would have traded your left leg for three aces."

"I'll see you after the fight," George said, patting the other man's cheek. "And have my money in large bills. Small bills make my pockets lumpy."

As he trotted up the stairs he could hear the snap of leather punishing flesh over the cries of the crowd, like small firecrackers going off. The two men he had squeezed by earlier were now standing midway up the dim staircase. But as he pushed between them this time, they didn't move. Suddenly one of them was pinning George's arms back. The other man lit a match on his heel and brought the light up to a cigarette in his mouth. George recognized the brutal, piggish features of Owney Madden, the gunsel Arnold Rothstein had brought to the casino.

"Mr. Rothstein asked me to look you up. Mr. Rothstein said he wanted you to have something more to think about while you were considering his offer. He said you'd understand."

Madden blew out the match. George heard the snap of the fighters' gloves again as the man behind him tightened his grip on his arms. He barely saw Madden's fist before he felt it smash into his ribs. He heard the snapping again, but this time knew it was his ribs cracking. Before he could take another breath Madden's fist landed again, just under his rib cage, doubling George over.

Madden was puffing. "Mr. Rothstein said not to mess up your face 'cause you got a girlfriend. Mr. Rothstein said don't leave marks. But I got my professional pride to uphold. So I'm going to break your nose, McManus. And every time you look in a mirror for the rest of your life, you'll remember Owney Madden."

He grabbed the front of George's shirt and pushed him upright. Madden then drew back his fist with a wide grin. George barely managed to jerk his head aside as Madden's hand crunched through the wall. Madden groaned as he tried to pull his broken hand out of the hole. George spun quickly, slammed the side of his fist into the second man's throat. The man gasped for air and George hit him with his shoulder, sending him flying down the stairs. When George turned, Madden was still trying to get his fist out of the wall.

"My compliments to Mr. Rothstein," George said as he calmly kicked Madden in the groin. The other man went white, then gray. He tumbled backward down the stairs, ripping out a large section of wall still connected to his hand. At the bottom of the stairs both men lay motionless.

George touched his ribs and winced at the pain. He straightened up gingerly and arranged his clothes, then went slowly upstairs.

"What happened?" George sat carefully beside Elizabeth.

She was intently watching blood trickle out from a cut under McGraw's left eye as he was being worked over in his corner.

"Ravelli chased him around some more in the second. I think the Irish fans of the manly art of self-defense are ready to toss McGraw on the first potato boat home. Boxing is brutal, ghoulish, inhuman—and you know what?"

"What?"

She smiled. "I like it."

She put her arm around George's waist and gave him a happy squeeze. He gasped with the pain. Elizabeth looked at him, concerned.

"Somebody beat you up." It was a statement, not a question.

"I fell down the stairs."

She touched his face. "You're flushed and hot, like you've been running—or fighting."

"I ran back up the stairs after I hit the bottom."

"Uh huh. Do you want me to take you to a doctor?"

"No, I'll be all right. Just kiss me, don't hug. Okay?"

She nodded, ran a finger lightly over his rib cage. He even winced at that.

"I hope you kicked him in the balls," she whispered, kissing his cheek.

George laughed once, holding his side.

In the third and fourth rounds Ravelli kept up his pursuit of McGraw, like the hare chasing the hound. The Italian threw everything he had, reaching from the floor to deliver his punches. McGraw wobbled, ran, hid in the crab, clinched, stuck to the ropes like a babe to its mother's breast. At the end of the fourth someone threw a dead fish at McGraw's feet. He picked it up with both gloves and angrily threw it back at the crowd, which got him a standing ovation from both Italians and Irish because it was the first thing he had thrown all night.

In the fifth Ravelli came out with another rain of punches. But suddenly McGraw wasn't running. Ravelli began moving slower and slower. His gloves were now floating in with all the sting of a fruit fly. This had not escaped Mike McGraw's notice. He actually smiled as Ravelli hit him flush on the chin.

"I smell something funny," George muttered as the crowd began to sense what was happening.

Elizabeth sniffed the air. "It stinks in here. But nothing unusual."

"A rat, toots. I smell a big, dead rat."

McGraw tossed a light left at Ravelli's head and the Italian, exhausted and his reflexes slowed to a crawl, barely deflected it. McGraw threw a combination, then another. Left, right, left, right. Suddenly Ravelli was reeling. A left cross caught him square on the nose. Blood gushed out, spattering those in the front row. A right uppercut, a left hook. Ravelli was down and the crowd was hysterical.

George took Elizabeth's hand and led her up the aisle to the exit door. She was looking over her shoulder as Ravelli rose slowly, nodding shakily at the referee, trying to get his eyes back in focus.

"It's not over. It's not over," Elizabeth shouted.

They stopped at the door and looked back. "Yes, it is," George said quietly.

As the referee got out of the way McGraw moved forward. He was smiling. He started with a heavy left to the stomach, then a sharp right to the temple. Ravelli would have gone down but McGraw was holding him up. The blows became quick, rhythmic, like a boxer working out on a punching bag. Ravelli's knees sagged. Blood trickled from one ear.

George led Elizabeth down the dim stairway and through the training area to the street. When they were outside they stopped for a moment, and both took deep breaths. They could still hear the crowd shouting upstairs, still hear the regular blows. He put his arm around her.

"I hope he doesn't get badly hurt," Elizabeth said.

"Ravelli? Listen, toots, he's been punched more often than the down button on an elevator. He'll be okay."

They walked toward the car. George was whistling something jazzy under his breath. He bent and kissed her hair.

"I don't believe you." She looked up at him. "You're actually happy."

"Why shouldn't I be?"

Elizabeth was staring at his car. All four tires were slashed and flattened. And someone had viciously cut up the leather seats and pulled the stuffing and springs out.

"Well, that's one reason, darling. And it was such a pretty car. I think somebody doesn't like you very much."

George bent and looked at the dashboard. A note was jammed into the edge of the glove compartment door. He unfolded it and read: "Mr. R. says to be extra careful of your health." He crumpled the note and threw it into the street.

"It looks like we have to take a subway home, toots."

"Do we have a nickel each?"

George smiled. "Haven't you ever heard of jumping the turnstiles?"

"It's funny," she said, "my father builds subways, but I've never been on one. Are they fun?"

"Oh, sure. Every train comes with its own clown and performing monkey act."

She laughed and took his arm and they began walking again without speaking. The streets were quiet now, and so dark even the shadows had shadows. Sometimes broken glass crunched under their feet as they walked. But she was happy and he was whistling again. Far ahead they could see the big globe lights that marked the entrance to the subway.

They had gone about two blocks when a black Cadillac pulled to the curb next to them and the driver honked the horn. Dancer Hyams stuck his head out the window.

"I've been hunting for you, Georgie," he called. "No hard feelings, huh?"

George looked into the car and saw the Basher sitting next to Hyams. The Basher gave George a big wink.

"It's just business. You understand," Hyams was saying. "It would have broken me if I'd had to pony up all that money."

George shrugged. "I don't care about the ten dollars anyway."

"What ten dollars?" said Hyams. "I'm talking a hundred and eighty thousand potatoes."

George looked at the other man and patted his cheek for the second time that night. "The way I look at it, Dancer, I came to you with ten bucks and now my pockets are empty. So I only lost ten bucks."

Hyams chuckled, looked at Elizabeth, then back to George. "Hey, that's pretty good, Georgie. You ought to be writing for the papers. Yeah, that's funny." He pulled his head back into the car. They heard the grinding of gears as the Dancer drove off, shaking his head and saying, "That's one for the papers, all right."

George watched the car disappear down the street and around a corner. Even after it was gone he stared at the dust the car had raised. "Writing for the papers," he mused. "Sure, why not?"

"It's been quite a day," Elizabeth said, taking his hand as they began walking.

George stopped, took her into his arms, kissed her deeply.

Then he held her at arm's length and looked at her. They could hear the rumble of the subway beneath them as it slowed for a turn before easing into the station across the street.

"And if we hurry and make that train," he said, "we can still make it quite a night."

They ran together, George holding his side.

18

WALLY HILGENBURG was older than his printing press, which made him the oldest man in Sullivan County in New York's Catskill Mountains. The press had been new when Grover Cleveland was President and had, in fact, been used in the second Cleveland election to print up phony ballots to stuff boxes throughout eastern New York State. The press had been idle for years, however, since Wally was sent up the river for using it to counterfeit stock certificates. He had only been out on parole a week when George McManus came to him. Hilgenburg thought it was damned decent of Tammany to provide him with work so fast.

McManus ran his index finger through the dust on one of Hilgenburg's impossible-looking iron Linotype machines as he studied the old man. Hilgenburg was short and thin with horn-rimmed glasses that kept slipping down his nose. Liver spots dotted his mostly bald head. The years in prison had left him with an almost funereal pallor and bad lungs. But he was the right man for the job, Hines had said. Hilgenburg could copy anything.

McManus placed a leather briefcase on a paint-spattered table and pulled out that afternoon's *New York American*. He showed it to Hilgenburg.

"Do you think you can counterfeit that typeface and head-line style?"

Hilgenburg took the paper from McManus's hands. "If Hearst can do it, Hilgenburg can do it." The voice sounded as if it needed dusting.

"I need a million copies of a one-page broadside by Monday noon."

"No problem," the old man rasped. "I'll set the copy now and start running it off tonight. You'll have everything by Sunday night."

"I don't have the stories with me. But you'll have them by five. Good enough?"

Hilgenburg nodded. "I'll need some supplies—ink, paper, cleaning oil. . . ."

"Just make a list and I'll get it."

"And if it's not too much trouble, a bottle of Canadian Club."

"It's not too much trouble," McManus said. "Believe me, it's not too much trouble."

The night hours at the club and the good life had taken their toll on Izzy the Stub. His eyes were red-rimmed and puffy. There was the beginning of a paunch at his waistline. George watched as Izzy jammed half of an overstuffed pastrami sandwich in his mouth.

"It was a cinch," Izzy said between bites. "It only cost a fiver. I met this printer I know in an establishment around the corner from the paper."

He wiped his hands on the tablecloth and pulled a large, crumpled sheet of paper from his pocket.

McManus whistled as he looked at the copy of the front page of the newspaper. No wonder Walker was worried. The headlines screamed: "Walker Caught in Sex Tryst," "Subway Baron Bribes Jimmy Walker," "Mayor Hylan Deplores Loose Morals of Opponent." The pictures were missing but the captions underneath the empty spaces were clear enough.

"I've got another job for you, Izzy. You have any pals who can drive trucks?"

"I suppose so. If you can drive a car you can drive a truck. What do you need them for?" He picked a stray piece of meat off the table and popped it into his mouth.

"I'll tell you later. Have forty drivers at the club at seven A.M. Monday. And tell Chins to come along. I've got something special planned for him and Rats."

•

"The main has to be fixed at three o'clock. No earlier. No later. Got it?"

George could hear Hines scribbling furiously at the other end of the telephone.

"And I want traffic rerouted on Chambers and South Broadway. I think we'd better arrange for some problems on the Brooklyn Bridge, too. What do you think?"

"Yes. Nice touch," Hines breathed, scribbling again. "Anything else?"

"Do you know Father Donahue at the St. Bartholomew Orphanage?"

"Of course," said Hines. "A fine man. A saint."

"Does he owe Tammany a favor, too?"

Hines laughed. "Everybody owes Tammany a favor."

"Then I'd like to borrow about a hundred of his kids for some civic service."

"You've got them." More scribbling. "Anything else?"

"That should be it."

"McManus?"

"Yes?"

"I'm proud of you. Keep up the bad work."

19

THE SIRENS of the police escort wailed. Gears ground under the touch of inexperienced drivers. Forty trucks loaded with newspapers rolled into Manhattan at 1 P.M. Monday, spreading out from there to Brooklyn, Queens, and the Bronx. And on a thousand different corners the conversation was the same:

"Why so thin?" the newsstand operator would say.

"Special edition," the driver would answer.

"Where's the regular guy?"

"Sick."

Slowly at first, then with the inevitable impetus of hot gossip, the word spread. Over and over again, on the subway, at lunch counters, in offices, readers clucked their tongues and read. So Honest John Hylan has been taking bribes, they said. Didn't we guess it all along? So Will Hearst is going to hook up with Tammany. Should have done it years ago. And isn't it crazy that Hearst has finally endorsed Jimmy Walker? That's politics for you.

At 3 P.M. a grimy sewer worker hammered at a joint on a thirty-six-inch water pipe beneath Park Row just down the street from the plant and offices of the *New York American*. He gave it one last whack, then picked up his tools and left. In moments, water under tremendous pressure was squirting from the joint, suddenly rupturing the weakened pipe. The force of the water shot a manhole cover on Park Row forty feet in the air, forming a new municipal fountain. Soon the entire north end of the street was under three feet of water and the crest of the flood was moving quickly toward the middle of the block.

Inside the *New York American*, plant dispatchers were already loading the election special into trucks. Behind the trucks the *American*'s presses were rolling on schedule. A stream of water had started to trickle into the loading docks but no one seemed to notice. The drivers of the loaded vans gunned their engines and began to move slowly out of the plant. Truck number one turned left on the one-way street and ran right into the flood. He signaled to the other drivers to follow him and sped up, trying to race through the torrent. His truck went ten yards before the engine coughed, sputtered, and stalled.

The driver got out of the cab and automatically threw open the hood but he already knew the problem. There wasn't a dry wire in the engine. Two other trucks had followed him and also stood dead and useless in the surging water.

Other trucks turned and were threading their way up the street against traffic when an enormously fat man stepped off the curb and was brushed by a truck's bumper. The fat man landed hard on the pavement and lay still. Heads turned throughout the City Hall area at the squeal of the tires and the ear-splitting moans and groans that immediately followed. A crowd quickly gathered. The truck driver leaped from his cab to the fat man's side.

"My back. My back," Chins Hamner cried. "I think I broke my back." Pedestrians surged forward to get a better look. Storekeepers appeared in doorways, drawn by the commotion. At the edge of the crowd a hot dog vendor set up shop.

The driver scratched his head. He bent and looked for blood, then touched Chins' shoulder. The fat man's groans were heard a block away. The crowd grew larger.

Behind the stopped truck two dozen more Hearst trucks were waiting, the drivers honking their horns and gunning their engines. Water from the other corner was licking at their tires but the fat man and the crowd around him blocked the narrow street.

Two drivers began pushing the fat man, trying to roll him to the curb. They could barely budge him. They called to other drivers to help.

Chins opened his eyes wide and a look of sheer horror covered his face.

"Oh my God," he cried, pointing up. "He's going to jump!"

The crowd instantly turned to where his finger was pointing. High above them a small man in brown straddled the railing on the sixth-floor ledge of the Capital Hotel. He threw his other foot over the railing and people could see his lips moving. The crowd did not know Rats Wolnik was praying that the ancient wrought iron would last one more day. He was taking no chances, however. He had already tied a rope around his waist, with the other end securely fastened to the big brass bed in the room behind him.

People shouted at him. Women fainted. Rats waved. It was hard to decipher just what they were yelling but their concern made the little man feel good. Rats leaned farther over the railing and the crowd alternately sighed, then roared, not sure exactly what they wanted either.

From his vantage point Rats could see City Hall, the Tweed Courthouse, and most of the streets feeding into Park Row. Traffic was nearly at a standstill. Cars were being abandoned throughout the area, as far south as Wall Street. People were pouring out of the subway stations. And dozens of children in uniforms of white shirts and black trousers now raced about the streets in small packs. The children broke traffic lights

155

with stones, set small fires in garbage baskets, turned in fire alarms. In the milling crowds they were hardly noticed. Rats noted that there was not a policeman in sight.

He watched as Chins Hamner slowly got off the pavement, dusted himself off, and strolled into the crowd, heading for the hot dog wagon. The astonished drivers around Chins quickly dashed back to their trucks. But there was nowhere to go. The streets were hopelessly snarled by traffic and the thousands of people watching Rats Wolnik eat a banana on the sixth-floor ledge. When he threw down the peel, dozens scrambled to catch it as some sort of bizarre souvenir. It was after five now and, as offices closed, additional thousands streamed into the street. They wandered gaily through the throngs, asking people what was going on.

At 5:30 a half-dozen burly printers dashed from the *New York American* building and raced through the crowds to the Capital Hotel. Within moments Rats could hear them pounding on his door. It took only five minutes to break through the door, but another fifteen minutes to pull away the heavy dresser, the bed, the chair, and the night tables that Rats had moved in front of it. Sweat was pouring off the first man through the door. He gasped for breath. Rats threw his arms around the man.

"You saved my life," he cried. "I owe you a beer."

As the other men barreled into the hotel room, Rats slipped out in the confusion. There were even more people in the streets when he got outside. They were coming from all over the city now, attracted by the ad in George McManus's phony newspaper. The ad proclaimed a victory rally for that evening outside City Hall. The ad also promised free beer.

On one corner a Salvation Army band heartily clanged out "Bringing in the Sheaves." The children in uniform who had finished destroying street lights now turned their attention to the cars that filled the streets, deflating all the tires. Then they let the air out of the tires on the newspaper trucks, sneaking between the drivers' legs.

Speakeasies on Chambers Street next to the courthouses opened early. Bucket brigades were set up passing pails of beer outside. Shops that normally closed at five stayed open for business. Restaurants and small groceries in the neighborhood were soon running out of everything edible.

Finally, two uniformed motorcycle officers from police headquarters near Canal Street inched through the crowd and reached Park Row. They fought their way to a police call box and reported what was happening. They were ordered to a domestic disturbance in Brooklyn.

At 6 P.M. the small factories downtown closed, feeding the crowd again. A juggling act performed on the corner of Centre Street. An old socialist harangued a thousand people on the lawn of City Hall. A violinist played Bach on the steps of the Tweed Courthouse. A mulatto trumpeter played Dixieland on South Broadway. And on Park Row the crowd was singing along as the Salvation Army band wheezed out "That Old Rugged Cross."

The music wafted to the East River and Hudson docks and sailors from American, Irish, and Italian merchant vessels raced over looking for action. The crowd swelled and swelled again, until it seemed Manhattan had to tip over like a rowboat with everybody at one end. Yet, as darkness fell, the thousands of people stayed on. No one knew what was happening, but no one wanted to go home either.

By 9 P.M. Times Square had emptied. Dogs and an occasional drunk wandered down the middle of Broadway. Theater marquees lit up empty sidewalks. The party was downtown and no one wanted to miss it.

At 10 P.M. the word went out from the *American*'s office. Each driver and every other Hearst employee was to take two bundles of newspapers and spread them around town by bus, cab, or subway. A few thousand papers finally reached the streets this way. But in the fine, cool, late-summer night the crowd found a better use for the bundles. The children dressed in black and white grabbed most of the bundles from the trucks and started dozens of small bonfires through the crowd.

People pressed close for the warmth and the camaraderie. They told stories, laughed at jokes. Boys hugged girls close as the glow of the flames lit their faces and reflected eerily from the thousands of windows in the office buildings around

157

them. And, as they often do, the dreams of many men went up in smoke.

20

SHE SLEPT HEAVILY, her hair covering her face. Occasionally, as he watched, her cheeks would twitch or her lips would curl. Sometimes she smiled. Elizabeth could never remember her dreams when he asked about them. He himself never dreamed in bed, he once told her. His dreams were for the waking world.

She was sleeping on his arm. But she was so thin that the weight did not bother him. He lay quietly on his side in the dim light, listening to her breathe. And thinking. At first he barely heard the tapping. Then it came again, louder. He gently lifted Elizabeth and slipped his arm from beneath her. She sighed as he swung his legs over the bed and slipped into his robe.

When he answered the door he could tell immediately that Izzy the Stub was drunk. His red sport coat was stained with beer. His green shirt was missing three buttons and billowed out over his pants. The dancing-girl tie hung from a coat pocket. And his eyes jumped about like someone suddenly confronted with an old debt.

"You should have seen it, boss. Oy, you should have seen all those people." Izzy slurred the words. He tottered to the sofa and sat heavily.

"It was beautiful. Gorgeous."

"It worked, then?"

A bubble of spit popped on Izzy's lips. "Like clockwork, my friend. Like Swiss movement with seventeen jewels. It was as if the messiah had come. All those thousands of people, laughing and wondering what was going on."

"Nobody got hurt?"

Izzy waved his hands wildly, shook his lead. "Like lambs, boss. Those wonderful people were peaceful lambs. And you know what? A couple hundred are *still* there. It's almost dawn and they're still there."

158

George was relieved. "And what about Hearst's paper? Any get out?"

"Not to worry, boss. A few, enough maybe to make hats for those little animals you got from that orphanage. Nobody is going to see this paper."

Izzy pulled a copy of the *American* from his pocket and threw it on the sofa. Behind him Elizabeth came out of the bedroom, tying the sash on her robe. Her eyes were heavy with sleep.

"What's going on?" she yawned. She saw Izzy. "Did your plot work, George?"

"It worked," George told her.

She flopped on the sofa, pushing the hair out of her eyes. Izzy started talking loudly again and George led him to the vestibule. She heard them go out in the hallway and close the door behind them. Outside, their voices were muffled.

She picked up the newspaper Izzy had left on the sofa and skimmed it idly before she realized what it was. Her eyes went to one story, then to the picture above it. It was poorly done, obviously faked. The likeness of the man dumping a briefcase full of money on a desk was very muddy. But as she stared at it she knew it was the face of her father.

She studied the picture for a long time, until she heard the click of the door latch. George came back and sat beside her, looking at the newspaper in her lap.

"This sure would have cooked Tammany's goose if it had come out before primary day," George finally said. "But when Walker gets the Democratic nomination today, he'll have every judge and city official burying these charges for him. Hearst might as well have accused him of jaywalking."

She was still looking at the photograph.

"How long have you known about my father—and this?"

He put his arm around her. "I was at Tammany when he made the payoff."

"You never said anything." She looked at him.

George shrugged. "Scratch an honest man and you'll usually find a thief. Why should your old man be any different?"

"But all that scheming," she said. Elizabeth took his hand. "You did it for me, didn't you? You saved him for me."

159

"No, I did it for me."

"I don't believe you. And I love you for lying."

She got up, turned off the light. When she came to him in the darkness, they laughed.

1926

"TAMMANEE, Tammanee . . . swamp-um, swamp-um . . . get the wampum." They sang it all over town as they cheered Jimmy Walker's inauguration on January 1. It was open season, they knew. Anything goes. Twenty-three skiddoo, kiddo. Get the wampum.

Fill your flask, roll up your skirt, roll down your stocking tops. Sing, dance, get rid of old Henry's black Model-T, and did you see the snazzy new Chevy coupe yet?

Can Dempsey take Tunney? Will the Bambino hit 50? Who'll fly across the Atlantic first for a handful of glory?

It'll take 250,000 cops to enforce Prohibition in New York, they laugh. And another 250,000 to police the police. So what'll it be, bub? Drink up.

How's about panther whiskey in a smoke joint, with half of every bottle wood alcohol? Or yack-yack bourbon with lead, ether, or iodine as a chaser? Or should we have the good stuff, the real stuff, the $30-a-bottle hooch from lovely Ireland? Well, the label's from Ireland, anyway. The hooch is from the Bronx. It doesn't matter. Drink up and let's dance.

Drink up and let's cash in on the Florida boom.

Drink up and let's cash in on the California boom.

Drink up and buy Radio.

Drink up and buy Steel.

Drink up for our heroes are grand and life is heroic. Like the poet says:

> My candle burns at both ends
> It will not last the night.
> But ah, my foes, and oh, my friends,
> It gives a lovely light.

Drink up.

21

THE SUN GLARED DOWN on the flat brown field, creating little mirage shimmers of water in the distant dust. Sometimes the sun struck off a pebble just right and reflected a startling pinprick of glare, like a star being born and dying in one flash. George McManus scuffed at the dust with his shoe and a little cloud rose and drifted away. He was watching the mechanic as the man methodically crawled over, under, and about the flimsy-looking biplane parked on the edge of the runway.

The mechanic talked quietly as he worked, droning like the small planes that buzzed about the airport in the distance. His name was Alvin, according to the patch on the front of his greasy overalls. Alvin pulled his head out of the engine cowling, gave a couple of wires one last caressing check, then banged the metal covering into place and tightened the bolts. He backed away a few feet and looked lovingly at the plane as he wiped his hands with a black rag.

"Nope, they sure don't make 'em like this old Jenny anymore," said the mechanic. He had a drawl that sounded like Texas and a weathered, outdoorsy face to match. "And the lady made some purty nice changes. That's a spankin' new Curtiss One-eighty behind that prop. She'll turn a hundred easy. Purty nice."

George wasn't listening. He looked beyond the plane toward a small shack at the end of the field. A wispy flagpole stood beside the shack. At the top of the pole a cone-shaped windsock danced gaily in the slight breeze. Behind the shack was a row of low trees, and just visible far beyond the trees were the tips of Manhattan's skyscrapers. Watching them, he felt almost homesick.

The mechanic shoved the rag in a back pocket and picked up a small can of brown paint and a brush that sat near the plane's tail. He pried open the can with his dirty fingernails, carefully dipped the brush, and began to paint over letters printed between the forward and rear cockpits. George moved closer and looked over the other man's shoulder. The letters formed a name—Bobby Cooper.

"Who's that?" George asked. "Who's Bobby Cooper?"

The mechanic looked up at him, eyes thin slits in the sun's glare. "Boyfriend. Heard they was goin' to get hitched for a while."

He turned back to the plane, delicately laying some more brown paint over the letters, forming a perfect rectangle on the plane's canvas fuselage. "Before this Cooper it was some stuck-up joker named Wingate. And before that the name was a Dennis something-or-other." He said it matter-of-factly.

George laughed and the mechanic squinted at him again. How like Elizabeth, he thought, as the mechanic went back to painting. Other women could wear their love on their sleeves. Only Elizabeth could wear it on the side of a biplane —and think it perfectly normal. Tire of a man and all it takes to get rid of him is a coat of paint. He wondered what these other men looked like, what they said when they found someone else's name on the side of her plane, and laughed again.

The mechanic went off to putter in the cockpit, pushing the rudder and testing the tail flaps. George leaned against the wing, feeling the warmth and roughness of the taut canvas on his palms. He ran his fingers over the thin supporting struts and the fine guywires that held the wings together, marveling at how fragile they were to lift the weight of the plane and the people in it. Even that was like Elizabeth, he realized. Fragile, yet strong.

In the heat the thin coat of paint dried quickly. The mechanic went to a nearby shed and returned with a can of white paint and a new brush. He blew on the patch he had just painted and, satisfied it was dry, opened the other can. He took a piece of paper from his pocket, checked it, and began lettering carefully. The first letter was a G. The second was an E. George smiled.

"You?" the mechanic said. He had his tongue between his teeth, concentrating on the lettering.

George nodded.

"She must be some woman, pardner," the mechanic said, looking up briefly. "Some woman."

She came out of the shack at the far end of the field just then. She had changed clothes. Now she strode across the field purposefully in leather boots, jodhpurs, a leather flight jacket and leather helmet. He had to look twice to make sure it was her and not a man. But it was her walk, her cast of the shoulders, her chin held high. Yes, that was Elizabeth's stride, like she wasn't afraid of anything, like a lovely cossack. He followed her with his eyes. Look at those shoulders, he marveled. She could show more disdain with one shrug of those bony little joints than most people could muster in ten minutes of cursing.

Like the night at the opera last winter. She had put her head on his shoulder in the middle of a dull aria from Tosca. Then she had kissed his ear. Then his mouth. When someone behind hissed at them she stood and unleashed those shoulders.

"Such bores," she said very, very loudly. And with 3,500 people watching, she swept out holding George's arm. Even the orchestra stopped to watch her leave.

Sometimes she exhausted him. In December he took a week away from the club and they went upstate to Saratoga. He wanted to play some nice, restful poker. They went ice skating instead. He wanted to shoot craps, she insisted they go ice fishing. He caught two catfish and a cold. In the evenings when he wanted to be alone with her she wanted to go dancing until dawn. And one morning, when he wanted to sleep, she took him skiing. Somehow he broke the middle toe on his right foot and had to walk around with half an ice cream stick splint taped to the toe. That night she came to him and kissed his toe, among other things, until, miraculously, he felt no pain.

In February, Big Bill Dwyer invited them to Miami for the racing season. Dwyer said he had a modest cottage on Biscayne Bay. It turned out to be a forty-two-room French villa with a three-story-high central courtyard and enough exotic birds to fill a zoo. Elizabeth loved the birds—so much so that she insisted on going to the Everglades to see more of them. Instead of going to the races they spent five days in a canoe poling through the swamps with a Seminole guide who could barely grunt English but knew how to ask a great blue heron the time of day. Elizabeth learned every bird call she could, jamming various fingers in her mouth, breathing through reeds, squawking from deep in her throat. And in the damp night in their tent, while the mosquitos and moths gently committed suicide on the lantern outside and the bullfrogs called their mates with much huffing and puffing and bravado, Elizabeth would coo bird calls to him and hold him and love him until he knew he would follow her to the North Pole to watch penguins moult if that's what she wanted.

They might still be watching the loons go loony if Izzy the Stub hadn't wired that Detective Sergeant Johnny Broderick was sticking up the club for more protection money and should he pay or tell Broderick to take a long walk off a short pier. They hurried back to New York by canoe and train. George bought Broderick off again for another $5,000.

And now it was flying. She stood in front of him, her legs slightly apart and hands on her hips, looking like Eddie Rickenbacker in drag. But she was so lovely he couldn't laugh at her. Actually, she was inspecting *him*, and then laughed herself.

"You dope, you can't go up like that." She shook her head. "I told you to wear something appropriate and you come in a pin-stripe suit, silk shirt and tie, and that old fedora."

"I figure I'm getting killed today, toots. So I dressed for a funeral."

She took off his hat and handed him a soft leather helmet she took from the cockpit. She pulled it on his head and buckled it under his chin.

"Thanks," he said. "Now I really feel safe."

Elizabeth hugged him, looked up at his face. "I know you don't want to do this. I know you're only flying with me because I asked you. But you'll love it, I know you will. So get in and shut up, darling."

He took a deep breath, crossed himself, and clambered up onto the wing, then gingerly stepped into the rear cockpit. The mechanic reached in and buckled the safety straps for him. There was a small smear of white paint on his left hand.

"How's my name look?" George nervously tapped the side of the plane.

"Beautiful, pardner." The mechanic winked. "None of the others rated white paint."

168

The mechanic went around to the front of the plane and put the propeller into a horizontal position as Elizabeth climbed into the other cockpit.

"Switch on," he called. She gave him the thumbs-up sign and he heaved the propeller around. With a gasp, then a roar, the engine caught and they were slowly rolling across the field. George gripped the sides of the cockpit as Elizabeth briefly smiled back at him.

"Don't worry, pardner," called the mechanic. "What goes up must come down." Uh huh, thought George. That's what bothers me.

She taxied to the end of the field near the shack, then deftly turned the plane around and gunned the engine. The plane bounced heavily, then more gently on the ruts and grass stubble as it picked up speed. Then they were skimming just above the ground, the wind whistling through the wing wires. Just as he thought they were going to crash into some trees she pulled up the nose and they zoomed into the sky. She took the plane higher in lazy spirals—a thousand, two thousand, then four thousand feet.

"How do you like it?" she shouted back to him, the wind whipping her words around.

George could only grimace through tightly clamped teeth as he stared from side to side at the ground far below. She flew toward the towers of Manhattan, following the northern shore of Long Island. Once they caught up with a gull who looked startled to see them. The bird seemed to stare George in the eyes, then finally veered off with a look of disgust at the intruders. I don't blame you a bit, George thought. I wouldn't want you in one of my poker games, either.

Slowly he relaxed, coming to recognize that Elizabeth knew what she was doing. She seemed to hold the plane steady with effortless ease. He watched the control stick between his legs and could barely see it move as she lightly touched the stick up front. He became absorbed in the view. Up here the world looked so clean and orderly. He studied the carefully laid-out grid pattern of the farmers' fields, with roads snaking through them. As they got closer to the city more factories and homes appeared, then the densely packed streets of Queens and the Bronx. The geometric shapes on the ground fascinated him—the silvery splinters that were ships on the Sound, the gleaming railroad tracks. Then they were over Hell's Gate and flying down the East River, Manhattan flashing and sparkling on their right.

Over Forty-second Street Elizabeth turned and flew west, toward Times Square. She dipped the plane lower and now he could clearly pick out people as they scurried through the streets, oblivious to his eyes, intent on their little lives. Up here, in the sky, the worries of the ground don't matter, Elizabeth had told him. Problems become squeezed, diminished, until you soar over them, leave them behind. The world isn't real, she had said. Only the wind and the sun and the sound of the engine matter. Now he knew what she had meant. He looked up and saw that Elizabeth had been watching him. She nodded, knowing what he was feeling.

On they flew, down the Hudson River and over the Jersey piers, stubby ferry boats cutting blunt-nosed vees through the harbor below. She flew twice around the Statue of Liberty, swooping past the crown and missing it by only inches. Then over Staten Island, back past Liberty Island to the Battery in Manhattan. She buzzed a tall office building and George could see a man pouring himself a drink from a green bottle. He had a pleased, anticipatory look on his face. Then he heard the plane, hurriedly looked up, and dropped his glass. As they soared away George thought the man was going to cry.

Finally Elizabeth flew west over New Jersey toward a low range of hills. They landed at a small airport far out in the countryside. When they touched down, George realized that he was sorry to be back on the ground.

They bought fried chicken and a bottle of lemonade at a roadhouse across from the airport. Elizabeth led him to a nearby field and they sat on the bank of a small stream. He helped her pull off her heavy boots and they ate as they dangled their feet in the brook. He watched her, sometimes pushing a stray hair away from her face.

"I'm happy," she finally said. She lay her head on his lap.

"That was really something," he said dreamily. "I was sorry to come down. I feel . . . I feel like . . ."

"As though you had just made love?"

"Yes. Crazy, isn't it?"

"Not really. It strikes me that way too, sometimes," she said. "Flying gives you a great sense of well-being."

"Like gambling," he mused. "When you're winning."

She stretched, making her body taut. "Such a romantic."

He bent and kissed her eyes. She sat up and rested her chin on her drawn-up knees, looking at George. "Sometimes I think you'd like me better if I were the queen in a poker deck, back to back with three more just like me. Four of a kind that couldn't talk back."

He stared at her, wondering if she were serious or joking. Sometimes it was hard to tell with her. She could be like a cat, purring but with claws out. "I love you exactly the way you are, Elizabeth," he finally said. "Exactly."

She smiled. He only called her Elizabeth when he was very, very serious, she knew. Most of the time it was toots or Liz or even baby—although he knew she hated being called baby. But now he had called her Elizabeth.

"I'm hot and dusty," she said, rising and unbuttoning her blouse. "Come in the stream with me?" She pulled off her blouse, peeled down her pants.

"What? Here? What if somebody happens along?"

"That sounds familiar somehow," she said, leering at him. "Like something I once heard in Central Park." In moments she was naked. She looked at him challengingly, her hands cupping her breasts. Then she splashed into the shallow stream, ducked under the surface and came up with a great spray of water, pushing hair out of her eyes.

When did this begin? he wondered. When had she started putting him on the defensive like this? How was it that she was now calling the shots, somehow challenging him? And he was letting her do it. He studied her naked body in awe as she stood in the stream, wanting to throw off his clothes and rush to her. The water ran down her breasts and arms, coursed over her hips and down her fine legs. She bent and grabbed handfuls of water, throwing them up in the air. The droplets glistened in the sun as they fell around her, peppering the surface of the stream. She was so beautiful. She turned, laughed, wiggled her hips sensuously at him as she splashed like a water nymph. When had she taken over? he wondered again. Why was this affair now out of his control? Sometimes

171

lately he felt like a child around her, an infatuated child hopelessly and helplessly wooing his beautiful teacher. With a word, a look, a gesture Elizabeth could send him into ecstasy. No other woman had ever had such control, such power over him. He struggled endlessly, trying to understand the emotion instead of just the word *love*. It was as simple as that.

"Oh, what the hell," he told himself. He tore at his tie, pulled off his clothes, and scrambled into the stream. She ran from him, shrieking with laughter, until he caught her by the waist, pulled her under the water, then brought her up and pressed her to him. She shook her hair in his face, spun around, and ran the other way, still shrieking. He splashed after her again, tackled her around the thighs. They both went under the water and came up sputtering and laughing. But this time she did not run from him. She wiped the water off his face as they kissed. His hands found her thighs, moved up them as she caressed him, clawed his back, brought her breasts to his face for him to taste. He sat on the bed of the stream. She lowered herself onto him and they reveled in the rush of the stream as she moved rhythmically against him. He moaned once, twice, again, as Elizabeth cried out, thrashed about. Then they were sitting quietly in the water, arms tightly about each other.

"Why don't you marry me?" he finally murmured into her wet ear. "Then we could buy our own stream and do this every day."

"I wish I could. You don't know how long I've been waiting for you to ask. But . . ." she breathed into his wet ear.

He drew back and looked into her face. "But what?"

She hugged him again, ran her fingers through his soaking hair. "I'd feel a little foolish married to a man who goes swimming with his shoes and socks on."

He raised one foot out of the stream. Water ran out of his shoe.

"I guess I got a little excited. You could get a job in burlesque any time with those hips."

She kissed his neck, rested her head on his shoulder. "I don't know, darling."

"About burlesque?"

"About marriage." She could feel him stiffen.

172

The stream gurgled and popped past them. He listened to the water, watched as it splashed the ends of Elizabeth's hair. Not this time, he decided. She wasn't going to toy with him this time. He was going to get his own way, and she'd like it. He began to move gently beneath her, rocking her, his hands on her hips.

"I run from marriage," she explained, looking at him earnestly. "I'm afraid of it. You know about my wedding. You want to end up chasing me down the street, too? I wouldn't want to do that to you. What are you doing? Hey, I'm trying to talk to you. Mmmm. Stop that! Hey, listen to me!"

He held the plane steady at five hundred feet, careful to do what Elizabeth had told him. George gingerly stepped on the rudders and felt the little plane gently slip left, then swing back right. He nudged the control stick and the plane nosed down slightly, then came back to level as he eased back. He looked up, past the top wing to where the crescent moon shone palely in the darkening sky. He could just make out a few stars over the hazy horizon.

Elizabeth hadn't looked back at him since they left New Jersey. They had dressed in silence beside the little stream, she angry because he would not listen to her arguments but only make love to her. She had tersely explained how the controls worked, then taken off and let him fly the plane. He flew badly at first, Elizabeth correcting his errors. Then he got the hang of it and as they flew over the Hudson River she left the plane to him.

He watched her shoulders, wisps of still-damp hair brushing them. Sometimes they went stiff—with anger, he thought. Then they would relax, soften. Several times he thought she would turn and look at him. But then the shoulders stiffened again.

Perhaps he should have listened to her, he thought. Maybe her fears were legitimate, although they didn't bother him. There were times for discussion and times for action, and that was a time for action. He was touched that she would be afraid to marry out of consideration for him. But he knew it was fear, too, as she said. Fear of that lasting commitment, something that you can't simply walk away from. Was she ready? Is any-

173

body ever ready for marriage? You had to take a chance, risk all, draw to that apocryphal inside straight. As he watched her shoulders he knew she was debating with herself. But he knew who would win—even if she didn't.

They were over Long Island Sound when she finally turned around. Her eyes were soft and wet. Her lips moved but he couldn't hear what she was saying. He cupped his ear in a gesture of trying to hear. Her lips moved again, slower, and he could tell she was shouting. But only snatches of words came to him. He shrugged, shook his head.

Suddenly he jumped. She was getting out of the cockpit, putting one foot over the side onto the wing! She fumbled with something in front of her and he quickly took the plane down, pleading with her to stop. In seconds they were zooming low over a wide beach. Now she had both legs out and pushed herself onto the wing. He shouted at her to get back in the plane, swinging his arm wildly as he desperately tried to control the plane with his other hand. The ground rushed up at him as Elizabeth gingerly stepped along the wing, finally putting a hand on his arm. He struggled with the plane as he hauled her into the cockpit with him.

There was an abrupt jolt and he could feel something tearing away beneath the wings. Elizabeth put her arms around his neck as the plane settled to the beach with a little bump, then skidded through the surf, spray mixed with sand flying in all directions. With a last groan and a tearing of canvas the plane spun to the right, then came to rest leaning on one wing.

"What the hell was that all about?" he yelled, wiping sand out of his face.

She smiled at him. "I thought you'd like to know. I'll marry you."

22

"Congratulate me."

Horace Wainwright slowly and deliberately lit his cigar before asking why he should congratulate his daughter. He really didn't want to know, he decided. Once, when she was fifteen, she had used those words to prepare him for the announcement that she was going to swim across Long Island Sound from New York to Connecticut. He had said no. She went anyway. A sudden summer squall came up and she was missing in the water for two hours before a fisherman found her, still swimming valiantly against the tide.

Congratulate me. She also said that when she decided she was going to become the first woman to fly solo from New York to California. Was she eighteen or nineteen then? Again he had said no. She was over Iowa when her engine sputtered out and she crash-landed in a cornfield, breaking an arm and a couple of fingers.

"I'm afraid to ask, child. What shall I congratulate you for this time? Are you going to fight an alligator barehanded? Have you decided to run off to the circus and become a hoochy-koochy girl?"

"Worse," she said, and gave him her most dazzling smile. "I'm going to become a married lady."

His cigar slumped in his mouth and nearly set his silk smoking jacket afire. He hurriedly brushed away the ash and embers, then sat heavily on the sofa. He rubbed the arm of the sofa, admiring the feel of the soft leather, and trying to think of what to say to Elizabeth next. Besides no.

He stared at her. She stood across the room, in front of a vast array of roses in a Chinese vase. She still wore her leather flight jacket, jodhpurs, and boots. Her hair and her clothes were dirty and streaked with sand, as if she had been playing in some adult sandbox. He wanted to ask her where all the sand had come from if she was flying. But then he thought better of it. There were more important things to discuss.

"I notice you didn't say that you'd like my permission to marry. I assume that means you've made up your mind?"

"Father, it's nineteen twenty-six—not the Middle Ages." She stalked across the room and sat on the couch beside him. Wherever she walked, he noted, she left a faint trail of sand behind. And did she have to look so damnably happy!

"I suppose I should be flattered that you mentioned your

175

betrothal to me at all. After all, it *is* nineteen twenty-six. Is your intended this hoodlum you've been living with for the past six months?"

"He's not a hoodlum. He's a gambler," she countered, realizing how weak and defensive that sounded. She watched her father's face. It was stony, expressionless. But the sarcasm in his voice was as thick as maple syrup.

He puffed deeply on his cigar, exhaled a thick cloud of smoke that drifted toward the roses. He turned the cigar in his fingers, examining it from every angle, as if some great decision were involved with it.

"So now what?" he finally said. "Do you seriously expect my blessing, or some such old-fangled notion that we dinosaurs have?"

She sighed, then set her jaw in determination. "If you knew him, maybe you'd understand. . . ."

He rose and walked to his big square desk in the corner of the library under the tall windows. He opened a drawer and took out a single sheet of paper. He held it so the yellow light from the desk lamp shone on the paper.

"George Michael McManus," he read. "Age thirty-one. Height six feet. Weight one eighty-five. Marked scar over right eye. No brothers or sisters. Parents John and Colleen McManus died in influenza epidemic, nineteen-oh-four. Raised by Jesuit fathers in West Side orphanage. Left at age fifteen. Lived with aunt, Violet Cushing, in tenement on West Forty-eighth Street. Several minor scrapes with the law— petty theft, street brawling, hooliganism. Held on burglary charge in Hoboken, New Jersey, nineteen eighteen. Released for lack of evidence. Turned gambler five years ago, eventually staging high-stakes poker games. Now partner in speakeasy and casino called Paradise Rehearsal Club, Broadway at Forty-sixth. Major partner is convicted bootlegger William Dwyer. McManus associates with other known gamblers and mobsters. Now resides at Park Central Hotel in Manhattan. McManus has a reputation as a ladies' man. Formerly lived with dancer named Marie Flynn, who now works in his speakeasy. Now living with . . ."

Wainwright looked up from the paper. "But you already know that, don't you?"

176

"Did you hire detectives to look under the bed, too?" she asked. "Very thorough. Even I didn't know his middle name was Michael. I like it."

"There's more, if you'd like me to read it." Wainwright watched her closely.

She ran her fingers through her hair, shaking some of the sand out onto the Persian carpet. "That won't be necessary, Father. I don't think you've got anything there that will shock me."

He slammed his hand on the desk and waved the paper in the air. "Come to your senses, Elizabeth. Grow up. This man isn't for you. Of course, you're infatuated with him now, I can see that. He must be exciting to a young girl. But dammit, he's a crook. Do you think it will be exciting visiting him every other Wednesday in Sing-Sing?"

She slipped off the leather jacket and brushed idly at the streaks of sand and dirt on it. "People who live in glass houses, Father, shouldn't accuse others of being crooks."

"What kind of nonsense are you talking now?"

She got up and walked to him. She put her arms around her father. "Please. I don't want to hurt you."

He held her at arm's length. "What do you know about me?"

"I saw the story in the *New York American* about you and Tammany." She looked at him evenly.

He let her go and turned toward the desk hunting for his cigar. "Bah, a lot of Hearst hokum to try to discredit Walker. I'm amazed you would believe such political drivel, child. You just don't understand these things."

"George McManus saw you at Tammany, Father. He saw you dump money on Jimmy Walker's desk. Bribe money."

Wainwright forgot about his cigar. "It's a lie," he finally managed to say, not very believably.

She shook her head. "No, it's true, Father. And there's more. It was George McManus who arranged to have that issue of the *American* stopped. He saved your skin, Father. So you'd better be careful whom you call a crook."

Wainwright stumbled back to the sofa and flopped down as if all his joints had inexplicably loosened. Suddenly, Elizabeth thought, he looked like a very old man.

177

She sat beside him and hugged him to her. "I want you to meet him. Say you'll do that."

He could only nod.

23

HER VOICE was low and mellow, custom-made for the torch song she was wailing. The new singer at the Paradise Rehearsal Club was a well-stacked blonde dressed in a skin-tight bright-red frock slit up one side to the top of the thigh. The song was one of the hits of the season—a plaintive ballad about her lover beating her and mistreating her, but she'd never leave him because she hated being alone.

Her styling was first rate. She'd been hired away from one of the top uptown clubs. But she might as well have been Jojo the dog-faced girl singing the "Marseillaise" stark naked for all the attention the crowd paid her.

Even the couples on the dance floor ignored her. The singer could hear their questions as they swayed in front of her cheek to cheek. "How much do we have left?" whispered a woman in blue. "How much did we win?" shouted a girl in black. "When can we come back?" said one. "When can we leave?" moaned another. The singer finished the lament and turned to the five-piece band. She snapped her fingers three times quickly and the band began a brassy up-tempo rendition of "Alexander's Ragtime Band." That ought to grab them, the singer thought as she belted out "Come on and hear, come on and hear . . ."

But only the two men at the bar were really listening to her. Big Bill Dwyer sipped a glass of white wine and tapped his foot in step with the tune.

"Nice, Georgie. As good as Helen Morgan. Maybe better." Dwyer leaned back against the bar and looked around. The club had changed in the months he'd been in Miami. Another crap table had been added. A poker game was going in one of the rehearsal rooms. And a row of one-armed bandits—slot machines—lined the dance floor below the casino to accommodate the usual overflow crowds. The man doesn't miss a trick, Dwyer thought, as he watched George move off to okay an IOU.

He watched George McManus closely as the other man bustled about the club. McManus smoothed customers' rough edges, warned Marie Flynn and Izzy who was going to be trouble, greeted friends and ordered them free drinks and bottles of champagne. McManus was still hungry, Dwyer knew. He did everything but polish the dice.

The band finished the ragtime number and the singer, deciding to please herself, began another blues tune. Dwyer looked dreamy as the song began. He loved sad songs. Like most true Irishmen he was never happier than when listening to a ballad of lost loves or lost wars. "Hurt me, desert me," the woman sang as a furtive little man pushed his face close to Dwyer's right ear.

"Pssst," he began, "Izzy the Stub says we can do business. Got some toney little items to sell."

The man wore a too-large tan topcoat over a brown pin-striped suit and two-tone red and black wingtips. A strawberry-colored birthmark covered most of the right side of his face.

He introduced himself only as "Izzy's pal—from the war," then pulled a shiny, gold and jewel-encrusted bracelet and matching ring from the breast pocket of his topcoat. The baubles dazzled in the dim light of the casino. They looked real, Dwyer thought.

"My mother's," the man whispered. "I wouldn't part with 'em but she needs an operation. And my little girl needs braces on her teeth. You know how it is."

Dwyer nodded solemnly. He knew how it was.

"Been in the family for years. Mama cried when I told her we gotta sell 'em." The little man seemed near tears himself. "But I ain't had a real job since the war. And Izzy says you'll give a fair price."

"How much do you need?" Dwyer asked as he sipped his wine again.

"Two-fifty. But I'll take a couple bucks off for you, on account Izzy says you're a stand-up guy. They're worth it. See?" He took the ring and scraped one of its white stones across the base of Dwyer's glass, scratching the crystal.

Dwyer pulled out a wad of bills and peeled off three hundreds. He handed them to the man.

"Keep the change. And come back here tomorrow night. We may be able to find a job for you."

The little man smiled and nodded, giving Dwyer a where-have-you-been-all-my-life look. He started to leave, then turned back. He flashed open his overcoat, revealing two dozen pockets brimming over with rings, watches, bracelets, necklaces, jewels of all kinds.

"My aunt's, my father's," he began, fingering the merchandise until a hand grabbed his shoulder and spun him around.

"Hit the road," George McManus warned. "Next time I see you up here I'll make you eat a watch."

The little man gave one longing, backward glance at Dwyer, then scurried out of the casino.

"Christ, they come out of the woodwork when you're around, Bill. Don't you ever say no?"

Dwyer shrugged. "I know what it's like to need money and not have it. You should remember, too, George."

"I do. But nine times out of ten these guys are conning you. Why hand out money to every hustler with a sob story?"

"That's where we're different, Georgie." Dwyer shifted on his stool. "I'd rather pay off ten cheats than deny one honest man in trouble."

"An honest man? What's that? Don't come running to me when you run out of money, Bill."

"I'll never run out of money," Dwyer said mildly, "as long as George McManus is running this joint."

George lowered his voice. "But the word is you're in trouble again. Rothstein says you dropped two hundred thousand to him the other night. You know how Mr. Rothstein likes to talk."

"It was only fifty thousand. That Rothstein would lie about the number of guests at the Last Supper.

"But talk about losing money," Dwyer went on, "I fixed a race in Miami and still lost. Bought off seven jockeys in an eight-horse race and put half a million on the other animal. A real longshot—fifteen to one. I spread the money with book-makers all over the country so no one would catch on. Even Rothstein took some of the action.

"Anyway, by the head of the stretch my longshot was twenty lengths in front and I was screaming so loud you could hear me in Ohio. Then, fifty yards from the finish my horse broke a leg and went down. You should have seen it, George. The other riders pulled up and stopped for three full minutes before deciding to pass the horse. It must have been the longest race in history."

"And you're out half a million." McManus shook his head.

"It was worth it to be able to tell the story, Georgie. Anyway, I've got a little shipment coming in next month that will replenish my wallet. I'm bringing it in through Long Island Sound to avoid all those bandits off Jersey. There's some very dishonorable people out there on Rum Row, you know."

George refilled Dwyer's wine glass from the bottle on the bar. "I know you limit yourself to one glass a day, but this is a half-a-million-dollar toast." George raised his glass.

"Well thank you, Mr. McManus. I'm genuinely touched." Dwyer raised his glass.

"To ill-gotten gains," George said quietly.

As they drank, Marie Flynn wove through the crowd and tapped George on the shoulder. He put an arm around her waist but she gently backed away, lowering her eyes.

"There's a geezer downstairs who wants to see you," she told him. "He's dressed like money but he doesn't look like he wants to gamble. When I patted his cheek he just turned red. Didn't even try to play grabass."

McManus nodded and she walked away.

"Lovely," Dwyer said, following her with his eyes. "But it doesn't seem like she wants anything to do with you anymore. Losing your touch?"

"Hell hath no fury like a redhead scorned." George downed the last of his drink. Over the edge of his glass he saw Izzy directing a well-dressed man in his sixties toward him. He felt a flicker of recognition as the older man looked toward the bar. Then George knew where he had seen him before. Horace Wainwright pushed Izzy aside and bulled his way through the crowd.

181

"You McManus?" the old man demanded. Wainwright sounded calm but a vein in his neck was an angry purple. It throbbed rhythmically. George nodded.

"I want to talk to you. Alone." Wainwright glared at Dwyer, who turned his head and resumed listening to the singer.

"Let's go somewhere more private," McManus suggested. He put a hand on the older man's shoulder but Wainwright pulled away from his touch. Wainwright followed him but he was not walking very steadily, George thought. He was breathing heavily through his mouth. His eyes were locked straight forward as they walked through the money room, as if he feared glancing from side to side might deter him from his mission. He never even seemed to notice Otto Berman or the stacks of bills piled around.

The office door slammed behind them and for a moment no one spoke. Wainwright began circling about McManus like a stalking cat. McManus half expected the old man to urinate on the floor to mark his territory. Horace Wainwright didn't look much like his daughter, George decided. Only the slightly weak chin and fiery gray-green eyes were similar. On further inspection he realized that even the eyes were different. There was warmth in Elizabeth's, only intensity in Wainwright's.

"How much?" Wainwright said finally.

"How much what?"

Wainwright took off his hat and unbuttoned his coat. He reached into an inner pocket, pulled out a packet of money, and threw it on the desk.

"How much to leave my daughter alone?"

Elizabeth always said her father never wasted time on subtleties, George thought. He picked up the bills. Hundreds. He thumbed the edge of the stack. There were at least a hundred bills.

"Name your price, McManus. Anything within reason."

"Sorry," George said, "but I'm not for sale."

"Everyone's for sale." Wainwright produced another wad of bills and slammed it down on the desk.

"Let's quit haggling. How much do you want?"

McManus shook his head. No wonder Wainwright was a

182

successful businessman, he thought. He not only refused to take no for an answer, he refused to even hear it. And he certainly knew how to use his money for dramatic effect.

"Save your money for a wedding present, Wainwright," George said with a smile. "Or should I call you Dad?"

Wainwright's eyes bulged with rage, but he held his tongue. He licked his lips twice.

"Now, look here," Wainwright began. His voice had softened but the eyes still looked like they could set asbestos on fire. "You think you're in love with my daughter. And she thinks she's in love with you. But, believe me, son, it's only infatuation. I know Elizabeth."

"Or maybe Pops. No? Father? No, that's too formal. Dad it'll have to be." George sat behind his desk and locked his hands behind his head.

"Not enough?" Wainwright said as he pulled out two more packets of bills and his checkbook. "Fifty thousand? How about a hundred thousand?"

McManus took a bottle of scotch and two glasses out of a desk drawer. He poured and pushed one glass toward Wainwright.

"I'm glad you dropped in, Dad. This gives us a chance to talk about the wedding. We . . ."

Wainwright sighed. "Take the money, McManus. Now. Before Elizabeth tires of you. . . ."

". . . just want a small affair. Two or three thousand of our closest friends. I think I know where I can get the liquor real cheap."

"She *will* tire of you, you know. She always tosses men aside eventually." Wainwright swallowed the scotch and was surprised at how smoothly it went down. Prewar hooch. At least the boy had taste. Wainwright opened his checkbook and began writing. "I'll make it two hundred thousand."

"The name's McManus," George said. "Not Walker."

Wainwright stopped writing. So he *did* know about the bribe. Wainwright had a vague recollection that someone else had been in Walker's office that day, but he no more remembered McManus from that encounter than he remembered the face of the boy who shined his shoes that morning. He would

183

have to be more discreet in the future. Wainwright sat heavily in a chair and pushed his whiskey glass toward George, who filled it to the brim.

Wainwright picked up the glass and studied McManus's craggy face. There was no reason he should remember him, he decided. A strong face but still typical shanty Irish. What *did* Elizabeth see in him? He had brains. Wainwright could see that from the casino and his clientele. But Elizabeth had never chased anybody for his gray matter before.

"Elizabeth tells me I'm in your debt." Wainwright sipped the scotch. It flowed easily down his throat and left a satisfying warmth. He hadn't had anything this good in years, he thought. Even his club had run out of the good stuff. Damned Prohibition. The wrong people were being denied the pleasures of life. He pushed his glass toward George again.

"It was nothing." George shrugged and poured. "Our interests coincided."

"Still, I like to pay my debts." Wainwright opened his checkbook again and uncapped his pen. "Say an extra fifty thousand?"

George frowned, stared at Wainwright. "Okay, you want me to name a price. Here it is."

Wainwright sat forward and put down the glass.

"I'll give *you* one million dollars to get out of my way and leave Elizabeth alone," George said. "Is she worth a million to you, Wainwright?"

The other man stiffened, the vein in his throat throbbing again. "Do you really think I'd sell my daughter to a bastard like you—even for a million?"

George shrugged. "Not enough? You're a man who loves money, Wainwright. I've seen you in action. How about a million and a quarter? All right, all right." George raised his hands in exasperation. "Let's not quibble. I'll give you an even million and a half. A lot of currency for a hundred pounds of flesh."

"You're a fool, McManus. And you're trying to make a fool out of me." Wainwright rose, put on his coat. He stuffed the packets of bills and his checkbook into a pocket and walked slowly to the door. He looked slumped, dejected. As if,

184

George thought, the reality that there was something money could not buy had taken the life force out of him. Wainwright was halfway out the door when he turned.

"You're a gambler, McManus. A wager. For Elizabeth. Are you game?"

George looked at the other man, weighing him, trying to tote up the worth of his soul. Perhaps he wasn't just a money belt with a body attached. Maybe there was flesh and blood and feeling there.

"A turn of the cards?" he finally asked.

Wainwright nodded. George led him from the room and through the crowd to the bar where Dwyer was still sitting. Dwyer looked at them with interest as George asked the bartender for a new pack of cards.

"Not you. I don't trust you to cut them," Wainwright said as George pulled the wrapper off the pack.

"You wound me to the heart." George pulled the cards from the box and deftly spread them on the polished bar. "Do you trust the bartender, then?"

"I don't want you or anybody that works for you to touch the deck, McManus." Wainwright quickly looked around and his gaze settled on Dwyer. He looked him over carefully. From his clothes and his bearing he judged him to be someone of quality. His honest eyes and sober face convinced Wainwright.

"Would you do the honors for us, sir?" Wainwright asked. "We have a wager going. Would you please cut the cards for each of us, as I don't trust this . . ." He searched for a word, then gave up. He looked to George. "If that's acceptable to you?"

George nodded. "Winner take all."

"Yes," murmured Wainwright. "Winner take all."

Dwyer looked from man to man. Wainwright was sweating inside his coat in the heat of the club. His eyes were on the cards. George's look was noncommittal. Dwyer wondered what they were cutting for. He picked up the deck and carefully began to shuffle, still looking from one man to the other. Finally he held the deck in front of him in one palm. He nodded to McManus.

"This is for you," Dwyer said. His long, tapering fingers split the deck. He turned his hand over. "An eight of spades, gentlemen."

"And now for you, sir." Dwyer turned to Wainwright. He put the two halves of the deck back together, carefully making the stack even. With a flick of the wrist he cut the deck and showed the bottom card.

A six.

McManus breathed deeply, turned to the bar, and poured himself a drink. When he turned around Wainwright was gone.

"Did you con him?" George asked matter-of-factly.

"What an awful question," Dwyer replied, "to ask an honest man."

24

ON A BRIGHT DAY in early June, one hundred Negro children left a costume shop on Thirty-seventh Street and scattered through the city. Each child was between the ages of nine and twelve, and each wore a scarlet silk tunic and breeches, a scarlet turban, white hose, black pumps, and a yellow silk sash around the waist. Each child also carried a parchment envelope nearly a foot square and sealed with red wax.

As might be expected, and as was intended by Horace Wainwright, their presence was soon remarked upon. As the children scampered through the streets from mansion to mansion and office to office, puzzled men and women laughed at the tiny apparitions before them, tore open the envelopes, and read the enclosed cards inviting them to a costume party July 4. The bottom line of the cards asked the recipients not to mention the invitations to anyone else. That was all that was needed. Within hours people were on the phone to each other all over the city asking who had—and hadn't—been visited by the children in their outlandish costumes.

By late afternoon Cholly Knickerbocker's gossip column in the late editions was already proclaiming that you weren't anybody if you hadn't received an envelope. And Cholly reliably reported that at least one matron who hadn't received an invitation had dressed up her maid's son in scarlet and paraded him up and down in front of her Fifth Avenue address until the neighbors got the idea.

There hadn't been this much curiosity about a party, noted Damon Runyon in his sports column the next day, since the victory banquet in Rome after the Lions swept the Christians in a double-header.

At the end of the week, people finally found out why Horace Wainwright was in a celebrating mood. On Friday the papers were full of pictures of Wainwright and Mayor Jimmy Walker shaking hands after the city contracted with Wainwright to build a subway tunnel connecting Brooklyn and Manhattan. Most of the papers quickly ran editorials lauding the mayor for getting the subway project going after so many years of anti-traction politics and delay.

In a modest article the *New York Times* questioned the bidding procedure by which the contract was awarded. But it was a lonely voice in the wilderness. The unions praised the creation of so many new jobs. Steelmakers, iron foundries, cable and brick makers, cement manufacturers all clamored for supply subcontracts. Tammany quickly put out the word that hundreds of jobs were available for laborers and sandhogs who had loyally supported the party in the past.

"Every man, woman, and child in New York City will benefit from this Herculean undertaking," gushed one newspaper. "Not to mention America and the world at large."

"Marvelous. I'm getting to be a bigger man than the governor," said Horace Wainwright with a satisfied smacking of his lips. He passed the folded newspaper to his daughter and reached across the breakfast table for the marmalade to smear on his toast.

Elizabeth picked up the paper and scanned the editorial praising Wainwright for his "industrial prowess" and "princely business acumen." It also compared his "grand achievements" to those of Henry Ford and Thomas Edison and "other kings of industry."

"Industrial prowess," she mused, thoughtfully chewing on

187

scrambled egg. "It makes you sound like you shoot bricks instead of sperm."

Wainwright glanced at his daughter. "If you were a few years younger and I wasn't so pleased, I'd wash out your mouth with soap."

"Ah yes, mustn't talk dirty around the old folks." She playfully pinched his cheek. "I'm not a child anymore, Father."

He studied her as she went back to eating and laughing at the newspaper article. No, she wasn't a child anymore, he realized. It was the same face, the same body. But there was assurance there now. The eyes had become mature, the features sharper, more defined. His eyes strayed to the cleavage her silk dress revealed and he felt slightly ashamed that looking at his own child could arouse him. She was a woman now, beautiful and aware of it. He felt, somehow, betrayed. That was something else he had George McManus to thank for.

"Let me tell you why I asked you to join me this morning." He pulled his eyes away from the sight of her breasts as she leaned toward him.

She laughed. "You make it sound like one of your board meetings, Father."

"Well, it *is* a matter of business. Your mother did a real fine job outfitting those silly-looking colored boys and making up the invitations. Now I want you to take over this whole costume party for me. Spend whatever you want, but make it memorable. I want this whole town to talk about Horace Wainwright. There'll be lots of wealthy people at the party, child, and I don't want them to lack for anything. The best of everything. Knock their eyes out, Elizabeth. What do you say?"

She studied her father, amazed at seeing him so excited about spending money. Usually his enthusiasm was reserved for making it. But there was a sparkle in his eye and a flush in his cheek that told her he was serious. This party was to be his ultimate status symbol, she realized. His mark that he had made it big, his passage into a world that measured your worth by the millions you possessed—however those millions were gained.

She looked down at the newspaper again and the phrase

"kings of industry" caught her eye. She suddenly remembered when she had been in school in Switzerland and the class had gone on holiday to Paris. They had spent a whole day at the Palace of Versailles and she had wandered the ornate rooms and corridors and impeccable gardens as if in a fairy tale. In the Hall of Mirrors she had stared at herself and her friends in the glass, but instead of schoolgirls she had seen reflected handsome ladies of the French court with brocade gowns heavy with jewels and ornate hairdos piled high on their heads. And in the background sat Louis XIV, the Sun King, in long, curly hair and fine silks, regal on his throne while the wealth of the world was strewn at his feet. It had been a beautiful fantasy. One she had never forgotten.

"All right. But it won't be just another costume party, Father. We'll have a grand costume party. A theme party. Everyone will come as French nobles—and you shall be Louis the Sun King. How does that suit you?"

He slapped the table and the plates jumped. "That suits me right down to the ground, daughter. Make it big, grand."

"I'll begin making arrangements this afternoon. And of course I'll have to let the guests know about their costumes. We'll use the Negro boys again, Father, if that's all right with you. On July fourth the Sands Point cottage will become the Palace of Versailles."

He took a last sip of coffee, then put his hand over his daughter's hand. "I'm glad we'll be, well . . . working together. Maybe we can sort of get to know each other again, Elizabeth. It's been a while since you've been under this roof, you know. Your mother and I have missed you." He pushed away from the table and stood up, a little embarrassed by his remark, as if it were an admission of weakness.

Elizabeth took his hand and pulled him back down to the chair. "You haven't heard my price, Father."

"Price?"

"You don't build subways or bridges or roads for free, do you? Why should I handle this party for you for nothing? It'll be lots of work, you know." She tried to look innocent but wasn't succeeding very well.

"Then what's it going to cost me?" he said suspiciously.

"It's not really going to cost you anything, Father. It's going

189

to gain you something—a son. I want you to announce my engagement to George on July fourth."

Wainwright absently pushed some bread crumbs around the tablecloth while looking at her. For a moment he thought he recognized the look in her eyes. It was like the look of excited anticipation she had given him when he had bought her a pony at the age of six. It had been a beautiful pony, he remembered. With red saddle and bridle, and mane and tail braided in red ribbons. How she had loved it. She had even insisted on sleeping in its stall for days. He had always enjoyed giving her things, beautiful things.

A few months later he had given her a child-size two-masted sailboat, perfect in every detail, to sail around the small pond at the Long Island estate. The pony had quickly been forgotten. He finally sold it.

"You asked me to meet this McManus," he finally said. "I didn't like what I saw. He's not . . . the man for you. . . ." His voice trailed off. He knew he sounded feeble and uncertain. He wondered if McManus had told her about their bet.

Anger clouded her face but she held her temper. "I'm going to be his wife one way or the other, Father. I'd rather have your approval. I won't argue with you about what kind of man he is. I just won't."

He saw the futility of debating with her. It was not the time to be stern, authoritarian. He stood up and walked to the large windows of the dining room, overlooking the garden. Beyond the hedges, across Fifth Avenue, he could see men and women strolling happily, hear the traffic bustling by.

"All right. July fourth. If that's what you want." He sighed.

She jumped up and ran to him, hugging him and pressing her face to his back. He did not turn around. He did not want her to see his face.

25

THE WHITE SATIN GLOBE hung four feet above the polished ballroom floor, a gossamer-thin silk rope holding the globe to the chandelier in the center of the room. As it swayed gently a slight man with thinning red hair and white kid gloves extracted a near-transparent blue-green butterfly from a smoked glass tank and carefully guided it through a hole in the globe. He could hear the flutter of delicate wings as it joined the two hundred other butterflies inside.

Around him glass tanks and cases were scattered about the ballroom floor, each containing dozens of specimens of the order Lepidoptera. Red and gold Sulphurs imported from Cuba. Peacock butterflies from Europe. Green Sphinx moths from Brazil. There were a thousand of them in all. Orange and blue, green and red, all the colors of the rainbow, from nearly all the continents of the world. The young man worked slowly, taking care not to injure a single one.

The big double doors squeaked behind him and he turned his head in time to see his employer step out of her shoes, take a running start, then slide in her stocking feet across the slick ballroom floor. Elizabeth Wainwright stopped suddenly as she hit an unwaxed spot, fought to keep her balance, then fell backward, laughing. The startled man dropped the butterfly in his fingers. It darted away and landed on a large glass tank near Elizabeth. It was a particularly lovely one, she thought. Brilliant blue-purple wings, each cut across with a shock of bright orange. She reached for it and the butterfly drew its wings over its head, revealing a dull gray underside. It stood stock-still on the glass case and Elizabeth watched, fascinated.

The man picked up the insect and announced, revealing an unmistakable pride in his expertise, "*Kallima tribonia*. From Sumatra."

"Of course." Elizabeth nodded knowingly and wondered where Sumatra was.

The man placed the butterfly in the palm of Elizabeth's left hand, stealing a long look down the bodice of her low-cut green silk dress. He didn't meet many women like her in his line of work. The average female butterfly fancier, he mused, was sixty-five, unmarried, and had a face like a potato.

"It pretends to be a dead leaf whenever it's frightened," he explained.

Elizabeth studied the gray underwings. The insect did in-

191

deed look like a dead leaf. She gently stroked the butterfly and it slowly spread its wings.

"It won't pull that camouflage trick tonight, will it, Mr. Beasley?"

"Oh, no," he assured her cheerfully. "No, Miss Wainwright, he'll be so happy to get out of the globe, he'll fly around for hours. They all will. You'll see."

Elizabeth handed the butterfly back to him. It would be a beautiful sight. At the stroke of midnight the satin globe would open and hundreds of butterflies would cascade down and dance over the ballroom. It would be the pièce de résistance of the party. The moment no one would ever forget.

Elizabeth wandered about the butterfly cases, gazing at the specimens. The red-haired man tried to describe them all, pleased at the opportunity to show off his knowledge to a beautiful woman. But Elizabeth excused herself and wandered out of the ballroom just as he was explaining the finer points of the family Papilionoidea. He felt his heart racing as he watched her walk away. Finally he sighed and returned to his butterflies.

Elizabeth was drawn away by the aromas escaping from the kitchen. The fragrances of vanilla, ginger, garlic, roasts of beef and pork combined with less identifiable spices and dishes to produce one delicious smell. It hung in the air as she stood half drooling in the pantry. She felt a sharp hunger pang and suddenly realized she hadn't eaten all day. She wanted to go in and make herself a sandwich but she knew the foppish French chef she had hired for the party from the Waldorf would complain about her presence in his squeaky little voice again.

She took one last deep smell, then turned and walked from the pantry to inspect the rest of the ground-floor rooms. The library, the music room, the sitting rooms, even the chess room and the conservatory had been redecorated with copies of furnishings from Versailles. She watched as maids dusted and arranged the ornate commodes, bureaus, desks, chairs, and sofas. Satisfied, Elizabeth went out the French doors to inspect the formal gardens. The gardeners were putting in the last touches—fountains formed of frolicking nymphs and satyrs. A huge tent sat on the lawn.

Behind her came the tap of a baton on a music stand. Two flutists, an oboeist, two clarinetists, and a bassoonist began a light chamber piece. It sounded pretty, she thought, if dull. She was glad she had also hired a Dixieland group, a dance band, and the torch singer from George's club to play in the tent and throughout the house. Hours of chamber music would bore to tears all but the most fanatic classical buff, she knew. And Elizabeth wouldn't let anyone be bored for a moment. She had planned something for everyone—exotic foods from abalone soup to *zuppa inglese*, a giant fireworks display, a water ballet in the pool, roving madrigal singers. She had even invited a handful of gigolos to cater to the homely, the widows, and the neglected wives on the guest list. She expected much giggling.

Beyond the tent, on the curved drive of the estate, stood a black-and-gold coach with four white horses. Behind that coach were a dozen others. The coaches would meet the guests as each of the special trains her father had hired reached the local station. The drivers and footmen all wore bulky overcoats, called doublets, of black and gold, white breeches, and high black leather boots with silver buckles. Each coachman wore a long, brown curly wig and a three-cornered black-and-white hat.

Finally, she walked up a little grassy hill near the house, sat down, and tucked her knees under her chin. She looked back at the house, the gardens, the tent, the coaches—it was her fantasy of Versailles come to life. She imagined it as it would look tonight, with the lights and servants and hundreds of people strolling gaily in costume. She saw herself dancing in the arms of George McManus. And the excitement at midnight when her father would announce their engagement. The butterflies would flutter everywhere, the fireworks would begin, the band would play for them.

Other thoughts crowded into her mind even though she tried to push them away. She thought of the stony silences from her father that greeted every mention of George McManus. No shouting anymore, no dire warnings, just silences when he would not meet her eyes.

She heard the creaking of springs and the cadence of horses' shod hooves. The coaches were heading to the station to pick up the first guests. She stood, straightening her dress. She put her arms up and stretched, taking deep breaths. It was time to put on her costume. As she walked back down the hill she thought of how she pitied those people who couldn't afford to make their dreams come true.

Captain Francis O'Brien impatiently studied the late-afternoon sun through the trees on Mt. Misery Point. Whoever had named this spit of land on the north shore of Long Island had certainly known his business, O'Brien thought. Ugly, twisted, scrub trees, bare sandbars, and stony beaches surrounded the little cove in which his ship sat, waiting for darkness. Not so much as a fisherman's rowboat had entered the cove all day.

O'Brien had been up since dawn, when he pulled the rusty old submarine chaser into the cove. He and his lookouts constantly watched the beach, the entrance to the cove, even the air, for Coast Guard patrols. This trip the old ship was called the *Catherine Moulton,* after Dwyer's favorite manicurist. Next trip her name would be something else. Changing names frequently helped confuse the Coast Guard.

O'Brien crossed his arms. He would be happy when they got underway and made for City Island off the Bronx. He would be even happier when Dwyer's motorboats met them off City Island and sped his cargo of scotch whiskey, rye, and gin to piers all over New York City. O'Brien could feel the ship rock slightly in the low waves slapping into the beach. She was too heavily loaded to move about much, certainly too heavy to outrun any patrol boat.

But there was nowhere to run in these narrow waters in the western Sound anyway. From City Island it was just a short run to Hell's Gate, the East River, and Manhattan. A ship the size of this would hardly be able to maneuver at all in the shallows and swift currents, O'Brien knew. That's what he had tried to tell Dwyer. She would be a sitting duck. Maybe that's what I ought to name this old lady, he thought. The *Sitting Duck.*

He stroked his full beard contemplatively as he looked at the sky again. Two hours to full sundown, at least. Maybe the

194

Sitting Duck would make its move a little early, he decided. In and out. Fast. That's the ticket.

"You'll have to suck in a bit, sir."

"Goddammit, I am sucking in. If I suck in any more, my belt buckle will bruise my spine."

Horace Wainwright's normally florid face was a shade short of purple as he tried to cram his ample belly into the royal blue and gold brocade coat. He cursed again. Nothing seemed to fit. The black velvet breeches were too tight. The white linen and lace shirt hung on him like a sack. The satin waistcoat cut into his stomach so badly he was sure it would leave a mark for weeks. And the white silk stockings and black leather pumps made him feel like some foolish escapee from a French operetta.

"Did people really wear ridiculous get-ups like this?" he shouted at no one in particular. "No wonder the damned French empire fell. No one could breathe, for God's sake."

Wainwright sucked in hard and this time the valet pulled the coat together, fastening it quickly before the old man could breathe again. The valet was a short, pale, sad man with wrinkles on his wrinkles. He thought Wainwright was a pig as he tied a gold silk sash around his waist, then pinned a white silk cravat in place with a diamond and emerald stickpin. Finally the valet picked up a long black wig, its curls flowing down his arm.

Wainwright scowled as the valet placed the wig on his head, gently straightening and smoothing it until it fit snugly. Wainwright thought he detected a small smile in the corner of the valet's mouth. If he's laughing at me I'll twist his nose off, Wainwright promised himself.

"What nonsense," he muttered. "How did I ever agree to this. And the cost! Do you know what this little soiree is going to run?"

"I'm sure I've no idea," the valet said, walking around Wainwright for a last inspection.

"Of course you don't, you pipsqueak. Two hundred thousand if it's a penny, that's what. And to think I told Elizabeth to spend whatever she liked. I must have been insane!"

195

"Yes, sir," the valet agreed amiably. He half-pushed, half-led Wainwright to a full-length mirror in the big bedroom. Then he placed a diamond and ruby crown on his head at a rakish angle.

"Magnificent, if I do say so myself," the valet sighed. "What do you think, sir?"

But Wainwright wasn't talking. He was too busy staring at the image in the mirror before him. He had been transformed from an aging, overweight businessman into a prince, a monarch, an emperor. The doublet hid his paunch. The wig and crown did away with his thinning hair. The silken ruffles covered his double chin.

Maybe this get-up would make things easier tonight, he finally thought. Emperors had no compunction about doing what needed to be done. They had no need for outmoded scruples. When an emperor spoke, his daughter listened. Maybe the world had been simpler—and better off—in those days. He turned around before the mirror, checking himself from several angles. Definitely regal. And why not? This wasn't just a party tonight, it was a proclamation. I'm going to make millions off this subway tunnel, it announced. So many millions I can afford this lavish nonsense tonight. The others would understand, his peers in business. They would know what he was saying. Maybe they wouldn't kiss his hand tonight the way people used to honor regents. But they would certainly kiss his ass.

Besides, he thought, it's not every night a man is supposed to give away his only child and heir to someone he despises. That's certainly a cause for excessive celebration, he thought bitterly.

"Get out," he told the valet. "Go find out how my daughter and Mrs. Wainwright are coming along. Ask them if they need another gallon of rubies or pearls or something."

When the door closed behind the valet, Wainwright walked from the mirror to his bed. He opened the drawer of the nightstand and took out a photograph. He sat and studied the photograph for a minute, brushing the curly wig out of his face several times. It was a poor picture, taken at a distance. But it was good enough. Finally he took off the crown and wig and put them on the bed beside him. He lay back on the bed and propped the photograph up against the ruffles of his silk blouse. After a few minutes he heard the jingle of coach harness outside. With a grunt he sat up and put the crown and wig back on. He took a last look at the picture of George McManus. Then he tore it into small pieces.

Lieutenant Joe Smith ambled around the control room of the Navy submarine he commanded, idly studying the dozens of gauges and dials. The submarine had been sitting on the floor of Long Island Sound for almost an hour and there had been no reports of leaks or other pressure problems. He touched a steel table and his fingers came away only slightly damp. That meant the air filtration system was working well.

He ran a hand over a dial next to his head, tapping it to be sure the needle wasn't stuck. He loved this ship, he thought. It was his first command and he had been told by veteran sailors that a man loves his first ship as he loves his first wife, with the unbridled passion of the naive. He had laughed when he first heard that, because he had a new wife, too. In fact, Constance would be waiting for him when his submarine sailed into Groton harbor late tonight. They would drive to that little hotel in Mystic where they had their three-day honeymoon the month before. And then they would resume the honeymoon where they had left off, before he had taken the S-51 out for sea trials.

The lieutenant looked at the brass-bound chronometer high on the bulkhead. Another hour on the bottom and then he would take the ship through several more crash dives, emergency surfaces, and damage-control checks. After that they would make for Groton. He studied the chart on the table beside him. Groton would be about seven hours steaming underwater, five hours on the surface.

He thought of Constance again and the memories sent a rush of warmth through him. He remembered their wedding night, her musky smell, the curve of her hips, her hair over her bobbing breasts, the feel of her lips on his stomach. When he had turned off the light she had turned it back on, refusing to let him sleep.

A few more hours, he thought. Maybe he'd take the fast route to Groton.

Around and around they spun, faster and faster, the lights and people flying past them like scenes viewed from a speeding train. The others moved away from them, relinquishing the center of the floor to their dancing feet, sensing something special was happening. But George and Elizabeth took no notice of the others. He danced with her tightly in his arms, their faces close together, her full skirt swirling around both their legs. He pressed his lips to her brow, smelling her perfume, tasting the salty perspiration on her skin. Only when the music stopped did they become aware of the others around them. They stopped, looked about. Polite applause greeted them. Then the music resumed and everyone began moving again in a kaleidoscope of colors.

"I need air," Elizabeth told him.

"I need you," George answered. "But I'll settle for a place to park this damn sword."

He took her arm and led her to the big French doors that opened onto the garden from the ballroom. Outside he dropped his black cape, unbuckled the sword on his hip, and put them on a bench. Then he threw his tri-corner hat with the two-foot peacock plume onto the pile.

"That's better," he said, taking her in his arms. "Remind me never to dance carrying a sword again. A man could get into serious trouble that way."

"But you look so grand, darling. Like a swashbuckler." She studied his red velvet coat and pants, the ruffled blouse, the knee-length boots. "You could steal a poor, innocent girl's heart away."

"There's nothing innocent about you." He bent and kissed her bare shoulder, brushing his cheek against the tight ringlets of her hair. He looked from the demure lace cap on her head to the ruby necklace that plunged to her half-bare breasts. "Is that really what they wore in the good old days?"

She ran a finger down his cheek. "That's why they're called the good old days."

They laughed and she took his arm. They strolled through the gardens, marveling at the fountains and lights, the dewy grass tickling Elizabeth's feet. Laughter and music flooded from every window of the house as they rounded the corner and walked past the huge tent. Inside they could smell the rich foods and see dozens of people hovering around the well-stocked tables. The string quartet played gaily even though no one was listening. Shrieks, laughter. A young man chased a girl from the tent into the gardens. They saw him catch her and half drag her behind a sculptured hedge. The girl didn't protest.

"Come on, I want to show you my favorite spot, a little hill. You can see everything from there." She took his hand.

"Will we be alone?" George asked.

"Definitely."

"Then what are we waiting for? Lead on."

But as they walked past the front of the mansion a man called Elizabeth's name and ran toward them. He was tall, hawk-nosed, aristocratic looking.

"Oh, no," he said, "I won't let you duck me again, Elizabeth. I've been trying to get a dance with you all evening. And there are about two dozen others in line behind me."

"Chester Morgan," she said, introducing him to George. "One of *the* Morgans. But Chester never earned an honest penny in his life."

"You do say the nicest things, Elizabeth. Now come on, love, and dance with us poor boys. After all, George will have you for the rest of your life after tonight."

Elizabeth looked surprised. "Who told?"

"You can't keep a secret in high society, lovey. It's positively immoral, you know. Shall we dance?"

She looked at George and shrugged. "I have to, this one last time, darling. See you later, okay?" He nodded and she kissed him on the cheek, then walked back to the house with the other man.

He sat down on an ornate wrought iron bench and looked about. It was truly a beautiful spot, he thought. Little lights twinkled in all the trees and bushes. The statues were backlit with different color bulbs. The huge house virtually glowed in the dark. Over the music he could just make out the sound of the surf from the nearby shore.

"Got a minute?" Horace Wainwright sat down heavily beside him.

"I'm not going anywhere." He looked idly at the old man.

199

Wainwright pulled off the wig and scratched at his scalp. "This thing is killing me. It itches like mad." When he stopped scratching he unbuttoned his brocade coat and waistcoat and let his stomach bulge out with a sigh.

"I think it's time we had a talk," he finally said, caressing his protruding gut.

"I thought we already had one. At the club," George said nonchalantly.

"Then we have to have another talk, McManus."

"I don't know. I found talking with you kind of useless."

Wainwright smacked his lips. "Forget all that other stuff I said. I'm not going to try and kid you and tell you I'll love you like a son, because I won't. But I'm in your debt again."

"For what?"

"You didn't tell Elizabeth about our bet. The one I lost. At least she never said anything about it."

George crossed his arms, rested one boot on the other. "I didn't see any reason to say anything to her. After all, I won."

"And I thank you for that, McManus. If you had told her she probably would never have spoken to me again. She's strong-headed, independent. She'd never forgive me for gambling with her future like that. You see what I mean? Of course," Wainwright raised an eyebrow, "if you *had* told her, she might have walked out on you, too. We both could have lost."

George just nodded.

"Don't get me wrong, McManus. I still think you're a low-class conniver who'd steal the coins from a corpse's eyes. But if Elizabeth is going to marry you, I guess I'll have to live with you."

"Yeah, I think you're a sweetheart, too. But what the hell, let's call a truce."

They shook hands.

Wainwright held up the wig, sneered at it, then put it back on. "Look, you gave me some pretty nice scotch at your nightclub. I think it's only fair that I return the favor. I've got a bottle hidden in my den that even the thieving maids don't know about and it's smoother than a baby's behind. Interested?"

200

"Always."

"Good, let's go before somebody drags me back into the party and wants me to sit on the throne."

George followed him across the lawn and through the house, down a corridor away from the ballroom. Wainwright led him into a small, musty office crowded with filing cabinets and bookcases and dominated by a large desk covered with engineer's blueprints. There was dust on everything.

"This is my private place," Wainwright explained, digging behind a row of textbooks and pulling out a bottle. "Nobody comes in here unless I ask them. Not even to clean up."

"You'd never know," McManus said, looking around. He pushed some papers off an armchair and sat down while Wainwright uncorked the bottle and poured. He gave George a glass and sat behind the desk. They raised their glasses and drank the scotch quickly.

"What'd I tell you, huh?" Wainwright smacked his lips and poured again.

The scotch brought heat to George's face. He coughed and didn't see Wainwright slip a tiny yellow pill into his drink. "Damn, but that's nice stuff," George said. "It makes breaking the law sheer pleasure."

Wainwright handed him the glass and they drank again.

"You know, I'm a rich man, McManus. Very rich. You know how much I stand to make on that subway tunnel alone?"

"Ten or eleven million if you cut enough corners and don't fuck up."

Wainwright looked up sharply. "How did you know that?"

"Let's just say I have friends in high places, too."

"Yes, well . . . "

But George interrupted. "And now you're going to say something like why don't I go legit, dump the Paradise Rehearsal Club, come into the business with you, and make an honest woman of Elizabeth because there's plenty of money to go around. Right?"

The old man gave him an angry look, the curly wig making him look slightly ridiculous.

"Well, the answer is no, Wainwright. See all the time I've saved us both? Now how about some more of that excellent stuff." As he rose to get the bottle, George stumbled, then

201

rubbed his brow. "That *is* good scotch. A couple of drinks and I already feel lighter than a cloud."

Wainwright looked at him intently. He got up and came around the desk and poured George another.

"Listen, McManus. There's a little private party going on upstairs that I want you to come to. After all, you're the guest of honor here tonight. And I think you might have a few laughs. Just a few of the boys—you know." He nudged McManus with an elbow.

George drank down the scotch. "All right, lead on, Pops. I'll follow you anywhere tonight." He was surprised to find that he was slurring his words.

Wainwright had to help him out of the office and up the back stairs to the third floor because McManus's legs weren't working too well. Suddenly everything was spinning around him, the stairs alternately going up and down like a roller-coaster car. He wondered what was happening to him, why his cheeks felt so numb, why his hands wouldn't grasp the rail.

Finally Wainwright pushed him through a door on the third floor. The room was brightly lit and crowded with men. The air was full of smoke and the odor of liquor. The men were shouting and laughing and he began to laugh, too, even though he didn't know what he was laughing at.

He heard Wainwright saying something about the guest of honor being here. And then George was half dragged to the middle of the room where a huge metal tub was sitting on the floor. The tub was full of something that smelled sweet and sticky. Champagne! A tub full of champagne. And then the others started shouting and whistling because a girl was walking to the side of the tub. A tall, beautiful girl. She took off her robe and stepped naked into the champagne. Slowly she sat down. Somebody popped corks and began to pour champagne on her breasts and shoulders.

But the girl didn't even seem to notice. She never took her eyes off George McManus.

The quarter moon flitted in and out among the thickening clouds, revealing low whitecaps on the sea. The wind brought the smells of land—trees, flowers. Finally, shortly before midnight, the sky clouded over completely and the moon disappeared, to the relief of Frank O'Brien. He stood rooted on the bridge of the rumrunner, staring out to sea and feeling the thrum of the engines as they pushed the ship sluggishly through the water. Only tonight it felt like his ship was sailing through molasses. He pulled out his pocket watch and flipped open the gold cover. It had been two hours since they sailed from Mt. Misery Point and O'Brien could still see a glimmer of light from Bridgeport harbor far behind them.

He had a bad feeling, a premonition that something was going to go wrong. In the twilight just before they sailed from the cove three people had been spotted on the beach. Through the binoculars he made them out as two teenage boys and a young girl. They chased about the beach, hunting crabs, wrestling with each other, picking up driftwood for a fire. And then they had spotted the ship. He had seen one of the boys point it out, a boy with pimples. They had looked at the ship curiously. That was when O'Brien had ordered the anchor raised. They had sailed from the cove even though there were still fingers of lavender light in the western sky. He knew small boats might be able to pick up their silhouette in the lingering light and think it suspicious that the large ship was running without lights.

Suddenly a lookout on the prow was waving his arms, pointing somewhere ahead of the ship. O'Brien squinted into the darkness. Out of a low fogbank several hundred yards ahead a large coastal steamer crossed in front of them. The other boat was brightly lit. He could see people moving on deck, and for a moment, fancied he heard a burst of laughter.

"Stop engines," he ordered quietly.

With a ringing of bells a crewman registered the order. In a moment the vibration of the engines subsided and O'Brien could feel his ship coasting to a stop. The steamer was within a half mile and he could see the wet, gleaming hull, the red-painted lifeboats looking like pouting lips throwing him a kiss. Then the steamer veered off and sailed directly away from them. When it was just a point of light he ordered full speed. As the rumrunner plowed through the sea again,

O'Brien scratched his chin through his beard. He watched the last glow from the other ship and tried to shake his premonition.

At that moment, Lieutenant Joseph Smith was also watching the lights of the coastal steamer, hunched over the periscope of his submarine. When the lights disappeared he turned the periscope 360 degrees, face pressed to the eyepiece, cap on backward. He felt snug and safe as he scanned the horizon again. Nothing in sight.

He stepped back and lowered the periscope. Lieutenant Smith looked around the control bridge and saw that everyone was watching him, waiting for his orders. They had already performed two emergency blowout ascents and two crash dives tonight, but he heard no complaints.

"Once more into the breach, gentlemen," he said mildly. "Blow all tanks. Emergency. Take her up!"

The crewmen leaped to their tasks, throwing levers, pushing buttons, adjusting the pressure. Lookouts stood at the ladder beneath the conning tower hatch, ready to scramble up as soon as the sub broke the surface. Lieutenant Smith heard the roar of the compressors forcing water out of the ballast tanks, replacing the water with air, and buoying the ship to the surface. He grabbed a ladder as the helmsman steered the ship up at a sharp angle until everyone was bent as though walking uphill. Despite the pressurized hull, Smith felt his ears pop as the sub rushed to the surface, the seawater swooshing past the steel plates with the clanking of a locomotive.

With a last tremendous heave the submarine threw itself out of the water. Smith felt the exhilarating surge, the change in the submarine's motion as it finally reached the surface. He smiled, men sat back from their controls, someone scrambled up the ladder and began to open the hatch.

Suddenly the entire ship shuddered. Smith fell, cracking his shoulder painfully against the deck. He heard the wrenching, screaming sound of steel being torn and twisted. Around him, men began to shout. Someone hit the claxon and the clanging alarm sounded over and over. Dazed, Smith tried to lift himself from the deck, then realized with surprise that he was soaked, that seawater was rushing in around him. He swallowed a mouthful and, half choking, fought his way to his feet,

The lights on the bridge went out. He heard men screaming in the total blackness of the ship, the roar of water rushing around his knees now, numbing him with cold. Someone blundered into him, knocking him back into the water. When he tried to rise the floor was no longer level, the water up to his waist. He heard men crying, screaming, pounding on steel. There was a tremendous bubbling noise and the loud hiss of escaping steam. Valves and pipes burst around him like popcorn and a piece of metal glanced off his skull. He sank downward slowly, his feet no longer able to find the deck. He knew he was dying as he clawed uselessly for air. He knew his ship was sinking beneath him.

"Constance!" he tried to scream as his lungs filled with water. "Constance . . ."

High above, Captain Francis O'Brien picked himself off the deck and stared wide-eyed. At first he thought it was a whale that had hurtled into the air directly in front of his ship. And then the impact had made the entire ship quiver and he knew it was not a sea creature. In the darkness he stumbled down a ladder and ran to the bow. The scene below him was chaotic. He could make out two bodies floating in the water next to the black hull of the half-submerged submarine. The bow of his ship had smashed halfway through the sub and now held the wreckage pinned. But with each roll of the ship there came the noise of steel being wrenched apart. Oil spurted from the side of the submarine. The conning tower was bent crazily to one side.

Ideas rushed through O'Brien's brain. Should he save his ship, his cargo? Should he back off and try to shake the crippled submarine? But it would sink for sure, he knew. Should he lower boats, throw lines, try to save any survivors? His instincts battled with his practicality. Other crewmen ran up beside him and gawked at the scene below. Some threw lifelines and ran off, another vomited over the side. They had to get out of there, O'Brien finally decided. Run as fast as the damaged bow would allow. The sub might have radioed for help. Other ships could be on the way already from Connect-

205

icut or Long Island. He was not going to spend the rest of his life in prison for this. Run. Get away. The submarine was a dead ship. Run. Fast.

He began to push men away from the rail, shouting for them to get back to their jobs. He waved to the bridge, trying to get the helmsman's attention through the growing rain. Lights began to come on all over his ship. No, no, he shouted. Douse the lights. Full back. Make for a safe harbor. He began to run down the slippery deck when he heard a strange popping noise. Suddenly the sky lit up like high noon and he saw an emergency flare floating gently down toward him. Then another and yet another flare shot up from the rear of his ship.

He waved his arms, shouting to stop the flares, but no one heard him. Flare after flare went off, bathing both vessels in eerie white light. He looked about and, in the distance, could see several faraway boats already converging on the lights. He staggered to the rail just as one last terrible screech of steel came from the bow.

In the glare of the flares he watched the broken submarine slip underwater.

He saw the lights, eerie and wavering, on the horizon far beyond the window. Through the smoke in the room they looked like long, impossibly drawn-out lightning flashes. But where was the thunder? he wondered. Can't have lightning without thunder. Then someone was shouting about fireworks and nearer, as if in answer, right over the house, rockets exploded in a shower of dazzling red and green and purple sparks, dwarfing the lights far out at sea.

But he didn't care about the lights anymore. He stared at the girl before him. The tips of her nipples had a bluish tint. Goose pimples covered her arms and legs. Her hair was drenched with champagne. The blonde in the tub shivered slightly as a cool breeze swept through the window where the others crowded to see the fireworks. Someone poured two more bottles of champagne over her shoulders and George leaned over to catch the drops in his mouth as they cascaded off her breasts. The movement made his head swim and he nearly fell on top of her. He clutched the sides of the tub, but his fingers were too numb to hold and he fell to one knee, laughing, bumping his chin gently on the edge of the tub.

Someone handed him a bottle of champagne and he took a long drink before pouring the rest on the girl. He looked at her face and marveled at how much she looked like a blond Elizabeth. Was it Elizabeth?

The room was fuzzy, out of focus. How long had he been here? he wondered. He vaguely remembered Wainwright leading him up a narrow, dark stairway to this room. But the shouts and laughter of the men around him sounded distant now, miles away, like the fireworks and the lights on the horizon. Only the girl was real. Only she was nearby. Elizabeth?

He could not take his eyes off her. And she did not stop staring at him. Her deep-set dark eyes flirted with him, caressed him. No words had been spoken but her message was clear. She wanted him. Now, later, in front of this crowd, alone, whenever.

He watched as her thighs parted slightly, invitingly. He reached out and stroked the inside of her right leg until someone grabbed him and pulled him back from the tub. No touching, he heard a voice say. But the blond Elizabeth's huge, sad eyes kept calling him back. Keep coming, they said. We're alone in this room. No one else exists.

McManus picked up a cup from the floor and dipped it into the tub. He drank half, then offered the rest to the girl. She smiled and held his unsteady hand as he raised the cup to her mouth. Out of the corner of his eyes he could see the old man. Stern, humorless. Why was Wainwright hanging back on the edge of the crowd? Watching? Waiting? McManus filled the cup again and raised it to Wainwright. The old man's expression didn't change. Sober again, George thought. Poor fellow.

More lights outside, white flashes, red, blue, explosions. But he didn't look. The girl had her fingers on the front of his coat. She was pulling him to her, trying to whisper in his ear. He couldn't hear. Her voice was too soft. The others' voices were too loud. But he understood. Join me, the eyes said. Her hands reached for him.

The blonde deftly unbuttoned his coat and let it slip to the floor over his shoulders. The girl's eyes were smiling now, beckoning him. He fumbled with the ruffles that covered the buttons on his silk shirt. His fingers were slow and thick and he finally just ripped the shirt open and peeled it off.

He threw it back over his shoulder. Someone leaped and caught it and the rest of the crowd cheered. McManus heard the shouts but it did not register that they had anything to do with him. Come to me, Elizabeth, he mumbled. Come to me.

Her hands were on his chest. Rhythmic clapping pounded in his ears. The room was spinning but the girl stayed before him—calm, loving. Elizabeth. He leaned over and kissed her right nipple. Her soft hands held his head at her breast for a moment. She moaned softly in his ear. Someone pulled George away.

A red rocket exploded outside the window and was reflected in the blonde's eyes. Then more explosions, a rainbow of lights. The excited men rushed from the room, somehow carrying George along. He looked longingly at the girl in the tub. He tried to fight his way back but it was like fighting the tide. Two men were laughing as they carried him down the stairs. His feet never touched the ground. They did not release him until they reached the lawn outside, where hundreds of people stood watching the dazzling fireworks.

The cool, misty night air was like a slap in the face. He shook his head, trying to expel the dizziness, the liquor. He stepped forward and his knees nearly buckled. His legs were as sturdy as tapioca. He held tightly to a stone pillar as a wave of nausea hit him. Brightly-costumed bodies whirred past him.

He heard muffled laughter. Under a table loaded with fruit was a young couple, pawing and kissing with great passion. George remembered the blonde. Where was Elizabeth? He wanted Elizabeth.

Then he saw her, her crooked finger beckoning him to follow. Was it Elizabeth? But she was blond. She vanished behind a hedge. George tried to run after her but when he reached the hedge she was gone. Then she reappeared twenty feet away. She smiled at him, then slipped out of his sight again. He followed slowly, dizziness returning. Not now, he thought. I can't be too drunk now. He leaned against a fountain, his head spinning.

Suddenly she was at his side, taking his hand, pulling him

through the maze of hedges to a white bench. She said nothing. McManus sat down heavily and she slid next to him. He leaned back and closed his eyes. He could barely hear the rest of the party, only a distant hum of voices and music.

He felt her small hand touch his thigh. The hand began moving higher and higher on the inside of his leg until it reached his groin. He looked at the girl with half-closed eyes. She knelt before him, began kissing and licking his stomach, then his chest. Elizabeth, he murmured. Elizabeth. Her mouth moved to his right nipple and she began sucking. McManus could feel himself rising as the girl unbuttoned his breeches and reached inside. Her hands, her mouth, were all over him, caressing him, devouring him, until he could stand it no longer.

He grabbed her, fumbling with the buttons on the back of her dress until her gown somehow tumbled to the ground. She wore nothing underneath. McManus fought for equilibrium. He blindly swayed as he laid her on the bench. He entered her and her legs wound around his back. Elizabeth still smelled of champagne, he thought. The girl began breathing heavily in his ear as he thrust into her again and again. He heard voices, footsteps. He closed his eyes and burst into her. More lights, more explosions.

Then a bright light shone in his face. He opened his eyes and looked past the glare of a flashlight. Wainwright and Elizabeth stood before him. Elizabeth's face was white. The girl pushed George off, grabbed her dress, and walked calmly away into the garden. He moved slowly, barely understanding what was happening. Where was Elizabeth going?

He pulled his pants up and stood unsteadily, rocking back and forth. Wainwright was coming toward him but he made no effort to move. The old man raised his hand and smacked McManus across the mouth. He went sprawling, then sat up in time to see Elizabeth run off.

Wainwright pulled something from his pocket and threw it at McManus's chest. George looked down. It was a deck of cards, scattered on the grass.

"Win yourself another bride, McManus. You just lost this one." The old man walked away.

•

She ran blindly through the garden, up to the veranda, then suddenly stopped. The others needn't know. She didn't want anyone to know. What now? she wondered. Caught in the act. It was almost funny. If it had happened to someone else she would be laughing madly.

She smoothed her dress, took a deep breath. Then Elizabeth stepped into the pool of light that emanated from the house. She walked slowly up to the French doors. Inside, in the ballroom, the band was playing something fast and the girls were kicking off their heels to dance. The Charleston. What a silly time to play the Charleston, she thought. What was there to dance about?

She'd walk through head high, she decided. No tears. Not yet, anyway. And nobody would guess anything. She'd walk through the ballroom and then go upstairs and pack a bag and go somewhere, anywhere away from here. And tomorrow, when word got out, maybe they'd all say how brave she was, how they never guessed that her heart was breaking, poor thing.

A young man and then two older men, friends of her father, grabbed her arms and asked her to dance. But she just brushed by them as she walked the length of the ballroom. It was midnight, a girlfriend told her. When's the announcement going to be made? Midnight. That struck a chord in Elizabeth. Then she remembered. She looked up to see the satin globe swinging high above the room, dangling from the sun-bright chandelier. She'd have that much of her fantasy anyway, she decided.

She ran to the wall where the cord that held up the globe was tied to a light sconce. Frantically she picked at the knot but couldn't undo it. Finally she jerked the cord. The satin globe flew upward and ripped open on the chandelier. She watched as the hundreds of brightly colored butterflies spilled out and fluttered through the air. But they weren't flying, she saw. They just fell to the polished floor. Someone shrieked, the band stopped playing as the butterflies cascaded down. Elizabeth ran to the center of the room as everyone looked up, astonished.

A red-and-blue moth landed lightly on her shoulder. She picked it up gently between two fingers, but it didn't move.

She stroked the wings. It was warm to the touch, brown around the edges, baked by the lights of the chandelier.

Finally, she began to cry.

26

THE LONG MARBLE CORRIDOR was jammed with reporters and photographers jostling each other to get close to the massive bronze doors of the courtroom. In the middle of the crowd Otto Berman stood dejectedly, his shoulders slumped. He was crying. Two burly policemen came out of the courtroom and began moving the noisy crowd of newsmen down the corridor, sweeping the little man with them. George McManus reached out and pulled Otto Berman inside the men's room.

"Anything yet?"

Otto shook his head from side to side, still sobbing.

"Jesus, get a hold of yourself," McManus ordered. "You're no good to Big Bill this way." He handed Otto a handkerchief. The little man shrugged and blew his nose mightily.

Detective Sergeant John Broderick left the courtroom and walked to the bathroom. He took a look at George McManus, then sauntered over to a urinal. He farted as he unbuttoned.

"Well?" McManus demanded.

Broderick sighed as he relieved himself. "Well, nothing," he finally said. "Dwyer is screwed eight bleeding ways from Sunday. No way your bucko is going to slip out of this one. Everybody wants his royal arse."

"What's the official charge?"

"You mean charges, McManus. Everything from murder to jaywalking. The federal boys want his hide for the deaths on the sub, destruction of federal property, violating the Volstead Act, various conspiracy charges, unlawful entry into the country, and—are ya ready for this one?—piracy on the high seas. Now, the state boys, they're satisfied to go with murder and tax dodging because this little escapade happened in state waters. And the city? Well, they arrested Dwyer on a parking violation even before the federal warrant was issued, so the district attorney is still thinking up his charges. That's why the court was cleared of those fuckin' reporters, so the lawyers don't make public arses out of themselves trying to decide who gets what piece of your friend Dwyer."

Broderick buttoned up, went to a mirror, and began to adjust his uniform. "But when they get finished, there surely won't be many pieces left."

Otto Berman began to sob again.

McManus leaned on a sink and studied his shoes. He didn't feel well. His brain was still fuzzy from the party and something nagged at the back of his mind, something he knew he should do. Izzy the Stub had come banging on his door at dawn, yelling that Dwyer was arrested at the club and something about ships crashing. McManus hadn't been able to get a straight story out of him. It was only when they arrived at the courthouse and he saw the early papers that he understood what was happening. The story had been sketchy, the only pictures some old shots of Dwyer. But two things were certain: Dwyer's rumrunner had rammed and sunk a Navy submarine. And no one from the sub had survived.

For hours McManus had been trying to figure out what it all meant—to him, to the club, to Dwyer. He knew that Dwyer and O'Brien were going to prison. The expression on Broderick's face told him that.

McManus finally looked up. "Get back to the courtroom. Tell the lawyer if he needs any help I'll send him a platoon of legal beagles. And keep in touch."

"This is going to cost you," Broderick said, turning at the door. "I only do favors for me friends. And you ain't one of them."

Before McManus could answer, Broderick went out. At the same moment Izzy the Stub came in with a half-dozen papers under his arms. McManus grabbed them. More pictures of Dwyer, but now they had photos of the submarine's sister ship and one of Dwyer's rumrunner being towed into harbor. The headlines were four inches high and everything else had been pushed off the front page. There were profiles of Dwyer and the sunken submarine's skipper, with quotes from his young bride. The U.S. attorney called it a heinous crime that deserved to be punishable by death. The Coast Guard and the Navy vowed an all-out crackdown on bootleggers and rumrunners on the East Coast.

He threw the papers into a garbage can, where Izzy fished them out. His head hurt too much to read. He went to a sink and washed his face. As he was drying it on a towel his jaw started to throb and he remembered Wainwright's slugging him. Not a bad punch, either, for an old man. Then he remembered the blonde and the look on Elizabeth's face. He would have to call her, to apologize, when this Dwyer business was cleared up. He'd tell her that girl didn't mean anything, that he was drunk. The more he thought, the more his head hurt.

Broderick stuck his face in the door. "They're coming out. Dwyer wants ya. And that's another hundred you owe me, lad."

McManus adjusted his fedora in the mirror. He was walking out when Izzy called him.

"Hey boss, I think you should look at this." Izzy was holding one of the newspapers.

"Later," McManus said, and pushed out into the noisy corridor. Flashbulbs were bursting like solar flares and reporters were peppering Dwyer with questions as McManus walked down the hall. Dwyer looked strangely calm now, he thought. Not a hair was out of place, his suit was well-pressed, his shirt spotlessly white. McManus wondered how Dwyer had managed to get valet service in jail. Next to him his three court guards looked positively disheveled.

Dwyer put his arm around George's shoulder, pulling him toward the wall. The court guards fended off the reporters but the flashbulbs still popped like mad.

"Quite a show, huh. Looks like I'm famous, George." Dwyer put his mouth near McManus's ear.

"It looks like my luck has really run out this time, partner. My lawyer says I'm going away for sure, that there's no way I'll get off with just a fine. But the shyster says the prosecution is so screwed up over jurisdiction that he can maybe get me three to five if I plead to reduced charges. Same for O'Brien."

McManus turned angry. "What do you mean, three to five? Let me get you another lawyer, Bill. I'll get you the best. Darrow maybe."

"It's no good." Dwyer shook his head. "I've seen the looks on those vultures in court. They'd like to sit me on the electric chair until I resemble overdone bacon. This submarine business is just too big. I figure I'll live with a couple of years in prison, sort of a vacation. But I need a favor."

"Just name it."

"Okay, then, I want you to take everything over for me. The boats, the trucks. The club. Watch the store. Otto can give you the details. You're the only one I'd trust not to rob me blind. Will you do that for me?"

McManus looked closely at Dwyer. "I don't know. I don't like this, Bill. The minute you're gone, every shark in Manhattan will be muscling in on you."

"You can handle it, Georgie. I've been watching you closely for a long time. You're tough and you've got more moves than Dempsey. You'll be all right as long as you stay a jump ahead of them. Say you'll do it." Dwyer held out his hand.

George took it.

"A couple more things, George. Take care of my wife, okay? And Otto. See that O'Brien and his boys don't lack for anything either. And there's a two-year-old at the Jersey farm. Crazy Quilt. I think he's Derby material next year." A wistful look came into Dwyer's eyes, but he shook it quickly.

The doors of the court opened just then and a short, dark, wiry man in a rumpled white shirt came out flanked by two more policemen. The photographers, weary of shooting Dwyer, began snapping pictures of the other prisoner, who looked totally perplexed.

"There's justice for you," said Dwyer, watching the dark man. "The poor dope got off the boat from Sicily Saturday. Last night he's walking to a party with two bottles of dago red under his arm and the cops grab him. He doesn't know Prohibition from prostitution, of course. His case came up just before mine. The judge gave him two years in the slammer."

Dwyer laughed bitterly. "I'm going to get three years for murder. He gets two years for going to a party. Who says this isn't the land of opportunity, Georgie."

Dwyer walked over to the Italian, who still looked totally bewildered. Dwyer whispered something to him, hugged him, and shoved a handful of money in his shirt pocket while

214

the flashbulbs popped. Then the guards took Dwyer back into the courtroom. He winked at McManus over his shoulder as he went.

McManus and Izzy left the building and climbed into a cab. They were driving uptown when Izzy snapped his fingers and pulled the newspaper from his pocket. He opened the paper to a particular page, folded it, and handed the paper to George.

McManus threw it back. "Read it to me," he told Izzy, pulling his hat over his aching eyes.

"If that's the way you want it." Izzy held the paper up so the light hit it. "It's Cholly Knickerbocker. The column is all about this swell party you was at last night. Says they had everything but trained seals swimming in the punch."

"Spare me the details," McManus muttered.

"Well, here's the part you might be interested in." He cleared his throat and read: "This morning the host of the party mysteriously put his daughter, the lovely and eligible Elizabeth Wainwright, aboard the liner *Franconia* for the sumptuous six-month Millionaire's Cruise. Can you imagine how the caviar will run like tap water? First stop for the moneybags bunch is London, England, to say cheerio to the queen. Cholly's advice is watch out for those seagoing fortune hunters, Lizzie. And hurry back, because lots of nightclubs are draped in black over your departure."

Izzy snorted. "And this guy gets paid to write this crapola."

But McManus wasn't listening. He grabbed the paper, reading it quickly. Then he ordered the driver to pull over.

"You get me a ticket on the next boat to England," he said, jumping out and leaning in the cab window. "Anything that floats. I'll meet you at the club later. Get going, Izzy!"

George watched the cab pull away, then dashed into a drugstore on the corner of Twenty-fourth Street.

"The phone. Where's your telephone?" he half-shouted at the bored clerk behind the big, copper-colored cash register. The clerk nodded toward the rear of the store.

George ran in that direction, digging in his pockets for change. He jammed a nickel into the phone's slot and dialed quickly. The phone rang five times at the other end before someone answered. It was a maid. He asked for Elizabeth and the maid went away for several minutes. George tapped the phone nervously until a man's voice came on. He recognized the voice.

"Where is she, Wainwright?" he demanded. "If you don't let me talk to her, I'll come over and kick in your door."

"You can break the door if you wish, McManus, but Elizabeth's not here. Right now she's probably a hundred and fifty miles out at sea. So start swimming."

"You bastard. You forced her to go."

"On the contrary, she wanted to go. To get away from you. Did you really expect her to take it lightly when a hood like you insults her in front of her own father? I told you, McManus, that you really didn't know my daughter."

"You're cute, Wainwright. You set it all up. Planned this from beginning to end."

"Did you really think I'd just give her to you, McManus?"

"Did you tell her about our little deal, Wainwright? The bet you lost?"

But the only answer was a click at the other end. Then the phone went dead.

27

IT WAS A HIGH WALL—ten feet high—made of yellow bricks and mortar. On the other side of the wall he could hear the ominous sound of waves breaking and the rushing of water. As he looked at the wall it suddenly began to crack. Pieces of brick broke loose and fell to his feet. The wall seemed to shrivel up like the face of an old woman. And then something began to leak through the cracks. Something golden but transparent. He shouted in panic as the leaking droplets became thin streams flowing through the wall. But no one heard him.

He rushed here and there, back and forth, as fast as he could stuffing dirt and stones and pieces of his clothing into the cracks. Suddenly a big fissure appeared high on the side of the wall. He threw his hands up, fingers tight together, desperately trying to keep the golden torrent back. But the wall kept breaking open, wider and wider. Bricks fell on him and he threw his hands over his head to protect himself. Then, with a great noise, the wall burst and the torrent was on him. He was swept away, floating on the crest of the wave. Then he went under, sputtering, his lungs afire, finally realizing that he was drowning in a sea of whiskey.

"We're here, boss. Boss?" George McManus woke with a start as Izzy the Stub shook him.

The limousine was parked in front of a row of blank-faced red-brick warehouses in the South Bronx. McManus shook the sleep out of his eyes and looked around. Except for the car the street was deserted. Foot-high weeds grew from the cracks in the sidewalk. The noon sun bathed everything in a harsh glare. This didn't look any more promising than his dream, McManus thought. He was tired. Very tired. It seemed as if he hadn't slept at all, as if he had been constantly running for the three days since Dwyer's arrest. And he kept having that dream.

Otto Berman was out of the car and opening the back door before the chauffeur could make a move. McManus climbed out wearily but couldn't help admiring the long, shiny lines of the car at the same time. It was Big Bill Dwyer's limousine and he had wanted George to use it. But when Otto first saw him climb in the back and give orders to the chauffeur the little man had looked stricken. What the hell, McManus thought. If I'm going to inherit Dwyer's headaches I might as well get to them in comfort.

Otto rushed to the massive warehouse doors and knocked four times. A narrow entrance within one of the big doors opened and they all stepped through. The inside of the warehouse was empty, dusty sunbeams streaking through from a couple of big skylights. A dark, rather dapper, curly-haired man stood in front of them rubbing a bump on his forehead. He had an odd expression on his face, as if he were trying to hide a smirk. McManus recognized him as Tony Licata, one of the crewmen from Dwyer's speedboat.

"What did you want to show me, Otto?" George finally asked, looking around. "I don't see anything here."

"That's just it, it's empty." Berman was nearly dancing in his agitation. "There were eight hundred and fifty cases of scotch, bourbon, rye, and gin in here last night. We've been hijacked."

McManus tensed. "Who was guarding the stuff? You?" He looked squarely at Tony Licata, who nodded. He was still rubbing the lump.

"Somebody conked me last night. I don't know how they got in. When I woke up this morning the place was cleaned out, so I called Otto." Licata still had that half-smirk on his face.

"What are you going to do about it?" Otto demanded of George. "This is the second warehouse full of hootch hit in two nights. Somebody is getting inside information. How else could they know where it all was? You've got to do something!"

George turned his back on Otto and touched the bump on Licata's forehead. The smirk disappeared as the man winced.

"Hurts, huh? They sneak up on you from behind?" George asked, studying the angry red lump.

Licata nodded, the half-smile back on his face. "Sure. I was lookin' around 'cause I heard a noise. And somebody cold-cocked me from the back."

"Then why is the lump on your forehead?" George looked at him from under the brim of his fedora. Licata only stared back sullenly.

"You want me to give him some lumps to match?" Izzy asked, balling his fists and moving toward the other man.

But McManus just waved him off, then turned abruptly and walked from the warehouse back to the car. Izzy and Otto got in and the chauffeur drove off. They rode for five minutes before Izzy spoke.

"If you let him get away with that you're going to be hijacked by every bum in town, boss."

Otto snorted his agreement, turning in the front seat and looking suspiciously at McManus through thick lenses.

George shook his head. "Not now, Izzy. Licata will be around when we need him later. He'll talk. Just shut up now, okay?"

The others looked straight ahead as George settled back into the plush leather seat. He had things to think about, things that were whirling through his mind like horses on a

merry-go-round. Too much was happening too fast. Two hi-
jackings now. People were calling McManus demanding to
know when they'd get more liquor delivered, even getting
ugly and threatening. Dwyer's trucks disappeared, three motorboats were grabbed by the Coast Guard. There was hardly
an ounce of liquor moving on the East Coast since the sinking
of the submarine.

Meanwhile, Dwyer's lawyer was always hovering around
the club, like a habitually needy relative. He was passing out
hundreds of thousands to everybody with five fingers in an
effort to buy Dwyer some leniency in sentencing. Only
Dwyer didn't have any ready cash, according to Otto Berman.
So George was dipping into his own pocket for a fortune.

On top of that, every down-and-outer within ten blocks of
Times Square was camped out in front of the Paradise Rehearsal Club looking for a touch from George. Word was out
that he had taken over from Dwyer, and Big Bill had always
been good for an extra few bucks. It wasn't the cash—that was
just nickels and dimes. But they scared away some of the big
money. Especially the bums who smelled. The rich could
endure poverty, but not bad odors. Last night George had
bought a gallon of cheap cologne and had some of the worst
ones doused. In the Tenderloin it was already being called
Saint George's Baptism.

And then there was Elizabeth. He pulled a long white envelope from his inside coat pocket and took out the contents.
The envelope contained a hastily procured passport and a
ticket for a first-class berth on the liner *Hanseatic,* departing
New York for Southampton, England, at 3 P.M. today. The
ticket was gaily colored, imprinted with a drawing of the great
ship. It seemed to promise things to George as he held it. It
promised that he would find Elizabeth somewhere in England. It promised that he could explain what had happened
between them. It promised that she would come back to New
York with him. It promised that he would feel her touch again,
hear her voice.

"You leave now, boss, and you'll be lucky to have two pair
of pants left when you get back." Izzy watched him as he
toyed with the ticket. "You going to kiss it all good-bye for a
dame?"

McManus put the ticket and passport into the envelope, then slipped the envelope back into his pocket. "But what a dame. What would you do if you were in my shoes?"

Izzy crossed his arms and looked out the car window. "Well, the way I see it, you busted your butt to build the club, boss. How you going to give that up now? Plus, you got responsibilities to Dwyer now. If you crap out, him and his organization go down the tubes, too. I figure you owe Dwyer, boss."

"You make it sound simple, Izzy."

The other man smiled, took off his straw hat, and flicked dust off it. "There's only one dame I let wrap herself around my throat, boss. And that's this one." Izzy unbuttoned his coat and showed George another tie with a dancing girl painted on it. This one was different colors than the tie George remembered.

"I've got a whole set now," Izzy explained, making the girl twitch. "Ain't she grand?"

Izzy went on talking, but George wasn't listening anymore. He settled back, lost in his own thoughts, until Izzy wound down into silence. They drove on through the afternoon, out of the Bronx and into Manhattan. At Seventy-second Street the chauffeur crossed to the West Side of town and the Hudson came into view. They drove down the elevated highway and got off at Twenty-third Street. The chauffeur stopped at Pier 14. The pier bustled with stewards, stevedores, passengers, and friends, many of them heaving luggage toward the giant ship lying next to the three-story Germanic Lines terminal. George stepped out of the car and stretched. He studied the ship, a sleek three-stacker with red and white trim. Smoke already rose from the forward stack in preparation for departure. Booms quickly lifted cargo nets full of provisions and luggage from the dock and swung them aboard. In the water two tugboats were slowly chugging into the slip, ready to ease the *Hanseatic* into the center of the river.

The chauffeur took two bags out of the trunk and handed one to Otto and one to Izzy the Stub. They followed McManus through the terminal and up the passenger walkway. At the top the white-uniformed purser checked George's name on a long list, then clicked his heels in salute and directed them toward his stateroom on A-Deck. The decks and corridors were crowded and pulsing with excitement as people hugged one another, shed tears, laughed gaily, or just roamed confusedly looking for their staterooms. Crew members and children rushed about adding to the noise.

They found the stateroom and walked in. The room was large, decorated in blue and handsomely furnished. George threw his hat on the bed and put the tickets on the dresser as the others dropped the luggage with a bang.

Otto Berman rushed to the bed, wide-eyed. "Are you crazy? Putting your hat on the bed is bad luck." He grabbed the hat and laid it on the dresser next to the ticket. "More bad luck we don't need already."

George smiled. "You too, huh? I swear I'll be back in two weeks, three at the most. I'll tie Elizabeth up and drag her back if I have to. Just hold the fort." He shook his head. "Jesus, but you two are worse than wives."

Izzy was already popping the cork on a champagne bottle he found next to a basket of fruit. "At least the Huns have the good sense to buy French bubbly. I figured them for Rhine wine."

He poured the champagne into three glasses and handed out the other two. As he raised his glass the ship's horn blew three long blasts. Someone knocked on the door once and announced: "Fifteen minutes. All ashore who's going ashore." Then footsteps trailed off.

"To the boss," Izzy called, raising his glass again. "The prisoner of love. May he quickly get a parole." They drank.

"Now get out of here," George said, "and watch over things until I get back." He pushed them toward the door, jamming Izzy's hat on his head.

Suddenly the door burst open and Marie Flynn flew through. She flopped on the bed puffing madly and trying to catch her breath.

"I got lost," she gasped. "Boat's so goddamn . . . big. Broderick . . . at the club." Her chest heaved and her red hair was disheveled.

George shook her. "What are you talking about? What about Broderick?"

"The cop's at the club . . . says he's taking over. Says the

221

...croupiers and waiters...even the band work for him now.... Taking over." She coughed, patted her hair, and looked up at him imploringly with her blue eyes.

"The hell he is," George said under his breath. Then louder: "The hell he is. I'll kill him before I'll let him take the Paradise."

He looked around quickly, his eyes red with anger. He picked up his hat and threw the boat ticket at Otto.

"Get my bags off this tub, fast," he told the others. "Get to the club and keep Broderick there any way you can, Marie. I'll be at Tammany." He ran out slamming the cabin door.

Marie and Izzy looked at each other and then, solemnly, shook hands.

"You did beautifully." Izzy kissed her on the cheek. "Shakespeare couldn't have done better. And now, my friends," he said, turning to Otto, "I suggest we depart for remote sections of the great borough of Brooklyn because I, for one, don't want to be within the vicinity of the boss when he finds out we tricked him into staying."

"But what am I supposed to do with this?" Otto, looking confused, held up the boat ticket.

"Well, the least you could do," said Izzy, "is send us a postcard."

1927

Where the apple reddens
Never pry—
Lest we lose our Edens
Eve and I.

    —ROBERT BROWNING
      A Woman's Last Words

28

GEORGE PACED around his desk, nodding every so often at what the other man was saying. Finally he idly placed a hand on the small, blue and green world globe on his desk and spun it. Elizabeth had presented him with the globe on his birthday nearly a year ago. For days afterward they had played with the new toy, spinning and spinning it, planning romantic trips to exotic places.

Now he used it to chart her progress. She was somewhere in South America, he knew. The last leg of the six-month cruise. Maybe soon . . . He didn't complete the thought. She hadn't answered any of his cablegrams. Dead silence. As far as she was concerned, it looked as if George McManus no longer existed. But still . . . George turned his head sharply as Izzy the Stub's voice became louder, more insistent.

"He sold out Big Bill and now he's doing it to you, boss. You needed him before. The rest of Dwyer's rummies didn't know bootlegging from bootmaking. But you sure don't need him now. Not after yesterday."

McManus waved at Izzy to stop talking. He didn't need to be reminded. The Dwyer organization had been riddled with thieves when he took over. He had paid them all off and gotten them out of the way within the first week. All but Tony Licata, who knew almost as much about the business as Otto Berman. And that had been a mistake. Licata had gotten too greedy.

Still, it was no surprise that Licata had sold out to Rothstein. George had suspected it all along. But he had needed Licata. Besides, Rothstein paid better wages than the devil—and was so much more accessible.

"Okay, let's kill him," George said matter-of-factly, sitting down.

"Kill him?"

"Sure, what'll it be? Cement overshoes, a ride in the country? How about cutting off his head? I'll let you decide, Izzy. You take care of it."

"Boss, this is not Chicago. Don't go crazy on me. But maybe you're on the right track."

"What do you mean?"

Izzy cleared his throat and squinted with the effort of deep thought. "Well, if you just pay off Licata and tell him to get out of your sight, I think maybe you're telling everyone who works for you that it's okay to screw George McManus, you should pardon the expression. People will talk, you know. But maybe, if you could fix Licata's trolley—and Rothstein's, too . . ."

"And how do I do that?"

Izzy stroked his tie, another of the dancing-girl numbers, this one in puce and green. "I don't know, boss. Maybe you could start by kicking Rothstein out of the Paradise Rehearsal Club. I mean, he's here drinking your booze and winning your money every night. That doesn't look right."

McManus said nothing for a moment. He didn't care how it looked to Izzy. He knew it would look far worse to his customers if he kicked a winner out of the club. Besides, Arnold Rothstein's brooding presence was a drawing card. The out-of-towners especially could not get enough of stealing furtive glances at the man who fixed the 1919 World Series.

"Is he out there now?"

"Nah. He's in his office collecting for the keep-Rothstein-rich fund. Must be around Sixty-first Street by now."

"How's he doing?"

"You know Rothstein. He's so lucky he could fall in the East River and come up dry."

"I need some air. Even money starts to stink eventually," George said, jumping out of his chair and grabbing his hat and overcoat. Izzy opened the office door and followed George through the money room and into the jammed casino. The noise was just a few decibels short of painful. Was it a Friday or Saturday? George wondered, only a little surprised that he couldn't remember. It took him nearly ten minutes to wend his way through the crowd and reach the big door. Everyone wanted to have a drink with him.

Halfway down the street stairs he heard a familiar voice

calling his name behind him on the landing. He turned and saw Marie Flynn at the top of the stairs in a gown slit up both sides to the tops of her thighs. Someone stood behind her, his arms around her and his hands on her breasts. She gently slapped the hands away.

"You're not leaving?"

"Just for a few minutes. I'll be back."

"I'll be waiting," she said, smiling, then took the man by one hand and went through the door.

McManus shivered as he hit the street. The damp, late-January cold sliced through him like a cruel remark. He pulled his coat closer around his shoulders, tugged his hat down on his head, and slogged through the gray remnants of the last snowfall. As he turned the corner onto Broadway a banner hanging on a wall and proclaiming "Merry Christmas" in six-foot letters snapped in the wind. Red and green lights twinkled all along the street.

Despite the cold and the lateness of the hour the streets of the Tenderloin were far from deserted. Newsboys hawked the bulldog editions. Hustlers pulled their latest cons on shivering marks. Honest citizens huddled against the wind and scurried from speakeasy to speakeasy. And a sleek black Reo touring car moved slowly along Seventh Avenue following a man in a fine cashmere overcoat and top hat. Rothstein.

McManus watched as he stopped in front of a disheveled beggar wearing dark glasses and holding a tin cup. The car stopped with him, as did a husky man who had been walking three paces behind.

This was Arnold Rothstein's office. Every night, in all seasons and all weather, he toured Seventh Avenue and Broadway, collecting his cut from the bookmakers and loansharks and prostitutes and con men who worked the Tenderloin. His bodyguards always followed close behind. Rothstein rarely had problems with slow payers.

The beggar handed a paper bag to Rothstein, who opened it and began counting the money inside.

The beggar pushed his dark glasses down his nose and peered over them. "It's all there," he said. "Don't you trust a blind man?"

Rothstein tossed a quarter in the beggar's cup. McManus

knew the beggar. He had gone blind two years ago. Before that he had been deaf and dumb, but there was more money in blindness.

"Stay away from the ponies," Rothstein advised, walking away. McManus followed but his path was blocked by the bodyguard. When Rothstein saw George he nodded at the other man to let him pass.

Rothstein stamped his feet in the slush. "It's cold enough to freeze your kishkas tonight, Georgie. What say we stop in somewhere for a shot or two? I'll even buy."

"Why do you do it, Arnie?" George asked, ignoring the offer. "You've got more money than the Treasury Department, but you're out here every night taking two-dollar bets from shop clerks and newsboys and bums. How come?"

"It's not so difficult to understand, my friend." Rothstein watched his steamy breath. "I never know when I might need the two dollars. Now how about that drink? But I can't stay long. I have a party on Fifth Avenue."

They walked side by side for half a block before George asked: "Is that why you keep muscling in on my booze business? Because you might need a couple of extra bucks?"

Rothstein called to his bodyguard, who was right on their heels. The man handed him a silver flask and Rothstein took a quick sip. "Ahhh, that's better," he sighed. He offered the flask to George, who shook his head.

Rothstein jammed his hands back into the pockets of his expensive coat. "I don't know what you're talking about, my friend."

"I'm talking about how some goons hired by you grabbed one of my trucks last night, winged the driver, and made off with fifty-five cases of the real thing."

Rothstein tsk-tsked a couple of times. "My condolences, Georgie, but you don't have the culprit. I understand there are a few other people in town who like liquor besides me. Maybe they did you in."

Before George could answer, Rothstein turned into a narrow doorway leading to a second-floor walkup that George knew was a brothel. The door was open and warm air shimmered in the dim light. A woman stepped from the shadows behind the door, pulled Rothstein toward her, and kissed his cheek while Rothstein's thin, almost feminine hand reached into the bodice of her dress. He plucked a roll of money out and put it in his coat pocket. The woman quickly broke the embrace and pushed him away. He returned to McManus's side.

"Well, if you won't drink with me, my friend, then I'll have to find other amusement." Rothstein beckoned and the black car drew up to the curb beside him.

George could just make out the cheap perfume the woman had left on him. "I'm not through talking to you yet."

Rothstein climbed into the car and rolled down the window as his bodyguard got in the other door. "Yes you are, Georgie. It's been a pleasure."

The car roared away, spinning its tires on ice. George watched it turn the corner, feeling slightly foolish. He stood in the snow for a minute, wondering how Rothstein had managed to win this round, too.

As he walked back to the club his mind drifted back to Elizabeth, as it did often. Pushing through the slush and dirty, black-speckled snow he could picture her in the sun at the rail of the big ship. The water was deep blue. In the distance was a palm-tree-laden island with a wide white beach and misty green mountains rising behind. She was gay, laughing, carefree. She wore a white blouse that showed her shoulders. There was someone beside her. She wouldn't be without a man, he knew. Even for a short time. He wore a white suit and had dazzling white teeth to match.

George tried to push the picture out of his mind, hoping they both went snowblind from all that whiteness. He thought of Marie, instead. She never wore white. "I'll be waiting for you," she had said. And he knew she would be, as if Elizabeth had never existed, had never tormented him. Why hadn't he gone after her? he asked himself for the millionth time. Why had she gone? came the too-familiar reply.

When he got back to the club, Izzy and Otto Berman were waiting in the office.

"Did you talk to him?" Izzy wanted to know.

"He offered me a drink," George said as he took off his coat.

"Amazing. That's one drink more than Rothstein ever offered anybody else, boss."

"I turned him down."

Otto coughed very obviously as George slid behind his desk and pulled a bottle of scotch and a glass from a drawer.

"All right, Otto. What's eating you?"

"It's time for a board of directors meeting, Mr. McManus," the little man said, his eyes huge behind thick glasses. George tried to remember if he had seen Otto smile or crack a joke in the time he had known him. The only image he could raise was of the little man hunched over a pile of money and counting dutifully. The human adding machine, Big Bill Dwyer had called him once.

"Otto, there's me and you and this casino. This is not the Ford Motor Company and we don't have a board of directors. So why do you insist on calling board meetings? Can't we just talk?"

"It's strictly a matter of good business practice, Mr. McManus. Now here's the agenda for tonight." Otto handed him a sheet of paper. It was typed and very businesslike. George looked at Izzy and shrugged. Once a week it was the same routine. Otto followed him around the club like a nagging wife. Board meetings. Agendas. You have to decide. We must discuss this. And no matter how many decisions George made, Otto always found more unresolved problems.

"The first item on the agenda is the Arnold Rothstein situation. I understand you're working on that, Mr. McManus, so we won't go into it. But I have to warn you it is causing a cash-flow problem. We're not in business to have him steal from us. Mr. Dwyer won't like it."

George rubbed his eyes wearily and nodded.

"Next on the agenda is the radio syndicate in Jersey. I told you it was a bad idea to try to buy in under the table. But Mr. Dwyer said it was up to you," Otto said with a shrug. "And now this Everett Lonsdale you hired as a front wants another fifty thousand dollars. He says it's for administrative expenses."

"Too much silver hair and teeth," Izzy said, making a sour face. "You can't trust Protestants, boss. No soul. They'll slap you on the back with one hand and pick your pocket with the other."

George sat back in his chair. He could just hear laughter

from the casino and the clatter of a ball skipping around one of the roulette wheels. Prohibition wouldn't last forever, he knew. Nor would Jimmy Walker. And when they went, the Paradise Rehearsal Club wouldn't be far behind. But he wasn't going back to poker games in his apartment. He'd invest his money, even under the table and through dummy corporations when necessary to avoid tax problems. And radio was getting bigger and bigger all the time.

"Give Lonsdale the money, Otto. But tell him that's all. Either the sale goes through or I back off."

"If that's what you want." Otto pursed his lips as he scribbled in a notebook. "Next is the brewery. I know Tammany practically made a gift of the place to you, but it's losing money every month."

"How can a brewery lose money during Prohibition? That's like a desert oasis losing money selling water."

"Well, as I understand it, it works like this," Otto began. "The place is legal and licensed. After they brew the beer the law says they have to take out the alcohol. So you end up with near beer. But the near beer you can't give away because it tastes so bad. Besides, you're competing with yourself, since you're bringing in good liquor at the same time. Why would people drink bad legal beer when they can have good hooch or bootleg beer?"

"Tammany did me a real favor setting me up with that place," George said, shaking his head. "So how do I make money out of this white elephant?"

Otto riffled through some papers and pulled out one sheet. "I've been looking into that, Mr. McManus. First, you make the beer taste better by finding another brewer. I can take care of that. Second, you give the beer more punch by keeping more alcohol in."

"How do you do that if the federal inspectors are around?" Izzy rubbed his thumbs over the tips of his fingers.

"Oh, yeah. Pay them off." George rubbed his eyes again. "I must be very tired if I didn't think of that first. I suppose you'll take care of that, too, Otto?"

The little man nodded and scribbled in his notebook again. "Now one last thing. The farm. I know Big Bill loves it, but it's a loser. You could invest somewhere else if you sold it.

233

The horses aren't much, but the land is worth something. And the main house and outbuildings."

If he was going to be a businessman, George knew, Otto was right. The only people who made much money in horse-racing were the crooks. And you didn't have to pay to feed and stable horses to be one of those. So why keep the farm? Still, all the horses couldn't be plugs, could they? What was it Dwyer had told him months ago, at the courthouse?

"What about that three-year-old Bill was so high on?" George finally said. "The Derby prospect."

"You mean Crazy Quilt?" Izzy chuckled. "He needs oxygen after six furlongs. The Derby is a mile and a quarter. The only way he could win is if you shot every other three-year-old in the country. But at five or six he's perfect." Izzy rattled off Crazy Quilt's dismal racing record.

"Now I've been assessing the value of the horseflesh," Otto began, consulting his sheaf of papers. "A lot of the mares are poor quality or older stock. They could go for dogfood. Then a few of the horses certainly could be sold to other stables. I make the animals worth a total of seventy thousand. And the land and the buildings should bring two hundred to three hundred thousand. So what shall I do, Mr. McManus?"

"What'd you just say?" McManus suddenly asked, looking at Izzy.

"I said he'd never have a chance in the Derby."

"No, after that."

"Crazy Quilt never lost a six furlong race in his life?"

McManus nodded. "How many people know that?"

"You, me, Big Bill, the trainer, a few stable hands." Then Izzy's face began to light up. "Oy vay, but it just might work, boss. He hasn't had a good race in ten months."

"Get down to the farm," George told Izzy. "I'll meet you there in the morning."

He turned to Otto. "I don't think we'll sell the place just yet. This meeting is adjourned."

McManus stretched out on the couch after the others left. He closed his eyes and listened to the muffled strains of "The Lonely Man Blues" from the casino. He could make a bundle, he thought. Take Crazy Quilt to a small track where

234

no one knew him. Spread the bets around. More money. But it didn't solve the Rothstein problem. Or did it?

Just then the door opened. Marie Flynn slipped in and locked it behind her. She slid out of her blue evening gown and lace slip as he watched her appreciatively. No subtlety with Marie, he thought. He always knew where he stood. Marie leaned over him and kissed his right ear as he drew her to him. He kissed the hollow of her throat and glanced over her shoulder at the globe on his desk. South America. So close. He closed his eyes and let Marie touch him.

29

WAVES SLAPPED QUIETLY against the steel cocoon of the big ship. Bright moonlight streamed in through the open porthole. As if from far away she could hear murmuring voices drift through the hull and then dissipate in the heavy breathing of the man who had his arms around her on the bed. Elizabeth tried to relax as the man held her closer, his stubbly chin scratching her forehead. But still she stiffened when his hand touched her hip.

He could not be put off much longer, she knew. And she was not sure she even wanted to put him off anymore. She had not intended to be celibate on this crazy trip. But here she was, quivering with uncertainty.

"Whoa, boy." Elizabeth put her hands on his chest and pushed him back a few inches, frankly assessing the man in the dim light of the stateroom.

Philip Thorndike had the hard, lean body of a man who lives off women. He looked like a matinee-idol sheik—flashing black eyes, slick black hair heavily pomaded, aristocratic nose, high cheekbones. He claimed to be the illegitimate son of King Edward VI and an American actress. Elizabeth guessed he was more likely the son of an impoverished Cockney frycook. Her father would despise Philip Thorndike. Maybe that was part of his attraction.

Thorndike leaned across her body and picked two empty wine glasses off the night table. The bed creaked under his weight.

"All right. I understand, love. Can't play a love scene without champagne," he said in a too-perfect Oxonian accent. He held both glasses in one hand and filled them from the already-opened bottle in the ice bucket. He handed one glass to Elizabeth as she wondered how many moneyed widows he had thrilled with that trick.

"Do you always seduce by the script?" She sipped the wine and coughed as the bubbles went up her nose.

"Always." He smiled and clinked his glass against hers. He had exquisite, even, pearl-white teeth. Elizabeth wondered what they cost.

"It's a point of pride. I make all the stops along the way." He shook his head. "You Americans. Bang-bang and it's all over. No style. No romance."

How generous, she thought. He was going to give the unloved but wealthy American lady the benefit of his worldly knowledge. Would Philip kiss her fingers next?

He began to nibble on her fingers as she lay back on the bed. She couldn't keep from smiling. He took it as encouragement, moving up to lick her palms. She realized the ship had grown very quiet. Most of the passengers had retired early, she guessed, resting up for tomorrow's celebration. They would be in Rio by morning, just in time for Mardi Gras.

Elizabeth was not looking forward to it. She was getting sick of faraway places and colorful people and quaint customs. She had seen untouchables in Calcutta, whirling dervishes in Istanbul, saffron-robed Buddhists in Bangkok, leprous beggars in Jerusalem. She longed for a glimpse of a bum on the Bowery.

Now, she realized, she just wanted to go home. The cruise seemed to go on endlessly. She could have rowed around the world in less time.

And always the gold diggers, swirling around her like dinghies in a whirlpool. They came in all shapes and sizes and nationalities. A few had booked passage on the ship. But most were too poor for that. So they watched the shipping columns

236

and haunted piers all over the world as if they were famished seagulls waiting for the garbage scow to dock. She wondered if there was a professional gigolo grapevine, perhaps a newsletter published monthly and sent to gold diggers all over the world by some oily Frenchman in an ascot. *"Attention Naples: Wealthy American widow en route. Likes finger kissing and bonbons. If all else fails resort to champagne at dawn. Victory or death. Maurice."*

They were everywhere—wooing and courting in Honolulu and Vancouver and San Francisco and Tierra del Fuego.

But Philip Thorndike, who had now worked his way up to kissing the crook of her arm, was the most persistent. He had booked passage on the ocean liner in London after they had met at a private party in Mayfair. Thereafter, he had roses delivered to her door every day, whether aboard ship or in hotels.

When she got into difficulties with other men, he was always there to help. He dogged her footsteps all over the world. He sent her love notes, candy, liquor. He arranged to sit at her table aboard ship, waited hours in a deck chair under the broiling sun just to watch her read a magazine. He was always a willing partner in shuffleboard, bridge, and Mah-Jongg. He escorted her to dances and dinner when she could find no one else. When she said she liked mustaches, he grew one. Then cut it off at her whim.

And now, finally, she was beginning to give in. After all, he deserved it for his persistence alone. In the time he had spent on her, Philip could have gigoloed a dozen other women. Good God, she wondered, had Philip broken the first rule of gold digging—never fall in love?

He was tiring of hands and arms, she realized. He brushed a hat box from the bed and moved up next to her, murmuring in her ear. His hands began to move quickly, sensing the green light. In moments he had undressed her, tossing her gown and undergarments on the cluttered floor. To her surprise, she didn't stop him. He caressed her breasts, his fingers kneading the nipples. She squirmed, thought briefly of pushing him away. But she didn't.

Why should she? she thought. For George McManus? But

why wasn't he lying here next to her now instead of this man? Why hadn't he come after her, instead of just sending a few pitiful cablegrams? After all, it was George who had wronged her by getting caught with his pants down. What did she owe him anyway? Certainly not chastity.

Philip sat up and began to peel off his clothes, uncovering each part of his body as if it were buried treasure. She thought he looked silly doing his strip, but promised herself she wouldn't laugh at him. He rejoined her on the bed and pressed his body against hers. He felt warm, taut. It reminded her again how long it had been since she had been with a man. But George's body had been strong, mature, muscular, she remembered. Philip's was sleek, sensual.

She told herself to stop thinking of George McManus, to concentrate on the man beside her. If he could live without her for six months, she could live without him forever. She would conduct no romance by correspondence. What did George even look like anymore? she wondered, trying to picture his features. She hadn't brought a picture, but if she couldn't even remember his face . . .

Philip slowly and sensually made his way down her body with slow kisses. He stroked her thighs gently and they parted almost without her realizing it. She could feel a warm rush overtaking her. This was nice. His lips returned to hers and she kissed him back, their tongues dancing together.

Suddenly he leaped on top of her. She felt no more hesitation as she pulled him close, her fingernails digging into his back. With the urgency of a man who had waited six months for this moment, he entered her, her legs winding around his back as he began moving faster and faster. His eyes were slightly glazed, hers tightly shut. Sweat glistened on his face. She smiled as a drop hit her nose. She pushed with him, held on tighter until she shuddered violently. Philip groaned and suddenly stopped. She could feel a warm wetness filling her. Philip hugged her tightly, whispering in her ear.

"I love you, Elizabeth," he said.

"I love you, George," she replied.

30

GEORGE MCMANUS patted the stocky bay's nose. The horse snapped at his hand.

"That's a sign of a good one," the ruddy-faced trainer said in a rough Scottish burr. He leaned against the scarred door of the stall. "All the good ones are a bit mean."

McManus rubbed his hand where the bay's teeth had just nicked the skin. "Too bad his legs and lungs aren't as good as his teeth."

The trainer frowned as he slipped a bridle over the horse's nose. He led Crazy Quilt out of the stall and through the barn. George and Izzy followed, picking their way carefully around piles of manure. The trainer limped badly and George noticed that one leg was shorter than the other. The infirm training the infirm, he thought.

The trainer stopped suddenly and turned back to McManus. He spat a nasty-looking thick brown liquid at the ground near McManus's feet.

"He won't lose at six furlongs, if that's what you're worried about."

"I'm afraid he'll have to, Campbell," George said. "Just this once."

The trainer glanced quickly at Izzy, who looked equally surprised. They had spent the last three hours plotting Crazy Quilt's first victory in ten months. Was McManus now pulling a switch?

"I thought you were going to make a killing on this race," Campbell said finally as the horse pulled him to a dusty trough and drank with loud, sucking slurps.

"We are." George ran his fingers through his slick black hair and yawned. He had been up for nearly twenty-four hours.

"You see, I have a score to settle with . . ." Then he decided against saying more. ". . . with this fellow. And he's very fond of betting sure things."

"Then you'd better find another horse," Campbell said somberly. He affectionately patted Crazy Quilt on the shoulder and George wondered why so many miserable human beings could only give their love to animals.

"Mr. Dwyer didn't name him Crazy as a whim. Once the race starts nobody on God's earth can stop the beast. He runs like the wind until he tires. You might be able to slow him down, but I wouldn't vouch for it."

Campbell nodded as if agreeing with what he just said. "That fellow you're trying to gull, you'd be doing him a favor putting him on a horse like this." He looked at Crazy Quilt as if the colt were winged Pegasus.

George frowned. The old racetrack saw had it that there were a thousand ways to lose a race but only one way to win. And now he couldn't even guarantee himself a loser when he wanted it. George toyed with the idea of entering the horse in a race at seven furlongs—a race Crazy Quilt was sure to lose. But Rothstein was no fool. He wouldn't bite at that bait.

George watched the dust motes floating in the beams of sunlight that shot through the barn windows. Around him three dozen horses munched their hay industriously. Hay that he had to pay for. Izzy and Duncan Campbell watched him with equal interest, the grizzled trainer gently stroking Crazy Quilt's mane while Izzy tried to breathe the pungent barn air without inhaling.

"How about drugs?" George finally asked.

Campbell shook his head. "I won't have any of my stock drugged, Mr. McManus. That wasn't Bill Dwyer's way. You could as easily kill a horse that way as to shoot it in the brain." His fingers played with the horse's ears. "Besides, even if you were to drug Crazy Quilt, he might still win. The needle is too uncertain."

George crossed his arms and leaned against a post. "Do you have any ideas, then?"

"It's simple enough," said Campbell. "If you must do this, get another horse. A ringer."

Izzy and George looked puzzled as the trainer resumed walking Crazy Quilt. He stopped before a stall at the end of the barn. George followed and read the nameplate on the horse's halter. Slow Burner.

Campbell tied Crazy Quilt to a post and led Slow Burner out. McManus looked at the new horse, then quickly glanced back at Crazy Quilt. They were nearly identical. Both were short, compact, dark bays with three white stockings. The only difference was the triangular white blaze on Crazy Quilt's nose.

Campbell scratched Slow Burner behind the ears and the horse nuzzled his chest. He pulled a lump of sugar out of his pocket and put it between his teeth. The horse gently snatched it away and gobbled it daintily.

"They had the same sire," Campbell explained. "And their dams are sisters. They were even born on the same day. Go ahead, pet him," he said to George. "This one won't bite."

George tentatively touched the animal's back. Slow Burner turned his head and rubbed against George's shoulder.

"The only difference between them is the patch of white on Crazy Quilt. And the fact Slow Burner can't outrun a dead man."

George and Izzy looked at each other and at the two animals.

"This is a million-dollar piece of meat you have here, boss. They could be twins."

"If you painted a white blaze on Burner's forehead," George asked finally, "could you tell them apart?"

"I could," the trainer said. "But no one else could."

"Boss," Izzy said, "I think we're going to the races."

The music was lousy. Repetitious melodies. Inane words. The book was improbable, too. More coincidence in ninety minutes than Arnold Rothstein had come across in his entire life. Arch dialogue. He got none of the jokes. The actress playing the ingenue would never see forty again. The costumes were garish and tasteless.

The perfect investment, he decided.

This musical would run for years. Rothstein nudged the balding, thick-set man sitting next to him in the fifth row of the Orpheum Theater.

"How much?"

"Fifteen thousand. For that you get fifteen percent."

Rothstein shook his head. "For that I get twenty-five percent."

"Are you crazy?" the producer shouted. Then he lowered

his voice, though no one had heard. The cavernous theater was nearly empty. He had scheduled this performance solely for Rothstein's benefit. "Either take fifteen or I'll go somewhere else."

Rothstein laughed. It was not a kind laugh, more of a wicked snicker. He nodded at two nondescript men who sat near the wall on the other side of the theater. They wore nearly identical gray suits and black derbies and carried nearly identical black leather satchels. The two men nodded back at Rothstein. One managed a tight smile.

"Now we both know, Dolan, that you can't go to someone else. You haven't got time. Either those two gentlemen get their money by five o'clock or this play goes out of business. Correct?"

"But I can't give you twenty-five. It's not mine to give."

"I won't waste time dickering." Rothstein rose and stepped into the aisle, straightening his suitcoat.

The producer sat with hands clasped. "How about twenty? I can give you twenty." He looked up at Rothstein, his shining, chubby face pleading.

"Agreed," Rothstein said. "But only if you throw in a few more girls, Dolan. And more feathers and razzmatazz." He nodded to a handsome, muscular man in an expensive suit who sat two rows behind them. Legs Diamond reached into his inner coat pocket and pulled out a wad of bills. He flicked the rubber band off the roll and counted out $15,000 loudly.

Dolan looked like a man whose sentence of thirty years at hard labor had just been reduced to two weeks in Palm Springs. He snatched the cash from Diamond's hand and raced toward the two bill collectors. They took their money and disappeared silently, oozing out of the theater.

Rothstein watched as the producer skipped over to the orchestra pit and whispered to the conductor. In midbar the orchestra switched into a spirited rendition of "Angel Child." On stage the actors and dancers had started to whisper among themselves.

"Reprieve," someone shouted.

The producer waved at a lighting technician perched high above the stage and pointed to Rothstein. The light man

242

swung a glaring yellow spot on him and the entire cast and crew burst into applause.

What fools, Rothstein thought, as the clapping died down, the spotlight switched off, and the shadows about him returned. How he loved doing business with show people. They were always desperate for cash. And a few dollars earned their eternal gratitude.

The curtain had fallen but the orchestra still played loudly. He heard the sound of sets being moved backstage. Then the curtain was raised again, revealing a dozen actors, in full Indian regalia, complete with tomahawks, loincloths, and headdresses. They began singing a number which Rothstein decided was the worst of the lot.

"Great show," said Legs Diamond, his long, thin fingers tapping violently on the back of the seat in front of him. One of the actors began a silly half war dance, half Charleston, and soon tears were streaming down Legs's cheeks.

"Your taste is all in your mouth," Rothstein grunted, sitting next to him. "But with a hundred and fifty shows on Broadway you have to have this kind of costume nonsense to attract an audience."

The music stopped and Legs wiped away his tears. "If you don't like the show, Arnie, how come you're putting money into it?"

Rothstein looked at the stage. "Because I'm basically such a nice person."

The curtain fell again. The house lights came on. Legs stood up. "Well, it's okay by me, Arnie. It's your dough."

"And speaking of money," Rothstein said, slipping on his gloves, "sit down and tell me again what Tony Licata had to say last night."

Legs sat, unbuttoning his coat. The butt of his gun just peeked out past the lapel. "Like I told you, McManus is running this longshot at Bowie, name of Crazy Quilt. The horse is a lock. No way it can lose at the distance, Tony says."

"McManus. How do I know Tony is on the level? I wouldn't put it past McManus to try and pull a con on me."

"Well, Licata's always been reliable in the past. And now, since McManus got rid of him, why would Tony be doing him favors?" Legs reasoned. "Besides, he got the dope by accident from a croupier at the Paradise Rehearsal Club. A little weasel named Rats Wolnik who'd go over Niagara Falls in a barrel if he saw two bits floating at the bottom. Wolnik was drunk and spilled the beans. He said McManus has been setting up the race for five weeks, spreading bets around."

"I don't believe in accidents," Rothstein said.

"I don't either, Arnie. But I've checked it out." Legs pulled a crumpled scratch sheet from his inside coat pocket. "See for yourself. Fourth race tomorrow at Bowie."

Rothstein glanced at the entries, taking a fountain pen from his pocket and making notations. Dog meat. He made some quick calculations. The eight horses had lost their last races by a total of 127 lengths. The sheet didn't show Crazy Quilt's winning sprints.

"He can't lose," Legs said again. "And they're running him down at Bowie where no one knows him. So you should get good numbers."

"How good?"

"So far five to one in Maryland and seven to two up here. Word's starting to get around, Arnie. McManus must be going in heavy."

Rothstein still stared at the newspaper, as if the numbers might suddenly leap out and give him an answer. There was only one other contender in the race, he decided, and it wasn't good enough to carry Crazy Quilt's horseshoes. The perfect setup. So why did he have reservations? Because McManus was involved. Both of them winning—where was the kick in that?

Rothstein peered over the scratch sheet at the stage. A lone woman dancer was practicing a routine, humming her own music. He hadn't seen her before, he thought. Maybe she had been hidden in the chorus. She had short legs for a dancer. The rest of her was just as tiny.

The overhead lights left her face in shadow but he could still make out her small nose and wide mouth. Her eyes were on him as she tapped rhythmically, her knees and arms pumping. He smiled at her and she smiled back.

"How much should I get down?" Legs asked.

Rothstein raised his eyebrows at the dancer and her lips formed the words "Meet me backstage." He nodded.

"I have to start soon if I'm going to spread the bets around," Legs urged.

Rothstein turned back to the scratch sheet. He still didn't like it. It was too easy. His eyes lighted on the record of the other contender, a chestnut colt named Storm King. What if he wins? he thought.

"Oh yeah. Licata wants to put down five hundred on Crazy Quilt with you," said Legs tentatively, puzzled by the other man's inaction. What was Rothstein hesitating for? It was a sure thing! Cold! A lock!

"Hey, Arnie. . . ." he began again, touching Rothstein's sleeve.

Rothstein finally looked up from the paper. "Legs, I want you to find Tony and bring him to my office later. I think I've got some business for him at Bowie racetrack."

"But what about the bets?"

Rothstein stood and pulled on his coat. "Hold off for the time being, Legs. I'll get some money down. But it won't be on Crazy Quilt."

31

A CAR HORN BLASTED on the street far below. George Mc-Manus glanced out the window as two nannies wheeled their charges past a row of waiting cars and headed for Central Park. A fat woman in a full-length fox fur ran down Fifty-sixth Street after a galloping gray wolfhound that was attached to the leash in her hand.

He heard the bells of St. Patrick's Cathedral strike nine times and watched the shops across Seventh Avenue immediately fling open their doors. McManus wondered if he'd ever seen a day so sunny, so bright. The air was still brisk, but the promise of spring was unmistakable. A lone panhandler walked jauntily down the sidewalk tipping his hat to all he passed. What a day, George thought. Even the bums looked good.

George rubbed at his eyes. He had been too excited to sleep, managing only three hours. Even that was restless, full of dreams, full of plans. He padded across the bedroom in his robe and bare feet. His eyes strayed to her cablegram on the bureau. He didn't have to read it. The words were etched in his memory. "Ship docks tomorrow. Stop. Must see you. Elizabeth." Would he see her? Nothing short of death would stop him. He started as a heavy knock sounded on the door.

Izzy the Stub began talking as soon as George opened up.

"Tsuris, boss." He shrugged his coat off and threw it over the suit of armor in the foyer. "Rothstein didn't fall for it. He's going down heavy on another horse in the same race today."

McManus said nothing. For a moment he didn't even know what Izzy was talking about. Then he remembered. The race at Bowie, the Rothstein setup. Izzy stared at him, waiting for some reaction to the news. Izzy still sported the deep-purple tuxedo he had worn at the club last night. But now it reeked of tobacco and beer. There was a thick brown stain on his yellow bow tie. His face was red and he puffed excitedly.

"How do you know?" George asked finally.

"From Dancer Hyams. He let it slip last night after the sixth boilermaker. I've been checking it out ever since."

"And?"

"And? And the bookmakers say Rothstein has at least five hundred thousand on Storm King. He didn't bet a dime on Dwyer's colt."

George frowned and toyed with the sash of the silk robe. "Did he find out about the ringer?"

"I don't know that he did. Only you, me, and Campbell know about it. But that Rothstein, he can smell a rat from here to Buffalo, boss."

George paced across the living room to the windows. He watched a burly cab driver curse at an old man walking slowly across Fifty-sixth Street against the light. The old man was grinning.

The telephone rang and Izzy picked it up before it could ring again. He handed it to George, who quickly recognized the rough accent of Duncan Campbell on the other end.

246

"The ringer's been drugged," the trainer said in a hurried whisper. "I'm at the track and he can barely walk. The stewards will never let him run."

George motioned to Izzy to pick up the bedroom extension.

"Do you hear me, Mr. McManus? I say the ringer's been drugged," Campbell repeated. "I'll have to scratch the animal."

It was beginning to make sense now, George decided. Comes the dawn. It had the Rothstein touch all over it.

"No," George said quickly, "don't scratch the horse."

"But I'm telling you, man, he looks like he's been on a three-day toot," the trainer protested. "He's so wobbly his knees are knocking. As soon as the stewards see him—"

"Then make sure they don't see him," George ordered. "Just sit tight till I call you back." He slammed the earpiece onto the hook.

"How did Rothstein figure this out, boss?" Izzy ran out of the bedroom. "I'm not sure I even understand myself what's going on anymore."

George sat on the sofa and stared at the ceiling. "I don't think he knew about the ringer after all," he began. "Rothstein just figured I was going to make a killing with Crazy Quilt and decided to stick it to me a little. He doesn't know he had a ringer doped. How's that sound?"

Izzy shrugged. "Could be. Got anything to eat, boss?"

"Never mind that." George got up and steered Izzy toward the door. "Because I think I can stick it to Mr. Arnold Rothstein anyway. What've we got, five hours to post time? Now, here's what I want you to do. . . ."

George gripped the steering wheel so tightly his knuckles were white. He weaved the long car rapidly through traffic on the highway, leaving a trail of honking horns and squealing tires behind him. Every few minutes he'd look back to see if the red trailer was still hitched to the limousine. It was still there, jerking violently along behind as he veered from lane to lane. He hoped Crazy Quilt wouldn't be too sick to run after this ride.

George looked at the speedometer. It registered eighty-five miles an hour. Where the hell was the racetrack? he wondered. It should be right along here. He was so used to having a chauffeur that he didn't even bother to notice how to get to places anymore. Was he lost?

He glanced at the clock on the dashboard. It was after 2 and the race went off at 2:45. If he didn't make it he was going to be out an awful lot of money. But when he looked up there was a sign: "Bowie Racecourse 4 miles." He put both hands back on the steering wheel and tore around a slow-moving Model A full of waving children, leaving them in a cloud of dust.

When he reached the track he followed the fence until he found the horsemen's gate. He jerked to a stop at the booth, wincing at the thud as Crazy Quilt banged into the side of the trailer a fraction of a second later.

"Where's Duncan Campbell's barn?" he shouted at the uniformed guard who carried a clipboard.

"Third from last on the right," the guard answered. "But you can't go in. You ain't got a windshield sticker, buddy."

"I'm in a hurry. Where do I get one?"

"At the track office," the guard answered nonchalantly.

George looked up at him. "You mean I can't get in without a sticker. And I can't get a sticker until I get in, right?"

The guard shrugged. George took a hundred-dollar bill from his wallet and held it out the car window. He let it float out of his fingers. As the guard bent to retrieve it the limousine and trailer squealed away. In the mirror he saw the guard pick up the bill, slip it in his pocket, and calmly scribble something on the papers on his clipboard.

The limousine rolled along the line of barns. Finally George found Campbell and Izzy the Stub sitting on a bench and pulled to a sudden stop. There was another thud from the trailer.

"Where's the chauffeur?" Izzy said, running around to open George's door.

"I couldn't find the bugger. I drove myself." George jumped out and ran back to the trailer, where Campbell was already unloading the horse.

"What'd you do to the beast?" Campbell demanded, holding the halter and staring into the horse's eyes. "He looks punchdrunk."

"I had to make a couple of fast stops. I think he bumped his head."

"You think?" Campbell said with a snort. "He's got a couple of goose eggs growing on his noggin and his eyes are glassy."

"But can he run?"

Campbell nodded. "I'll get him sponged down and then to the paddock right away." He led the horse away, followed by a short groom with a bucket full of brushes, sponges and bandages.

George turned back to Izzy. "Did you change the bets okay? Any trouble?"

Izzy shook his head. "It's all on Crazy Quilt now. And I put a few shekels of my own on him, too, boss. I got you a box, by the way." Izzy handed him a ticket.

George straightened out the wrinkles in his suit, pulled his fedora low over his forehead. "I need a drink."

Izzy handed him a flask.

It was only a few minutes before the fourth race when George settled into his seat. He glanced about the crowd. It was a workingman's racetrack, all right. Most of the men had more rings around their neck than on their fingers. A woman a few rows away in the grandstand was wearing an odd-looking fur that George decided was made of the skins of alley cats.

The track itself was graceless, a drab factory for horses. The colorless oval was frowned upon by the dingy, paint-peeling stands. Most of the box seats around him were empty. A few were broken. Only the desperate or the greedy went to Bowie. George wondered which category he fit into.

The trumpeter blew the call to the colors and the horses for the fourth race were led onto the track. At the end of the line Izzy and Duncan Campbell led Crazy Quilt, who wore a mammoth set of red blinkers. They turned the horse over to a lead rider.

George checked his program. Rothstein's horse was number six. The colt didn't look like much, he decided. He didn't limp and he didn't drool. But all four legs were encased in knee-high bandages like most of the other nags. It was beginning to look better and better.

"Beautiful day for the races, eh Georgie?"

He turned sharply. Arnold Rothstein was leading an entourage into the box next to McManus. A trim blonde in a mink so new it still had creases from its packing box held his arm. Legs Diamond and a no-necked goon George didn't recognize followed closely behind. They all waited for Rothstein to sit before sitting down themselves.

"I understand you have a horse in this race," Rothstein said amiably.

George nodded. "He's Dwyer's. But he's a good one. Big Bill thinks he might make the Derby."

"Only if you shoved a motor up his ass," Rothstein said with a straight face. The bodyguards and the blonde laughed.

"I want a drinkie-poo, Arnie," the blonde said. Rothstein ignored her.

George looked up at the gray sky flecked with patches of blue, then smiled.

"Ah, you're probably right. Dwyer just has this thing about winning the Derby some day. But I think he's a good bet today."

Rothstein and Diamond looked at each other knowingly, staring through the blonde between them as if she were invisible.

"I'm a sporting man, Georgie. Would you like to make a little wager on the race? Just to keep it interesting, of course."

"Well, I really just came down for the Maryland air, Arnie. Trying to get some of that smoke from the club out of my pipes. But for you . . . say a hundred bucks?"

There was no change in Rothstein's expression, but his eyes blinked eight times, very fast. Without thinking, he reached down and snapped the garter on his sock, concentrating on McManus.

"Please, Arnie. I need a drink," the blonde pleaded.

"A hundred is barely worth reaching into your pocket for," he finally said to George, ignoring her again. "How about a hundred thousand?"

"You're on," George said, probably too quickly. But it didn't matter now, he thought.

The lead riders put the spur to their ponies and the thoroughbreds with the jockeys gingerly balanced on their backs extended their gait. The crowd began to buzz and George raised his binoculars. As George watched the eight entries, Crazy Quilt seemed to dance around the other horses, his hooves barely touching the dirt. The banging in the van hadn't hurt him, George thought thankfully. If anything, the horse was too much on the muscle. The jockey held him on a tight rein but could barely keep him from bolting.

George looked over at Rothstein, who put down his binoculars with a frown. He leaned toward Diamond and whispered something. If only I could read lips, George thought. Legs quickly left the box, passing Izzy on the way out.

"Arnie doesn't look too joyful, boss," Izzy whispered.

"Does he have any reason to be?"

"Nope," Izzy murmured. "Not one."

On the track the horses neared the starting line. The crowd grew noisier and George raised his glasses again. The other horses were flat-footed, waiting for the race to begin, half asleep. But every muscle on Crazy Quilt was tensed, bulging. He was itching to be turned loose.

The starting pistol sounded and Crazy Quilt exploded. He was three lengths in front at the head of the turn. Then four, then five. Izzy was on his feet shouting with the rest of the crowd as Crazy Quilt crossed the finish line ten lengths in front, his jockey standing up straight in the saddle and waving his whip in triumph. Rothstein's horse loped in a well-beaten second.

The roar of the crowd shut off like a faucet being twisted. George quickly looked over to Rothstein. His box was empty. Scattered on the floor were bits and pieces of the program.

George looked over his shoulder and caught a glimpse of Rothstein walking away down the stairs, the blonde in her tight skirt struggling to keep up. Behind him Legs Diamond was shouting something at Rothstein, his arms waving wildly.

Izzy nudged George. "We have an old saying on Delancey Street, boss. Stealing money from a poor man is a sin. But stealing it from a rich man is a dangerous mistake."

George stuffed his binoculars into the case. "Let's go find out if that's true."

George knew where Rothstein would be. And he heard his voice in the barn even before he saw him. Rothstein pushed aside a groom and let himself into a stall. The colt in the stall looked like a sick version of Crazy Quilt. His eyes were glazed. He leaned drunkenly against the walls. Rothstein turned as George and Izzy entered the barn. Diamond still looked excited. He must have had his own money on the race, George thought.

Then they heard the sound of hooves and Duncan Campbell led the sweaty Crazy Quilt into the stable. The short groom began wiping the colt down.

Rothstein studied the sweaty bay for a moment, then turned back to the sick colt in the stall. He reached in and touched the white blaze on the drugged horse. White paint came off on his fingers. He stared at it dumbly.

"Okay," he said softly. "So that's how it is." He looked at George.

"Give him the hundred thou," Rothstein told Legs.

George could read nothing in the gaze. But he was glad they still had the death penalty for murder in Maryland.

Rothstein looked at Izzy the Stub and then at Campbell as if he were memorizing their features, while Legs angrily counted out the cash and slapped it into George's hand.

"Now, Arnie? Can I have that drink now?" the blonde asked plaintively.

Rothstein turned his gaze on her, then picked up a water bucket in the corner of the stall and emptied it over her head.

"There's your drink," he said, stalking out of the stall with a last angry glance at George McManus.

The blonde pushed her wet hair out of her eyes and dashed after Rothstein.

"It's okay, Arnie. I didn't want a drink anyway," she called. "You don't want your coat back, do you honey?"

"I thought he was going to pee in his pants. I never saw Rothstein so mad." Izzy laughed. He'd been laughing ever since they left the roadhouse outside Baltimore. He took the silver flask from his pocket and handed it back to George, who sipped the whiskey gingerly. It tasted like kerosene.

He gave it back to Izzy behind the wheel. He'd had enough to drink anyway, he thought. A fifth of scotch with Campbell after the race, two magnums of champagne at the roadhouse. He was feeling good. Very good. But not drunk. He couldn't get drunk tonight. Plenty of time to celebrate after he saw Elizabeth.

"And Diamond," Izzy continued, tears rolling down his cheeks as he steered the car all over the road. "If looks could kill, my mother would be sitting shiva this moment. Boss, you fixed them good this time!"

George coughed at the taste of the whiskey and looked out the limousine window. He could see the lights of Manhattan far off in the distance. They were in Jersey now—only a few miles away. They'd reach the city just in time to close the club for the night. The word should be all around the Tenderloin by now, George thought. He was looking forward to his next meeting with Rothstein.

He pulled the dog-eared cablegram from his coat pocket. He wanted to read her words again, but it was too dark. Just a few more hours and he'd see her again. He knew what he would say to Elizabeth. But what would her answer be?

He rolled down the window and took a deep whiff of the country air. The car must be passing a dairy farm. He couldn't see the cows but he could smell them. A sweet and sour odor. Maybe they'd get a place in the country, he thought. Izzy sneezed twice violently. George closed the window.

Bright headlights behind them lit up the inside of the limousine. A car zoomed by, then cut sharply in front of them. Izzy hit the brakes with a curse and spun the steering wheel hard to the right. The limousine skidded onto the soft shoulder of the highway, then stopped suddenly in a rain-filled ditch. Izzy flopped over the steering wheel. George's knees crashed against the back of the front seat.

George rubbed his bruised right knee. He turned sharply as his door was ripped open. A husky young man reeking of garlic grabbed George by the shoulders and pulled him out of the car. He tried to push the man away but another man, just as burly but a little older, appeared before him. He held up a shiny, silver-plated pistol.

"You're comin' wit' us," the older man growled.

George looked back in the car. Izzy's face was white, his eyes on the pistol.

"I think I'm going with them," George told Izzy as the two men prodded him toward their boxy black Ford.

Izzy regained his courage, threw open his door, and bolted after George. The man with the gun fired a warning shot in the air. Izzy shrugged and trotted back to the limousine. For good measure the gunman turned his pistol on the car's front left wheel. McManus could hear the tire hissing as he was pushed into the back seat of the Ford. The two men got in on either side of him.

George studied their faces as a fat, pimply driver started the Ford and drove off. The gunman's skin was unusually pale—as if he'd been a guest of the state for a few years. His partner in back didn't look old enough to vote. Tough guys. All muscle and no brains. You could pick them up on any corner of the Tenderloin.

"Okay, boys," George began lightly. "What's this all about?"

No response.

"I may be wrong, but I get the idea you're upset about something."

Still no response. On George's left the younger man pulled a blue steel revolver out of a holster on his belt. He caressed the gun.

The older man called across George's body: "Where you wanna get breakfast, Eddie, when we're done?"

"Up to you, Ralph." The other man shrugged.

"I know a good hash joint in Newark," George said brightly. "Great coffee and the waitress looks like a Ziegfeld girl. Tell you what, I'll even buy."

Ralph smiled strangely at George, revealing a row of gold-filled teeth.

"You hear that, Eddie?" he sneered. "He thinks he's goin' wit' us."

Eddie chuckled softly.

"You wanna tell him where he's goin', Eddie?" Ralph said.

"Nah, we don't want to scare him to death before we kill him. The boss might not pay off."

Ralph thought that was pretty funny. Even the driver grinned. George wished they wouldn't talk about him as if he wasn't there. The Ford slowed and turned down a dirt road.

Eddie began playing with his revolver. He slipped a bullet out of the cylinder and peered closely at it, looking for defects.

The young gunman laid gun and bullet on his lap and pulled a chamois pouch out of his pocket. Now, George told himself, go for the gun *now*. He glanced quickly at Ralph. The silver pistol was pointed at George's head.

"You'll never get away with this, you know," George said casually. "Too much evidence. Too many witnesses. The cops'll arrest you as soon as they find my body."

Ralph snorted. "If they find your body."

The voice sounded like death—cold, flat, eternal. But George relaxed a little against the back seat. At least they're talking to me now, he thought. He wondered who sent them. He was pretty sure he knew.

"Oh, they'll find me soon enough," George said. "Didn't you notice that strip of tar we passed through a few miles back? You've left a trail even a dumb cop could follow."

Ralph quickly looked out the back window. It was too dark to see the road. George was counting on that. Ralph looked back at George.

"And didn't you see my boy jotting down your license number when you drove away?"

Izzy had probably been too scared and too full of whiskey to do anything of the kind. But Ralph didn't know that. George sensed he had struck a nerve. Some of the bravado had gone out of the gunman's manner.

"I sure don't envy you boys a few months from now, when they strap you—"

Ralph cut him off. "You'll say anything to get out of this. You're lying like a rug."

A real wit, George thought, but he kept silent. Let the doubts set in. A biting, pungent odor filled the Ford. Eddie plucked a clove of garlic from his chamois pouch and sliced it in half with a pocketknife. He rubbed the garlic on the bullet in his hand. George noticed Eddie's hands were shaking slightly.

Eddie emptied the other bullets out of his revolver. He placed the garlic bullet in one chamber and spun the cylinder. The gun fell apart in his hands. Ralph cursed softly as Eddie groped around the floor of the car looking for the parts.

A small spring lay on the seat next to George's hand. He picked it up.

"You looking for this?"

Eddie snatched it away and snarled. The snarl looked rehearsed, George thought, as if Eddie practiced it for hours in front of a mirror. The Ford kicked up stones as the road got rougher. No time left, George decided. Go for the kill.

"How much you getting for this? Couple hundred? A grand?" George shook his head solemnly. "Not enough to risk the chair."

"Rothstein's paying us plenty," Ralph snapped.

"Ah, Rothstein." George nodded knowingly. Suspicion confirmed. He never dreamed the Jew would get that angry. It was only money.

"Well," George went on, "you boys are in even worse trouble than I thought."

Ralph looked puzzled. Eddie was still trying to put his revolver back together. He kept coming up with extra parts.

"Hell, Rothstein will probably turn you in himself," George said. "We're good friends, you know. Sure, he's mad now, but he'll get over it. He always does. But if I get hurt, he's going to send some mean-looking people after you."

"Look, McManus," Ralph said flatly, "you can't talk your way out of this. We was hired to take you for a ride and we have our professional pride to think of. We got a job to do."

"You do if you work for Rothstein, but not if you work for me."

There was a dead silence in the car. Neither man caught on. You're moving too fast, George told himself.

"How much is Rothstein paying you?" George asked again.

"Five thousand," Ralph said proudly.

George didn't know whether to laugh or cry. Was that all his life was worth?

"I'll double it," George said finally. "No, I'll triple it, if you come to work for me."

Ralph shook his head doubtfully.

George reached into his coat pocket and Ralph quickly shoved the pistol against his chest. George heard the hammer click back.

"I'm just trying to get to my bankroll," he said weakly. Ralph eased off as George pulled the wad of bills out.

"There's a hundred thousand here. You guys can split it. A

downpayment on your salaries." Rothstein's money, George thought. How ironic.

Ralph grabbed the roll and began counting. George could almost see what he was thinking: He'd been a crook for years but had never held that much money in his hands before. Dishonesty simply wasn't paying as well as he had planned.

For the first time the driver spoke. His voice was a high, nasal whine.

"Supposing we just kill you and keep the money?"

"Come on," George said, trying to smile, "you're all bright boys. There's plenty more where that came from. You've heard of my place, haven't you? The Paradise Rehearsal Club."

"Hey, you *that* McManus?" the driver whined.

"Shut up, Manny," Ralph told the driver.

The Ford turned onto a muddy road next to a foul-smelling swamp. The sun was beginning to light the eastern horizon. Ralph was silent for what seemed like an eternity. His brow was furrowed. He nervously clicked the hammer of his pistol. Thinking, George decided. He was probably a virgin at it.

Finally Ralph nodded. He tucked his gun in his belt and he offered his right hand to George.

"You just bought yourself three boys."

George shook Ralph's hand. Eddie was smiling but looked a bit perplexed, as if events were moving too fast for him. Manny headed the Ford out of the New Jersey swamplands, then through the Lincoln Tunnel into Manhattan. He stopped the car at a red light.

"Let me out here," George said. The Ford pulled over to the curb. George looked at the street sign on the corner. Eleventh Avenue and Thirty-sixth. Nice neighborhood. Hell's Kitchen. Home. George climbed over Ralph and got out of the car.

On the sidewalk he slammed the door. "Tomorrow you boys go up to the club and tell Otto Berman you're working for me now. Got it?"

All three nodded.

George turned away, then stopped abruptly and patted his pockets. He turned back to the car.

"Can you spare ten bucks, Ralph? I seem to be a little short and I have to meet a lady."

Ralph peeled a fifty off the roll George had given him earlier.

"Keep the change, Mr. McManus," he said with a grin.

The Ford pulled away and George took a deep breath of the dawn air. It smelled sweeter than ever before. The sun glinted prettily off office windows as he walked briskly up Eleventh Avenue, whistling loudly. The docks and Elizabeth were only a few blocks away.

32

SHE SWUNG the big metal door closed behind her, cutting off the noise from the salon. It was nice on the deck, calm and quiet and cool. Elizabeth walked to the rail and flicked her cigarette in the choppy Atlantic waves, wondering why she had had a cigarette in her hands since she didn't smoke. Nerves, she guessed.

She leaned against the rail, looking out to sea, toward tomorrow and home. A lone piano tinkled blues in a lounge on another deck. She heard faint, teenage giggling from a covered lifeboat a few feet away. As she watched, the lifeboat swayed gently and the giggling tapered off. Someone's having fun tonight. She smiled at the thought.

She turned around and studied the elegantly dressed people behind the windows, in the big salon she had just left. The bright room was too hot and the faces of the heavy, older men and their youngish women glowed with a sheen of perspiration and excitement. Without the sound, they seemed to move in some elaborate, bizarre pantomime, as if they were all players in a show performed just for her.

A tall, lean man in a tuxedo weaved his way through the impossibly silent players. Philip Thorndike was looking for someone. Then he spotted her through the window and waved. She waved back, wondering why.

He disappeared into the crowd and a minute later emerged from the door. He crossed the deck and looked at her.

"Bored, too?" he said quietly. "We could go to my cabin for a more private party, love."

"Oh, damn it, Phil. Not tonight. Not again," she said sadly. "Don't you ever think of anything else?"

He lit a cigarette and the match illuminated his lean, dark features.

"Sorry, love. It's all I know." He blew smoke out through his nostrils. "One of the tricks of the trade. When all else fails, swoop the victim off her feet with an outpouring of passion."

For a moment she smiled. "I haven't been a very good victim, have I?"

"Damned frustrating, if you must know." He studied her in the darkness in her simple white gown. "You're not even that beautiful, you know. Or that wealthy. A ship full of fabulously rich widows and lubricious, romance-smitten maidens and I picked you. And when I finally force the castle defenses and bed you after months of siege, what do you do? You call out another man's name."

"Poor, poor Philip," she said. "It's not too late, you know. Janet Helman has been aching to get her claws into you ever since Bombay. She salivates every time you come near. We won't be in New York until tomorrow morning so there's still time for a whirlwind courtship and marriage by the captain."

"Are you trying to tell me my business, love? No, no, you've spoiled me for other women," he said mockingly.

Elizabeth couldn't help but laugh. "That line has whiskers two feet long."

"Three at least, Lizzie." He took her hand. "If it's to be our last night together, then at least come and dance with me. Friends?"

"Friends," she said, nodding.

He led her across the deck and through the door. The salon was even more crowded than when she had left. It was the last night of the cruise and everyone was partying. As they weaved through the crowd to the dance floor many people said hello and asked her to join them. But she begged off and Philip realized that she didn't want to talk tonight.

Finally they found some open space near the orchestra and he took her in his arms. They moved about the floor slowly to

259

the strains of a sedate waltz. They could hardly hear the music for the noise in the ornately decorated room.

"I sent him a cable," Elizabeth said after they had been dancing for a few minutes.

"Who?"

She looked up at him. "Who do you think? George Mc-Manus. I asked him to meet me when the ship docks."

"Ah, the ever-present George. My bitterest rival. Will he come tomorrow?"

"I'm not sure. It's been so long since . . . I'm not sure how he feels anymore."

"Will you do me a favor?" he asked. "Will you forget him, just for tonight, and have some fun? If this George doesn't meet you tomorrow, then so be it. *C'est la vie!* But tonight, let's not be a drudge, love."

At his words she felt a tremendous sense of melancholy. So George still had a hold on her. The possibility that he might not meet the ship, might not care about her anymore, made her feel weak and her stomach churn. When had falling in love become such a horrible thing to happen to a person? Or was it a wonderful thing—to care so much? But Philip was right. What if George didn't come? A drudge. Was that what she was becoming? Would she be one of those dried-up prunes of women who sat about in shawls and petted cats and pined for the one perfect love that they had let slip through their fingers? Not me, she decided.

"All right, you win," she told Philip brightly. "Let's get out of here and have some fun."

"Now that's the Lizzie I know and love." He grabbed her hand and pulled her through the crowd to a stairway at the back of the salon. They ran downstairs and down a corridor to a pair of swinging doors. Loud laughter rolled out.

They walked in and were greeted by a formally dressed maitre d' who handed each of them a chilled bottle of champagne.

"Captain's orders," he said. "Have to drink this up or the Prohibition agents will confiscate it when we dock in New York."

A waiter dressed like an Apache dancer escorted them to a

small table near a grand piano. The ballroom had been converted into a Parisian nightclub. Dim lights, crowded tables, and almost enough room for a floor show. A redhead in a slit skirt and beret sat on the piano and belted out torch songs in the worst French Elizabeth had ever heard. Then, as if at a prearranged signal, the singer and the young black pianist switched to American jazz. And the room came alive.

The patrons pounded on the tables, tapped their feet to the rhythms. A dour-looking blonde, high on champagne and jazz, leaped on the top of a spindly table and began to shimmy, finally falling into her escort's arms.

Elizabeth and Philip joined the laughs and cheers. The music and champagne carried them, blotted out their memories, reduced reality to a rhythm. Philip looked at her across the tiny table. Somehow their lips met and Elizabeth didn't pull away.

A jumble of images flashed through her mind: Philip and George, the ship, the music. Her exile had been much too long. She was confused. All she could think of was getting out of the room, away from that noise. She bolted for the nearest door, Philip chasing after her.

She found herself in a group of men and women crowded around a pair of dice in a room blue with smoke. A man she knew as a millionaire automobile builder elbowed Elizabeth out of his way and tossed the dice. "Baby needs new shoes," he cried.

"Wait a minute, I've got to talk to you," Philip shouted above the noise at the crap table.

Elizabeth looked for another door but couldn't find a way out. She raced past poker and faro tables and settled for the relative quiet of the roulette game. She sat next to the balding croupier and fumbled in her bag. She bought one five-dollar chip and plunked it on number 13 as Philip reached her. The croupier spun the wheel.

"We have to talk about this," Philip pleaded.

"Thirteen black," said the croupier.

She let the money ride. The wheel spun again.

"It didn't mean anything. It was just an innocent little kiss," she argued.

"No, I think you're in love with me, Elizabeth. Don't try to deny it. This McManus person is only a romantic memory. Look, I'll even"— he half gagged as he said it— "marry you."

"Thirteen black again for the lucky lady." The croupier pushed a pile of chips toward Elizabeth. Without thinking, she swept the chips away from her, onto number 25. The croupier shrugged as he twirled the wheel once more.

"Stop saying crazy things," she shouted at Philip. "I need time. I have to see him again. Then maybe I'll know."

"Twenty-five red. The lady wins big."

Philip gasped. "Lord, Elizabeth, do you realize you've just won over two hundred thousand dollars?"

"Will you settle for a check, miss?" the croupier asked, shaking his head. "You've broken the bank."

She nervously twisted her handbag. The last thing she needed was more money. She simply wanted a quiet place to hide.

"Please, Philip, take me back to my stateroom."

He caught her mood, put a gentle hand on her shoulder. Leaving the croupier with his mouth open, they found the door and walked together down the ship's serpentine corridors. At her door he kissed her once more, but on the cheek.

"If McManus doesn't show up tomorrow, or if things don't work out . . . I'll be staying at the Plaza." He walked away quickly.

In her stateroom Elizabeth fell on the bed without undressing. She lay still a long time before finally falling asleep.

One eye opened and was nearly blinded by the sun streaming in the porthole. She snapped the eye shut and buried her face in the silky pillow. After a moment she opened both eyes and tried to shake the sleep from her brain. Slowly, very slowly, she pulled herself out of bed. The morning was never her best time. Mornings, she reflected, should be consigned to battles, work, and all the other unpleasant things of life.

She washed and dressed slowly, pulling on a demure white chiffon frock with puffy sleeves and flowers sprinkled about the bodice. Her father would approve, she thought.

Looking in the mirror, she crossed her eyes and made a face at her image before applying just a touch of lipstick—the only make-up she wore. She thought about calling the steward to help her pack, when she was drawn out of the stateroom by a racket of horns and whistles.

Stepping on deck out of the dim corridor she was stunned by the scene around her. Dozens of small boats crowded around the *Franconia,* darting around fireboats spewing tall, graceful streams of water that caught the sun and turned into rainbows. As the ship slowly approached the Statue of Liberty, freighters, tugs, barges, and ocean liners of all descriptions hooted and whistled a welcome. And on every ship men crowded the rails, waving to the *Franconia.*

Excited gray-white gulls swooped gaily about the ship and dove into the water as Elizabeth walked quickly to the foredeck, expecting to find Philip as she had for months.

Passengers crowded the rails and waved as three tugs carefully came alongside and began to nudge the ship into the Hudson River. The proud towers of lower Manhattan gleamed in the morning sun as the liner eased around the Battery for its berth at Fourteenth Street.

She finally saw Philip on the deck below, being petted and wooed by Janet Helman and her mother. He would be all right, Elizabeth decided. If Janet wouldn't have him, the Helmans had five other unmarried daughters and at least twice that number of millions.

The *Franconia* shuddered slightly as its engines reversed. Slowly the tugs, churning the dirty harbor water into a boil behind them, turned the great white liner and inched her into the pier. Elizabeth stood at the rail and watched hundreds of people waving on the dock, wondering if George McManus was one of them. On a warehouse wall a huge banner read "WELCOME HOME, MILLIONAIRES." Simple but touching, she thought.

The moment the liner brushed the pier a band on the dock began to play marches. Crewmen quickly threw out lines and the ship was secured, the tugs giving little toots of farewell as they steamed away.

Elizabeth scanned the pier for her father and mother or George, but couldn't find them. Behind her, passengers scurried about on deck followed by crew members struggling with bags and trunks.

263

She was surprised to find that she was sad the voyage was over. As the green-clad bandsmen energetically belted out Sousa she felt as if an innocent phase of her life was abruptly drawing to a close, a gentle interlude that had allowed her to run away from an upsetting reality. Now that reality stared her in the face again. Welcome millionaires. Welcome, indeed.

She turned and was heading back to her cabin when she heard urgent shouts competing with Sousa. She went back to the rail. On the dock people were pointing to a cargo net being lifted high into the air by a crane. A man rode on the net, a black-haired man in a blue suit and fedora. He took off his hat and waved to the crowd on the dock as the net was lowered onto the ship. He scanned the deck anxiously.

"Elizabeth," he shouted as he spotted her. His face lit up. "Liz, it's me!"

"Georgie," she screamed, and ran toward the bow where the net was coming down.

She leaped into his arms, crushing the faded carnation in his lapel. He held her tightly, swinging her around twice, covering her face with kisses.

"I couldn't stand to wait for you another minute," he said with a laugh, squeezing her even harder. "So I slipped the crane operator a fiver and he flew me up here air mail!"

"God, I'm so confused but so happy!" She pulled his head down and kissed him long and deep, oblivious to the crowd chattering around them.

"We can't talk up here," Elizabeth said finally, looking about. "Come to my cabin."

"That sounds like a great idea, toots," he said, unable to take his eyes off her. They walked arm in arm down the deck.

"I don't know if it's just that you've been gone so long, but you look even more beautiful than I remembered. I wanted to send you flowers, a whole cabinful of flowers, but I had a little bad luck last night. It doesn't matter now, though. Nothing matters." He spoke quickly, breathlessly, as if everything had to be said that instant.

As she opened her door he picked her up, carried her inside and laid her on the bed.

264

"Now, George, don't be silly. Take it easy. I've got so many things I have to say to you." She sat up on the bed.

He kicked the door shut and sat beside her. He stroked her hair and kissed her neck.

"There hasn't been a day when I haven't thought of you, dreamed about holding you again," he whispered, pushing her back on the bed. "The months felt like years . . . like a hundred years."

He unbuttoned the front of her dress and slipped it off her shoulders.

"Please, Georgie, I've changed, everything isn't the same. We have to talk," she murmured. But she held him tightly as he kissed her jaw, her throat, then exposed one breast and began to stroke it. She purred now.

"That's funny, everything looks the same to me," he whispered. He ran a hand up one stockinged leg.

"Welcome home, toots."

33

THE TAXI tore around the corner of Sixth Avenue and raced up Forty-sixth Street with a squeal of tires. It jerked to a halt at the curb in front of the corset shop. George McManus threw a ten-dollar bill at the cabbie and pulled Elizabeth out of the taxi, across the walk, and up the narrow stairs to the Paradise Rehearsal Club. Izzy the Stub was toying with a slot machine when he heard them rush across the floor.

"Boss! My God, are you okay?" he shouted. "I went to your apartment when I got the car fixed, but you weren't there. I called everybody. I didn't know if I should go to the cops. . . ." Then he saw Elizabeth.

"Never mind that," George said quickly, pushing Izzy toward the door. "Go buy some flowers. Lots of flowers. And be back here in fifteen minutes because you're going to be best man."

"But what about those two apes? . . . Best man? For what?"

"For the wedding," George again shoved Izzy gently toward the stairs. "Go. Flowers."

Izzy looked at Elizabeth over his shoulder. She shrugged at him, then smiled. "I'm as surprised as you are."

"I don't think so," Izzy said, then walked out.

She turned to George. "Maybe we *are* being a little abrupt. I'm not even dressed for a wedding, especially my own. And there isn't time to tell anybody. Not even my father."

He took her in his arms. "Don't you think I thought of that? We don't need anybody else to get married. Especially your old man. Let him read about us in the papers after we're gone. I'm not taking any chances on losing you this time."

"What do you mean, gone? Where are we going?"

"On our honeymoon. Don't all newlyweds go on a honeymoon?"

She reached up and kissed his ear. "But where?"

He thought a moment. "Where haven't you been?"

"The North Pole."

"That's out. Room service is lousy."

"I love you," she said. "And I'm sorry I ran away and hurt you. Did I tell you that yet?"

"You can prove it on our honeymoon."

"But you still haven't told me where we're going."

He took her hand and they went up to the casino. "You'll know it when we get there."

The casino was empty of customers. Rats Wolnik and Marie Flynn sat at a corner table talking and sipping drinks. The bartender was washing glasses with his sleeves rolled up. A couple of the musicians were idly shooting craps at one of the big felt-covered tables. The janitor was mopping the dance floor. Everyone looked up at them.

"It's not exactly high mass at Saint Patrick's Cathedral, but it'll do," he said to Elizabeth.

Rats scampered over and took Elizabeth's hand as George shook his head, warning him to be silent about Rothstein. "I'm so glad you're back, lovely lady. So good to see you again. The boss has been as useless as a blintz without sour cream ever since you departed. Are you staying for a while, perhaps?"

Elizabeth laughed. "Thank you. I guess I am staying. We're going to be married."

"Married?" Rats shouted. "Wonderful. Wonderful. I was

married three times myself, you know. Each one had a bigger mouth than the last. But that's another story. And when is the happy day?"

"Today. Right now," George said. "You've got ten minutes to clean the place up before the judge gets here."

Rats rubbed his hands together. "I wonder if the band knows the Wedding March," he muttered to himself, running off.

"How are you going to get a judge in only ten minutes?" Elizabeth looked skeptical.

"Somebody at City Hall owes me a favor," he reminded her. "I'm going to make a call and cash in on it. You powder your nose and I'll be right back."

She looked around the casino. The band was struggling into tuxedo jackets. The bartender was breaking out a magnum of champagne and a tray of glasses. Rats was covering up the roulette and crap tables with silken dropcloths. Only Marie still sat where she had been. She stared at the glass before her, slowly pushing her red hair out of her eyes.

She *was* lovely, Elizabeth realized. The blue eyes and the hair were like fire and ice in the same vessel. She was flashy in her tight gown, stripes of orange and blue—like the butterflies that night at the costume party. Elizabeth wondered if Marie and George had had an affair while she was away. She walked toward the table and Marie looked up at her, her face tinging an angry red. Elizabeth had her answer. Well, she decided, I'm going to be big about this.

"You heard?" Elizabeth said, sitting across from her.

Marie nodded, eyes back on her drink. "Lots of luck."

"I hope you mean that. I'm a little dazed by how fast things are happening. But I'd like you to stay for the wedding."

Marie looked at Elizabeth and smiled dryly. Then she rose and walked away in the slinky gown, her striped hips undulating like a sidewinder on sand. She went out past the big, reinforced casino door. A few moments later Elizabeth heard the whir and chatter of a slot machine downstairs. She picked up Marie's glass and finished her drink.

By the time George returned Izzy was back with a bouquet for Elizabeth, followed by two men from the florist with several big wreaths of flowers. One of them read "Rest in Peace."

"Wonderful." George pointed to the wreath. "It's a wedding, not a funeral."

Izzy shrugged. "The florist says next time you should give him more than ten minutes' notice. But he says he'll make it up to you when you die. He'll give you one no charge that says congratulations."

Rats and the janitor were setting up a makeshift altar using two tables when Jimmy Hines arrived with a gray-haired, pudgy man in tow. The man had a hard time standing up straight. Occasionally he'd weave too far to one side and nearly fall over.

"The Honorable Harrison Doheny, presiding judge of the Circuit Court," explained the Tammany boss, slapping the judge on the back and nearly sending him to the floor.

"I had to pull him out of a speak on Fourteenth Street, which explains why he's three sheets to the wind. But we grabbed a police escort and hightailed it up here as fast as we could. By the way, congratulations, McManus. I take it this must be the lucky lady, since she's the only female in the joint."

Hines pulled the cigar out of his mouth and loudly planted a kiss on Elizabeth's cheek.

Everyone assembled in front of the judge, who managed to remember most of the wedding ceremony, even though his eyes seemed to go in and out of focus. George and Elizabeth stood solemnly before him as he mumbled and muttered. But when he asked for the wedding ring George slapped his forehead.

"Goddammit," he groaned. "Izzy, run down to that hock shop around the corner and get a fat ring. I want a stone you can club somebody with. Okay, toots?"

"Mmm. Something terribly flashy," Elizabeth said, nodding.

"But boss, that bandit at the hock shop? He'll sell you jelly-jar glass for a diamond," Izzy warned. "Lemme run over to Tiffany and pick the lady something nice."

"That won't be necessary," interrupted Hines. He took the fat cigar from his mouth, pulled off the bright red paper band, and handed it to George.

"In the eyes of the law you can get married just as well with an El Ropo as with a diamond. Right, judge?"

"Oh yes, but of course," the judge agreed, his head bobbing loosely on his neck.

The ceremony was quickly finished and everyone kissed the bride. The janitor caught the bouquet.

The limousine was waiting at the curb when the wedding party got to the street. Izzy quickly hustled them inside and told the chauffeur to get to Grand Central as fast as possible.

"Is Cuba okay, boss?" Izzy said as he stuck his head through the window. He handed Elizabeth a handful of brochures on the island. "They were the first things I grabbed at the travel agency on the way back with the flowers. The travel agent said the Southern Flyer pulls out of Grand Central in twenty minutes. You'll be in Miami tomorrow. Then you make a connection with a steamer to Havana."

The car started to roll and Izzy trotted with it.

"How does a honeymoon in Cuba sound, Mrs. McManus?" George asked.

"It sounds marvelous, Mr. McManus. Thank you, Izzy." Elizabeth kissed his cheek as it bobbed in the window. He winked and pulled his head out.

The car picked up speed and the others ran alongside, shouting good-byes. No one had brought rice, so they threw handfuls of poker chips.

George and Elizabeth kissed as the limousine sped through red lights, the chauffeur honking the horn repeatedly at pedestrians. At Grand Central they dashed for the ticket window. There were no private rooms left on the train and only one upper berth still available in the sleeping car.

"Do you mind sharing a berth, Mrs. McManus?" the ticket clerk asked.

"Not as long as he's in it, too." She pointed to George.

He bought the tickets and they ran for the gate. They found the right pea-green-painted car, clambered up the metal steps, and were barely in their seats before the train started off with a jerk. They held hands as the train wound through the pitch-black tunnels under Manhattan and the Hudson River. They smiled at each other's reflections in the window. When the train emerged from the tunnel into the sunlight of New Jersey, she rested her head on his shoulder and they watched the countryside slip by.

"I don't believe it. Mrs. George McManus," she whispered, clutching at his coat. "It's happening too fast."

"Believe it," he whispered back. "I love you."

"Daddy is going to be very angry," she told him later over steaks in the dining car.

"Good."

That night they lay side by side, her hips pressed against his stomach, in their narrow upper berth. He raised the shade and they watched the mysterious, detached lights as the train rhythmically clattered south.

"I never asked. Do you beat your women?" she murmured.

"Hardly ever anymore." His hands cupped her breasts, felt the nipples stiffen. She rubbed her hips against him, shuddered slightly.

"Will we be happy?" She rolled over and faced him, her lips almost touching him. She traced a circle on his chest.

"Always. We'll always be happy. We'll probably be so happy we'll get sick of happiness and long to suffer." He kissed her, pulling her body to him, touching her hair. "You're so beautiful."

She held him in her arms. Her hand found its way down his back, over his stomach to his groin. Their tongues met briefly as they kissed. She squeezed and he sighed.

"Where will we live when we get back to New York?" She bit his neck and her breath was hot.

"Maybe we'll just spend the next couple of years right in this upper berth," he whispered. Then they made love.

In Miami the next afternoon they shopped for clothes, then found the Cuba steamer docked downtown. Elizabeth brought five large suitcases full of new clothes aboard. The ship was a grimy coastal packet with room for only ten first-class passengers. The captain was an oily man named Alvarez with a perpetual five o'clock shadow and coffee stains on his tie. Captain Alvarez insisted they dine at his table and regaled them with stories of his exploits at sea.

George was chewing on a radish and trying to be polite

when he felt something touch his knee, then crawl slowly up his thigh. He looked across the table at Elizabeth. She seemed engrossed in the captain's tales. He reached under the table and found that the object brushing his thigh was a foot. A petite, feminine foot. The foot slowly rubbed his leg as it worked its way to his groin. When he pinched the toe, Elizabeth jumped.

He slipped off his own shoe and searched for her with his foot. He found her shin, then slipped his foot under her long skirt. She still stared at the captain but George could see her face flush as his toes worked past her knee, along her silk-stockinged thigh. He felt the bare flesh above the stockings, then the sheerness of her panties. And her warmth. He watched her closely. She was beginning to squirm.

"Excuse me, captain." She interrupted him in the midst of a tale about pirates on the Dry Tortugas. "But I feel slightly dizzy. I think it would be best if my husband took me back to the cabin." Her voice was unusually high, George noticed.

"Seasick again, dear?" he said. "I swear, she gets seasick in the bathtub, captain."

"Please, señora. I understand perfectly. You must lie down. The sea affects many people in such a way." Captain Alvarez rose and bowed as George put his arm around Elizabeth and helped her from the table. The captain watched her as she limped to the door, thinking how sad that such a beauty should be deformed. Then, puzzled, he noticed she wore only one shoe.

Just after dawn the next day the ship steamed past the ominous bulk of Morro Castle prison on the heights and into the harbor of Havana. The dock was a confusion of peddlers, passengers, seamen, mountains of cargo, and prostitutes in brightly colored dresses. After the drabness of the small ship, Havana was like landing on an artist's much-used palette. The handsome white stone buildings of merchants around the quay were set off starkly by the azure sea and the lush green of the nearby hills. And everywhere were crazily-painted taxis, barking dogs, darting children, the smell of exotic foods from dark alleys and inns, the screaming of arguments, the cajoling tone of bargaining, the creak and clatter of wagons and trucks, the sound of ships, the cries of women, and, over everything, the combined smell of flowers and garbage in equal measure.

Elizabeth and George stood at the ship's rail for a few minutes. Then he led her off the ship followed by sailors with their bags. They were besieged by a dozen taxi drivers clamoring for their attention and grabbing at the luggage. Finally George chose a moon-faced man in a spotless white shirt who said his name was Castro and who quickly hustled them into his taxi.

"Where are you staying, señor?" Castro asked as he slid behind the steering wheel.

George shrugged. "We've never been to Havana and don't have reservations anywhere. You pick a nice place for us, okay?"

Castro smiled, showing bad teeth. "Are you rich, señor?"

"Filthy rich, Mr. Castro," Elizabeth said.

"Then you will have a wonderful time in Havana, my friends." He released the brake and the car started rolling. "This is a town where the only sin is not to be rich."

They drove around the edge of the harbor, then into the city, the taxi finally rounding a point that jutted into the ocean. Castro turned into a long driveway lined with purple and white orchids and jacaranda growing on a low stone wall. At the end of the drive Castro stopped at the canopied front entrance of a four-story building. The building was long and narrow and shaped like a ship. A bronze plaque next to the door proclaimed it was the Hotel Christoforo Colombo.

The lobby was green with potted palms, gardenias, and American tourists with money. Castro escorted George and Elizabeth to the desk and helped arrange for a suite of rooms. George tipped him heavily and asked him to return the next morning to give them a tour of Havana. Castro half bowed and happily showed his bad teeth.

The suite was heavy with handsome rattan furniture, blue silk wallpaper, and more palms. A broad balcony with a splendid view of the Caribbean and the harbor ran the length of the sitting room. They stood on the balcony, arm in arm, after the young bellhop left.

"It's so beautiful. It makes me hungry," Elizabeth sighed.

"I don't understand that, Mrs. McManus."

272

"The banana trees and the coconut palms. They make me think of food. And we didn't have any lunch."

George turned to her. "Are you going to become one of those women who get a man and then happily eat their way into the size of a zeppelin?"

"I promise I won't get all lumpy. But I guess love has given me an appetite."

"Me too." He unbuttoned her dress and slipped his hands inside.

Later, after lunch, they changed into slacks and shirts and walked through the lobby in bare feet, to astonished stares. They went down the broad lawn and crossed the highway to the deserted beach. They walked in the surf, hunted shells, then lay on the sand in each other's arms for a long time and watched the sun set. The sweet evening breezes flowed gently over them as the tropical constellations rose in the sky. Sometimes they heard snatches of laughter and radio music from the hotel, with the announcer speaking in both Spanish and broken English.

Finally, the sky crowded with stars, they shook the sand off their clothes and went back to the hotel. They were standing at the elevator when they heard shouts from a room on the other side of the lobby. They walked over and looked inside. It was a small room painted stark white and glittering with lights. Perhaps three dozen expensively dressed people were crowded around several long tables, holding money or chips in their hands.

Elizabeth squeezed his arm happily. "This looks like something you may be familiar with, husband. Why don't we change and try our luck?"

"I'm right behind you, toots."

They dressed quickly and were back in the casino in fifteen minutes. Elizabeth was drawn to the roulette table and George followed her, sipping a dark rum drink handed out by a black-faced Cuban in a starchy white jacket. George watched Elizabeth play, studying her face as she won and lost, watching the other men around the table admire her verve and beauty. The expressions on the faces of the others gave him a proud feeling of possession, as if she were a smart new car he had just purchased. He wondered if he should tell

273

her about his feeling. Probably not, he decided. She was so proud of her independence. She'd probably punch him in the nose.

"Banco!" someone said excitedly at a table in a far corner. George turned, his reverie broken. He saw several men around the table playing cards, others watching them.

"Banco!" came the call again.

Restless, George strolled over to the corner and looked on. The game appeared to be similar to blackjack, but the values of the cards were different. One of the players announced "Cheval" and the dealer gave him an extra hand. They flipped cards quickly across the table. The dealer lost and the cards were relinquished to the next man.

"Do you play, señor?"

George looked up. A dark, willowy man wearing a white linen suit and a thinly elegant mustache stood next to him. The man nodded gravely, his face very serious.

"Permit me to introduce myself. Guzman. Francisco Guzman. I manage this hotel."

They shook hands and George told him his name.

"Ah yes, you are here with your wife. From New York, I believe?"

"You must enjoy reading your guest register."

"It is my business to know who is staying in my home. I think of the hotel as my house, you see." He looked back down at the card players. "You are interested in baccarat?"

"I've played some cards in my time, but I've never seen this game before."

Guzman put his head close to George's. "It is a very elegant game, señor. Simple but elegant. One wins or loses very quickly. Many Americans like to play baccarat because of that. Americans must have everything at once, you see. Your countrymen have no patience." Guzman shook his head, then went on. George listened intently, watching the players' cards as the other man explained the game.

After a few minutes one of the players tired and left the table. At Guzman's urging George sat down. His fingers automatically found the cards and began to shuffle. Just a few minutes, he told himself.

After an hour at the roulette wheel Elizabeth realized she

was hungry again. When she cashed in her chips a good-looking American in a blue suit offered to buy her a drink, but she declined and went looking for George, finally finding him at the corner table.

She bent over him. "Hungry. Eat. Sex," she breathed in his ear. "Not necessarily in that order."

He glanced up at her quickly, then looked back at the table and picked up another card. "A couple of minutes, toots." She thought he looked almost annoyed. George and cards. Of course.

Elizabeth drifted over to the crap table and lost a few dollars. Her empty stomach was starting to make little whimpering noises. Fifteen minutes later she leaned over George again. "Food. Sustenance. Victuals. Now!" she whispered.

He finished the hand, sweeping his winnings in front of him.

"Why don't you go upstairs first, toots? Order a couple of steaks and some wine from room service. I'll be up in ten minutes. Two more hands." He pecked her cheek, handed her the room key, and turned back to the card players.

She was a little annoyed as she rode up the elevator with an elderly American couple. She didn't even notice the man staring intently at her cleavage, or the woman nudging her husband to stop. What is this nonsense? she thought. She didn't come on this honeymoon to play second fiddle to a pack of cards. She didn't like going to the room by herself while he stayed downstairs. It reminded her of some married couples she had heard about who took separate vacations. Very modern. Very chic. Very bored with each other. But who ever heard of separate honeymoons?

When she opened the door of the suite, though, her anger disappeared. The sitting room was full of flowers—buckets and vases of roses, jacaranda, gladiola, daffodils, lilacs, and violets. What a beautiful surprise, she thought. He planned this. He ordered all these flowers and then wanted me to find them like this. What a marvelous man. Suddenly she was ashamed of herself for thinking badly of him.

She quickly arranged for dinner with room service, then undressed and took out a filmy negligee she had been saving for this night. She put it on and looked at herself in the mirror.

The negligee was low cut, showing most of her breasts. It barely reached the tops of her thighs and was thin enough to read a book through. Perfect, she thought, looking at herself from every angle. This would even drive a Valentino wild. George McManus would be foaming at the mouth.

There was a knock at the door and a voice announced that it was room service. She threw on a robe and let the waiter in. He carefully arranged the handsome silverware and dishes on a table, laid out the food, and lit two candles, then left. Elizabeth took off the robe, draped herself on the couch in the filmy negligee, and waited for George. And waited.

He came in almost three hours later to find the candles burned down and flickering. Most of the food was eaten off both plates. Elizabeth lay sound asleep on the rattan sofa, the remains of a steak bone in one hand. He picked her up lightly and carried her to the bedroom. As he lay her gently on the bed she stirred and looked at him through half-closed eyes.

"The flowers . . ." she murmured, smiling. Then she was asleep again.

He pulled a silk sheet over her, took the steak bone out of her hand, and arranged mosquito netting around the bed. He turned off the light and went back to the sitting room, feeling like a heel as he saw the flowers everywhere. She must have thought he sent them, George realized. He'd make it up to her. He'd send her a truckload of flowers tomorrow. And there'd be no more baccarat.

He found small cards tucked into some of the pots. Most of the plants were from Izzy and Jimmy Walker, with one big arrangement from Hines. There was even a bunch from Big Bill Dwyer. Otto must have told him of their marriage. He wondered how Dwyer managed to order flowers sent from his prison cell at Fort Leavenworth.

He found a small, rectangular flower box next to the telephone. In it was one white rose and a card that read: "I would have sent more but I'm a little short right now. You understand." It was signed "Rothstein."

George wondered how everyone had tracked them down in Havana. They must have called every major hotel. He took a last look at the flowers, then went to the bedroom and wearily took off his coat and tie. He was almost undressed when he heard a knock at the door. George pulled his pants back on and opened the door to find the same bellhop who had brought them up in the afternoon. He looked as crisp as he had then.

"Telegram for Señorita Wainwright," he said sharply, holding out a yellow envelope. George threw him a quarter, took the envelope, and closed the door.

He walked out onto the terrace, wondering who would cable Elizabeth as Miss Wainwright. But he knew even before he tore open the envelope. "Shocked at rumors of wedding. Cable it's not true. Father."

Exactly ten words. Even in his anger Horace Wainwright believed in getting his money's worth. George read the telegram once again with satisfaction, then slowly tore it into small pieces and tossed it off the balcony into the flower-scented night.

Castro was waiting for them in his cab at ten o'clock the next morning. He spoke nonstop as they left Havana and drove through dusty little villages full of blocky, white stone houses with high-walled stone churches in every square. Here the poverty was more apparent, the women walking barefoot and vacant-eyed through the streets, the thin, black-eyed men and raggedy children watching the *norteamericanos* suspiciously when they stopped for lunch and gas.

"*Muy interesante,*" Castro would say over and over about whatever he happened to be telling them about—whether it was an old church, the bandits that infested the eastern mountains in Oriente Province, the current dictator Machado, or the fact that most Cubans died before they were forty-five. "*Muy interesante.*"

In midafternoon they finally reached their destination, the natural caves of Bellamar. George and Elizabeth had a drink in a local inn, then hired a guide to take them into the caves. They were a fairyland of crystalline caverns, soaring stalactites and stalagmites, sparkling underground streams. She wanted to stay longer, but George insisted on leaving.

"You were right," she told Castro when they came out two hours later. "*Muy interesante.*" He laughed.

They drove straight back to Havana, with Castro telling

them of a fine little restaurant he knew of in Cathedral Square. Elizabeth asked Castro to dine with them and he happily showed his teeth again.

George spoke little during dinner so Elizabeth chatted with Castro. But later, after more drinks, Elizabeth took George's hand and they strolled toward the mammoth stone cathedral in one corner of the square, leaving Castro behind.

They stood on the steps outside the tall bronze doors of the cathedral and heard a strange buzzing as if the church were full of bees. Only as they stepped inside did they realize the buzz was from dozens of women in muted prayer crowded around the glowing altar. They walked down the aisle, almost overcome by the scent of hundreds of burning votive candles.

The church was so warm they left after a few minutes. Elizabeth raised her face to catch the sweet breeze on the church steps. They strode silently back through the square.

"You're so quiet," she finally said. "What's the matter?"

"I guess I'm not a very good tourist." He picked his words slowly. "I keep wondering what's going on back in New York. At the club."

"We'll be back soon, darling. Another week. Are you that anxious to get away from me?" The question was too obviously coy.

He put an arm around her waist. "It's not you, toots. You know that. I'm just restless. You have to understand, I've been hustling for so long. While you were gone maybe . . . maybe I changed a little. Somewhere I started living for the hustle instead of the reward. And now I feel at loose ends without another con, a game. Does any of this make sense to you?"

"But you're a rich man. You don't have to grub for a living. You don't have to hustle people anymore."

"No," he agreed. "I don't have to. I just like to."

She stopped walking, puzzled, and looked up at his face. Here was something different, she thought. A George Mc-Manus she hadn't really seen before. Of course there were going to be changes. She'd been away a long time.

"Is it me? Am I doing something wrong?" she asked earnestly. "Is that really why you're restless?"

He kissed her brow. "Don't be a fool."

"Then maybe I can help you forget it. For tonight anyway."

278

She pulled his face down and their lips met. His arms squeezed her tightly.

They walked quickly back to the restaurant and found Castro, who drove them to the hotel. Back in the suite they undressed each other hurriedly. He turned out the light and found her in the cool bed, between the silken sheets. He made love to her powerfully, not even waiting until she was ready. His lips crushed hers and there was sudden pain when he entered her. Then she wrapped herself around him, holding him fiercely, feeling his thrusts in her teeth, her fingertips, until they both lay exhausted and the sheets were sweat-stained.

She murmured things to him, suddenly half asleep and not even knowing what she was saying. She thought she would close her eyes for a moment.

When she opened them again he was gone. Startled, she looked around. The clock next to the bed showed she had slept for two hours. She pulled the sheet around her and went into the sitting room looking for him. Nothing. She went back to the bedroom and sat on a fancy carved-rattan chair, thinking. She went to the closet and saw that his tuxedo was gone. Elizabeth dropped her sheet and began to dress.

She left the suite and rode the elevator to the lobby. It was empty except for the night desk clerk, whose eyes followed her with lecherous interest as she crossed to the noisy casino. At the door she looked around, blinded for a moment by the lights reflected from the mirrors. Then she went directly toward the far corner of the room, pushing purposefully through the crowd, ignoring the glances she got from the men.

He was there, sitting in the same seat at the table he had occupied the night before. As she watched he swept up two cards, then said something to the dealer and pushed chips to the center of the table. She walked around the table so she could see his face. He was a poker player and she knew a good poker player never shows emotion. But she saw excitement, anxiety, contempt on his face. And then, when he lost and the dealer swept the chips from the pot, she saw another emotion. Contentment.

The man George had told her was named Guzman whispered something into his ear. He nodded, put more chips into the pot. She noticed Guzman staring at her. But as she turned and walked out of the casino George never looked up. She went upstairs, back to bed. But she couldn't sleep. She thought of his restlessness, of what he had said that night. Hours later, when he came in, she pretended to be asleep.

The next morning they made small talk over breakfast, then dressed casually and found Castro in the lobby. The Cuban told them he would drive them to the village of Batabano for *"muy interesante"* fishing—sailfish and sharks. But then he lapsed into uncharacteristic silence as he drove. Too much rum last night, Elizabeth thought.

As they rode south out of Havana she finally turned to George.

"I saw you last night, in the casino. I woke up and you were gone."

She didn't know if she expected an apology or a challenge. But his only reply was a noncommittal, "Well?"

She took his hand. "I hear the fishing is really great on the Hudson River this time of year."

He told Castro to turn the car around. That night they caught a boat for Miami.

34

THE WOODEN GATE slammed shut, a bell rang twice, and with a great heaving and moaning of cables and winches and steam pressure the broad elevator began its descent into the depths of the earth. It moved slowly down inside the scaffolding—sand, clay, soil, and landfill garbage gradually giving way to the solid, drab schist on which Manhattan is built. On the way down, electric lights sunk into the stone every fifteen feet threw crazy shadows over the two men in the elevator so that they could have been imps returning to hell after a night out, instead of mere mortals.

The elevator reached the bottom of the deep shaft and stopped with a jolt. Horace Wainwright stepped off, followed by the second man. They walked down the eerily-lit thirty-foot-high tunnel toward the sounds of men hammering. The second man was blocky and muscular but much shorter than Wainwright and half ran to keep up with the older man's long, nervous strides. They skirted piles of rails and ties and by the time they reached a small narrow-gauge electric locomotive with a flatcar attached, Thomas Dempsey was winded from chasing Wainwright. They climbed onto the crudely built bench on the flatcar and Dempsey waved to the engineer. The small train began to move, picking up speed as it followed the tunnel's gentle downward slope.

They quickly reached a section of muddy tunnel laced with wood scaffolding on both sides of the track. Dozens of welders sent showers of sparks flying as they pieced together steel girders to reinforce the tunnel walls and ceiling. The hammering noise grew as they reached a crew of gandy dancers laying a section of the second track and driving spikes to hold the rails. The workmen looked up as the train passed, then bent back to their tasks.

Wainwright smacked his lips, satisfied with the progress he saw. Nearly a quarter-mile of tunnel dug in just over a year. The shaft already connected to the existing Whitehall Street station in lower Manhattan. Track laying was well along. And work was progressing at the Manhattan face. He wished the reports from the Brooklyn end of the tunnel were as glowing.

"This looks fine here," Wainwright called to his chief engineer.

Dempsey held a hand to his ear, signifying he couldn't hear what Wainwright was saying.

"Good work," Wainwright shouted over the heavy whine of the engine and the clatter of the steel wheels. Dempsey nodded his sandy-haired head. His gruff, broad-nosed workman's face creased into a very modest smile. He had learned not to smile too much when Horace Wainwright handed out a compliment. It was usually followed quickly by a complaint.

He warily watched the old man sitting next to him as they sped through the tunnel. How long had he worked for Wainwright—nine years? In that time he had risen from ditchdigger to chief engineer, while building everything from sewers to roads and now this subway from Manhattan to Brooklyn. And in all that time he had never seen the man so tired, so driven. He was pushing hard, cutting corners, skimping on supplies and tools, working overtime to finish this tunnel fast. And what for? Dempsey wondered. To make another million bucks? The man was already rich as Croesus.

Not that Wainwright had been above cutting a few corners in the past if he could turn an extra buck. A cheaper grade of cement for a road? Why not. Who would know if the specifications were not met?

When Wainwright had built the city's trolley car garage on the West Side he had shaved a little off costs, too. It was simple, really. Wainwright had just built the huge, two-block-long trolley barn about eight yards shorter than ordered, saving a fortune on bricks and steel. On something that big, no one noticed the slight discrepancy. And even if some city building inspector had, Wainwright always knew who to see to take care of any problem.

It was just good business, Wainwright always said when he explained things to Dempsey. And Dempsey did as he was told. He had a sneaking suspicion that that might have played a part in his rapid rise to chief engineer. But it was a suspicion that he carefully kept to himself. He and his wife had their own home out in Brooklyn now, thanks to Wainwright's money. And his children had a nice yard to play in. Just good business.

But he knew, of course, why Wainwright was pushing so hard on the tunnel. Why he was at the construction site nearly every day. Why he pored over the blueprints into the night. Why he even picked up stray nails and bolts and pieces of wood to salvage. Everybody in the company had seen the gossip in the papers about his daughter running off with a bootlegger. For a couple of days the secretaries had talked of nothing else but the marriage in a speakeasy. One had foolishly tried to console Wainwright and he had sent her packing with five minutes' notice, fired after eleven years with the company.

And then, just when the tongues had stopped wagging, Wainwright had done it. He bought advertisements in every city paper announcing that she was disowned. The gossips had a field day.

Dempsey couldn't help but feel sorry for the old man. Since that day a week ago he had turned haggard, grayer. He hardly went home anymore, burying himself in his work. Even in this dim light in the tunnel Dempsey could see that Wainwright's eyes were red-rimmed. He slumped on the flatcar bench. When he pointed out a rusted girder, his hand shook.

The little train slowed and stopped in front of a winking red warning light about an eighth of a mile into the tunnel.

"They're going to blast down at the face," Dempsey said, climbing off the flatcar. "But that spot I told you about is just around the curve, Mr. Wainwright. We can walk it while the engine waits for the signal to change." He lit a lantern and helped the old man down. They walked single-file, Dempsey in front, following the track for about 150 feet. They stopped before a narrow puddle of water that began at the wall and almost touched the near rail.

Dempsey held up the lantern and Wainwright inspected the wall. His shaky fingers found the small crack in the rock through which the water trickled.

"It's one of those underground creeks, like I told you." Dempsey knelt next to Wainwright.

"Bah, it's nothing. Just plug it with concrete," Wainwright ordered, standing and massaging the small of his back.

"I don't know, Mr. Wainwright. The rock seam looks weakened to me. That trickle could be the beginning of bigger trouble." Dempsey still knelt, looking at the crack. "And there's been so much construction south of Wall Street in the last couple of years that some of the other streams could have diverted down here, too. They could undermine a whole section of tunnel."

Wainwright looked at him with those tired eyes. "So what are you saying?"

"You should probably go in, inspect, and then reinforce the section, sir. That's what that city inspector Vescuso said, too. He saw the crack yesterday."

"It'll cost time and money." Wainwright looked back down at the puddle of water. "I'd have to divert a crew, stop blasting at the face. Could set the tunnel back a week or more. Is it worth it?"

283

Dempsey knew what Wainwright wanted him to say. Just good business. "It will probably hold fine with just some patching, Mr. Wainwright."

The old man was already walking away, back around the curve.

"But what about this Vescuso? He's due back next month. He could shut you down."

Wainwright never broke stride. "You get the Brooklyn crew cracking. I'll take care of Vescuso."

Roberto's was all red—red wallpaper, red carpeting, red leather seats, red tablecloths, and good, red steaks and boiled lobster. The waiters wore red and handed out red menus. Even the checks came on red slips of paper. Its proprietor, one Agnes Roberto, had once run a successful house of ill repute nearby, across the street from the New York Stock Exchange, before going into the restaurant business. It was all meat, she had reasoned. But she missed her old line of work so much she decided to adapt the old decor.

Still, even the friendly pats on the cheek by Madame Roberto, as everyone called her, couldn't cheer Horace Wainwright. He sat alone at a choice corner booth, surrounded by the bankers and stockbrokers and businessmen and politicians who ran New York City, the state, America, and most of the rest of the world that mattered. They ate with gusto, sometimes waving gaily at Wainwright when their eyes met across crowded tables. He would swiftly acknowledge the waves, then lock his eyes back on the goblet of beer before him, contemplating it dolefully.

No one approached him. The table he sat at was known as The Pit. It was reserved for important business transactions. So everyone knew Horace Wainwright was waiting for someone to join him. Someone important.

Wainwright picked up the goblet and swallowed some beer. He couldn't taste it. He couldn't even feel it roll down his gullet. His nerves were too on edge. How could she have done it? His only child. He kept asking himself the same question. He had been asking the question for days. He would be talking to someone, a friend, even his wife, and the question would bubble up like gas out of a tar pit. How could she have defied him so? Shamed him?

Once he had heard someone say he had the taste of ashes in his mouth. That was the way he felt. He knew that when Jimmy Hines got to Roberto's they would both order rare steaks. And share a bottle of wine. But he knew he wouldn't get any pleasure out of the food. Ashes in his mouth.

At least, he had thought, disowning her publicly would help. At least gain that much satisfaction. Hurt her the way she had hurt him. He had told Flora what he was going to do and she pleaded pitifully with him to let it go. She had even cried. That was more passion than he had seen in his wife in twenty-eight years of marriage. But he had been adamant.

He had driven around to the newspapers personally, handing out the advertisements that he had written up himself:

> Horace Wainwright will not be responsible for the debts or conduct of his errant daughter, Elizabeth Anne Wainwright, after this day, April 1, 1927.

Wainwright stressed especially to the clerks who took his ads that the word *errant* must appear without fail. That's what she was, he had decided. Errant. He had even looked it up in the dictionary. It meant straying from the proper path.

And yet, where was the satisfaction? His own flesh had wounded him badly and he had struck back. But to what avail? Where was she now? he wondered. Probably off on a honeymoon with that gambler who wasn't half good enough to open doors for her. Did she know he had disowned her? Did she care? He took another sip, but the taste of ashes would not go away. His only child. His Elizabeth.

When he looked up again Madame Roberto was shepherding Jimmy Hines to The Pit, trailing thick clouds of smoke from his ever-present fat cigar.

"How's the old man?" the Tammany boss said gaily, slapping Wainwright on the back as he sat. "Glad you called. Glad you called."

Wainwright was aware that many eyes around the room

were watching them. He didn't see Hines looking in shock at his face, surveying the new wrinkles, the unhealthy color. Hines dropped his eyes to Wainwright's hands and was surprised to find dirt under the fingernails. The old man had always been so fastidious. Hines twirled his cigar in his mouth thoughtfully.

After they ordered—from a waiter who even had red hair —Hines settled back, wondering how to begin. "You're making quite a splash in the papers lately, Wainwright. Everything going all right?"

The other man looked at him dully. "That's my personal affair."

"Not when you involve everybody who's got a nickel to buy a paper, it isn't. I believe that's called airing the dirty linen in public."

"I came here to talk business, Hines."

"He's not so bad, you know, your son-in-law. Elizabeth could have done a lot worse in marrying some useless dandy with a closet full of clothes and nothing upstairs." He tapped his head. "In fact, the mayor thinks very highly of George McManus. Lots of get-up-and-go. Sharp as a tack."

"He's a second-rate hoodlum who'll undoubtedly end up in prison—or worse," Wainwright said viciously. "He stole my child from me."

The waiter brought a bottle of wine and poured for Hines, who quickly waved him away. "Well, I don't know where McManus will end up, Wainwright. But he's going first class all the way. There's nothing second-rate about him." Hines paused for a moment.

"I was at the wedding, you know."

Wainwright looked at him angrily, his old reddish color flushing through the gray skin for a second. Then he caught himself.

"That doesn't concern me anymore, remember? I'm filling your face with steak because I need a favor, not to talk about ancient history."

Hines sighed. "Well?"

Wainwright explained that an inspector in the building department, named Vescuso, was snooping around the construction site and causing trouble. Nothing big, Wainwright said.

286

Just a lot of little niggling violations that were delaying work and causing headaches. He wanted him assigned to other duty or transferred to another department.

"We can do that," Hines said slowly through a cloud of cigar smoke.

"I know you can do that," Wainwright half sneered. "The question is, how much is this favor going to cost?"

Hines held up his arms in a gesture of surrender. "Now don't go off half-cocked, old man. This won't cost you anything. It turns out Mayor Walker needs a favor from you in return."

It was the first time Hines had ever seen Wainwright look surprised.

"It's like this," he went on. "You know about Freddy Dunnigan?"

"Never heard of him. I . . . uh, haven't been reading the papers too closely lately." Wainwright stared at his beer again.

Another sign of deterioration, Hines thought. He used to know about big things before they happened. This thing with his daughter was serious.

"Dunnigan's one of the mayor's oldest political cronies from the Albany days. The mayor appointed him to run the health department in February. But Dunnigan got a little ambitious and started taking kickbacks from milk dealers. Nothing real bad, mind you. He just started living a little too high and bragging about his connections. One of Hearst's reporters did some digging and now Freddy is arse deep in shit. He's been indicted by the grand jury. You didn't know?"

Wainwright shrugged. "What can I do about it?"

"How far along is the tunnel?"

"Quarter-mile dug on the Manhattan side, less in Brooklyn. I've only been on the job a year. But the rough work on the stations at either end is nearly finished. Why?"

Hines did a bit of silent calculating before answering. "Freddy's trial comes up in mid-June and the mayor would rather it didn't get a lot of publicity. You understand. So he was thinking that maybe we could dedicate the Brooklyn tunnel with lots of hoopla that week. Parades, testimonial dinners, lots of important people from out of town. A week-long affair, to kind of get people's minds off the trial. The judge has guaranteed us the case won't take more than four days."

"But the tunnel isn't finished. How can you dedicate something that isn't completed?"

Hines raised his glass. "Think of it as . . . oh, like dedicating the cornerstone of a new building. Those are never finished."

"I suppose it could be done—if you take care of Vescuso for me." Wainwright looked at Hines suspiciously. "It couldn't be that the mayor is afraid this Dunnigan is going to implicate him in the kickbacks? Is that why he wants to hush up everything, because Dunnigan is threatening him?"

"Be careful you don't ask too many questions," Hines hissed as the waiter brought their food—thick steaks and baked potatoes.

"We have a deal then?" Hines asked as he cut into his meat.

"You'll get your tunnel dedication. Lots of hoopla," Wainwright agreed.

"Fine, fine. And don't worry, this inspector what's-his-name is going to be inspecting fire plugs in Staten Island by tomorrow afternoon."

Wainwright pushed a forkful of steak into his mouth. For the first time in days it didn't taste like ashes.

35

THEY WALKED through the huge, empty house slowly, footsteps echoing off the handsome parquet floors and gilt-trimmed walls and ceilings. The man in the elaborate morning coat and striped trousers always stayed several paces in front of them. But his deference was obvious in his constant glances back over his shoulder and the way he scuttled half sideways as he led them along.

The overdressed man, who was named Emil Tanzer, kept up a constant patter, pointing out features like ornate, stained-glass French windows and the library's rosewood bookshelves and the huge walk-in icebox in the kitchen. His steady stream of talk made him sound more like a fish peddler than someone who was selling a million-dollar estate. At any moment, George McManus expected him to offer a dozen fishheads if they bought before noon. George and Elizabeth, arm in arm, looked at each other and smiled, realizing they were both thinking the same thing.

"And now, the *pièce de résistance*," announced the salesman, his pencil-thin mustachios curving into an elaborate smile that showed a gold tooth. "The conservatory."

With a little prance of pleasure he took them down a narrow, arched gallery. Bright bare spots on the drab, painted walls showed where large pictures had once hung. At the end of the gallery was a pair of glass doors. He led them through into the large, glass-enclosed conservatory. Towering palms and ferns grew raggedly, dead leaves and litter partially blocking the curving pathway. But the air was pleasantly moist and fragrant and a bird that must have come through a broken pane chirped gaily high in a tree.

The salesman beckoned to them to follow and walked to a small court surrounded by thick greenery. In the center, in a large fountain, a smiling marble angel ceremoniously urinated water into a shallow birdbath, to the delight of frolicking marble swans and nude nymphs.

The salesman saw their looks of bemusement.

"The last owners . . ." he said with a shrug. "Nouveau riche," he added with a quick, contemptuous look, as though that would explain everything.

"No, no, I think it's amazing." Elizabeth laughed brightly and the salesman looked relieved. "One of a kind. It should never be touched."

The salesman ducked behind a tree and produced a tray table bearing a chilled bottle of champagne and three glasses. He filled the glasses and handed them around.

"Mmm, champagne. Pretty classy," Elizabeth said appreciatively.

"Well, we're not exactly haggling over fish here, are we, Mr. and Mrs. McManus?"

"Not exactly," George agreed, wondering if the salesman caught the irony in his voice.

"Tell me, Mr. Tanzer," he went on, "who owned this place last? Why'd they move out?"

"I can't tell you the name, Mr. McManus. We deal in the strictest privacy at Harmer and Weeps Realtors. But I can tell you that the owners lost everything in the stock market. I believe he was some big wheel in a car company that foundered, if you'll pardon the pun."

"How can anybody lose money in the market nowadays?" George said. "Prices are going through the roof and margin money can be had for a song. Every day you read about a mailman or a tailor or a shopgirl who suddenly strikes it rich on the right stock."

"Ah, but the nouveau riche," the salesman said, sadly shaking his head as he invoked what was obviously his favorite expression. "Here today and gone tomorrow. You would be surprised at how many people move into the big homes on Long Island and in Connecticut with money they made overnight—and have to move out again in six months. Why, more of the big estates around here are empty now than are occupied."

Suddenly the salesman looked stricken. "But of course, I don't mean to imply that you are not people of substance. . . ."

"Don't worry, Mr. Tanzer," Elizabeth soothed. "We're old money, aren't we, darling?"

"Some of it goes back almost three years," George said. "Is that old enough?"

The salesman smiled feebly. "And now, I'm sure you'll want to talk privately about the house, so I'll leave you alone. Please have some more champagne," he added as he bowed out of sight past the trees.

"It's not a half-bad old heap, toots. Let me buy it for you," George said when they were alone.

Elizabeth looked away, the gaiety gone from her face. "Look at that fountain. Can you imagine the crazed mind that must have thought that up? A marble maniac."

"So we'll rip out the fountain. I'll put in a giant tub and turn the whole joint into a huge bathroom, trees and all. What do you say?"

She shook her head. "I just don't like the house. Because—"

"Because it reminds you of your father's estate at Sands Point, right? That's what you said about the three other mansions we've looked at since we got back from Cuba," George said with a sudden trace of exasperation. "You know, it's funny how most houses look pretty much alike. They have walls and floors and doors and kitchens. What do you want, a thirty-two-room wigwam that won't remind you of your old man?"

Elizabeth sipped champagne. "I just don't like the house. It's too old. And drafty."

George took away her glass and put his arms around her. "Okay, if you don't like it, I don't like it," he said tenderly. "I just want to make you happy."

Later, in the limousine as they drove back to Manhattan, Elizabeth turned to him, biting her lip. "You do make me happy. You have to know that."

"I know." He looked out the window. "But I know he's gotten under your skin, too. Is it because he disowned you? Is it the money? Or is your pride bruised because some of those blue-plate friends of yours have been snubbing us?"

She turned silent as the car hummed along, thinking about his questions. It certainly wasn't the money, she knew. George had more than even she could spend. And the social snubs at parties or nightclubs were trifles, mostly by her father's older friends. Since they had been back in New York most of her own friends were fighting over them to hear the whole story. In truth, they were more envious than shocked at her abrupt marriage to George McManus, to George's amusement. She knew most of them—even playboys like Bobby Cooper or Harvey (the Veep) Beltaire—would never have the nerve to disobey the tenets of their caste and marry an outsider. Society matches were as rigidly ritualistic and businesslike as corporate mergers, not something to be disrupted by anything as mundane as love.

So what was the answer?

"At first, I think it *was* pride," she said tentatively, turning back to George as the car rolled onto the Manhattan Bridge. "Remember the day we came back and Izzy met us at the station? He couldn't look me in the eyes when he told me what my father had done. God, I was angry and embarrassed. Imagine publishing that in the papers! I could have killed him.

"But it's funny, darling, now I'm just sad for my father. And

291

myself, too, I suppose. I must have hurt him terribly for him to disown me. After all, he has nothing else in life except me and Mother. To cast me away like that he must have been half insane with anger and jealousy."

George looked at her. "What do you mean, jealousy?"

"Oh, you know what the big brains say about fathers. That they can't stand to lose their little girl to another man. It's all supposed to be very sexually involved. So how do you think he felt when he lost me to someone he totally disapproves of, with no warning?"

"I wouldn't say he totally disapproves of me," George said. "I'd say he hates my guts."

"I don't know, darling. I'm not sure how he feels right now. He has my temperament—and I'm not mad anymore. So maybe he's sitting in his office regretting what he did as much as I am. But we're both too proud to make the first move. My mother says he's been burying himself in his work on that tunnel since we got married. She's hardly seen him lately, but she says he looks terrible—not getting any sleep and losing weight. And when he does come home he spends the whole night at his desk."

George touched her chin, turning her troubled face to him. "Why don't you make the first move? Go see him if this is how you really feel?"

"But what about you? You know he'll never accept you. Can you live with that?"

"I love Horace Wainwright's daughter, not Horace Wainwright. Like I said before, I only want what makes you happy. So I'll settle for an armed truce instead of a shooting war. I just don't want that old man to come between us."

Her emotions swept across her face like clouds over the sun. "Do you really think I could see him?" She grabbed George's pocket watch. "Let's see, he'd probably be in his office at the Flatiron Building right now, after lunch. God, I can't do this! What if he tells me to go to hell?"

"Take a gamble," he urged. "What have you got to lose?"

Most people never stand out in a crowd. But there are some human beings so unremarkable, so nondescript, that they are overlooked even standing alone. Giuseppe Vescuso was one of the latter, a slightly goggle-eyed forty-two-year-old, balding man of modest height in a blue serge suit. Joey, as everyone who knew him called him, never understood why it had become his lot to be a nonentity in a world full of individuals. All he knew was that his entire life was one of standing in front of others, waiting to get their attention while he was invariably ignored or innocently overlooked. In short, he had about as much presence as an earthworm.

Even today, sitting on the bench in Riverside Park across the street from William Randolph Hearst's fancy apartment house, Joey Vescuso knew he was a nonentity. The policeman who guarded the canopied front entrance of the building had been looking at him for three hours, and yet never seemed to see him. If anybody else had been loitering here like this in front of the home of a rich and famous man, he would have been hustled off hours ago.

But he was glad of his low profile today, because he was still nervously trying to make up his mind whether or not to go across the street and into the apartment building. His appointment was for three o'clock, only fifteen minutes away.

As he sat, his fear see-sawed with his anger. He was afraid that if he crossed the street and went up to Hearst's apartment he might lose his job—a job that meant everything to Joey Vescuso. For the first time in his life he was able to tell others what to do thanks to that job. It had taken him years to qualify for the position of New York City construction inspector. Years of night school and trying to be nice to bosses who made him sick.

Yet his anger was such that he was willing to risk even losing that job. His anger boiled over once again as he thought of how he had been wronged simply for doing his job. And an important job it was, he told himself. He had a responsibility to the city, the taxpayers. Yes, he would do it. He would cross the street and keep the appointment he had made with Hearst. They couldn't treat Giuseppe Vescuso like this. He was somebody, after all.

Precisely at 3 P.M. he walked past the bored policeman, who still ignored him, and into the lobby of the big apartment house. An aging butler with a face wrinkled like a peach pit was waiting for him. They rode up together in Hearst's private elevator.

Vescuso was not an ignorant man. His family had immigrated to New York from Florence and he felt that imparted to him a certain degree of culture. He had never been to the Louvre in Paris or the Prado in Madrid, but he thought they must look a lot like Hearst's apartment. The butler padded silently ahead of him through rooms jammed with statuary, antique furniture, medieval tapestries, suits of armor, rare books in illuminated cases, and hundreds of paintings, vases, lamps, and handsome carpets.

"What does Mr. Hearst do with all of this stuff?" he asked the impeccably correct butler in awe.

"Why nothing, of course," the butler sniffed, unsmiling, and continued through the endless rooms. Finally, at the head of the third flight of stairs they had climbed, the butler indicated that Vescuso should wait and disappeared through a massive iron door carved with religious scenes. Vescuso was studying a large painting on the wall beside the door when he noticed that the butler had reappeared.

"Botticelli, sir," the butler explained.

"No, no, Vescuso," Joey reminded him, piqued that even on this crucial occasion people couldn't get his name right.

The butler blinked, then crossed to the other side of a large bright sitting room and opened another door. "Mr. Hearst will see you."

Now that the moment had arrived, Vescuso was suddenly afraid again. But he swept his derby off his head and plunged bravely ahead to find William Randolph Hearst in pink silk pajamas, sitting on the edge of a huge, canopied bed. A copy of the *New York American* lay on the floor at his feet and he was turning the pages with his toes. Occasionally he would bend over and scrawl some comment on a page in red ink.

Hearst was in his sixties but still bluff and hearty and powerful-looking, with only a touch of jowliness. As Hearst studied the paper a lock of hair fell boyishly over his forehead. Vescuso shifted nervously from foot to foot but Hearst seemed oblivious of him. The story of my life, Joey thought. Looking around the richly appointed bedroom he saw a life-size portrait of a woman in a gypsy costume. He recognized the face of the actress Marion Davies. Posed hand on chin, she seemed to be staring at her mentor petulantly.

"My editors call this process my daily urinalysis," Hearst suddenly said with a laugh, startling Vescuso. Hearst picked the paper off the floor, carefully folded it, and laid it on the bed with a sigh.

"They're almost like children, you know. Give editors too much freedom and pretty soon they think they own the paper. What's the matter, cat got your tongue?"

Startled at being the center of attention, Vescuso suddenly froze. "I . . . I don't know how to start, sir."

"Try the beginning, my friend. You called my secretary and told him you had some information about this ridiculous subway tunnel that my papers might be interested in. That right?"

"It won't work," Vescuso said enigmatically.

"What does that mean, if you please?"

"I'm sorry. I mean there's defects in the construction. The whole thing could go poof one day."

Hearst looked up intently. The tunnel connecting Brooklyn and Manhattan was the pride of the Walker administration, which he hated and opposed editorially every chance he got. And it was being built by that crook Wainwright, whom he had unsuccessfully tried to expose. Tammany had managed to quash any grand jury investigation of the bribes that changed hands over the tunnel. No matter how Hearst's papers squawked, that was a dead issue. But here was something new and intriguing. If that tunnel collapsed, it could take James Walker, Tammany, Wainwright, and the whole City Hall mob down with it.

"Tell me more. Exactly what's wrong with the tunnel?" Hearst demanded.

Vescuso stood tall, proud that such an important man should be listening to him. Maybe he really *was* somebody, after all!

"It's a lot of things. Shoddy construction, poor inspection and quality control. This Wainwright Construction Company is rushing the whole job like they're all on fire or something. And they're skimping on materials. You know, second-grade steel supports. The track ties aren't seasoned wood either; they'll shrink and that could bend the rails. But the big thing,

Mr. Hearst, is this weakness in the tunnel wall." He was gaining confidence as he saw that Hearst hung on his words.

"See, there are lots of underground streams crisscrossing down there. It looks like a couple of them have converged and are undermining a section of the tunnel. They've cracked the wall already and the leakage gets worse every day. But they won't spend the extra money to dig out and reinforce the section. You have to make them do it, sir."

Hearst climbed off the bed and crossed to the big windows overlooking Riverside Park and the Palisades bluffs on the Jersey side of the Hudson. He stared out the windows in silence for several minutes, his hands clasped behind him. Joey Vescuso thought of how privileged he felt to be here with one of the most powerful men in America standing before him in baggy pajamas and bare feet. He knew Hearst wasn't as influential as he used to be in the old days, when he told presidents what to do and started wars. But he was a big man still, he thought, watching his back. Big enough to make Giuseppe Vescuso a hero.

"Why do you come to me, Mr. Vescuso?" Hearst said, his back still to him. "Since you're a city inspector, why don't you just report these serious problems to your superiors?"

"I did that," Vescuso answered vehemently. "Sure, I did that first thing when Wainwright's foreman ignored my warnings. I know my job. I know I have to report to my superiors. But they just tore up my report and transferred me to another job, away from the tunnel. You know what I do now? I inspect fire hydrants on Staten Island."

"Is that a bad job?"

"Hey, it's all rural out there, Mr. Hearst. They only got five hydrants in the whole place. That's why I came to you, sir. I sit around all day on my hands. This is on my record. If you don't do something I'll die on Staten Island."

Hearst turned and came back to the bed. As if at some silent command the butler entered the bedroom with a large tray of covered dishes. He set the tray on Hearst's lap and whisked away the silver covers to reveal bacon, eggs, toast, and smoked fish.

"Tell me one more thing." Hearst pushed eggs into his

mouth as he talked. "How long before this tunnel problem gets serious? Years, months?"

"It's hard to say, sir. Maybe two, three years. Maybe tomorrow. It depends on the pressures down there. But a lot of people could get killed if it goes like I think it will. That's why you have to do something right away, Mr. Hearst."

Hearst munched toast thoughtfully. "Thank you for coming to me, Mr. Vescuso. I'll look into this situation when the time is right. And I wouldn't mention it to anybody else if I were you. You could get into a lot of trouble."

Joey Vescuso looked shocked. "But don't you want me to talk to one of your reporters? I mean, they're building that thing right *now*. I didn't come here to get the brushoff, Mr. Hearst. You have to do something right away! Put it in the paper!"

But the wrinkled butler was already nudging him from the room.

The limousine stopped on the north side of Madison Square and Elizabeth stepped out.

"Don't take no for an answer," George said, rolling down the window. "He's a son of a bitch, but you're his kid. Make him see he's wrong."

He waved to the chauffeur and the car rolled away. Elizabeth took a deep breath, then crossed the street to the small park and walked alongside the wrought-iron fence toward the architectural freak that was the Flatiron Building.

How often had she walked this same way when she was a child, her small hand firmly gripped in her father's fist? She must have gone to his office with him like this a hundred times, looking forward to playing with the secretaries and bookkeepers and officeboys and engineers and draftsmen. She remembered how someone would seat her at a broad table on a high stool and give her a box full of rubber stamps. For hours she would happily stamp sheets of paper with different colored inks. And when she tired of that she would play with the switchboard operator or draw at the tilted drafting tables. The rich cigar and food smells of the long lunches at Delmonico's with her father and his friends swept over her again as she walked. She remembered the waiters bringing her endless chocolate éclairs and little French cakes and ice cream until she was ready to burst. How everyone fawned over little Elizabeth Wainwright, the rich man's daughter.

Maybe that was the problem. Maybe she still expected the world to fawn over her. And when it didn't, well, she would still get her way no matter what. If that meant walking over her own father, so be it. In fact, she suddenly realized, George McManus was about the first person in her life she hadn't been able to walk over or get around.

So maybe Horace Wainwright's anger at her was justified. She had walked over him once too often. And her marriage had been something too big for him to overlook or forgive. All right. She was ready to apologize, to meet him halfway. Even more than halfway. Despite her modern ways Elizabeth knew she was a sentimentalist. She needed her father. This trip back to his offices in the Flatiron Building—and the memories it stirred—showed her that. Damn George McManus, she thought. He was making her responsible. And vulnerable.

The lobby of the building, which was named for its peculiar triangular shape, was as she remembered it. The old elevator operators were gone, of course. And so was the blind man who used to run the candy and paper counter in the lobby— and give her free chewing gum. Now there was another blind man. But the marble corridor of the eleventh floor looked the same as she stepped off the elevator. And there was the same frosted glass door bearing the carefully stenciled words "Wainwright Construction, Inc."

Inside, she found the same three big desks partitioned off by a massive mahogany railing. The door to her father's private office was behind the desks. A corridor led off to the other offices. The same dark portraits of American presidents hung on the walls, glaring down as if in defense of this bastion of capitalism.

Elizabeth didn't recognize any of the secretaries. Two were fairly young women. But the third was a stern-faced woman with graying hair in a bun. She wore ugly pince-nez glasses low on her nose. She was writing in a large, leather-bound ledger, her desk a clutter of papers and wire baskets and books. Elizabeth stood before her for a few moments before she looked up.

"Yes?"

"I'd like to see Mr. Wainwright."

The secretary looked down her nose at Elizabeth's trim gray suit, black cloche hat, and black gloves, her eyes as emotionless and unblinking as marbles.

"Do you have an appointment?"

"No. But I know he'll see me. I'm Elizabeth Wainwright. His daughter."

At the word "daughter" the other secretaries quickly looked up from their clattering black typewriters. The sudden silence caused the woman in the pince-nez to look severely at them. Reluctantly they began typing again, glancing at Elizabeth out of the corners of their eyes.

"He's not in right now. I expect him back shortly," the secretary explained curtly. "Have a seat."

She sat on one of the two leather couches, which had been old when she was a child. She sat stiffly, feeling very out of place. She had once belonged here, but not anymore. Officeboys and other secretaries came and went, then three men in business suits, with toothpicks in their mouths, came in and walked down the corridor to their offices talking loudly. After a while the curious secretaries became bored with looking at her and went back to work in earnest. What did they expect? Elizabeth wondered. Salome in seven veils?

And then, suddenly, just as she was thumbing through a two-month-old copy of *Harper's Bazaar*, he came in. Wainwright walked quickly, talking to two men in banker-blue suits who trailed in his wake. He was almost past her, one hand on the swinging gate of the partition, when he turned toward her. The two men kept talking even though he fell silent.

He was much thinner and grayer. She noticed it right away. His gray suitcoat was stained and looked almost shabby. He needed a haircut. Now that the moment was here she froze, not sure what to say, forgetting everything she had rehearsed. She struggled out of the sagging couch to her feet. Say something, you ninny! she told herself.

"Hello, Father."

She watched his face, looking for a sign of welcome. By now the other two men were silent. The secretaries had stopped typing again, all three looking from her to her father.

For a moment Elizabeth thought she saw a glimmer of relief, even happiness, in the old man's face. Then his brows lowered. The eyes turned cold. He snapped around, pushed through the gate, and went into his office, followed by the two men and the secretary with the glasses. The heavy wooden door closed behind them.

Elizabeth stood numbly for a minute, not knowing what to do and feeling rather foolish as the secretaries watched her. She nervously twisted her gloves in her hands. What did that mean? she wondered. Did he think he was going to brush her off so easily? She was going to apologize whether her father wanted to hear it or not, she decided. She walked to the partition and pushed through the gate just as the office door opened and the older secretary came out. She closed the door behind her.

"He won't see you," she said, looking down her nose again.

"He has to see me. I'm his daughter." Elizabeth moved to brush by her but the woman grabbed her wrist. Their faces were only inches apart, the secretary's glasses reflecting the light from the windows. Elizabeth could see two perfect little miniature versions of the park across the street in the lenses.

"Mr. Wainwright said to tell you that he no longer has a daughter."

They looked at each other for a moment, Elizabeth stunned, her face flushed. Then she angrily pulled her wrist out of the other woman's grasp.

It was too much. He was going too far. The same pride that ruled her father also ruled her—he must know that. She would apologize, but not grovel; never grovel. And that was what he wanted, she knew. Elizabeth turned, viciously pushed the gate out of her way, and stalked to the front door. A gesture. She had to do something. She paused, her hand on the door knob. She couldn't just walk away like this, leaving him the upper hand. A gesture of disdain.

She whirled about, glaring at the secretaries. On the near desk the big ledger caught her eye. She picked it up and heaved it through the frosted glass door with her father's name on it. The shattered glass splintered on the floor with a very satisfying crunch.

She went out the door and slammed it behind her, breaking out the few remaining shards of glass.

"Give him a message for me, will you?" she called through the hole where the glass used to be.

"Tell him I no longer have a father."

36

IT WAS A BLIZZARD, an avalanche, a cascade of streamers and toilet paper and ticker tape and order forms and receipts and torn telephone books and anything else at hand that could be flung out a window to clog the air and turn the millions in the street below into springtime snowmen. But they didn't care as they waved and cheered themselves hoarse and pressed forward into the bulging police barricades until frazzled women fainted and men watched their straw boaters being tossed high into the maelstrom by zealous, long-armed strangers three heads away. It didn't matter, nothing mattered, because they were there to see the Flying Fool, the new idol, the kid with more guts than brains.

The bands passing before them knee-deep in paper played martial marches, but the mob had its own tune. In the thousands they harmonized snatches of his song above the tumult that swept the length of Broadway:

> *Just like a child he simply smiled,*
> *while we were wild with fear . . .*

They climbed up street lights and atop newsstands. They jammed every window in the stern office buildings that lined the long street. They lined roofs and hung from fire escapes for a glimpse of the new legend that flew from Long Island short days before into the laps of the gods. Could he be only a man, the object of this tremendous outpouring?

301

Suddenly the littlest details of his tender years were on every lip. Straight A's at the University of Wisconsin. Delivering air mail for the Army. Has he got a girlfriend? Why weren't there front windows on the *Spirit of St. Louis?* How could he see where he was going? Did you know it was built especially for Lindy in an old fish cannery? What's he going to do with the prize money? I hear he's going to buy another plane and go clear around the world this time. Boots like Lindy. Flight jackets like Lindy. Lindy scarves, Lindy caps, the Lindy Hop. Lindy madness.

And then he was before them, standing tall in a slow-moving open car surrounded by police motorcycles. They had all seen the pictures but they were astounded again by his youth, charmed by his boyish manner, endeared by his handsome smile and obvious innocence. The bands played "East Side, West Side" for the big-nosed man riding beside him. But nobody had come to see Governor Al Smith. He might as well have been invisible. It was Lucky Lindy they pushed forward to see, Lucky Lindy they threw the flowers at, Lucky Lindy they shouted their throats raw for.

Mayor James Walker was only a few feet behind the car that carried Charles Lindbergh, but he could barely make out the thin figure for the torrent of paper that floated about him. Every time he opened his mouth he would have to spit out another shred of ticker tape or scrap of the Bronx telephone directory. He wondered idly why it was the Bronx phone book that always went out the windows first in these parades up Broadway.

"What do you think?" he shouted to Jimmy Hines next to him. He had to repeat the words again to be heard over the rising waves of cheers.

"I think it's a great day for Alfred E. Smith." Hines puffed madly on his ever-present cigar, holding his tall silk hat on with both hands because the weight of the falling paper kept tipping it. "He'll grab a hundred thousand votes today easy. If the governor could get Lindy to tour with him all over the country he'd be a shoo-in for the White House next year."

"Never mind the governor," Walker shouted back. "It's a great day for us. How many reporters do you think are covering Fred Dunnigan's trial downtown? If there's one, I'll eat my spats."

Hines nodded vigorously in agreement, watching a piece of paper settle on the end of his cigar, flare into flame, and drift away. He turned in the back seat of the car and looked at the three dozen cars that followed them, cars full of ballplayers, congressmen, political contributors, Tammany bosses, and city officials. And at the end of the parade, half a dozen city buses full of reporters from all over the world, but mostly from New York. Lindbergh had pushed everything else off the front page since he touched down in Paris. Fred Dunnigan could walk into the courtroom in a clown outfit while leading a baby elephant and no one would see it but the judge, the stenographer, a couple of lawyers, and a guard. And chances were the guard was out watching the parade, too.

For a while Hines had worried that the dedication of the subway tunnel wouldn't be enough of a diversion despite all the publicity Walker had given it. He had even considered going back to George McManus for another little favor—maybe something like burning down the Chrysler Building the day the trial started. Anything to draw away the reporters. And then Lindbergh had appeared like a godsend. In a few hours Walker's dapper official greeter, Grover Whalen, had whipped up a ticker tape parade to put all previous parades to shame. There were actually sanitation men atop some buildings throwing tons of paper stashed just for the occasion.

Hines squinted at the car carrying the waving Lindbergh. How they cheered him! Hines's ears ached from the noise. Girls swooned as he rolled by. Here and there someone would break through the police lines and dash to his car just to touch him, as if some of his aura would rub off on them. And for what? All this for a young fool who flew off into the unknown and was lucky enough to get to the other side of the Atlantic without drowning?

Maybe everybody was just getting tired of crime and corruption and chasing the dollar, Hines thought. And then along comes Charles Lindbergh, Mister Clean, the Lone Eagle, untarnished, unsullied. Somebody everyone can believe in. He'd have to talk to Walker about that image for his next

303

campaign. Jimmy Walker, the man who bucks the crowd. Jimmy Walker, straight-shooter. He delivers what he promises. Yes, that had definite possibilities, Hines decided.

"Where to next? I'm starved," Walker shouted, leaning toward Hines again but waving to the crowd all the time.

To hell with this hat, Hines decided. He tossed the silk topper on the seat and fished in his coat pocket while bits of paper settled on his head like gigantic dandruff. Finally he pulled out a sheet of paper and consulted it.

"Yankee Stadium," he yelled to Walker. "The kid wants to meet Babe Ruth. Then you name a school for him in Queens. Lunch at City Hall at two-thirty with Lindy, Al, and three senators. Then the tunnel business."

"Shit. I don't need Wainwright now. Can I get out of it?"

Hines looked at the mayor and wondered who he was fucking now. Usually Walker enjoyed these public occasions, especially if his old political crony Al Smith was around. They thought alike, they liked each other, even if Walker's flashiness was costing the governor conservative support. If Walker wanted out for the afternoon it could only mean one thing. A woman.

Hines shook his head. "You gotta be there. We made a big deal out of it."

"Shit," Walker shouted again, still waving.

Eight cars back, George McManus watched in amusement as Elizabeth bounced on the seat next to him and waved to the crowd with both hands. They were both covered with paper and streamers and lengths of ticker tape and she was laughing madly.

"It's crazy. I love it. They don't even know who we are but they're all waving at us and cheering like we were movie stars. Why?"

"We're with the hero," George shouted to her. "Maybe they think we're his mother and father. Keep waving." He doffed his fedora to a pretty woman on the sidewalk who held a baby over her head to get a view of him.

Elizabeth was blowing kisses with both hands now. A young man in wire-rims darted out of the crowd with an armful of roses. The neck of a whiskey bottle protruded from his coat pocket. He ran to the car, dodging a policeman, and jumped on the running board.

"Are you Lindy's girl? Do you know him?" he cried as two cops pulled at his arms. When she shook her head no, he shrugged, kissed her quickly on the cheek, dropped the flowers in her lap, and let himself be led back to the sidewalk.

She sat back next to George, looking at the flowers in amazement. "How did you get us in this crazy parade anyway?"

"Remember my friend at City Hall? He insisted we come along and meet Lindy," he said close to her ear.

"We're going to meet him? When? Where?"

"Steady, lady. What happened to the old sophistication and worldliness? You're squealing like a girl," George said with a laugh.

"You're right, darling. I'm sorry. I shouldn't get so carried away. After all, I'm an old married woman now. And he's just another man who puts his pants on one leg at a time."

"That's better." George turned away from her and began waving to the crowd again.

Elizabeth pulled his hat down over his eyes and began punching him playfully. "If you don't tell me when I'm going to meet Charles Lindbergh I'll divorce you and find some gigolo and make you miserable for the rest of your everloving life."

"All right, all right! This afternoon," he shouted, adjusting his hat. "When they dedicate the new subway tunnel to Brooklyn we'll be with the official party."

She pushed away a strip of bunting that had fallen over her face and looked at him. She wasn't smiling anymore. "The tunnel my father is building?" she yelled over the noise of the crowd.

He nodded.

"Have a nice time and let me know how it all went," she shouted, "because I won't be there."

"Yes you will."

"What did you say?"

"I said, yes you will be there with me," he called in her ear.

Elizabeth threw up her hands. "I don't believe this, I'm arguing with a crazy man in front of two million screaming lunatics!" She brushed a mound of paper off her lap. "I can't go, George. You know that. After what he did to me I'd spit in his eye."

"Then start salivating, toots. Because Mr. and Mrs. George McManus are going to be there with bells on," he shouted. "It's time you got over this garbage with your old man anyway. You can't hide from him the rest of your life."

"Not now," she pleaded. "Someday, but not now."

He shook his head as a big wad of paper plopped onto him. Elizabeth couldn't help but laugh.

"That's not funny," he shouted, brushing away the scraps.

"Yes it is."

"Well, if you think this is fun, you should have a ball at the dedication."

"I told you," she shouted. "I'm not going."

Above all else—above the two acres of mealy mud, above the mounds of railroad ties and sections of track, above the mountains of rock and debris dredged up from the earth, above the rickety wooden sheds draped in bunting, above the stubby dumptrucks and bulldozers and cranes and the hundreds of men toiling—there was the sign.

It was a grand affair, twenty feet high and wide and painted in red. Its lettering in bold blue and white could be seen for blocks, almost up to Wall Street. The sign announced that this was the site of one of the greatest engineering feats of our time, the massive subway tunnel under the East River connecting Brooklyn and Manhattan. It announced that the tunnel was built with combined state and city funds. It identified the mayor, the governor, the chairman of the New York City Council. But it made clear in three-foot-high letters that Horace Wainwright was the builder of this marvel.

Under the looming sign the construction site bustled with activity as Wainwright made ready for important visitors. He was at the center of it all, directing the sprucing up of the new station and section of tunnel already dug. He worried whether the brass plaque to be dedicated would arrive in time this afternoon, and finally ordered two men to drive to Newark and pick it up personally from the engravers.

As he squished through the thick mud he decided that this

would never do either. He ordered that a trail of steel matting and railroad ties be laid from the street to the engineering shed and offices to the big shaft elevator.

"How would it look if this damned mud sucks off Lindbergh's silly boots?" he ranted at his chief engineer, Thomas Dempsey. "Can't have the damn governor in muck up to his knees, either. Even if he is a Democrat."

"You'd better listen to me, sir," Dempsey said for the fifth time, an edge of exasperation creeping into his voice.

"How about the flags, Dempsey? Have they come yet? I want flags everywhere. And more bunting, too. We've got to make this place look important, not just some muddy ditch with a hole in the middle. I promised the mayor."

"About the tunnel, sir. . . ."

"Yes, yes, I want it washed down thoroughly. The last thing I need is to choke everybody in dust. And set up a few more lights down there, Dempsey. I want it to look dramatic, important, like the goddamn Sistine Chapel or something. Can't have it pitch black. I want Walker to walk out of there whistling with approval. Got it?"

Dempsey was getting red-faced. He decided to plunge ahead. "I want to order another pump, Mr. Wainwright. The water at the fault is spilling faster and the one pump can't handle it anymore." He paused, then added: "And I don't like it."

Wainwright stopped abruptly, his rubber boots gently sinking into the mud. A truck ground past and splashed both their pants legs. "What don't you like, Dempsey?"

The stocky man took a deep breath and tugged at the brim of his battered brown hat. Now that the moment was here, he was not sure what he ought to say. Whatever he said he knew Wainwright wouldn't like it. But as he hesitated, his fear of the tunnel got the better of his fear of the old man.

"It isn't safe down there," he finally blurted out. "I . . . I'm not sure you should take all these bigshots through the tunnel to the face. Put the plaque in the station wall, sir. Have the dedication there. But don't go into the tunnel."

Wainwright looked genuinely shocked. "What are you talking about? What do you mean, the tunnel isn't safe?"

"Just what I say, sir. They blasted at the face yesterday. An

307

extra charge, like you ordered. And it seems to have scrambled the fissure worse than ever. There's more water pouring out every hour and the fissure seems to be growing." He threw up his hands, surprised at suddenly having nothing else to say. Even Wainwright should understand the seriousness of the situation now.

But the other man was glaring at him.

"You listen to me, Dempsey. You get that extra pump down there. Then you take care of the flags and the lights and get the station spotless. And you have the engine and three cars ready when everybody arrives at four o'clock. Because I'm taking them through the tunnel to the rock face as planned. And if you value your job, you won't mention your fears to anyone else. Understand?"

White-faced, eyes on the ground, Dempsey could only nod. He started to squish away when Wainwright grabbed his arm.

"One last thing. When the dedication ceremony is going on I want the pumps off. They roar like thunder in the tunnel and nobody will be able to hear the speeches."

"But without the pumps you'll have a couple of feet of water in that section in a few minutes," Dempsey said with growing alarm. "Mr. Wainwright, you're making a big mistake. . . ."

The old man's stern look silenced him.

37

THERE HAD BEEN a time when he had dreamed of events like this. Hobnobbing with the rich, rubbing elbows with important people. To someone on the outside, being on the inside often looks like the most important thing in the world. And then, having reached the coveted inside, you wonder what all the fuss was about.

George McManus was beginning to have the feeling of the surfeited insider as the well-dressed crowd jostled and shoved its way along the sidewalk of railway ties, under the gigantic sign that Horace Wainwright had erected to his own engineering genius. More accurately, George thought, the sign should honor the old man's genius for bribery. After all, being in the right place at the right time—with a satchel full of money, to boot—was no mean achievement.

Elizabeth walked carefully beside him, preoccupied with trying to keep on the walkway and out of the knee-deep mud. It was a difficult task because the other guests, the reporters, and the photographers were constantly pushing them aside to get closer to the mayor and Lindbergh and the governor. George knew, too, that Elizabeth was purposely dawdling. She was in no hurry to see her father again. In fact, he had the definite feeling that she was ready to bolt for the street at any moment.

"Lovely day for a stroll, don't you think?" he said, looking about at the mud and trucks and debris and low sheds and mud-spattered workmen who watched them.

"Couldn't we take a walk somewhere else—like California?"

"And miss your father's big day? It might break his heart."

"He hasn't got a heart, remember? Just a pneumatic pump thumping away in his chest." She took his arm. "Do we have to be here?"

He shrugged. "Walker himself asked me to come along. He likes to have his friends around him. I guess your husband is a bigshot now, huh?"

"I think I liked it better when my bigshot was a slightly smaller caliber."

George winced. "That's terrible."

"All right," she said, taking a deep breath, "let's get this over with. Maybe this time he'll even acknowledge my existence with a sneer or a kick in the rump. It would almost be a relief."

The big wooden construction elevator chugged back up to ground level, having already delivered the first load of VIPs to the station far below. The rest of them clambered aboard and the gate was lowered. With an audible groan of wood and steel the elevator lowered into the ground, past the eerie lights. Thirty seconds later it jerked to a stop at the station level.

The low-ceilinged station was so brightly lit that the lights glaring off a section of newly tiled wall dazzled George for a

309

moment. Then his eyes adjusted. He saw the engine and three open cars, arranged with benches, waiting on the track. On the platform most of the crowd were sipping from champagne glasses. In the midst of the crush he saw Wainwright and Walker posing for pictures with Lindbergh. The flier, in a blue suit, looked slightly ill at ease, like a wary bird trapped in a shoebox. And even at this distance George could see Wainwright's grayish, stubbly chin. He needed a shave.

George steered Elizabeth toward the little group, pushing through a thick crowd of Lindbergh admirers. Finally, as they came face to face with her father, George felt Elizabeth stiffen. The old man glared at them both, in surprise and anger. Suddenly Walker threw an arm around George's shoulders and introduced them to Lindbergh, who smiled interestedly if a bit wearily at Elizabeth as they shook hands.

With a glint of merriment in his eye, Walker then introduced George and Elizabeth to Wainwright as if they were strangers. The old man shook hands gingerly, nearly gagging as he fought not to say something and make a scene.

"Quite a little ditch you've got here," George said amiably. "I always figured I'd end up in hell, but I never thought I'd get a printed invitation."

With a snort, Wainwright turned on his heel and stomped away.

Walker smiled. "I think if it was up to him, you'd be there right now, Georgie. Come on, I want you to meet Al Smith."

They excused themselves and left Elizabeth and Lindbergh sipping champagne. Three other women already were zeroing in on the flier as they strolled away. So Lindbergh wasn't all that boyish and simple after all, George thought, looking back over his shoulder as the thin man touched Elizabeth's arm to make a point. Champagne and women. Public idols learn fast.

"What do you think of the hero?" George said.

"I know he'll never go anywhere in politics," Walker mused. "He's much too honest. You can read his face like an open book. Did you see how he looked at your wife?"

"I saw it, but I'm not worried. Elizabeth wouldn't tumble for anybody foolish enough to risk his life for a measly twenty-five thousand dollars. She'd hold out for a million, at least."

As Walker laughed, George noticed Wainwright at the other end of the platform arguing with a stocky man in a brown suit and battered brown hat. The way Wainwright talked to him with obvious disdain, George knew the other man could only be his employee. The stocky man kept shaking his head violently as Wainwright barked something at him. They argued back and forth for a minute, until the stocky man seemed to give in. Shoulders slumped, he walked angrily to a metal door and let himself into a room that looked like an office. George watched the man pick up a telephone, then lost sight of him as the crowd shifted.

George was looking for Elizabeth when the whistle on the engine tooted three times. Everyone scrambled for seats on the three open cars. He found her looking for him and they took a bench a few rows behind Lindbergh, the governor, Walker, and Wainwright.

"The boy wonder seemed to like you," George said as the train moved into the tunnel with a humming surge of electricity.

"He's sweet. Younger than his years, really. He hates having to meet all these people," she said over the noise of the wheels. She leaned close to him. "Did you see how my father looked at us? Like he'd like to kill us both. I'm afraid for him. He seems half crazy. I couldn't even bring myself to talk to him."

George shook his head. "This'll be over soon, toots."

"Not soon enough, I'm afraid," she said, glancing at the grayish-black wall of the tunnel rushing by.

George found the fast trip through the murky tunnel very disorienting, as if he were running headlong through a blinding rain with no idea of what was ahead. But the train slowed abruptly as it rounded a curve. Now the tunnel was suddenly brightly lit. Up ahead he could see a jagged wall of stone where the digging had stopped. The end of the line.

A band lined up next to the tracks began playing "East Side, West Side" as the train came to a halt. Then the musicians broke into a spirited rendition of "Lucky Lindy." On the other side of the tracks about two dozen miners and workmen cheered as Lindbergh, the governor, and Walker climbed off

the car and were shepherded by Wainwright to a small reviewing stand. The photographers quickly leaped off the rear
car and began flashing pictures of everything that moved.

When the crowd finally assembled in front of the reviewing
stand, Wainwright made a short speech welcoming everyone
and extolling the heroism of Colonel Lindbergh. Lindbergh
took a bow, acknowledging the applause. In the harsh artifi-
cial light he looked like a boyish wraith in a blue suit. Then
he let himself be led to the right side of the reviewing stand,
where a tarp was hung on the tunnel wall. While drums rolled
he pulled a silken tassel and the tarp fell, revealing the plaque
dedicating the tunnel.

Dutifully, Lindbergh said a few more words, then sat down
to more applause. Wainwright introduced Al Smith, who gave
a short, stirring speech that started by extolling Wainwright
and ended with all the reforms he would enact as President,
including the forty-hour week. That was cheered lustily by
the miners.

The band blared out another chorus of "East Side, West
Side" as Smith waved and sat down. Wainwright stood and
introduced the mayor, who beamed as he was loudly ap-
plauded.

As George clapped he suddenly felt something, a stirring,
beneath his feet. Alarmed, he looked about, but everyone was
still applauding, some happily, most dutifully. The sudden
surge of fear that had gone through him faded away. No one
else was alarmed—but what had it been? He looked at Elizabeth, but she was leaning forward to catch Walker's first
words and watching her father.

Then, there it was again, a little longer and more insistent.
He felt the stone ripple through the soles of his shoes. He saw
the man in the brown hat standing with his mouth open near
the reviewing stand. His face was white. The man was looking
up at Horace Wainwright, who suddenly stood and pushed
Walker aside.

"Ladies and gentlemen," he began, white-faced too, "it appears there may be some problem. Please get back on the
train and we'll . . ."

That was as far as he got as the stone shook again. George
could see the walls shake and puffs of dust fall from the ceil-

ing. Then there was a terrible, low rumble that raised the hairs on the back of his neck. A woman screamed as everyone began to push back toward the train at the same time. George grabbed Elizabeth's hand and pulled her through the crowd as fast as they could go, the musicians and the miners running beside them.

Wainwright and the man in the brown hat shepherded the governor, Walker, and Lindbergh aboard the train just as it began to roll. George lifted Elizabeth and sat her on the crowded edge of one of the cars, next to a trumpet player in his garish red uniform and tasseled cap. There was another rumble and pebbles dropped from the ceiling all about them. George could hear the steel supports keen as they bent and twisted.

The train picked up speed and a woman sobbed as she ran beside George, trying to keep up. He grabbed her by the waist and swung her up, jamming her in next to Elizabeth. The tunnel was full of dust now and he could barely see the engine as it surged uphill back toward the station. Elizabeth's eyes were huge and frightened as she watched him run. She held out her arm and he grabbed her hand. But the train was gaining speed all the time and slowly pulling away from him. He looked desperately for a spot to jump up on a car but there was no room. He ran as fast as he could, his lungs burning, but slowly Elizabeth's hand was pulled from his grasp. He had to stop, to breath. Just for a minute. He heard her scream his name as he slowed, tripped on a stone, and sprawled on the tunnel floor while the train rushed past him and disappeared into the smoke.

He lay still for a moment, his face next to the gleaming track. He could still hear the train, and the shouts of others behind him who hadn't been able to get aboard. Someone tripped over him, then got up and ran on. George pushed himself to his knees, then stood and brushed himself off. He noticed that his fedora was gone and looked about for a moment, suddenly realizing how foolish it was to worry about a hat.

Then there was another rumbling tremor and he almost fell as it shook him. He began to trot after the train, then realized he couldn't hear the sound of the wheels anymore. The train

313

had stopped. But why? And what about Elizabeth? He ran faster and soon reached the rear of the train standing in the tunnel. The cars were deserted. Up ahead he saw a line of people moving slowly alongside the track.

He pushed desperately through the crowd looking for her. When he got to the engine he saw that the track ahead was blocked by a ten-foot-high mound of fallen stone, mud, and water from a cave-in high on the tunnel wall. People were hastily picking their way over the stones, falling, cursing, and crying. But in the dust and the bad light he couldn't recognize any faces.

Then there was a gleam next to him and the red of a uniform moving through the darkness. He saw the trumpet and grabbed the man by the lapels.

"Where's the woman in the red dress who was next to you on the car?"

The musician looked at him dully and shrugged. "I think I saw some old guy helping her. But you better get out of here yourself while you can. See that?" He pointed to the roof of the tunnel.

George squinted and saw a huge slab of concrete and steel hanging precariously over the engine. Water dripped off the slab and made it sway slightly. When George looked back the musician was gone.

There was another, smaller tremor and he saw people scramble quickly over the rocks, pushing others out of the way. Someone was helping Elizabeth. That's what the trumpet player had said. Should he look for her back in the tunnel or should he hope she was already at the station? A shower of small stones fell from the slab above him and clanged off the engine. He pushed ahead, stumbling over the mound of rock on the track and calling her name again and again.

Finally he fell and rolled down the other side of the hill of rock. A few hundred feet ahead he could see the bright lights of the station. Dozens of shadowy figures limped or ran toward it through the choking dust. Someone fell heavily beside him, still clutching a big, boxy camera.

"What a story this is going to make," he muttered. George helped the man up and together they ran toward the station.

314

He saw Elizabeth immediately, sitting on the platform with her back against a pillar and her eyes closed. Her dress was torn and her face was dirty.

He bent over her and took her face in his hands. Her eyes flickered open.

"And you thought flying was dangerous," she said lightly.

"Are you okay?" He stroked her cheek and inspected her arms and legs. "I thought I was going to go nuts when I couldn't find you in the tunnel."

He touched her left foot and she winced. "Easy does it, big boy. I think I've got a sprained ankle. So you really do care, after all."

"This is no time for jokes. How'd you get out with the bad foot?"

She laughed and the others lying and sitting near them looked at Elizabeth as if she were insane.

"That's the biggest joke of all. It was my father who pulled me out. He found me lying next to the third rail almost unconscious, picked me up, and carried me here. How about that?"

George sat back and leaned against the pillar next to her. "Remind me to thank him. Where is he now?"

"He went back to help the others. You should have seen him. He was torn and bleeding and crying all over me when I came to. Then he just got up and ran back down there without a word. You've got to go help him."

"Huh?"

"We can't let him get killed now, George. Not now that I've got him back."

He stood and took off his coat. "Well, I guess I owe him one."

With a little wave he hopped back onto the tracks and trotted toward the mouth of the tunnel, past dusty people still streaming out. He asked several men if they had seen Wainwright and finally someone said he was back by the engine.

George ran on, then was knocked to the ground by another, louder tremor. A huge cloud of dust burst out of the tunnel and he heard shrieking again. He pulled out a handkerchief and put it over his nose and mouth, then ran on. He found Wainwright, covered with gray dust, pulling at a hand that

315

jutted from under a huge pile of rock. The rest of the body was buried. Wainwright was crying and cursing on his knees and pulling desperately at the hand.

"Come on," he shouted. "Damn you, you were right and I was wrong. Now come out. Let's get out together."

The third rail was sparking and buzzing loudly where a piece of steel had fallen across it. As he knelt next to Wainwright, George could barely hear himself.

"You can't help him now," George shouted, pulling Wainwright away from the hand. "He's dead. Save yourself."

"No, no, I can't. Don't you see, he was right all along," Wainwright screamed, trying to claw his way back to the crushed hand.

There was an ugly grinding noise from the ceiling. George looked up quickly and saw the huge concrete slab tip toward him directly overhead, ripping away the supporting steel wirework. Then there was another rumble and more stones fell around them. A rock glanced off George's skull and for a moment the sparks from the third rail were behind his eyes. With a last desperate lunge he threw his arms around Wainwright's chest and dragged the screaming man away as the huge rock fell and smashed on the ground in front of them with a roar.

The noise seemed to stun Wainwright. He no longer fought as George got him to his feet and half carried him a hundred feet down the tunnel before they both collapsed in exhaustion.

Suddenly the tunnel was eerily silent except for the trickle of water and the groans of the injured. George lay against the cold, rough wall and listened to Wainwright's quiet sobs. The old man rocked slowly back and forth. He clutched a battered brown hat in his arms.

38

SWEATY WORKMEN gingerly brushed dirt and pebbles from a grayish form, then wrapped it in a dusty white sheet. Wearily they turned their picks and shovels back to the slowly diminishing mound of rock and rubble as a sad-faced young priest with tear channels running through the grime on his face muttered a Latin incantation over the corpse. Another man tied a white cardboard tag bearing the number 11 around the body's ankle.

Horace Wainwright gave orders and the shrouded cadaver was loaded onto the flatcar, next to two other bodies. Wainwright's face was black with the dust of the tunnel, his eyes red-rimmed and bloodshot, the pupils dilated under the dim tunnel lights. His three-piece banker's suit hung loosely on his shoulders. He had not changed his clothes, had not slept, had not even taken off his coat for three days.

"Jesus! Another one!" called a muscular policeman with his shirt sleeves rolled up, a shovel poised in his hands.

Wainwright moved forward to look. He saw the foot first. Dainty, silk-stockinged and caked with dried blood and dirt. Then the still-shapely calf.

Suddenly Wainwright flung himself onto the pile of rock. His bare hands tore away the dirt and scraped against the shards of rock and metal.

"God help me, she's still alive, she moved," he croaked, falling to his knees as he worked. Then other, stronger hands pulled him away as he struggled weakly.

"It's only the shifting stone that made her move, mister," the policeman said softly next to him, holding his arm. "She can't be alive after all this time, not under all that stone, mister."

Horrified, Wainwright watched as the picks and shovels and crowbars uncovered more of the leg. He saw the mangled knee, where it had been severed from the rest of the body by a jagged piece of steel. Methodically the workmen began to uncover the rest of the body, shreds of green dress, a lone shoe.

Wainwright leaned against the cold stone of the tunnel wall. He would have vomited but there was nothing left to throw up. He felt hollow—cold and empty as the tunnel itself. He pressed his cheek against the rough wall, closed his eyes. Through the stone he could feel the throb of the pumps down the tracks, the slur of the shovels. The tired voices of the

317

rescue workers vibrated through the rock like imprecations from the dead still under the piles of rubble. So many dead.

He took a dirty handkerchief from his coat pocket and tried to wipe his sweaty face. The tunnel had always been cool before, he thought. How had it gotten so hot? There was blood on his hands. It was sticky, brown, nearly dried. He was trying to rub the blood off on his pants leg when someone touched his shoulder.

"You're wanted back at the platform." He turned to find another policeman, this one in a clean uniform and shiny shoes.

"I can't go. I can't leave now," Wainwright said as if it should have been obvious to this boy.

"He said to bring you any way I had to," the policeman went on. "He said to tell you his name was Hines."

Wainwright looked at the policeman in bewilderment for a moment, then nodded. He pushed past and walked up the tunnel, the policeman close behind.

Every few feet he passed workers, policemen, firemen resting from their toil in his tunnel. As he passed he could feel their eyes on him. In places, water streamed down the tunnel walls and boards had been put down on the ground between the tracks. As he walked toward the brightly lit platform his shoes and feet became wet and heavy, until it was an effort to move. He suddenly realized how tired he was. Every bone in his body ached. He stumbled over something and looked down. It was shiny, lying next to one of the boards. Wainwright tried to pick it up but it was jammed half under the steel rail. Then he realized it was a trumpet, all twisted and crushed, its brass already starting to rust. He wondered where the owner was.

Wainwright heard surprising laughter as he reached the mouth of the tunnel and coughed as the fresher air filled his lungs. He blinked several times to adjust his eyes to the brighter light. The relief crews lounged on sagging cots lined barracks-style on the platform. They were talking, joking, sleeping, playing cards, all with an easiness that Wainwright resented and envied. There were a few doctors and nurses on the platform but they looked bored. There was nothing they could do for the people who came out of the tunnel wrapped in sheets.

Wainwright dragged himself heavily up the steps to the subway platform. When he faltered, the young policeman tugged at his arm to help him. He picked his way among the knots of people who became quiet as he passed. The policeman led him toward the construction foreman's office at the other end of the platform where two burly men in dark suits stood outside on either side of the door. Wainwright could see Hines inside through the glass door. Wainwright stepped between the two big men, closed the door behind him, and slumped into a chair.

"Well, my friend, you certainly look like shit," Hines told him, toying with a slide rule while sitting on a pile of blueprints.

Wainwright looked at him dully. "What do you want?"

"What do I want?" Hines barked. "That's very nice, Wainwright. You sound like I'm interrupting something here. What I want is to save your stupid arse."

Wainwright put his face in his hands and wearily ran his fingers through his hair. "I have to go back in the tunnel. There are still people out there. So why don't you leave me alone?"

"Unless you're God himself and can breathe the breath of life back into their nostrils, I don't think you're going to do those people much good," Hines said.

Wainwright stood heavily, swaying with weariness. "I don't care. I have to go back. Don't you see?" He held the back of the chair to steady himself.

Hines put down the slide rule and walked over to Wainwright. "You're not going anywhere but home. You've caused enough headlines."

"Headlines?" Wainwright looked up.

"You mean you don't know?" Hines was incredulous. "Haven't you seen the newspapers?"

"I haven't left since . . . the incident," Wainwright said, falling back into the chair.

"The incident? Oh, that's lovely, Wainwright. Very genteel. But that's not what Hearst is calling it. He's calling it murder." Hines leaned over and practically spat the words into the old man's face.

"He's made so much noise that now there's going to be a grand jury investigation of your 'incident.' There's about two hundred reporters camped out upstairs waiting for you. And this inspector we took care of for you, Vescuso—he hasn't shut his mouth for three days. Hearst's been printing every word, got the whole town stirred up. Thank God you didn't kill anybody very important, Wainwright. Like the mayor. Though I don't think Hearst would have minded if you'd buried Jimmy Walker under a few tons of stone."

Hines beckoned to the two big men outside the office. "Come to think of it, it might have been better if Walker *had* been flattened. Then Tammany would have gotten some sympathy. Now there's going to be the devil to pay to sweep this mess under the rug. And a very big rug it'll have to be."

Hines looked at the bewildered Wainwright as the two men came in. "Do you understand what I'm telling you?"

"I . . . I didn't know," Wainwright said quietly. "I can't think."

Hines took a cigar from his pocket and thoughtfully peeled away the wrapper. "Look, Tweedledee and Tweedledum here will take you up, get you through the reporters, and see you home. You stay there and keep your mouth shut, and maybe we can all stay out of prison."

"What about the tunnel?" Wainwright protested.

Hines shook his head. "The district attorney's going to padlock this whole mess later this afternoon. Evidence for the grand jury. Once the last stiff's out, nothing moves."

Wainwright's eyes widened. "But my business. Everything I have is tied up in this tunnel project. If you close it down I'll go bankrupt in a few months."

"Nothing I can do," Hines said with a shrug, motioning to the two waiting men. "You should've thought of that before you dropped the roof on everybody. Look, maybe we can work something out in a couple months. Who knows?"

Wainwright tried to protest but each of the big men took an arm and propelled him out of the construction shed toward the big shaft elevator. The iron grill of the elevator quickly slammed shut behind them. As Wainwright turned, he saw the small switch-engine puff into view from the tunnel, hauling the flatcar behind it. There were four dusty shrouds neatly laid out on the bare wood of the car. Wainwright closed his eyes and covered his ears, but he couldn't drown out the screech of the elevator as it carried him up to his fate.

1928

In this world there are only two trage-
dies. One is not getting what one wants,
and the other is getting it.

       —OSCAR WILDE
        Lady Windermere's Fan

39

ONE DAY in 1928, high above the marquee of the B. F. Keith Theater on Broadway, one of the world's foremost flagpole sitters was calmly working on breaking the record of twenty-three days and seven hours. Bored with sitting on his lofty perch—for indeed there wasn't much one could do on a flagpole—he asked that a newspaper be raised to him on a rope.

As he thumbed through the financial section, black storm clouds began to scud in from New Jersey. Soon the rumble of thunder was heard, lightning flickered on the horizon, and the wind picked up, setting the flagpole swaying. As the first gusts of rain swept the skies over Manhattan, an associate sent up a note asking if it wouldn't be wise to come down.

"I'll be all right," the daring young man wrote back. "Send up my rain slicker—and buy a hundred shares of GM."

When Horace Wainwright read that story he began to laugh. In fact, he laughed until it hurt to laugh any longer. There was an irony in the flagpole sitter's unbridled optimism that stabbed him deep, thrusting into the bowels of his despair. For in a world where anything was possible, Wainwright was a man for whom nothing seemed possible any longer.

In the summer, after the tunnel accident, friends and business associates had rallied to Wainwright's side. But as the immensity of Wainwright's perfidy became more and more obvious every day in the venomous ink of William Randolph Hearst's newspapers, Wainwright's supporters began to fall away like leaves from a dying vine.

In the fall, when the grand jury began to consider the evidence in the tunnel accident that had killed so many, the touch of official frost chilled everything about him. The flood of phone calls of support subsided to a trickle. Lawyers dropped his case. In the winter, when city inspector Giuseppe Vescuso went before the grand jury, bits of testimony somehow leaked out, damaging bits. Visitors no longer came to Wainwright's home. His wife was shunned by the wives of other prosperous men. Contracts for building projects were canceled by men who somehow were now too busy to answer Wainwright's calls.

By spring, the newspapers waited breathlessly for an indictment to be handed down. It was no longer a question of whether Wainwright would be indicted—despite Tammany's best efforts to quash the investigation—but simply what the charges would be. Manslaughter? Negligent homicide? Murder? And each day, Wainwright sat in the library and wrestled with his black anger and helplessness, desperately searching for a way out of his travails, a way to restore his fortune.

It was yet another irony, Wainwright thought, that as the rumors from the grand jury room grew worse, the relationship between father and daughter grew closer. Indeed, Elizabeth often intruded when he did not want her to, breaking into his black moods, bursting into his office and home, and disrupting what little business he had left anymore, trying to cheer him. She would not take no for an answer, bringing flowers, books, his favorite candy, dragging him to lunch and dinner and even, once, a picnic in Central Park, where he had felt incongruous and uneasy in his black suit and equally black mood and anxious to return to his gloom.

He tried, but he could remember nothing of carrying his daughter from the subway tunnel. He wondered if he had really even known who it was in his arms in the smoke and dust and panic. She owed him nothing for that, he told her sometimes, often gruffly. But when he saw her once or twice a week, pushing into his office and his angry solitude, he had to admit that she was a solace to him. And sometimes, when he half expected her and Elizabeth didn't come, he turned angry again at George McManus for taking her away from him. Once the old man came close to asking her if she was truly happy with McManus. He didn't ask, though, perhaps for fear that she would tell him what he didn't really want to hear.

But by spring, with his troubles creeping up on him like a pack of stealthy wolves, even Elizabeth couldn't distract Wainwright. There had to be a way out, he thought as he waited to hear from the grand jury. There had to be something he could do.

40

THE BATTER rapped a sharp ground ball that skipped and skidded past the pitcher on the green-brown infield grass. Mickey Koenig, running bent like an old man with a bad back, streaked to his left, scooped up the ball with deceptive ease and, in one smooth motion, shoveled it underhand to Tommy Lazzeri at second base as softly as a butterfly landing on a flower.

With the grace of a ballet star Lazzeri nudged the bag with his toe, then pivoted in midair and fired the ball to hulking Lou Gehrig at first to ice the double play by two steps. The New York Yankees trotted back toward their dugout to the cheers of thirty thousand fans.

"Beautiful. Did you see?" Izzy the Stub waved his straw hat as he subsided into his seat. "Poetry, regular poetry."

"Interesting," said Elizabeth next to him. "But what's everybody shouting about?"

"Lady, are we watching the same game? This shortstop is a prince, a champion, a god. He flies through the air like he had wings."

"Oh, Koenig's not bad as shortstops go," said Elizabeth, crowding popcorn into her mouth and putting her feet up on the seat in front of her. "But he can't hit worth beans. And his bunting is terrible."

Izzy was red-faced. He wiped his eyes with his yellow tie. "Bunting? Who is talking from bunting? Schoolboys can bunt, *yentas* can bunt. We're talking bigtime baseball here."

"Besides, Koenig's got a bad knee," she added. "He can't last more than another season or two. Huggins ought to trade him."

Izzy bent and looked past Elizabeth to George McManus, sitting on her other side. "Now she is telling the manager of

329

the New York Yankees how to run his team. Boss, how can you live with this woman?"

McManus stared at the field, preoccupied, not answering.

"Boss?" Izzy called louder over the shouts of the crowd.

George suddenly shook his head and turned to find them both looking at him. "What?"

Elizabeth frowned. "Izzy thinks I'm a know-it-all about baseball, darling. He wants to know how you can stand to have me around."

George smiled. "You might not believe this, Izzy, but when we're alone we almost never talk about baseball."

Elizabeth took his hand. "A lot of our discussions involve wrestling, however."

George glanced at his pocket watch before absently adding: "Besides, you should never argue baseball with a girl whose father once owned a couple of minor-league teams."

"Now you've given away my secret." Elizabeth poked him.

"I am shocked, lady." Izzy put his hand over his heart. "Shocked that a person of your higher breeding would try to hustle a poor Jewish boy from Delancey Street."

"I'm sorry, Izzy. Do you want your money back on the bets we've made?"

"Lady, please," Izzy protested, "I am a gambler, like your loving husband. And a gambler does not ask for his potatoes back. He gets even."

"All right," Elizabeth said seriously, then pushed popcorn into Izzy's open mouth. "I'll let you cheat me once in a while."

"Boss, I think she's conning me again," Izzy said.

But when Elizabeth turned to her husband she found him staring at the field once more, lost in his thoughts. This time, Izzy didn't interrupt him.

If she wasn't so happy she would have poked George again, demanding his attention. But she knew something was on his mind. It had started with the telephone call during breakfast. He had come back to the table preoccupied, fidgeted with his food. But he had said nothing and she hadn't pressed him. Then suddenly he decided they were going to the baseball game. But even when Izzy picked them up at the Park Central he was silent. And now, during the game, he spent most of his

330

time staring at the faraway bleachers or up at the sky, interrupting himself only to check the time, as if he had an appointment. But at Yankee Stadium, in the middle of a game?

Elizabeth raised her face to the warm sun that sat beyond the left-field fence. Whatever was troubling George, he sat beside her now and nothing else mattered. With her eyes closed she felt engulfed by the crowd's gay, frivolous warmth. Children shouted. Men argued. The umpire scraped a stiff whiskbroom across home plate only a few feet away. On the steps of the dugout the players spat and grumbled noisily. Pigeons fluttered and called in the girders behind her. No, today she would not ask her husband any questions.

The crowd began to grow noisy again and she opened her eyes. Babe Ruth marched grandly from the dugout in front of her, preceded by his cannonball gut. He swung three bats easily over his shoulder, acknowledging the applause as he passed from the shade of the grandstand into the sunshine around home plate.

George looked at his watch once more, then stood up quickly.

"I'll get you some more popcorn, toots. And a hot dog."

"But I don't want . . ." she began.

Izzy jumped up and reached into his bright red coat for his wallet. "I'll go, boss. I know a guy here sells *tchachkes*. Souvenirs," he explained to Elizabeth. "He's got a little Yankee doll that when you knock off his head is a-hundred-and-eighty-proof Irish. Then this doll knocks off *your* head."

But George was already sliding past two-dozen knees to get to the aisle. For a moment Elizabeth watched him go. She almost followed. But as he disappeared up the steps she shrugged to Izzy and they turned back to the game.

In the cool, metallic shadows under the stands, George made his way through the crowd, hurrying past the vendors' booths. Suddenly a gigantic hand fell on his shoulder and he turned to look into a prominent adam's apple surrounded by a black shirt, white tie, black suit, and heavy blue jowls. The hand steered him through a nearby paint-scarred door and down a long, dim corridor of cardboard boxes and wood crates piled high on either side. Halfway down the corridor the hand almost lifted him off his feet as it swept him to the left around another stack of boxes. Arnold Rothstein was waiting under a bare lightbulb, cleaning his fingernails with a little gold pock-etknife.

"So glad you could make it," he said.

"How's about your right-hand ape gets his paw off me," George said, twisting in the big man's grasp. "He's leaving claw prints."

Rothstein nodded and the other man backed away into the shadows.

"Where do you find them, Arnie? Do you grow them on special goon farms somewhere?" George rubbed his shoulder.

Rothstein folded the little knife. His eyes watched George. "His name's Bruno and he'd walk through a wall if I told him to, wouldn't you, Bruno?"

A grunt came from the shadows.

"Sounds like he has to take his shoes off to count to twenty."

Rothstein smiled tightly. "It's been too long, Georgie. Too long since we've had a nice, long talk. I'd almost forgotten your authentic Hell's Kitchen charm."

"So that's why you set up this meet at the ball park and then had Goliath drag me into a storeroom. Because you missed me."

"Actually, it's a business matter." Rothstein tapped the lightbulb and it swayed slightly, chasing shadows around the room. "I won't beat around the bush. I hear around town you're in the stock market, Georgie. Heavy."

McManus leaned back against a cardboard box marked "Ex-celsior Hot Dog Buns—Five Gross." "I dabble a bit. Who doesn't nowadays?"

"Your dabbling is to the tune of twelve million dollars," Rothstein said.

"Now where would I get twelve million bucks, Arnie? A poor kid from Hell's Kitchen? I run a saloon, remember?"

"Please don't play stupid with me, McManus. My informa-tion is good. We both know that. I only buy the best."

George shrugged. "So?"

"So I'm going to do you a favor and let you in on the ground floor of a very good thing. The U.S. Radio Corporation."

"Never heard of it."

Rothstein tapped his forehead. "That's because right now it only exists up here. It's a new company I'm forming. Strictly legit. I've already signed up a couple of investors."

"Then why do you need me? I'm missing the ball game."

Rothstein stopped the bulb in midswing. "This is very secret, Georgie. You have to understand that. That's why I wanted to meet here like this. If people saw us together, they might talk before I want them to talk."

George watched him noncommittally. "I'm all ears."

"Much as it grieves me to admit it, Georgie, I have found that some people simply do not trust me. Somehow I have gotten a . . . reputation, you might say, as a sharp operator. This has put somewhat of a crimp in my plans for the U.S. Radio Corporation. That's why I need you as a partner."

McManus toyed with the tape holding down the top of the hot dog carton. "Let me guess, Arnie. You know that a lot of wealthy businessmen gamble at the Paradise Rehearsal Club. They know I'm in the money. And if they see that I'm going in on your investment scheme . . ."

"Not a scheme," Rothstein interrupted. "Legit, strictly kosher. We sell stock, issue certificates, have meetings. Capitalism in all its glory."

George nodded. "All right, then if certain businessmen see that I'm involved in your enterprise, they will be more willing to invest. Is that it?"

Rothstein stroked his soft, gray gloves. "I figure your participation will be especially convincing to our more solid citizens, since it's common knowledge that you and I have had our differences in the past. You see, if *you're* not afraid to come in with me . . . well, you get the picture."

George worried more tape off the carton. "Tell me, just what is it that the U.S. Radio Corporation is going to do? Make radios?"

Rothstein chuckled. "That's the beauty of it, Georgie. The company can do anything I want it to do. I mean, anything *we* want it to do. Radio is the magic word nowadays. It draws money like honey draws flies."

"Uh huh. So let me make another wild guess, Arnie. The U.S. Radio Corporation won't make radios, right?"

Rothstein nodded.

333

"And it won't sell radios, either."

Rothstein nodded again, smiling.

"In fact, about all it has to do with radio is that you might listen to one once in a while, right?"

"You take my breath away, Georgie."

"So what do you tell investors when they start asking where the profits are?"

Rothstein slapped the gloves into one palm. "Why, Georgie, *we* tell them that business is bad and we had to declare bankruptcy. Then you and I split the proceeds—a couple million apiece at least. What could be more legit than that? Companies go broke every day."

George looked at him in the dim light. "Very slick. And who are the suckers who have their money in this already?"

"You don't need to know that, Georgie. Not until we're partners. But I'll tell you this, one of them is your father-in-law." Rothstein looked for a response.

"Wainwright?" George said in surprise. "He doesn't have any money. Since the tunnel accident his business has fallen off to nothing."

"I didn't ask where he got it, Georgie. I just took it. But I hear he sold his house on Long Island and mortgaged the place on Fifth Avenue. Touching how he believes in me, isn't it?"

For a moment both men watched each other in silence, measuring each other. George heard Bruno breathing heavily in a corner, like a bull after the tenth pass at the matador.

"And if I say no to this golden opportunity?"

Rothstein shook his head. "Then, my friend, you'll have to negotiate with Bruno for a while. I need you on this one, Georgie. It's big money. Kindly don't screw it up."

McManus slowly peeled away the last of the tape on the box. He was thinking of Wainwright, and how far a man will fall if he is desperate. Maybe too far ever to crawl back out of the mire. Finally he shook his head.

"Sorry, Arnie. But I can't do it. Maybe, if it was people I didn't know. But you're asking me to con my wife's father. Even I have *some* principles. And then there's the problem of you."

334

"Me?"

George nodded. "You're a lying, conniving son of a bitch and we both know you're never going to change. You'd just try to con me, too, in the end."

There was another silence, then Rothstein began to pull on his gloves.

"What a shame we can't do business," Rothstein said with a sigh of genuine regret. "We have so much in common. Bruno?"

With a squeak of shoe leather the giant stalked out of his corner and made straight for McManus. When he was five feet away George suddenly swept up the box of hot dog buns he had opened and threw it in Bruno's direction. The big man stepped back for a moment in surprise, swiping the buns out of his face, then shuffled forward again. Suddenly he stepped on a bun and his feet flew out from under him. Bruno sat heavily on the floor, stunned. When he tried to rise, George picked up another box and crashed it over his head. Bruno lay peacefully on the concrete, the box over his face.

"Looks like negotiations are at a standoff," George said. Rothstein looked back at him blankly, then down at Bruno.

"You were wrong about Bruno," Rothstein said. "He can't even count to twenty."

George skirted the fallen man and began to walk away when Rothstein grabbed his arm, suddenly angry. "I'm not going to forget this one, Georgie," he warned in a controlled voice.

"See that you don't, Arnie," George said, pushing him away. "See that you don't."

Before Rothstein could say anything else, George went quickly up the long corridor of boxes to the door. On the other side, back in the crowds and the light, he trotted under the grandstand until he found the concrete-and-wire runway leading to the field.

"He should bunt," Elizabeth was arguing over the noise as George slid into the seat next to her.

Izzy groaned. "You want Lou Gehrig to bunt? If the man can hit the ball two miles, why should he bunt?"

"The other team won't be expecting it, Izzy—not with slow

335

runners like Grabowski on third and Coombs on first and two out. They'll expect Gehrig to hit away. Look where the infield is!" Elizabeth said vehemently.

Izzy shook his head. "Oh, no. No, not this time. I already lost two thousand to you on this game. But this time you are wrong, missus. Double or nothing says Mr. Lou Gehrig will not bunt."

"You're on." Elizabeth solemnly shook Izzy's hand. "But don't say I didn't warn you."

She turned to George. "You're going to have to give poor Izzy a raise, darling. So he can afford to gamble with me. I thought you were bringing a hot dog?"

When he didn't answer she looked at his face. "What's wrong?" she said quickly.

George watched Gehrig stride out to the batter's box as the crowd roared. "Have you seen your father in the last couple of weeks, Elizabeth?"

"Elizabeth? You called me Elizabeth. You don't do that unless something serious is happening."

"Have you seen him?" he asked again.

"Not for almost two weeks. You know that. I was supposed to go downtown last week, but we went to Philadelphia for the fights. And then we flew to Ohio to look at that racehorse you wanted to buy me, remember?"

On the first pitch Gehrig watched the ball sail past his knees while the runners on first and third danced near the bases. The crowd groaned.

"I think you'd better drop in on him," George said over the noise, leaning toward Elizabeth. "Your father's in some new kind of trouble."

"What kind of trouble?" she demanded, suddenly worried.

Gehrig squared around to bunt as the next pitch sailed to the plate.

"Ask your father," George said.

"Oy vay," Izzy moaned. Gehrig gently dragged the ball down the first-base line as the man on third thundered safely into the plate in a cloud of dust.

But Elizabeth wasn't watching. She was still looking at George, squeezing his hand.

41

UNDERNEATH the big picture of Calvin Coolidge the paint
had started to peel. There was a slight tear in the arm of the
overstuffed leather couch. The two young typists were missing from their posts in the reception room, the typewriters
covered, the desks bare. Only the stern-faced, gray-haired
bookkeeper Elizabeth had come to know as Miss Pruitt was
visible, scribbling steadily in a fat ledger, seemingly oblivious
to the emptiness around her or to Elizabeth's approach.

Elizabeth stopped at the wooden railing and put down the
wicker basket she was carrying. She cleared her throat but
Miss Pruitt pointedly ignored her and kept writing, her pince-
nez balanced precariously on the end of her nose. Elizabeth
noticed that all the entries Miss Pruitt made were in red
ink.

"Is my father in?"

The other woman nodded and, without looking up, pressed
a button on the brown console on her desk. Instead of its usual
"blaaat" the buzzer clicked anemically. Miss Pruitt pushed
the buzzer twice more but it still only chirped back at her like
a dying cricket. She shrugged and finally looked up at Elizabeth.

"It's broken again," she explained hopelessly. "Just go in."

Elizabeth picked up the basket and pushed through the
swinging gate. Somewhere down the long corridor to the
other offices someone pecked away slowly on a lone type-
writer. She heard voices, too, but they were subdued and
hushed like mourners whispering over a deathbed. Elizabeth
knocked on her father's door. Heavy footsteps rushed toward
her. The door flew open.

"Goddammit, it's about . . . oh, it's you." Horace Wainwright's face registered surprise and disappointment. He
looked beyond her into the front office.

"Is that any way to greet your own flesh and blood?" She
tried to make her voice light.

Elizabeth hugged him but he stood as stiff as if he'd been

starched. There were deep purple pouches under his eyes. A two-day growth of iron-gray stubble covered his chin. Tiny red lines were etched in the whites of his eyes like highways on a road map. Elizabeth leaned closer to kiss him on the cheek but he darted nervously past her into the reception room. She heard him mutter something unintelligible to Miss Pruitt, then came the sound, she thought, of a drawer being angrily slammed shut.

"You should have called first, Elizabeth," Wainwright said brusquely when he came back. "I'm expecting someone any minute. Someone important."

To punctuate the message he pulled his gold watch out of his vest pocket and opened it. As was his habit lately, he tapped the watch twice with his index finger to make sure it was still running. He had gotten thinner, too, Elizabeth thought. Even in the two weeks since she'd seen him last. The skin of his once-ample jowls lay slack and in folds like a punctured bagpipe. Elizabeth swung her basket onto his desk, nearly knocking over an open bottle of scotch.

"I thought we'd have a picnic," she said as gaily as she could manage. "Mother said you'd be working late. And I knew—"

"A picnic!" he nearly shouted. "I can't go on a picnic. I told you. . . ."

"Look at you." Elizabeth shook her head. "You're practically foaming at the mouth, Father. Come on, it'll do you good to get out. Cancel the appointment."

Elizabeth grabbed his coat and muffler from the hat rack in the corner of his office. She ignored his mood.

"I haven't got time, Elizabeth. I tell you, I'm—"

"Then make time. Now take your coat and don't try to fight me. I'm your daughter, remember? And every bit as stubborn as you are."

She pushed the worn coat into his hands but he only looked down at it, not moving. Finally she took it from him, held it up, and began to push his right arm into the right sleeve.

"Okay, if you want to be treated like a child, I'll treat you like a child, Horace Wainwright."

But when she looked up, instead of the anger she had expected the old man's face had softened, his eyes had turned moist. Suddenly he looked twenty years older and infinitely tired.

She finished pulling the coat over his other arm, then wrapped the scarf around his neck. He didn't resist but only smiled at her with a sort of sad admiration.

"Elizabeth, I know you're worried about me. I know what you're trying to do," he said. "But I can't go with you now. It's important I stay."

Suddenly embarrassed, Elizabeth slowly slipped the scarf off him, then took hold of the lapels of his coat. "I'm sorry, Father. But sometimes you make me feel so useless. I want to help you somehow."

"That makes you about the only one," he said with a bitter little laugh.

"Look, at least eat a sandwich for me, Father. It'll make *me* feel better. You look like you're starving to death." She patted his stomach and felt only folds of cloth. "You're beginning to look like a refugee from the Black Hole of Calcutta."

She went to the basket on the desk and pulled out a sandwich wrapped in wax paper. "How about cheese?"

He shrugged and she led him to the sofa against the far wall. She unfolded the noisy paper and Wainwright bit into the sandwich. But he couldn't seem to swallow. He chewed and chewed and chewed. Elizabeth looked over his shoulder at a portrait that hung between two windows. A portrait of her father that had been painted only three years earlier. The eyes were clear, sure, determined, the shoulders thrust back, the mouth slightly sneering, like a general about to do battle with an outnumbered and outclassed foe. Now his shoulders were slouched, she saw, his back bent like a dying tree. He finally swallowed the mouthful but seemed almost spent by the effort. She touched his hand. It was cold and clammy.

"What's wrong, Father? You look much worse, you're much more nervous than you were the last time I saw you. Why?"

He bit into the sandwich again. Outside the bells of the Dutch Reformed Church on the park began to chime an old hymn.

"So now you want to eat, huh?" Elizabeth took one arm and shook him in exasperation. "Tell me! Are you afraid you'll be indicted?"

He glanced at her sharply, then looked away. "This isn't a bad sandwich, you know."

She snatched the bread out of his hand. "Tell me what's wrong, now!"

"I don't want to involve you, Elizabeth. Stay away from me. As far away as you can. I don't want any of this to taint you."

She stared at him, wondering how to get through. "Is it money? Because I can help you with money, Father."

Wainwright smiled. "Money? Yes, I suppose that's what it always comes down to. Ask your husband, Elizabeth. He's a gambler. He knows about money and betting everything on one chance."

She struggled to understand what he was saying in his cryptic way. What did George have to do with this? "Look, Father. At least tell me this," she finally said. "Who's coming here today that has you so nervous?"

Suddenly Wainwright jerked upright, startled. She had reminded him. He pulled out his pocket watch again, then turned businesslike once more.

"I want you to do me a big favor now, Elizabeth. I want you to go, without any more questions," he implored her.

She stood up. "All right, if that's the way you want it, Father. But take this." She snapped open her purse and pulled out a white business envelope, one corner bent and dogeared. She pressed it into his hand.

"There's fifty thousand dollars there. It's George's emergency money. It's all I had in the apartment. But I'll get you more."

He pushed the envelope back at her. "I won't take his money."

"It's my money, too. And don't worry about paying it back." She stuffed the envelope in his breast pocket as someone knocked on the door. Beads of sweat suddenly broke out on Wainwright's forehead like condensation on a window pane. Elizabeth noticed that his hands began trembling.

"I'll go now," Elizabeth said. "But I warn you, I'm coming back tomorrow. And then you're going to tell me everything."

Wainwright silently walked her to the door, his mind obviously elsewhere. She kissed him quickly but he ignored her and pulled the door open. She was startled to find someone standing right in front of her, only inches away. He was a thin, well-dressed man with deep, black eyes that seemed to watch her in derisive amusement as if he knew her. In front of his chest he held a pair of gray kid gloves in one hand. The man stepped past her and Wainwright quickly urged her out, closing the door before she could even say good-bye. The last thing she saw was the stranger's eyes, still on her.

Elizabeth stared at the closed door for a moment. She had seen the visitor before. She knew the thin face, those cold eyes. But where? She turned and pushed through the swinging gate, walking past Miss Pruitt.

"No, no I won't," she heard a muffled voice cry from her father's office. "It's too high. You're asking too much!" The voice gradually trailed away to nothing.

Elizabeth could only hear the scratching of Miss Pruitt's pen as she slowly let herself, frowning, out the door to the cool corridor.

42

"IT'S CRAZY," Otto Berman complained.

He held a small metal cashbox on his lap with his fingertips, as if it were hot to the touch. Then he got up, flipped open the top of the box, and put it on the desk in front of George McManus.

George picked out one bundle of papers wrapped in a blue rubber band and fanned through it. "Okay, how much?"

"As of Monday," Otto said, searching through a sheaf of papers, "$894,003. It's crazy to have that much paper outstanding."

Izzy the Stub stirred on the sofa, where he was stretched out, and pushed his straw hat off his face.

"So what *goniff* stuck you with the three dollars?"

"It's not the three dollars that bothers me," Otto went on, blinking behind his thick glasses. "That money could be buying you more stock if you had it in hand instead of in IOUs. Mr. McManus, as your business adviser, I have to warn you that there are a couple of people who owe you almost a hundred thousand dollars apiece, and they're still out in the casino gambling on credit almost every night." Otto dived back into his papers. "Wait, I'll give you their names."

George shook his head and wearily tossed the bundle of IOUs back in the box. "I keep telling you, Otto, this isn't a bank. I deal in human frailty. Greed, excitement, the danger of taking a risk. Sometimes people get carried away and lose more than they can afford, God bless 'em. But most of them pay up eventually."

Otto blinked some more as he rearranged his papers. "All right, Mr. McManus. If that's the way you want it. All right," he said, unconvinced.

"Now, the next item on the agenda is the new liquor shipment coming in next week on two of Mr. Dwyer's boats. The connection at the Coast Guard has been making noises for more money again. This is a big delivery. I think he's probably worth an extra thousand this month. But not a penny more! There's been a glut of cheap liquor on the market for weeks and prices are dropping, cutting into profit margins."

Otto looked up. "Am I going too fast, Mr. McManus?"

George glanced at him. "No, Otto. But look, I trust you. You take care of the Coast Guard. I know you'll squeeze every penny."

Otto scribbled notes to himself for a moment. "Now, I'd like to talk about your investments next, Mr. McManus. I think you're a little heavy on Canadian copper stock—"

"Enough," George broke in, rubbing his temples. "Go count money for a while, Otto. We'll talk about the stock market later."

Berman put away his papers. "I understand, Mr. McManus. I'll come back later tonight. But I still wish you'd look at those IOUs. I have to write Mr. Dwyer a report and I'd like to clear up some of the debts."

"I promise. I promise," George said with a wave of his hand. He watched Otto leave the office briskly, soft piano music and harsher voices from the casino trickling through the door until he closed it behind him.

George got up from behind the desk and paced across the office, his hands in his pockets. He stopped in front of a long legal document hung on the wall in a gilt frame. For the thousandth time George read the court order that kept the police out of the Paradise Rehearsal Club. The language soothed him. It was very precise, very official. It was still a unique feeling for him, having the law on his side.

George paced across the office again, then back to the framed paper. He was restless, bothered, wary. Something chewed at the edges of his mind.

"Tell me something, Izzy," he said, still facing the wall. "When you're shooting craps or playing cards, do you ever know that the next card is going to go cold on you, or the dice are going to stop rolling your way? It's like a tingling in your fingertips?"

Izzy shrugged, looked at McManus's back. "I wish I did, boss. I'd be a wealthy man today."

"Well, I get that feeling once in a long while. It's kind of a sixth sense, Izzy. A warning that no one else can hear. Maybe that's what separates gamblers from people who just play cards."

"So?" Izzy asked.

George turned and came back to the desk, sitting on the edge. "I got that feeling this afternoon, Izzy. With Rothstein. And I have it now. It's like . . . like the sky is about to fall."

"What are you talking about, boss?" Izzy pooh-poohed. "You're doing terrific. The marks in the casino are strangling themselves to get to the tables. You've got millions in the stock market—the J. P. Morgan of Broadway, they're calling you on the street corners. You've got a knockout of a wife who'd fight lions for you. The safe's ready to blow up, you and Big Bill Dwyer got so much cash in it. And you think the sky is falling? It should only fall on me like that."

George picked up the box of IOUs and fiddled with it, opening and closing the lid idly. Finally he shook his head. "I just can't shake the feeling, Izzy. I keep thinking things are going too well, maybe it's time to cash in."

"It's just Rothstein." Izzy stood up and stretched. "He gets on your skin."

"Under my skin," George corrected.

Izzy shrugged. "You're the boss. So, what are you going to do?"

343

"For starters, I'm going to look both ways when I cross the street. Rothstein wasn't happy this afternoon. And when Arnold Rothstein isn't happy, a lot of other people get unhappy."

Izzy took off his straw hat and examined it. "Pardon my nose, boss, but I think you should tell your frau about Rothstein."

George shook his head. "No. No, it's bad enough I had to tell her her father's in more hot water. I don't want her involved with Rothstein in any way. And don't you say anything either, got it? Not a word. Ever." George looked at him sharply.

Izzy put a hurt expression on his face. "Boss, you know me. My lips are sealed."

There was a quick knock at the door and one of the redcoated waiters looked in. "Some old geezer wants to see you, Mr. McManus. In private. He looks like death's brother-in-law."

"Has he got a name?"

"Wainwright," the waiter replied.

George and Izzy looked at each other.

"Give me two minutes, then send him in, Tony."

"So what?" Izzy said quickly when the waiter was gone. "Big deal. Her father is here. Maybe he wants poker lessons."

George looked at him skeptically. "Get lost, Izzy. But don't go far. I may need you."

When Izzy left, George went behind his desk and sat down. He pulled the metal cashbox toward him, hardly conscious of what he was doing. He wondered why the old man would come to the club. Yet, at the same time, he guessed the answer. The feeling of foreboding he'd had all day swept over him again. His fingers tingled again and he began to sweat.

Wainwright didn't knock. He came in quickly and banged the door behind him, as if something were chasing him. He stood with his back to the door and the two men stared at each other, George shocked by the other man's appearance. He had expected Wainwright to look bad. Elizabeth had told him as much. But the man who stood before him was a bad copy of the Horace Wainwright he had last seen in the smoke and confusion of the tunnel. He seemed half the size, shrunken, wasted away. That Wainwright had been desperately full of life. This man was dead but refused to acknowledge it, George thought. Death was in the sunken cheeks, the tired half smile, the cast of the shoulders, the ugly pallor of the skin.

Wainwright finally went to the sofa and sat down, his bones rattling. In the strong light from the large chandelier over George's desk Wainwright seemed to shrink away even more. He hardly dented the cushion, George noticed.

Wainwright broke the silence first. "You could offer me a drink, McManus."

George took a bottle and two glasses from a desk drawer. He pulled the cork and poured two fingers of whiskey into each glass, keeping his eyes on Wainwright most of the time. He watched the old man drink it greedily, spilling a drop on his dark vest, holding the glass with both hands. Wainwright shivered with temporary relief and strength, smacking his lips.

"That's better," he said. "Can't talk business without a little something to grease the way." He tried to sound light.

"I didn't know we had any business to talk about." George refilled Wainwright's glass and handed it back to him.

The old man looked up at him warily. "You're not going to make this easy, are you? Still holding a grudge?"

"A grudge? We've never been the best of friends, Wainwright. You're my wife's father, so I'll listen to what you have to say, I guess I owe you that. But don't expect much else from me."

Wainwright swallowed the second glass of whiskey and a spot of color came into his cheeks, making him look almost clownish and grotesque. He coughed, ran his sleeve over his mouth.

"All right, McManus. No beating around the bush, then. I need money. A lot of it. And I'm willing to make you a partner in my company in return."

George almost laughed, but something in Wainwright's expression stopped him. "A partner in your company? Why don't you offer me half of the Brooklyn Bridge, or shares in the *Titanic*? You don't have a company. You have an office with your name on the door and a few desks."

345

Wainwright sagged on the sofa. "Has Elizabeth been telling you . . . ?"

"She didn't have to, Wainwright. It's common knowledge. I read the papers. And I have a few friends at Tammany. Nothing has moved at your tunnel project for almost a year. You're broke."

"I'm working things out, though," Wainwright said defensively. "I've been in trouble before. I've always survived." His voice trailed away.

George walked away from Wainwright, then turned around. "If you need money, why don't you go to your banker friends?"

"What makes you think I haven't? But with this grand jury business . . ." Wainwright waved his hands in a gesture of helplessness. "They all tell me they have other people to answer to. I'm a bad risk."

"Why should I help you then?" George demanded. "Why come to me?"

Wainwright stared at his scuffed shoes before speaking. When he looked up, George saw a defeated old man clinging to one last thread of hope.

"I'm close, McManus. I've never been so frightened in my life, but I think I'm close to saving my business. And myself. For months after the tunnel it was touch and go. Everything I touched turned to ashes, everyone turned away from me, except Elizabeth. I felt like a leper. People shunned me, my wife, in the streets. Do you know how it feels when people you've known all your life won't look you in the eye when you pass on the sidewalk?"

George said nothing. He went back behind his desk.

"It was the scandal, you see," Wainwright went on. "The tunnel thing, the bad business, they were secondary. Everyone has accidents and hard times. But the scandal wouldn't go away. The damn grand jury, the rumors of indictment. For a while I regretted I wasn't killed in the tunnel myself, instead of having this judgment hanging over my head like a sword every minute of the day and night."

Wainwright sat on the edge of the sofa, suddenly animated. "But now, now I have a chance again. A business proposition that can save me. There are millions in it, McManus. Mil-

346

lions. And he swears he can get the indictment killed, to boot."

"He? Who's he?" George wanted to know.

"I can't tell you that. But he's big, very big. He's very well connected at City Hall. Maybe better than you. And he says he can get me off." Wainwright grew more excited as he spoke. "But I need more money, McManus. I've given him everything I have. I sold one of the houses, even paintings and furniture. But I'm still short, McManus. That's why I've come to you." Wainwright was puffing as he finished.

"How much?" George said.

"Five hundred thousand. Not much for a life, is it? Make it a loan, if you don't want part of my business. I'll pay interest, of course. Better than the bank, if that's what you want. But I have to have the money tonight."

George thought for a moment. "You say he can get the indictment killed, Wainwright? But how? You're infamous. You killed too many people in that tunnel. Your name hasn't been out of the papers for a year. I made a few calls to Tammany about you—Elizabeth asked me to. The mayor himself said there was nothing that could be done, that you were certain to go to prison. And now you tell me you've got a savior?"

For a moment Wainwright paled, then plunged on. "Maybe I shouldn't tell you this, McManus, but this man, my associate, he knows things about the mayor and Tammany. Bad things. He's told me some of them, and they're big, much bigger than my dinky little campaign contribution. Tammany and City Hall, they've been stealing a fortune from the taxpayers. The things he knows would send the whole downtown gang to jail if they came out."

George shook his head. "Quite a business associate you've dug up. It sounds like his main business is blackmail."

"I'd make a deal with the devil," Wainwright said, suddenly quiet, "with the very devil himself if he could save me now. Will you help me, McManus? Tonight?"

George looked at his hands. The tingle that he had told Izzy about was coursing through him like a fire alarm. Every instinct warned him away from Wainwright. But instead, he stood and went to the big, black-steel safe in the corner. He knelt and spun the dial.

"There's just one more thing," Wainwright said warily behind him. "Besides the money, I mean. He—my business associate—wants you in on this new company he's forming. He was very explicit about that, McManus. He said I had to involve you."

The safe door was halfway open when McManus understood what Wainwright was saying. He swung it closed with a vicious clanging noise that set the tumblers spinning.

"Rothstein," George said in sudden anger. "You're in with Arnold Rothstein."

"But . . . how did you know?" Wainwright stammered out. "I never . . ."

"Never mind how I know," George nearly shouted. "You old fool, don't you realize he's the biggest swindler in town? He's taken you for everything you had, and wants to take me, too—through you."

"But he says . . ." Wainwright went on. "He said . . ."

"Rothstein's company is a phony, Wainwright. And so is his influence downtown. He's just using you to get at me. He doesn't give a rat's ass about saving your business or keeping you out of prison. All he wants is your money. And you gave it to him on a silver platter. But you're not giving him mine, Wainwright."

The old man struggled off the sofa, his lips moving but only unintelligible sounds coming out. As George watched, Wainwright seemed to deflate, collapse inward. His face went from red to white to gray then back to red. The shock of McManus's words left him groggy, dizzy. Slowly he staggered to the door, slumped against it with his shoulder, then let himself out of the office without a look back.

McManus went back to the desk and sat in his high-backed leather chair. His eyes were red with anger but he willed himself to be calm and steady. He sat forward and carefully opened the box of IOUs, taking out one bundle of papers. Then his fingers shook and he dropped the packet.

"Damn!" he burst out, sweeping the tin box and everything else off the desk. The box crashed against the opposite wall. "Damn."

43

A DRINK. He had to have a stiff drink. Something to bolster him, to help him think. But suddenly he felt so weary he wasn't sure he could make it to the bar across the crowded, spinning room. He ran heavily into someone but the man only laughed, slapped his back, propelled him to a long table around which many people stood.

The wood of the table felt hot and wet under his fingers. A woman's smooth, naked arm pressed against his side. She shrieked at something and shook her head and her long red hair slapped him across the face. He shut his eyes involuntarily. The tunnel again. The damp dark with pinpoints of blazing light, the rails curving away from him. Then there was smoke and noise and his eyes flew open. But it was only the noise of gaiety and the smoke of cigarettes.

What was happening to him? He felt so wan, so tired, as if his heart were missing on every other beat. Yet at the same time he could feel it racing deep in his chest, throbbing with the fear he felt. He knew he was sweating profusely. He could feel the little rivulets coursing down his back and under his arms. He rubbed his forehead and his fingers came away wet.

There were people all about him, but he could barely hear them. Their voices drifted to him like sunlight through seawater—bent, wavering, indistinct. He tried to catalog how he felt, wondering if he wasn't having a nervous breakdown or a stroke. Or even dying.

"Did you come to play or watch, sweetie? How about some fun?" The words floated to him on shallow laughter, slowly filtering to his mind.

He turned his head to find red hair, mischievous blue eyes, red lips, sharp little animal teeth.

"Got any money, honey?" Her laughter came through to him again. "That's a rhyme. Money, honey. Get it?"

Money. Yes, he had money. Not his own—he had nothing. He was broke, destitute. But he could feel the envelope, a thick lump in his right pocket, brushing his hand. It was Elizabeth's money, not his. Not for this pretty girl beside him. He

349

tried to move away but the girl held his arm, as much to keep him from stumbling or falling as leaving. She looked into his face.

"You look like you need a stiff one, lover. You don't look real well. Coming down with something?"

She put a glass before him but he only stared at it dumbly. What did she want from him? It wasn't his money. Didn't she understand? But he didn't resist when the girl took his hands and put them around the glass and made him lift it to his lips. He swallowed the contents in a gulp, not even knowing what he was drinking. The liquor burned, made him cough. But it was better. Now he could think. The liquor seemed to bolster him, jolt his brain, make him more alert.

"There. You look twenty years younger, honey. Now let's play, hmm? And Marie will be right here beside you."

As she spoke, he became aware that they were standing at the roulette table. He looked down at the green expanse cluttered with cash. He heard the clatter of the metal ball dancing around the wheel, the call of the croupier. He glanced at the girl, the others jammed around the table. Then his eyes came back to the money as the stickman deftly scooped it in and stacked it in neat piles. The money.

He felt his pulse quicken again, his breath came in short, shallow gasps. Why not use the money, he thought feverishly, amazed at his sudden lucidity. Take the fifty thousand and win what he needed. It was Elizabeth's money—but McManus's, too. Then he'd take his winnings to Rothstein, throw it in the Jew's face. Even if he couldn't deliver McManus, Rothstein couldn't ignore a small fortune. He would fix things at City Hall. Rothstein was as greedy as the rest of them. He'd keep him out of jail.

But what if he lost? He clutched at the edge of the table, pushing the idea away quickly, burying it. He had to win so he would win. There was no room for failure or doubt. That was for lesser men.

He was gratified that his fingers only trembled slightly as he slipped the envelope from his pocket. The girl took it from him, opened the flap. Her eyes widened. He felt her lips just brush his cheek as she pulled out several hundred-dollar bills.

"Honey, Marie Flynn is going to take care of you. You are

definitely no sucker. Let's see, you don't look like a man who bets numbers. So what'll it be, red or black?"

He swayed a bit as the alcohol began to wear off, leaving him even weaker. He raised a hand and pointed. The girl flipped the bills onto the black marker so quickly he couldn't follow her motion.

Maybe he'd take the money to Walker himself, he thought with sudden satisfaction. Dump the mound of cash on his desk like the last time and watch the mayor's snake eyes bug out. A half million, more if need be. Walker would clear him. Walker couldn't say no to that much. He'd stay at the table until he won enough for Walker and Rothstein both. He'd wear his gray suit to City Hall, he decided, as the woman beside him raked in his winnings. The gray suit was imposing. It made him look larger, more dignified. And Walker would look at him with new respect. They all would.

The girl took more money from the envelope but he didn't resist. It was as if he were hypnotized by her actions. She laughed something into his ear but he only nodded, not able to hear over the roaring noise in his head now. For a moment he wondered why the girl took more money from the envelope if they were winning. But then he had to hold his head, drink deeply to chase the roaring away, and he let the girl do as she would.

She was very pleased, he saw, as she pushed his winnings and the extra money onto a red space. He watched her openly put a single folded bill between her breasts and make it disappear into her gown. And then she kissed his cheek again. He could feel the wet spot. He watched the dark line where her breasts were squeezed together and suddenly thought how beautiful she was. Like Elizabeth. She had breasts like his daughter. Elizabeth helped him. She was a good child.

Across the room, on the far side of the table, he saw George McManus making his way through the crowd toward the bar. He shrank away, not wanting to be seen, hiding behind a broad shoulder while his heart thumped. McManus would stop him, keep him from winning. But McManus disappeared without looking his way. He touched his face and now was surprised to find it cold when he knew he was awash with sweat under his coat.

351

The girl was kissing his cheek again, her hands full of bills. She was flushed, pretty, alive. It surprised him that he felt shame and even guilt watching the girl. He hadn't noticed women for so long. But now the fine sheen of her perspiration suddenly tantalized him. A corner of one of the bills she had poked into her gown peeked out coyly as she bent toward him, over the table, and he felt a jolt of joy that he could not understand. It was as if he were a boy again, free, the sap of youth rising in him, worlds to explore, millions to be made. Yet at the same time he knew he was old, tired, crumbling from within. How was this possible?

"You sure are lucky with me, honey," she was whispering to him. He looked from her breasts to her face as she raked in more bills.

She hardly bothered to ask him what to bet now, but just put down the money herself. Sometimes she would rest her hand on his arm or brush his hip with hers in an easy intimacy and he would flush and feel the long-forgotten ache of sexuality. He knew what he felt was really not due to this girl. But her feel, her smell, her closeness kept forcing memories into his mind. Once she stroked the back of his neck with her fingers, as Flora had done when they were courting and first married, and the touch brought sudden tears into his eyes.

He quickly shook them away. The money. Concentrate on the money. That was the important thing.

Six months, a year maybe, he told himself, and he'd be digging his tunnel again. As soon as everyone had forgotten. The people, the city needed the tunnel. Progress. It would tie the sprawling boroughs together, the papers had said. And the money—the money he was winning from McManus—would finance other jobs. There was always something to build, a friendship somewhere to cash in on. The bankers would see that his business was booming. They would come running, buying him lunches. And he'd buy stock, get back the house on Long Island. Yes, then he'd throw a big party, bigger than the last one. Elizabeth would plan it for him. Flowers everywhere. The best people. Champagne. And everything would be as it once was.

It had to be.

But now the girl was leaning far across the table, carefully

352

pushing two piles of bills onto a black square. He watched her hips swell under the tight gown, studied the muscles of her bare back and shoulders. He gulped some more liquor from the glasses that constantly appeared in front of him, then reached out like a curious child and put a hand on her lower back, feeling the silky material of the dress. His heart boomed in his ears as he ran his hand slowly down, down over the smoothness of her hip and the curve of her rump. Then she was laughing at him, staring into his eyes as she gently took his hand off. She made a joke and the others crowded around began laughing.

His face burning with his foolishness, he picked up yet another glass and drank. He swayed, grabbed the edge of the table with one hand, looked up into the sparkling cut-glass chandelier. The lights refracted a million times as the chandelier swayed gently. The little droplets of glass revolved slowly as he blinked to keep them in focus. Galaxies of light were born, then gave way to new clouds of stars as he watched for a long time. They reminded him of something. They were like . . .

The girl was laughing again. "Sorry, lover, we lost that one," she said as she ran one hand across his cheek while the other hand drew more bills from the shrinking envelope. "But only a sucker quits when he's got money in his poke. Right, honey?"

He didn't stop her—couldn't stop her. He saw the bills leave him and began to tremble. Someone had opened a vein, was draining the blood out of him. But it wasn't red blood, it was red hair, and the girl was laughing again. She slid more bills from the shrinking envelope, putting one hand on his shoulder until she felt him quiver. She stopped a passing waiter and put another drink into his hands.

His head throbbed, his fingers ached as he put the glass to his lips. But when he put his head back to drink, the chandelier attacked his eyes like stark sunlight on ice. He forgot the drink, watching the interplay of light off the cut glass. How beautiful. How very beautiful.

Then something—the croupier's stick—touched a string of glass beads on the chandelier and the light turned glaring, garish, horrible. The lights burst in his face, flashing on and off like exploding suns. He remembered. Flashbulbs exploded before him. A crush of uniforms, sobbing men and women. Over and over the lights showed him bloody wounds, torn faces, grief, fear. People pulled at him, shouted, cursed. The lights followed, chased him as someone led him away. Elizabeth was holding him, shielding him. Yet still the lights tormented him, the screams would not go away even as he somehow rose over them. Frightened, he closed his eyes, put his hands over his ears.

He didn't hear the girl's disappointed laugh as she lost again. He didn't see her look into the envelope, push the last bill between her breasts, and drop the empty envelope onto the floor.

"What a shame, honey. And we were doing so good." The girl breathed into his face. "But it's only money, right, love?"

The money. Slowly, painfully he realized what she was saying. The money was gone. He looked dumbly around the table but the others had already lost their interest, were drifting away. There was a sudden, stabbing pain in his stomach. The roaring returned in his ears. His legs felt weak.

"You wouldn't happen to have any more fat little envelopes on you, would you, lover?" The sharp little teeth parted and her tongue moved over her lips. Then her expression changed to one of concern.

"Are you okay, honey? You're awful pale. C'mon, let's find you a place to rest for a few minutes."

She took his arm with both hands and moved him away from the table. He was surprised to find he could barely move his feet. When he stumbled the girl called a waiter over to help her. They half carried him back the way he had come, back to McManus's empty office, and sat him on the sofa.

The waiter brought him a glass of water, then left. The girl stayed for a few minutes, chattering. When he didn't respond she patted his arm, told him to rest, and promised to return soon.

He didn't hear what she said. He didn't hear her leave. Across the room a small mirror had caught his eyes. He stared at himself for a long time, until his reflection seemed to recede. It was as if he were on the rear platform of a moving train watching himself waiting forlornly back at the station.

His reflection grew smaller and smaller in the mirror until, finally, he could no longer see himself.

After a while, with a great effort, he got to his feet and stumbled to McManus's big desk. His fingers fumbled with his belt buckle until he pulled the belt off his pants. He tried to climb on the desk from the floor but it was too high, too much of an effort. He waited for a moment, marshaled his strength, then took a chair from the wall and pushed it next to the desk. Slowly, carefully, he climbed on the chair, then to the desktop. He stepped to the edge, reached up, and gently pulled the chandelier toward him, the little droplets of glass tinkling merrily.

He looped his belt through the buckle, then carefully tied the end of the belt to the chandelier. He pulled on it to test if it would hold, and was satisfied. Then he slipped the loop of the belt around his neck and pulled it tight. The metal buckle was cold against his throat.

Now that he was ready he hesitated for a moment. He was amazed to find that the noise in his ears, the pain in his stomach were gone. He was not frightened. Rather, he felt almost euphoric. This was something he could still do and no one could stop him. Not Tammany, not Hearst, not Rothstein, not the bankers. Not even George McManus. He wondered briefly, with some satisfaction, what McManus would say when he found him—how he would tell Elizabeth.

He closed his eyes. His tunnel was before him now, dark and cool and inviting; the tracks stretching away, beckoning him.

He stepped off the desk, down into the tunnel, and died.

44

ELIZABETH STEPPED OUT of the cab and quickly crossed the sidewalk. With a wave to Chins Hamner in his impossibly tight uniform she ran up the stairs, edging past an older couple in evening clothes slowly going up to the Paradise Rehearsal Club. Elizabeth hurried across the broad dance floor covered with slot machines and up the last steps. She could just make out the band playing something jazzy over the noise of the crowd as she went through the heavy door into the casino.

She was peering through the smoke and the crush of bodies, looking for George, when Rats Wolnik found her.

"Mrs. Boss, how wonderful to see you." He bowed slightly before her. "You know, you should come around more. You certainly class up this joint."

Elizabeth smiled, smoothing her sleek evening gown under her white fur without thinking. "Thank you, Rats. I'm always telling my husband you have uncommonly good sense and even better taste. Is George here?"

"I think you'll find the boss at the bar, dear lady. And I hope you can cheer him up because his mood is very poorly. I think he had a visitor who disagreed with him like a rotten fish."

Elizabeth touched Rats's arm, then hurried past him toward the bar. She clutched her small blue bag before her as she wove through the thick crowd. George had two shot glasses on the bar before him when she found him. When he saw her he looked troubled. She took his hand and pulled him toward a table near the band. George nodded to the musicians. They wound up their number, then put down their instruments and drifted toward the bar as George and Elizabeth sat down. Before he could say anything she pulled open her purse and poured a dozen diamond and ruby rings, several strings of pearls, and three gold necklaces on the white tablecloth.

"What's this?" he asked, too loudly in the sudden quiet.

"It's my good jewelry," she told him.

"I know that, toots." His hand toyed with a string of pearls that he had given her at Christmas. "But what's it doing here?"

"I want you to sell these things for me," Elizabeth said quickly. "I thought of it this afternoon, after I saw my father. He needs money, but he can't borrow any more. And he won't take anything from you."

George stared at the table. "Elizabeth, listen to me—"

"Don't try to talk me out of this," she interrupted. "I know you bought me most of these things, but technically they're mine, aren't they? And with all the connections you have, darling, you should be able to get at least a hundred thousand for these trinkets. Now isn't this a wonderful idea? By the way, I gave my father the fifty thousand from the safe in the apartment. I knew you wouldn't mind."

George looked at her shining face, wondering how to tell her. "Elizabeth, he was here. Your father was here tonight."

"I don't believe it," she said, mystified. "He came to you? What did he want?"

"What else?" George ran his fingers through his hair. "Money. He wanted to involve me in some business deal."

"But that's wonderful," Elizabeth said with a broad smile. "I mean, I can't believe he actually asked you. I know you haven't exactly been bosom buddies." Elizabeth leaned over and kissed George.

"You don't know what a relief this is, darling," she went on. "He looked so awful this afternoon. I don't remember ever seeing him so low—I was afraid for him."

"It's not that simple," George said somberly.

Elizabeth looked up at him. "What do you mean?"

"I turned him down."

"You . . . you didn't give him the money?" she said, confused.

George put one hand over her hands. "It's too late for him, Elizabeth. He's going to go to jail. Nothing I could do can help him. And now he's mixed up with some bad people to boot. He tried to involve me in their mess. Do you understand what I'm saying?"

"Where is he now?" she asked softly.

"I don't know. He stumbled out of my office in pretty bad shape. I don't know where he went. I had to do it, Elizabeth."

"That poor old man," she murmured. "He must have been very desperate to come here. And then you turned him away."

"There was nothing . . ."

George suddenly realized someone was standing next to them. They both looked up to see Otto Berman. His face was white. His jaw trembled.

"I went to get the IOUs . . . in your office," Otto blurted out, his fingers intertwining nervously. "You'd better come, Mr. McManus."

Otto glanced at Elizabeth, then looked away. "There's a man . . . I think he's dead. I told Marie. . . ."

George jumped up. "Stay here," he told Elizabeth.

But she was already on her feet, pushing through the crowd toward the club's office. He reached the door just in time to grab her arm and pull her aside. She was breathing heavily behind him as he pushed the door open. Then he froze.

Horace Wainwright swung in a slow arc from the chandelier, his head at an impossible angle on one shoulder. His tongue hung grotesquely from the corner of his mouth, the eyes bulging out of his blue face. And yet—somehow the face was almost serene, George saw with horror. Elizabeth must not see this. He forced himself to turn away, toward her. But it was too late. Elizabeth was beside him, her eyes huge, her mouth open, staring at her father.

Marie Flynn stood slumped, leaning on the desk, one hand over her mouth and her red hair in her face. Behind Elizabeth, Otto sobbed quietly. His glasses were off and he dabbed at his eyes with his finger.

For a moment no one moved. They were a tableau, a scene in a wax museum, perpetually frozen. George watched as Elizabeth looked from the body of her father to him. Her eyes were glassy, full of pain and questions.

He touched her shoulder. "Don't look any more, Elizabeth. Go back to the bar," he said, knowing how useless he sounded.

She brushed his hand away, then stepped forward into the office. The swish of her dress and the creaking of the overburdened chandelier were the only sounds in the room.

"Get him down," Elizabeth said through clenched teeth.

George quickly climbed onto the desk as Marie backed away. With one arm he lifted the body while he picked at the knot that held the belt to the chandelier. As he worked he thought how light Wainwright was, as if his body were hollow. He was careful not to look into the blue face only inches from his own. And all the time he listened for another word, some sound, from Elizabeth. But she was silent.

"I thought he was just another rich mark," Marie suddenly blurted out, brushing her hair back from her face, her voice faltering. "I didn't know he'd do this. How could I

358

know, George? He only lost fifty thousand. That's nothing here."

The knot came loose under George's fingers. He lowered Wainwright's body gently, carefully stepping from the desk to the chair next to it. Then he carried the body to the sofa and laid it down.

Elizabeth knelt on the floor and touched her father's face. She lowered his eyelids with her fingertips and forced his mouth closed. Then she took his lifeless hand and held it to her cheek, rocking slowly for a few seconds in an expression of grief as old as man. Otto blew his nose, took Marie's arm, and led her from the office, closing the door behind them.

George bent to Elizabeth but again she shook off his touch. He stood up, hands dangling uselessly at his sides.

"Come away from here," he said quietly, but he knew she would not listen.

Finally she looked up at him. There were still no tears in her eyes. "He came to you for help, George. He was that desperate."

"Elizabeth, I told you . . ." he began.

"But you turned him away. You were his last chance and you turned him away."

He angrily pulled her off the floor to her feet. "Stop it. Stop talking like that. He did this to himself."

"But that wasn't enough." Her voice was rising. "Then you —this place of yours—took his last cent. What was it, the crap tables? Roulette? Poker? Don't you have enough money yet? Didn't you know the money he was losing already belonged to you? It was the money that I gave him."

He tried to put his arms around her, to still her, but Elizabeth stiffened at his touch and backed away, toward the door. "I don't want you to touch him. I'll send an ambulance or a hearse or something to take him away. But don't you touch him. You've done enough to us."

He put his hands up, came toward her again, but she suddenly slapped him backhanded across the face. A hard, stinging slap that made him flinch and ball his fists.

She quickly ran to the door, pulled it open, and ran out. Stunned, George hesitated for a moment, then rushed after her. But a curious crowd was now pushing through the door,

359

forcing him back into the office like a powerful wave, surging around him to see the body.

He shouted her name, standing on his toes and searching for her over the bobbing heads. But she was gone.

45

IT WAS a fine day to be buried. New green shoots of grass cushioned the shuffling feet of the mourners and pallbearers. The spring sun glinted off the ranks of squat tombstones and tall monuments and warmed the backs of the people ranged about the open grave. Bees buzzed softly about the flowers that lay on the polished mahogany coffin. A soft breeze just stirred the young leaves on the trees and the rustling noise often carried away the droning words of the minister as he read from his Bible.

On a day like this, Elizabeth remembered, she and George McManus once drove to Coney Island and walked along the surf eating hot dogs. Later they bought homemade chocolate fudge with walnuts from a fat woman in a little booth on Surf Avenue and rode the Ferris wheel for hours without stopping, while George dropped money to the man who ran the ticket booth.

Elizabeth shook her head, as if to warn George away. She looked about her, half dreading he might show up now at the funeral. But there was only her mother next to the minister and the pallbearers. And across from them the familiar faces of the seven older men, friends of her father, who had been at the funeral home. They were quiet, somber businessmen in dark suits and gray hair who looked as if they felt at home at a funeral. Of all the hundreds of people her father had known only these few had bothered to see him off. Elizabeth thought she should be grateful to them. Yet they had left their wives at home, as if there were still something distasteful even in burying Horace Wainwright. Something genteel people should avoid.

Maybe it wasn't love, but guilt, that brought them to the

cemetery, Elizabeth guessed. Had her father asked them for help? Had they all turned him down? That would account for the dutiful but ungrieving looks on their faces.

On the other side of the grave the hired pallbearers could barely stifle their yawns. Thick, stolid men who looked uncomfortable in their coarse black outfits, they stood in a row, hands clasped before them, their thoughts miles away from the dead man before them.

"Lord, now your servants commit to you the mortal remains of our brother, Horace Wainwright," the minister said with sudden emphasis, raising his voice. He snapped the Bible closed with one hand and nodded to the pallbearers. They arranged themselves around the coffin and slowly lowered it into the grave on long leather straps. The coffin bumped gently to the bottom and the pallbearers stepped away.

The minister picked up a handful of dirt, then cleared his throat. "From dust we come, to dust we return," he explained with conviction, as though the others might have forgotten. Then he threw the dirt onto the coffin.

Elizabeth stooped and picked up a handful of dirt, gave it to her mother, and helped her toss it into the grave. The seven somber old men followed suit while the pallbearers fidgeted, ready to bolt for the limousines parked nearby.

The ceremony over, the minister solemnly shook everyone's hands and uttered quiet words of condolence. Elizabeth couldn't make out what he was saying, but nodded in agreement anyway. Her mother said nothing, but just stood quietly looking at the grave as the old men trooped by and patted her hand. Her mother seemed shriveled and dried up in her austere black dress, black hat, and veil. Since she had found out about her husband's death she had hardly said a word, Elizabeth realized. Alone now, she was more like a child than ever, somehow trusting that others would dress her, feed her, steer her in the right direction.

Elizabeth asked one of the mourners to take her mother back to the car. When he had lead Flora away, Elizabeth turned back to the grave. Alone, she raised her veil and took off her prim black hat. The gentle wind stirred her hair and for a moment she closed her eyes and secretly enjoyed the sensation.

When she opened her eyes she bent and picked up another handful of dirt. It was cool, moist, almost comforting as she worked it with her fingers. She threw it into the grave, rubbed her hands together, sighed.

Now what? Elizabeth had heard of people who talked to the dead, performed long soliloquies at graveside. It was comforting, they said. But she couldn't do that. She felt no guilt. Her father was just lifeless flesh and to tell him her problems would be useless. It was not grief that preoccupied her but all the troubles of her father's that had somehow, suddenly, fallen on her shoulders. From the moment he died she had been besieged by demands for loan payments from two banks, prying reporters who camped on her doorstep, suspicious policemen investigating her father's death, midnight telephone calls from cranks, and a funeral director who wanted to give her father the biggest send-off since Rudolph Valentino's funeral two years before, complete with cannon barrages. There had been no time to mourn.

Still, she wished she could find some last words to say to her father. Wasn't it a child's duty to send off a parent with some warm, loving thoughts? This was a time for compassion, not recrimination. But it was no use. Her father's grave was just a hole in the ground full of memories best buried right now. Better to save her compassion for the living, she decided. If that made her hard, so be it.

"Mrs. McManus?"

Elizabeth jumped at the sudden words behind her. She turned to find a portly man in his fifties watching her. He had thick gray-black hair, a thin mustache, and brows that ran together over deep-set eyes. He carried his hat in one hand and a briefcase in the other.

"Sorry, didn't mean to startle you. I've been waiting in my car for the service to end. My name is Quentin F. Arbogast, Mrs. McManus." His handshake was damp.

"My name is Wainwright," Elizabeth said flatly.

"Excuse me, but I understood you were married."

Elizabeth frowned. "I intend to do something about that." Her words surprised her as they came out.

"Well then, Miss Wainwright, if you please. I've been calling you for twenty-four hours, but you're a difficult person to get in touch with. I have a business proposition for you."

Elizabeth stared at him. "Mr. Arbogast, this is a cemetery. My father is lying over there and his grave hasn't even been covered yet. You could have found a more appropriate time to make a business call."

Arbogast moved his briefcase in front of him, holding it with both hands as if prepared to use it as a shield. "I know this is awkward, Miss Wainwright. But believe me, time is of the essence and I think you'll be very interested in what I have to say."

Elizabeth looked from the grave to where the limousines waited. "I'll give you two minutes, Mr. Arbogast, because you've got a lot of nerve. Talk fast."

"Fine. Excellent." He stood beside her and awkwardly opened the briefcase, coming up with a thin file.

"Miss Wainwright, when your father, uh . . . departed this life, he owed a great deal of money to many people. Banks, private investors. But of course, you know that. However, now those investors are getting ready to take over Wainwright Construction and any assets it may have within the next few days. Do you follow me?"

"Of course I follow you," she said impatiently. "I've been looking through my father's papers. But the will hasn't even been read yet. Nobody can do anything with the company until that happens. Your two minutes are running out fast."

Arbogast looked surprised. "You don't know?"

"Don't play games with me, Mr. Arbogast," Elizabeth said. "Know what?"

"There is no will."

Elizabeth was stunned, silent for a moment. "How do you know?" she finally got out.

"Because I was your father's attorney. Believe me, he left no will."

Elizabeth thought back to the two hours she had spent examining her father's big desk and files at home the day before. There had been hundreds of papers. It would take weeks to sort them out. Now she remembered seeing documents on Arbogast's stationery. But she had found no will.

"I don't understand. Even if there is no will, wouldn't my

363

mother inherit everything anyway? I mean, whatever is left," she asked.

Arbogast smiled, on surer ground now. "Not necessarily, Miss Wainwright. The creditors have a very strong case. By the time they get through, you and your mother will probably have nothing left—not even your house."

Elizabeth looked over at her father's marble headstone. Chiseled on it in flowing script were the words "HORACE WAINWRIGHT—LOVING HUSBAND AND FATHER—1863–1928." Loving father and husband. And yet he had left them in this fix. For a moment she felt like kicking the headstone over.

Finally she turned to Arbogast. "What's this business deal you mentioned?"

He took some papers from the file and thumbed through them quickly, awkwardly balancing the briefcase. "Besides being your father's lawyer, I also represent a very wealthy man with large business holdings in New York City. He's very interested in acquiring your father's firm. I'm prepared to make you a flat offer now for your and your mother's total interest in the company. My client will assume all risks, debts, and responsibilities of Wainwright Construction. You'll be totally in the clear, with money in your pocket."

"How big a cash settlement are you offering, Mr. Arbogast?"

"I can put a check into your hands right now for the sum of twenty-five thousand dollars." He looked up expectantly.

"But my father's business must be worth millions in equipment alone," Elizabeth said, suddenly angry. "And you offer a miserable twenty-five thousand. That's insulting."

He shook a finger in her face. "No, it *was* worth millions. Now the firm's worth is debatable. And to you it will probably be worth nothing, young lady. Now twenty-five thousand dollars is certainly a lot better than nothing, isn't it? Besides, even if you tried to keep it, you have nobody to run it. Face it, Miss Wainwright, it's a lost cause. Take the money."

Elizabeth looked at him squarely. "And what if I run it?"

"You?" He put his head back and laughed. "Madam, miss —whatever you are—you're just a woman. You have no engi-

364

neering or business experience, have you? Let's not talk fairy tales. I'm offering you hard cash."

"I can learn, Mr. Arbogast," Elizabeth said, stung. "I can learn about business and engineering. At least enough to run the company for a while. I'm Horace Wainwright's daughter. I must have inherited some business sense from him."

He was still smiling. "But Miss Wainwright. A woman? It just isn't done. No one, no banks, will deal with a woman. You're joking, of course."

"Furthermore, Mr. Arbogast, not only do I reject your offer, but I think you're a crook. I'm going to report you to the Bar Association for not counseling my father to make out a will— or not recording it if he did—and for representing a competing interest at the same time you were my father's lawyer. Good day."

The smile was gone from his face as she turned on her heel to walk away. "But Miss Wainwright . . ." Arbogast grabbed her arm.

"Let go of me," she warned.

"All right, I'll go to thirty-five thousand," he said, still holding her. "But that's my top offer! I'm doing you a favor."

Elizabeth put her hands on his chest and shoved hard. Arbogast stumbled backward a step, teetered a moment, then fell into the open grave, landing on the coffin with a thud. He got to his feet on the coffin lid, appalled at where he was, his face streaked with dirt.

"My God, get me out of here," he shrieked, struggling to pull himself out of the grave. "Help me, miss."

Elizabeth smiled down at him. "You just wait there, Mr. Arbogast. And I'll go see if I can't find a big, strong man to help you out."

And then she walked away.

Far away at the other end of the house the telephone kept ringing. Elizabeth could just hear the maid telling the callers that no one was available to talk to them today. Then, as soon as she would hang up, the ringing would begin again, filling the house, reverberating from room to room.

Elizabeth and her mother sat in matching wing chairs in the

365

library, a low polished table between them. They still wore the black dresses from the funeral an hour before. Flora sat with her hands folded in her lap, preoccupied with her thoughts. In the afternoon light her face seemed very young, her skin almost translucent. Sometimes she would move her lips, as if in some argument with herself that could not be resolved. Elizabeth wondered if her mother really understood what had happened today, that Horace Wainwright was gone.

Flora had been solemn at the cemetery, but like a child preoccupied with a very adult problem. Not a word had passed between mother and daughter on the drive back. Finally, after watching her mother for a long time, Elizabeth kicked off her shoes and walked to the tall French windows, studying the green-brown garden.

"Why did he do it, Elizabeth?" Flora suddenly asked, looking at her daughter. "Why did your father kill himself?"

Elizabeth turned and stared at her, surprised. "How did you find that out? Who told you he killed himself?"

"I heard the maid, on the telephone," Flora explained softly. "But she didn't say why. And I couldn't bring myself to ask her. I want you to tell me."

Elizabeth crossed the room and stood behind Flora's chair, gently rubbing her shoulders. "Money," she said simply. "Father was desperate. Things were going badly for him."

Elizabeth sighed and went back to her chair, putting her feet up on the table.

"We're pretty desperate ourselves, Mother. I wish you could understand. I wish I had someone to talk to that I could trust," she added, suddenly thinking of George McManus. "Now I'm afraid we're going to lose what's left of Father's company. The banks want two hundred and fifty thousand dollars by the end of the week. And a man at the cemetery told me some other people are going to try to take the company away from us."

Elizabeth brushed a speck of dust off her dress and looked up wearily. So much had happened so quickly. She didn't know where to begin, what to do. She could see that this pride business had its drawbacks. But troubling her mother would not help.

"I have money," Flora said, confused. "Why didn't your father ask me for it?"

"How can I make you understand, Mother? I'm talking about large sums of money, not a few dollars." Elizabeth began looking at the furniture in the room, trying to calculate what it might bring at auction if it came to that.

"It's in the soup tureen, on the top shelf in the pantry. The tureen shaped like a duck," Flora went on. "If it will help, Elizabeth, I want you to have it."

Elizabeth was only half listening to her mother. She had heard her ramble like this too often to pay much attention.

Flora rose and walked to the fireplace. She pulled the sash summoning the maid, then sat down again. When the maid came Flora told her to bring the tureen.

"Mother, wouldn't you like to lie down for a while?" Elizabeth said, a little concerned. "You shouldn't have to worry about money. Let me do the worrying. You've had a trying day."

But by then the maid had returned. At Flora's request she set the soup tureen on the table between them and left the room. Flora sat quietly, looking at Elizabeth.

"I want to help, dear," she finally said. "Please let me help."

Elizabeth shrugged, then smiled at her mother, humoring her. She reached over and took the top off the silly blue duck. The tureen was filled with crumpled green bills. She quickly dumped the money on the table, her eyes wide, and began counting. It took ten minutes before the last bill was laid flat.

Elizabeth looked up in awe. "There's over four hundred and seventy-five thousand dollars here. Where did you get all this, Mother?"

Flora looked solemn. Her mind drifted slowly back over the years. "Your father was a very generous man. He gave me so much more than I ever needed for clothes, household expenses. That's what I saved—a bit here, a bit there."

Elizabeth went to her mother's side, bent over, and hugged her.

"There's some change, too. In the big bureau in my bedroom," Flora went on quietly. "A lot of pennies, if you need more."

Elizabeth sat on the floor before her mother and laid her head in her lap, suddenly very weary. She looked up into her mother's face, searching for some logic, an explanation. But Flora just began stroking Elizabeth's hair, methodically, as one would stroke a kitten. It was beyond logic, Elizabeth thought, beyond understanding. A breeze rustled through the silent room and caught one of the bills on the table. Elizabeth watched it float for a brief moment before it landed on her hand. She pulled away quickly as if the piece of paper had burned her skin.

Elizabeth put her head back on her mother's lap and closed her eyes, retreating, feeling only the rough material of her mother's dress on the side of her face. The hours since the funeral, then the days since she had left George McManus, swirled through her mind, distorted faces and colors and images on a carousel. So much had happened so quickly, faster than she could comprehend.

When she opened her eyes again the blue duck was still there on its side on the low table, amidst the money. Somehow its vacuous, painted expression seemed to mock her, mock them all, as if this piece of crockery knew all along that it held secrets of life and death.

"He was a good man, your father," Flora finally said, almost to herself, staring at some place that only she could see.

Elizabeth closed her eyes again. Far away the telephone rang and rang and rang.

46

"DO YOU THINK this one is big enough?"

"Boss, if it was bigger the poor woman would have to hire somebody to help lift her head." Izzy the Stub inspected the pear-shaped diamond on a gold chain that George held up.

"I don't know. The color isn't that great. It's a little yellowish, see? Maybe I should send her some rubies. She always looked good in red."

Izzy shook his head. "Rubies you sent her two weeks ago.

And pearls the week before that, and emeralds last week. She's just going to send them back again like always. That's a very stubborn wife you have."

"Excuse me, Mr. McManus." The salesgirl smiled at him from behind the broad glass counter. "But it's almost five o'clock. Closing time. Have you decided what you want?"

George studied the large diamond, then handed it to the girl. "I'll take that one. But it has to be delivered to this address today." He took a gold pen from inside his coat.

"That's not necessary, Mr. McManus," she said, flattening out her order pad. "I know where to send it by now. Tiffany's will be happy to charge it to your account. And I hope your wife appreciates this one."

"How do you like that?" George told Izzy as they crossed the thick blue carpet to the door, where the uniformed doorman bowed them out. "Tiffany's knows everything about me but my underwear size. I'll bet the salegirls are snickering behind my back."

They climbed into the back of George's car. The chauffeur closed the door behind them, then dashed around to the other side and got in.

"You're surprised everybody knows your business?" Izzy grabbed the strap over the door as the car drove off. "First you marry a social butterfly. Then her crazy father says good-bye cruel world in your own establishment with a couple hundred witnesses around. On top of this, your wife is now getting her picture taken in half the saloons in town with men who are certainly not her husband. This can make people curious."

George looked out the car window.

Izzy shrugged. "I don't know, boss. But if she wants to run around and have a hot time without you, she could at least give the Paradise Rehearsal Club some of her business."

"Izzy, shut up," George muttered.

Izzy shut up.

A few minutes later the car rounded a corner and pulled to the curb in front of the corset shop. Chins Hamner rushed out of the club's doorway and ran to the car, folds of fat heaving under his tight uniform.

"You better hustle upstairs and see Otto," Chins puffed as

369

he dragged the door open. "He's jumping around like he's got St. Vitus Dance. And he won't tell nobody what's up."

"Didn't I tell you to let that coat out?" George inspected the huge man. "I can't have a doorman that looks like he's going to explode out of his uniform. It scares the customers."

"I did let it out. But then I went on this cheesecake binge. You know how it is," Chins said proudly, his hands on his girth. "A man's gotta eat."

"But not for six," George said over his shoulder as he and Izzy went up the stairs.

Before they reached the club's big door George could hear Otto Berman shrieking. Then they saw him hopping up and down in a corner, quivering like a blade of grass in a storm, while Marie Flynn and Rats Wolnik held on and tried to calm him.

When he saw McManus, Otto almost leaped into his arms. "He's getting out! He's getting out!" Otto shouted into George's face, his glasses flying off and skittering across the floor.

"Who's getting out?" George asked, shaking the smaller man.

"Big Bill," Otto gasped, out of breath. "On the phone, this afternoon . . . he told me . . . the parole's come through." Otto bounded away and then danced back. "It's a miracle, Mr. McManus, a miracle."

"A five-hundred-thousand-dollar miracle," Izzy reminded. "But who's counting?"

George grabbed Otto's hands. "Stand still, dammit, and tell me when Dwyer's being sprung."

Otto's body still quivered. There were tears of joy in his myopic eyes. "Six, maybe eight weeks, Mr. McManus . . . lots of paperwork. But he said to thank you, Mr. McManus." Otto pumped his hands. "He said you didn't forget him . . . and he'd never forget you."

Otto bounced away again and began pounding on the drums on the bandstand.

Marie touched George's arm, shaking her head. "That's more emotion than I've seen from the little twerp in three years. And he's been like that for two hours. Are we going to celebrate?"

370

"Sure we're going to celebrate," McManus told her. "You scrape Otto off the ceiling, then get on the phone and invite all of Big Bill's friends here tonight. Drinks are on the house."

"Well hello, sailor," Marie growled.

Their heads were close together, almost touching, so they could hear each other over the racket of music and shouts. George looked down into his glass, idly stirring the ice with a finger.

"I really hated you. When you married her, that day I could have torn your eyes out. There was never anybody else, you know. Not like you."

He looked up into Marie's eyes, only inches away. "Golly."

"All right," she admitted with a laugh. "So maybe there were one or two others."

"One or two dozen?"

She leaned closer, her lips brushing his cheek. "That was business. The suckers like me to kiss their bald little heads and goose them. It's a game. You know that. But it was never a game with you."

She ran a finger around his ear. "I knew you'd get tired of Miss Oysters Rockefeller after a while, love. And I was going to be here when you did." She slipped her tongue in and out of his ear.

Someone telling a loud story behind them smacked George on the back, spilling his drink on his sleeve. George held up the empty glass and motioned to a passing waiter. Two beefy, red-faced men reeled into the table arm in arm, crushing the back of a chair, then danced away clumsily, waving to George. The waiter straightened the tablecloth, put down another drink, and took away the damaged chair.

"Nice party," George said. "Big Bill would be proud."

"Why don't you take me home?" Marie breathed in his ear, her tongue busy again.

George shook his head. "You're too dangerous at close range. Besides, I'm the host of this affair."

There were shouts on the other side of the room near the roulette tables. George could hear fists landing, saw a hat fly into the air. There was the sound of a bottle breaking. Waiters

371

quickly converged on the brawl and broke it up. Rats Wolnik held a man by the beard as he led him toward the door.

"Somehow I don't think you'd be missed," Marie said with a sigh. "How about dancing with me, then?"

George didn't answer. He was watching Izzy make his way through the crowd toward the table, a bemused expression on his face.

"It seems your wife has decided to give you the business after all, boss," he said, leaning next to George. "She came in five minutes ago with a few couples and a fellow who looks like he should be in moving pictures."

Marie whistled. "You'd better get some soap, Izzy. I think Mr. George McManus is going to get his face rubbed in the dirt."

George stood and peered over the crowd, his face suddenly intense. He pulled Marie's hand. "C'mon, suddenly I feel like dancing."

"You're not crawling to her?" Marie protested.

"No, I'm dancing to her." George pulled her out of the chair. Marie looked at Izzy and shrugged.

He led Marie onto the crowded floor and slid a hand around her waist, his eyes searching the room over people's heads. They moved slowly to the music, Marie glancing up at George's face.

"You might look at me once in a while," she said. "I have the feeling you could be dancing with a side of beef and wouldn't know the difference."

"Huh? You say something?" George asked, still looking away.

"Your hair's on fire."

"Yeah, thanks," he said, distracted. Then his grip tightened on her hand. He steered Marie toward a knot of well-dressed people on the far side of the room.

Elizabeth danced close to a dark, handsome man with long, refined fingers spread across her bare back. She wore a sleek, jeweled blue gown with a matching headband. The rougher crowd of Dwyer's friends crashed into and receded from Elizabeth's elegant little group like coarse ocean waves battering a posh yacht club seawall.

With adroit use of elbows George maneuvered himself and

372

Marie next to them. He leaned toward the handsome man. "Dances good, doesn't she?"

"Very," the other man replied, surprised. He looked from George to Elizabeth as both couples swayed to the music. "Is this a friend of yours?"

"Not really," Elizabeth answered stiffly, avoiding looking at George. "This is Mr. McManus. He owns the place."

"Thorndike's the name." The dark man introduced himself with a nod. "Philip Thorndike. So you're McManus."

"And I'm Joan of Arc, if anyone wants to know," Marie tossed in.

The two couples danced in silence for a minute. George recognized some of Elizabeth's friends, but they quickly looked away in embarrassment when he caught them watching him.

As the band droned on, George nudged Marie and nodded toward Thorndike.

"Do your own dirty work," Marie whispered.

George kicked her lightly in the shin. "Big, dumb son of a bitch," she muttered, hopping on one leg and rubbing the other. "All right, all right."

Marie turned to the dark man, batting her lashes and showing her teeth. "I'm tired of dancing, Mr. Thorndike. Would you be interested in exercising the dice for a little while? I think Mr. McManus will take care of the lady."

Thorndike looked at Elizabeth. "Do you mind? I feel kind of lucky tonight."

Elizabeth shrugged, her face tense. Thorndike dropped her hands and turned to Marie.

"Tell me, Saint Joan, are you rich?" Thorndike was saying as they walked away arm in arm. George heard Marie's loud laugh as he looked at Elizabeth.

She avoided his eyes when he put his arm around her. "You always get your way, don't you?" Elizabeth said.

"I can't help it, toots, it's habit-forming." They began to dance, Elizabeth stiff and awkward in his arms, still refusing to look at him.

"Well?" she demanded. "Now that you've arranged everything, what do you want?"

"What do you mean, what do I want? What are *you* doing

373

here?" George tried to look into her face but she kept it turned away.

She shook her head. "I'm not here to see you, that's for sure. I came to this party to see Bill Dwyer. Where is he?"

George drew her toward him until her hair touched his cheek. "Dwyer won't be out of prison for weeks. Everybody in the place knows that."

"But Izzy . . ." She looked at him for the first time since they began dancing. "Izzy specifically called and said . . ." She hesitated. "So that's it. You had him trick me."

"Would you believe me if I said getting you here was Izzy's idea and I had nothing to do with it?"

"No," Elizabeth replied. "I know what a con man you are."

They danced on in silence. "You smell wonderful," George finally said.

"Thank you. You stink of liquor."

"A couple of drunks bumped into—" he started to explain, but she cut him off with a glance.

"Who's this Thorndike?" George asked after a few seconds, suddenly angry but not sure why. "I don't like his looks."

"He's from England. We met crossing the Atlantic last year. And I don't care whether you like his looks or not. Now please let me go. I'm not enjoying this." She tried to pull away, but he held her tightly.

"All right, no more small talk. Just one more thing." They stood together surrounded by dancing couples, Elizabeth glaring at him.

"Are you okay? Do you need anything, Elizabeth? I mean money—or anything?"

She pushed his hands off her waist. They stood like two boxers, wary of the next punch. "Even if I did need anything, do you really think I'd ask you? Not even if I was starving to death."

The band stopped playing and most of the other couples shuffled away from them, toward the bar or the gaming tables. They stared at each other. He was stunned by her bitterness.

"You're still my wife, Elizabeth."

Her chin came up as her anger became sudden confusion. "You don't know? You didn't get the papers yet?"

He started to say something, but she jerked away and ran

across the empty dance floor. George tried to follow but lost her in the crowd. When he saw her again, Thorndike was putting a fur wrap over her shoulders near the door. The rest of the elegant little group was preparing to leave, too, the women whispering to each other as they glanced at George. He started toward Elizabeth but Marie appeared beside him and took his arm.

"Give it up for tonight, love," she said softly. "Your timing is lousy."

George watched as Elizabeth left on Thorndike's arm. She didn't look back at him as the rest of the well-dressed entourage followed her slowly, like expensive toys on a string.

47

HE MADE LOVE to Marie angrily, viciously, biting her neck, her shoulders. His hands kneaded her breasts cruelly until she wanted to cry out with the pain as well as the pleasure, and when he sucked on her nipples he ground his teeth until she had to jerk his head away by pulling his hair.

When he finally entered her there was no warning, no preparation. He simply forced her legs apart, lying on her heavily, pinning her shoulders down as a wrestler would to hold her immobile. He didn't want her to move or react, she knew. He didn't want her to get any pleasure from this. He wanted to dominate, to control, to punish, to assuage the anger that was eating at him.

Marie understood but didn't care. She wrapped her arms and legs around him tighter, holding on joyfully as he thrashed about. She did what she could, trying to move her hips, covering his face with kisses. She hissed and snorted in his ears, darting her tongue in and out, finally grinding with him until, at the moment of climax, both almost forgot why they were locked together and who was trying to punish whom.

He rolled off her and they lay silent for a long time listening to the late-night sounds blending into the noises of early morning on the streets far below. A newsboy shouted some-thing about the market and "Getcha papah." An old man's distinct, wheezy cough. A girlish giggle. Grayish sunlight glowed around the edges of the curtains in the bedroom.

"You can get mad any time you want," Marie finally sighed.

"I wasn't mad at you," George told her quietly.

"I know."

He lay with his hands behind his head. In the dim light he could just make out a painting that hung over his bureau. Elizabeth had bought it for him as a birthday gift. It was a painting of a peasant girl, done by some Dutchman whose name he couldn't remember. The girl held a sheaf of wheat in her arms as she stood, half bent, before a dusty farm shed. She was dark, olive-skinned, enigmatic. Something about the girl's eyes had always reminded him of Elizabeth. They were mischievous eyes, full of mystery, deep secrets, quiet glee.

He rolled over on one shoulder, looking at Marie. There was no mystery about her, he thought. She was as predictable as tomorrow's sunrise. He ran a hand from her throat down to her stomach, then across to her right thigh, while Marie breathed rhythmically, her breasts rising and falling.

"How would you like to move in here? With me," he said quietly.

"Why? Your cleaning lady quit?" Marie almost laughed.

He poked her in the side until she yelped. "I like having you here, that's why. And I'm tired of sleeping alone."

She rubbed her ribs. "Since when does George McManus have to sleep alone? Do you think I'm a sucker? This is Marie you're talking to."

George lay his cheek on her breasts, listening to her heart-beat. "I'm not used to people saying no to me."

"Don't get me wrong, love." Marie stroked his hair. "I'm not saying no. But don't you think it would be a little crowded with the three of us?"

"What are you talking about?" George turned his head to look at her face.

"I'm talking about you and me and your wife."

George rubbed his chin on her soft skin. "What wife?"

"Oh sure. That's why you practically dragged me across the

376

club on my knees last night when Izzy told you she was there. Because you don't care about her anymore."

"What is it with women?" he complained. "Now you're playing hard to get?"

This time she did laugh. "Hard to get? All you have to do is snap your fingers, love. But are you sure you really want me?"

He snapped his fingers.

Marie pulled his face next to hers. "I must be crazy," she whispered as she kissed his lips.

A buzz from the door interrupted them. He picked up the clock next to the bed. "Who the hell is that at six-thirty in the morning?"

He got out of bed, took a robe off a chair, and tied the sash as he went to the door. Marie pulled the sheet about her when she heard the exchange of voices at the door. Then she heard the door close and George returned to the bedroom carrying a small package. He sat on the bed and stared at the package on his lap.

"Well, aren't you going to open it?" Marie finally said.

George slowly pulled away the paper wrapping. Out tumbled a smaller package in Tiffany giftwrap, the store's famous red ribbon around it. There was also a long, sealed envelope.

"This is for you," George said, tossing the package to Marie, who tore it open eagerly. Inside was a velvet-covered box. She ran to the window, losing her sheet, and pulled back the curtains. Then she opened the box. Inside was the big diamond on the gold chain.

"My God, it's beautiful! It's the biggest, most beautiful hunk of rock I've ever seen." She danced about the room naked, then dashed to the bed and jumped on George's back, throwing her arms around him. He didn't look up. He was staring at the sheaf of papers he had taken from the envelope. Finally he crumpled them in his fist and threw them to the floor.

"Divorce papers. That's what she was talking about last night, divorce papers." He sat staring at the floor for a minute, then threw off his robe and began to pull on a pair of pants.

Still kneeling naked on the bed Marie looked at the diamond in her hand, puzzled. "Wait a minute," she finally said.

377

"This wasn't for me at all, was it? You bought this for your wife. And like a sucker she sent it back to you, so you gave it to me."

"What's the difference?" George said, pulling a shirt out of the closet.

"You dirty, rotten, stinking bastard," she said, her voice rising. "A minute ago you were making love to me, now you're giving me your wife's leftovers. You're going back to her, aren't you?"

George searched under the bed. "I can't talk now, toots. I'll explain it all to you later—when I figure it out myself. Where's those damn socks?"

Marie jumped off the bed and went to the window. She didn't bother to open it, just threw the heavy diamond through the glass with a crash and watched it sail down toward Seventh Avenue.

"That's what I think of you and your gifts!" She stood with her hands on her hips, her naked breasts thrust forward.

"Suit yourself," George said, hurriedly tying a shoelace. "It only cost forty-two thousand."

Marie glared at him for a moment, then grabbed her panties and began to dress quickly, too.

"Where do you think you're going? You can't go with me." George pulled on his coat and shoved the crumpled papers into a pocket.

"Go with you?" Marie's red hair was in her face. She hopped toward the door in her wrinkled evening gown, trying to pull on a shoe.

"I don't want to go with you, you big dope. If I get downstairs real fast," she called from the living room, "maybe I can find that diamond before some other jerk does."

"Elizabeth McManus! Come out here, Elizabeth! Your loving husband wants to tell you something!" He banged on the heavy doors as he shouted, then listened with satisfaction as his words echoed from the buildings across Fifth Avenue and up and down the block.

The pinch-faced maid peered down at him from a third-story window of the mansion.

"I want to see my wife!" he roared, and the maid's face

378

quickly disappeared. In a moment a second-story window sprang open above his head and Elizabeth peered out in a bathrobe. She looked tired and drawn, as if she hadn't slept all night, he thought.

"Are you crazy? It's seven o'clock in the morning. You'll wake the whole neighborhood," she hissed. "Go away. You're not wanted here."

He pulled the crumpled papers from his pocket and held them up. "I just got your little surprise by messenger. And the answer is no. You're not going to get out of a marriage with me that easily," he shouted.

Elizabeth's face turned white. "Go away or I'll call the police and have you arrested."

"I love you, goddammit," he shouted at the top of his lungs, "and I don't care if all your neighbors know it."

Elizabeth stared down at him, mouth open. He saw her turn from the window and speak to someone behind her.

Suddenly the door opened under his fist. Philip Thorndike stepped out in a red robe bearing a crest over crisp blue pajamas.

"Now see here, McManus," Philip began reasonably, running one hand through his thick hair and blinking in the sunlight as he closed the door behind him. "This is no way for civilized people to act, making a scene in public. Strangers are gathering on the sidewalk and staring at this house. Be a good fellow and go away so everyone can go back to sleep."

Elizabeth turned back to the window. "Philip, you get back in the house. The police are coming," she called down.

George touched the crest on the robe. "Tell me, old boy. Are you sleeping with my wife?"

Thorndike looked from the crest to George's face, surprised. "Your wife?" He backed away. "She never said . . . "

That was as far as he got. George spun him around, grabbed him by the collar, and rammed Philip's head into the door with a resounding thud. When he let go, Philip slumped gently to the ground on his back. George stuffed the crumpled papers in the breast pocket of the robe.

Elizabeth leaned far out from the window. "What did you do to him?"

379

"He wanted to go back to sleep," George called. "I helped him."

Her mouth fell open again.

"Look, I've made my point," he shouted. "No divorce. Let me know when you change your mind and want to come back to me, toots. I'll be waiting."

Elizabeth spun about, then reappeared in the window with a vase in her hands. George was already going down the walk when she threw it. The vase missed him by a foot and shattered in the grass. He waved over his shoulder and kept walking.

By the time Elizabeth got downstairs and opened the door George was gone, walking away up Fifth Avenue. She knelt and lifted Philip's head, slapping his cheeks to wake him, but he was out cold. She could feel the bump already rising on his forehead. Elizabeth gently lowered Philip's head to the concrete and sat back against the door post, wrapping her arms around her knees. Through the trees Elizabeth thought she could just make out George's fedora across the street.

Behind her the maid was shouting something. A police car, siren blaring, was rolling up the drive. Philip began to moan beside her.

So why, she wondered, was she smiling?

48

THEY WATCHED HER, their eyes polished disks following her every movement, trying to read every gesture. Behind her the clock next to her father's portrait ticked steadily, the only sound in the crowded room. Some of them sat with their elbows perched on the long table, hunched forward as if ready to pounce. But most waited patiently with hands folded before them, or sometimes artfully rearranging pencils with points already perfectly aligned.

Elizabeth knew they were waiting for her to speak first, and that was why she hesitated. It was all part of the game. They were hoping to watch her fall on her face, expecting it, as they always did at these meetings. Someone sighed. A curtain swayed slightly. You could have heard an innuendo drop, Elizabeth thought.

She straightened the pile of papers before her, cleared her throat, and took in the engineers, accountants, salesmen, and executives before her.

"Well, gentlemen, why all the happy looks?"

A portly, balding man named Crisp rose from the first chair on Elizabeth's left, loudly scraping his watch chain against the table like a ghost hauling an eternal burden through a haunted house. He even looked ghostly—with fine, pale skin and shocks of white hair ethereally puffed over each ear.

"As vice-president of this creaking concern," he began, "it is my dubious honor to announce that we have signed contracts in the last week for two new projects." Crisp's lips curled back from his teeth in disdain.

"Two construction jobs, that's wonderful." Elizabeth looked up hopefully.

"Madam," Crisp resumed in his best lecturing tone, "your father built this company into an enterprise that constructed multimillion-dollar bridges, skyscrapers, engineering marvels. Our two new projects are for horse stables. One in the Bronx and one in Brooklyn. Horse stables!"

"How much money?" she asked impatiently.

"We estimate a total combined profit on both projects of eight hundred and seventy-five dollars. As the expression goes—chickenfeed. I only recommended we bid on them to keep some of our crews working. In my opinion, we cannot go on like this much longer." He sank back into his chair, again clanking the watch chain, frowning at Elizabeth.

Only $875. She winced, thinking of the huge sums she had already thrown into the company trying to save it. But how long would that money last with everything going out and almost nothing coming in? She wondered if her mother had any more soup tureens.

"Thank you, Mr. Crisp. As usual, you are an inspiration to us all. Mr. Connors?"

A serious young man wearing a white shirt with the pocket full of pens and drafting pencils stood up at the other end of the table. His shirt billowed over his belt. He carefully unfolded heavy glasses and put them on gravely, consulting his notes.

"Well, of the three other current projects Wainwright Construction has going, only the Westchester sewer extension is going full tilt," he explained carefully. "On the rest of the jobs material shortages are holding us up."

Elizabeth watched her reflection in the polished wood of the table. "Why aren't there enough materials, Mr. Connors?"

"I can answer that," Crisp joined in, stubby fingers habitually smoothing the twin shocks of white hair. "Our suppliers no longer trust us to pay our bills, madam. Every month we fall farther and farther behind financially and the word has gotten around that the company is a bad risk. Nor do they trust the new management."

"You mean because I'm a helpless little woman, Mr. Crisp?" Elizabeth said mockingly.

Her tone was lost on him. "There is no greater respecter of the fair sex than I," he said, standing, "but—"

"But the suppliers are reluctant to deal with a woman in any way, shape, or form. Is that what you were going to say— for the sixth week in a row?"

"Something like that, madam," Crisp agreed.

She looked away from him. "Let's get back to the more important things. Tell me, Mr. Connors, could you put some of our people back to work if I find you more supplies?"

"Of course." He took off his glasses and peered at her.

"And it would help our profit picture if we finished these contracts sooner, wouldn't it?"

"Yes."

"Well, there are acres of timber and other materials at the subway site just going to rot while lawyers haggle over the lawsuits. Could you use some of those supplies?"

Connors considered his pencils for a moment, then nodded. "Why didn't I think of that? Sure we could use the lumber, and a lot of the steel. We'll just cut it up to fit what we need. Plus there's concrete, tools, plaster, tile, paint—tons of it. I could get some trucks down to the site this afternoon." In his enthusiasm, he toyed with three pencils at once.

"Now wait just a minute here, Connors, Miss Wainwright,"

Crisp warned, standing again and hooking his thumbs in his vest pockets. Everyone looked to him.

"You cannot just raid the tunnel project like a pack of bandits. Those supplies and the whole subway job are in the midst of very delicate litigation since the unfortunate accident. Why you could even argue that the city owns those materials, not we. The company could get into serious trouble diverting them to other projects. I, for one, do not intend to be a part of this highly questionable affair."

Elizabeth stood and took a deep breath. Ten pairs of eyes turned back to her. "Mr. Crisp, as sole owner of this company, at least for the time being, I can do anything I want to do. And that includes taking risks as well as firing even my father's most trusted associates, no matter how long they've worked here. Do you get my drift?"

For a moment the old man and the young woman stared at each other, neither wanting to blink first, while the others looked back and forth as if following a tennis match. Then Crisp sighed and sat down, his face composed but his knuckles white.

No one spoke or moved for a long moment. Then, as if at some imperceptible signal, Crisp and the others rose and drifted out of the office and back to their jobs, talking in subdued tones among themselves.

Elizabeth went to the desk, falling into the chair with a sigh, trying to will away the knots in her stomach that always accompanied these meetings. She rubbed her eyes, wondering if there would ever be an end to the tension that gnawed at her every day.

She took a key out of a small box and unlocked the bottom drawer of the desk, then pulled a long, wrinkled envelope from the back of the drawer. She took some papers from the envelope and smoothed them out before her. She read the sheets covered with her father's pinched handwriting three times—even though she'd already looked at them so often the papers were nearly worn in half along the creases. Finally she sat back, staring at her father's portrait for a long time, wondering if she understood the papers correctly.

After a while she buzzed for the new secretary she'd hired to replace the battleship-gray Miss Pruitt. Elizabeth folded the papers and put them back in the drawer. She was locking it as her secretary, a young woman in a brown smock and sensible shoes, came in.

Elizabeth barely looked at her. "Any word from the mayor yet?"

The secretary flipped through the small dictation notebook she carried. "The mayor's office said he still isn't available to see you, ma'am. He had to go to a beer rally this afternoon. In Central Park."

Elizabeth shook her head. "Well, that's a new excuse, anyway."

"And Mr. Arbogast is here to see you again."

Elizabeth groaned. "That vulture? What does he want this time, as if I didn't know? Another offer to buy me out."

"I wouldn't know, ma'am," the secretary said. "But he's talking with Mr. Crisp right now."

Elizabeth looked up sharply, suddenly suspicious. The secretary stood silently before the desk, waiting for instructions.

"What shall I tell Mr. Arbogast?" she finally asked.

"Tell him I have a headache or I went to the park. Tell him anything. I don't care."

The secretary turned away efficiently and walked out, leaving Elizabeth drumming her fingers on the desk. She unlocked the drawer once more and took out the long envelope again. But this time she didn't open it. Instead, she seemed to weigh it in her hand. Then she put the envelope back in the drawer, relocked it, pulled on her hat and gloves, and slipped out through her private door.

Elizabeth smelled sausages. Grilled sausages on a vendor's wagon. The smell wafted across the small zoo tucked into the corner of Central Park, mixing with the odors of candy and popcorn and children and monkeys. The smell danced under her nose, tantalizing her, as she walked through a maze of baby carriages and nannies toward the steady pounding of a drum.

She climbed over a little grassy hill. Now the drumming was loud and she could hear the shouts of a large crowd as, through the trees, she saw the tail end of a raggedy parade snaking away from her. As she came closer she could make out some of the signs the marchers carried.

"Near Beer Is Near Awful," read one. "Bring Back the Real Stuff," demanded another. And around a five-year-old's neck hung a sign that asked: "My Daddy Had Beer—Why Can't I?"

Elizabeth cut across a road, walking quickly to reach the head of the column. The big drum boomed steadily. Walking a few paces behind it was a thin man in a dapper white suit and straw boater, waving left and right. She hurried through the crowd toward him. When she reached his side Elizabeth grabbed the man's arm tightly.

Surprised, Jimmy Walker peered at her. A couple of big policemen were coming through the crowd toward them but Walker motioned them away.

"Well, it's Elizabeth McManus, isn't it?" He waved to a knot of women pushing babies nearby. "I didn't know you were interested in the vital issues of our time, like beer. Wonderful stuff, beer."

"Yes, heady," she said over the noise.

Walker chuckled. "That's good. I'll use that sometime. And how's your husband? He's a good friend of this administration, you know."

Elizabeth clung to Walker's arm in the crush. "We've separated," she said loudly. "In fact, I'm using my maiden name now. You remember—Wainwright."

For a second Walker blanched, then recovered his composure. "Sorry to hear about you and George. But try not to use that other name around me. It still gives me nightmares." He smiled quickly for a photographer who darted in front of them.

"I need to talk to you. I need your help." She shouted into his ear over the beating of the drum.

"Anything for a former friend of a friend of the administration," he told her, still waving. "What can I do for you?"

Elizabeth took a deep breath, then leaned close to Walker's ear. "I want you to reopen the subway project."

Walker blanched again and tried to pull out of her grip, but she held on.

"Impossible," he nearly shouted, shaking his head for em-

385

phasis, no longer smiling. "This is why I've been avoiding you for weeks. Anything connected with your father and that damn tunnel is bad business. The reformers would dearly love to hang me up next to him. Sorry," he apologized quickly, looking past Elizabeth to wave to someone on the sidewalk. "Just a figure of speech."

"I don't care about that. Nothing can hurt my father anymore. But I'm going to lose everything if you don't help me," she pleaded. "I can't borrow a dime from the banks with the tunnel shut down. And I have to have money."

For a moment the throb of the drum drowned out Walker's voice. ". . . political suicide," she heard him say. "A little corruption is one thing, but that tunnel . . . ask me something hard, not impossible."

She knew he thought she was foolish and annoying. Her mind raced as she sensed he was losing his interest. In a moment he would call the two policemen, pull away from her. She could feel the tension in his arm. Her heart thumped with the drum. She knew she had no other choice.

"I'm warning you, I have some papers." Elizabeth leaned closer to Walker, almost stuttering over her words in her nervousness. "My father kept notes of his dealings with you— with Tammany—in his desk. If you don't help me . . ."

Walker's head spun toward her as if he had been shot. A child ran up and pushed a small American flag into his hand. He waved it half-heartedly.

"That's blackmail," he hissed through thin lips. "You're out of your league, aren't you, trying to blackmail me?"

Elizabeth stared at him.

"By God," he said with a strangled laugh, "there's a lot of George McManus in you, lady, separated or not."

They walked silently for a few paces, the big crowd becoming more and more boisterous. Elizabeth could see the platform where the rally was to be held up ahead. A smaller crowd waited there. The drum blasts grew louder, almost making her quiver, as a teenage boy beat with all his might.

Walker looked at Elizabeth again, his expression a mixture of amazement and dread, as if she'd suddenly grown a second head. "You must be crazy. Why don't you just go to Mc-

Manus? He's got more money than he knows what to do with."

"This has nothing to do with him," she said levelly, then took a deep breath. "Do I go to Hearst, or do you help me?"

For a moment he seemed to measure her, suddenly confused, looking for some outward sign of how desperate she really was. "I wonder if you're not bluffing, Elizabeth. Your father wasn't stupid. I wonder if you really have any papers."

Suddenly Elizabeth released his arm, made as if to walk away. For a moment she feared he was going to let her go. Then Walker grabbed her hand. He quickly took a matchbook and a pencil from his pocket and scribbled something on the inside cover.

"Maybe I can do something. I'll check around about the tunnel." There was a hard edge in his voice. "Meanwhile, you go see him. He's a money man. He'll take care of you." Walker handed her the matchbook.

Staring at her hand, Elizabeth stopped as the crowd surged around her. When she looked up a dozen hands were helping the mayor of New York up onto the bandshell. He was trying hard to smile, but his angry eyes were on her.

49

"MR. MCMANUS?"

"Yes, I'm here."

"This is the mayor's office calling. The mayor would like to speak with you, Mr. McManus. Hold on, please."

"Hello, Georgie?"

"How are you, mayor?"

"Tip-top. Couldn't be better. Did you hear about the mob that showed up in the park this afternoon?"

"I'm just reading about it in the evening papers in my office, over a slug of bourbon. Did you really sing them a couple of songs?"

"Sure, why not? I figure as long as Prohibition continues

and I'm on the side of the beer-drinking angels, I'll have no trouble getting reelected."

"You've got my vote, mayor."

"Listen . . . uh . . . how's the saloon business, George?"

"No complaints. There's a lot of gambling on stocks and bonds instead of craps and roulette now that the market's up. But I guess I can scrape up a contribution for the cause, if that's what this telephone call's about."

"No, no. Nothing like that. Uh . . . I hear Big Bill Dwyer's getting out soon."

"A couple of days."

"I'll drop down to the club when he gets back. We'll knock back a few, George."

"Anytime, mayor. Now what's on your mind?"

"Uh, well . . . look, George, your wife collared me today, in the park. She needs money. She wants me to reopen that subway."

"Did you turn her down?"

"My mother didn't raise any stupid children. I told her it was out of the question. That's when she started making threats, something about going to Hearst with the goods on me. You still there, Georgie?"

"I'm here."

"Any idea what she was talking about? Does she know about Wainwright's money?"

"Not enough to hurt you. What did you tell her?"

"Whattya think? I told her to go to you for the money. She gave me a look that would freeze an Eskimo's behind. Listen, uh, I got a little mad. I had to do something. . . . I gave her a name."

"Whose name?"

"Arnold Rothstein. But I was thinking it over and maybe it wasn't such a good—"

"Did you give her the address?"

"Yeah, the Park Central. But I thought maybe I ought to talk this over with you, George. You still there? McManus? Hello? Operator, this is the mayor. This line's gone dead. Hello, McManus? Where the hell are you? McManus!"

388

50

THE DECOR hadn't changed. Potted palms still sat in every corner under the blue silk wallpaper etched with gold fleur-de-lis. Leather chairs lined the walls of the busy lobby. The ornate brass plaque above the front desk still proclaimed it the Park Central Hotel. The balding desk clerk looked up as Elizabeth walked to the elevators. Then he quickly turned to a young couple laden with suitcases.

The elevator operator nodded at her wordlessly as she called out the floor. She felt a strange uneasiness as the familiar elevator rose, as if, were she to ride it to the penthouse and step out, she'd find her husband waiting as though nothing had ever happened between them, as if the past months had been a bad dream. She was surprised to find her palms sweaty, a twinge in her stomach, when the car finally clanked to a halt at the fourth floor. She stopped before a mirror in the hallway and looked at herself very deliberately. She straightened the seams in her stockings. Her outfit—a severe navy-blue suit with long skirt and white silk blouse—looked very proper, very efficient, very sexless. Too sexless, she thought, unfastening one button.

She walked down the hallway, found the door, and rapped twice. It opened almost immediately. She was halfway through the door when she recognized him. The mocking eyes, the thin face, the black hair pomaded close to the scalp. He was the man she had seen in her father's office on that last day, the day he had killed himself.

Arnold Rothstein smiled at her and tried to take the brief-case from her hands. For a moment she wouldn't let it go, not trusting it to this man. There was a silent, ridiculous tussle for the briefcase and then she released it, angry at herself.

As he put it on a table and took her coat she looked about the room. It was a shambles. The odor of stale tobacco hung in the air. The bedspread was half on the floor. Cigarette and cigar butts overflowed every ashtray and had spilled on the rug. In the middle of the room was a round table covered with half-empty glasses, poker chips, playing cards, half-eaten sandwiches, and five neatly stacked two-inch piles of paper money wrapped in rubber bands.

"I broke up a poker game to talk to you," he explained, one hand indicating the mess. "I hope you're worth the trouble. It was a very lucrative poker game."

He held up a bottle of scotch and Elizabeth nodded. He found two relatively clean glasses and poured, then led her to a rattan settee near the window. As she passed the table Elizabeth looked at the money and, without realizing it, licked her lips. Rothstein was smiling again as they sat down.

She sipped her scotch and tried to think of something to say, but her well-rehearsed speech had vanished from her head. She could hear a saxophone player practicing somewhere in a nearby room, going up and down the scales relentlessly. Rothstein watched her closely.

"You remember me, don't you." It wasn't a question.

She looked at him. "I saw you in my father's office, the day that he . . ." She waved her hands vaguely.

"Aren't you curious about what I was doing there?"

"Look," she said, her voice rising against her will, "Jimmy Walker gave me your name. He said you had money to loan. I don't care about anything else. I can't afford to."

Rothstein nodded slowly. "I see. Strictly business. What a shame, a beautiful woman like you, Mrs. McManus." His hand, which had been on the back of the couch, touched her shoulder.

"The name is Wainwright now," she said stiffly.

Rothstein looked surprised. "I understood you were still the wife of George McManus? That could have some bearing on any arrangement we might reach."

"We're still married officially," she admitted, confused. "But we're separated."

"I see," Rothstein said, his hand still on her shoulder in a gesture of intimacy that almost made Elizabeth shiver.

She stood quickly and found her briefcase, aware that his eyes followed her. When she came back to the settee she sat as far away from the dark man as she could. She unfastened the straps and took a thick manila folder from the briefcase.

"Let me show you these contracts," Elizabeth began. "I

think you'll find them good collateral for a loan. Business has been picking up some lately."

Rothstein stared at her. "Collateral? Mrs. McManus, you're my collateral. You see, I prefer to do business in a very personal way, avoiding all the legal niceties and official documents." He touched her hair. "Collateral is for banks, not friends."

The folder fell to Elizabeth's lap. "I don't understand. I thought you were a businessman."

He moved imperceptibly closer to her. "How much would you like to borrow, Mrs. McManus? I know you have many outstanding loans due by the end of the year. A half million should cover them, plus, say, another hundred thousand to tide you over for a while. Let's call it six hundred thousand in all. How does that sound?"

"Where did you learn so much about my business, about what I owe the banks?"

Rothstein ran a finger along her cheek, so softly she barely felt it. "Let's just say Wainwright Construction is a hobby of mine, Mrs. McManus. I may know more about it than you do."

She turned her head, pushing his hand away. "Please don't do that." But she looked at him evenly. "What kind of interest do you want?"

"Just ten percent," Rothstein said, his hand dropping lightly to her knee.

"Ten percent a year is a little high," Elizabeth said hesitantly, watching his hand, repelled by what was happening.

Rothstein shook his head. "My dear Mrs. McManus—Elizabeth. Can I call you Elizabeth? Not ten percent a year, ten percent a week."

She stared at him. "That's impossible. You're asking sixty thousand dollars a week interest? There isn't that much money in the world."

He shrugged. "I don't think you have any choice. Either you take my offer or you go bankrupt." He was squeezing her knee through her dress, running one hand along her thigh.

"I can't raise that much money every week," she said hopelessly.

He looked at her intently. "You could get it from your husband, couldn't you?"

She shook her head, her eyes wide. Elizabeth looked away from Rothstein, toward the stacks of money on the table. He followed her glance.

"There may be another way, Elizabeth. I could forget the interest." His hands were suddenly on her throat, slipping inside her blouse. "If I can't screw George McManus, then I can at least fuck his wife."

Rothstein ripped open the blouse, sending the buttons flying. Quickly he threw himself on top of her, his hands on her breasts. Elizabeth fought to free herself, staring into his black eyes as he pressed his mouth to hers. She shifted violently and slammed her shoulder against his ear. He backed off only a second, then slapped her viciously.

She felt his hands clawing at her hips, forcing up her skirt. There was a roaring in her ears, a pounding, as he half-smothered her, his teeth raking her breasts. She bit, punched, tried to scream, but his weight bore down on her. She could feel him push between her legs, fumbling with his pants as his flushed, sweaty face muffled her shouts. The pounding grew louder, then turned into the splintering of wood, the crack of hardware twisting and bending. Elizabeth and Rothstein both looked up at the same second, frozen in a tableau, to see George McManus standing next to the crazily bent door.

Rothstein turned pale, leaped off Elizabeth, and ran to the bureau next to the bed, tugging at his pants. When he turned around there was a shiny pistol in his hand.

"Get out, McManus. Get out or I'll kill you. This time I win," he shouted as George slowly walked toward him. Rothstein raised the gun from his waist, holding it at arm's length, pulling up his trousers with the other hand.

George saw the hammer of the gun draw back as Rothstein squeezed the trigger. Elizabeth screamed. But there was only a small metallic click. Rothstein looked at the gun stupidly, trying to release the safety as he held his pants in place with his elbow.

George hit Rothstein square on the jaw and sent him reeling over the bed. He dropped the gun, but picked it up quickly. As George came around the bed Rothstein finally snapped off the safety catch. At the same moment George grabbed his hand and tried to pry the gun loose. George stuck a finger under the trigger as Rothstein managed to point the gun at him. Then Rothstein drove his knee into George's thigh and pulled the gun hard. Elizabeth screamed again as the gun went off.

Rothstein stared at McManus in amazement, then looked down to see the spreading bloodstain on the left side of his shirt. His pants fell to the floor as Rothstein staggered against George, then lurched out the door and down the hall, his bony knees knocking above his garters.

George still held the gun in his hands. A few drops of Rothstein's blood were spattered on his coat. He let the gun drop on the bed.

Elizabeth stood up, stunned. She tried to smooth her skirt, pull together her clothes. She went to George and touched his arm.

"Are you all right? There's blood." She pointed at the stains on his coat.

He spun around without a word, picked up her briefcase and coat, and shoved them into her arms. "Get out of here. That shot will bring people running."

"But I want to explain."

George pushed her quickly toward the door. "It's a little late for explaining. I saw you and Rothstein together." He stared at her half-open blouse and red face. "I know why you came here. I know what people will do for money." He pushed her again, this time harder. "Take the stairs so you won't be seen. I don't want anybody knowing my wife—such as she is—was here."

Angry, humiliated, Elizabeth glared at him as she backed past the table toward the door. Then she suddenly stopped. The money. The five thick packets of bills. Her face a flaming red she opened the briefcase and quickly shoved the packets inside, avoiding George's eyes.

"Go ahead and take it," he said harshly. "You earned it."

Defiantly, the briefcase clutched in her arms, Elizabeth ran out of the room. In a moment he heard her footsteps on the stairs, then they faded away. George closed the splintered door and walked back to the bed. He picked up the gun, wiped it quickly with the edge of a sheet, went to a window, and shoved the gun through a rip in the screen. From far away there came the wail of a siren as he took one last look around the room, then slipped into the hall. George heard voices, the slamming of doors around the corner at the other end of the corridor. He took the stairs two at a time.

51

THE ELECTRIC LIGHT from the dime-a-dance parlor across the street blinked on and off incessantly. The screeching of children, the pounding of feet on ancient stairways blasted through the thin walls. The smell of boiled cabbage seeped into the dingy room, fouling the air, his clothes, even his hair with that rotting sweet smell. Did every tenement reek of boiled cabbage? It was the perfume of the poor.

George McManus opened the window shade a crack and looked down on Eleventh Avenue. It hadn't changed much since he was young. Children still played in the streets, dodging traffic, tossing stones at cars that dared to pass nearby. Idle men huddled over small fires burning in rusty trash cans. Across the street old women watched the world from their perches in upper-story windows. Women in too much make-up and too little clothing led faceless, nameless men to joyless rendezvous.

He released the shade and looked around his own bare room. Barely enough space to turn around, kitchen in the living room, bathtub in the kitchen. Too little heat. Too many bugs. The police weren't looking for him in Hell's Kitchen, George knew. But he was beginning to wish they would.

He tensed at the sound of a man's heavy footsteps in the hall, approaching the door. He inched toward the window with the fire escape, taking care not to make any noise. A fist rapped twice quickly, paused, then rapped three more times. George relaxed and opened up.

Izzy the Stub's expression was grim as he came in. He didn't carry the usual packages of groceries, only a folded newspaper. George quickly shut the door behind him.

"More *tsuris*, boss. A Hearst reporter found another witness under a rock someplace. And Jimmy Hines says this one could even be kosher." Izzy handed the paper to George.

He'd made the front page again, George saw, as he stood by the beat-up dresser. "WITNESS SAW MCMANUS LEAVE MURDER SCENE," the big headline screamed.

Izzy sat on a rickety chair next to the radiator and tried to coax some heat out of the metal. "This lady was supposed to be in a room down the hall sitting on a gentleman's face when she heard the fireworks. It's possible." He shrugged. "But Hines says Mr. Hearst is paying her five thousand dollars to refresh her memory. For that money I could remember seeing Lincoln give his address at Gettysburg—and the phone number, too."

"So we'll find another witness, too. A dozen witnesses—and all nuns," George said flatly, tossing the paper on the bed. "They still haven't got a case. Right?"

Izzy nodded but wouldn't look George in the eye. He was holding something back.

"Right?" George repeated.

Izzy sighed. "The truth is, boss, I don't know if even two-dozen nuns will help you. Hines says there is going to be an indictment. First-degree murder."

George slumped on the bed, his hands over his face. "An indictment? What the hell has that fat-ass been doing all this time? It was supposed to be smoothed over by now."

Izzy shrugged. "He said to tell you he's trying, boss. He arranged for the police to lose the fingerprint report. And he's trying to send the hotel desk clerk on a long vacation. But . . ."

Izzy paused. He saw that McManus's eyes were red-rimmed. He hadn't been sleeping, Izzy thought. He looked unhealthy. His skin had a grayish tone. There was a cigarette burn on the sleeve of his jacket.

"But what?" George demanded.

"Nothing, nothing," Izzy replied. "Only next time you shoot someone, maybe you could pick a person who is not so famous. Maybe next time you could shoot the President or the Pope or the chief rabbi of Brooklyn. But Rothstein . . . ? You know that there are now seventeen people who are swearing they actually saw you pull the trigger? Swearing. What was it, a convention?

395

"On top of that, Hearst is trying to kill you. A reporter even planted one of your old overcoats in Rothstein's closet. You have some wonderful enemies, boss."

Izzy got up and took the newspaper off the bed. "And this is only the early edition. Every paper in town is writing about you every day." He dropped the paper on the rickety kitchen table. "So now maybe you know why Hines is having a hard time pretending you are only guilty of jaywalking."

Heavy footsteps sounded on the ceiling, then muffled voices and the crash of crockery.

"Six o'clock on the nose," George said, checking his watch, almost welcoming the interruption. "Another example of marital bliss in action. They haven't missed a night in the three weeks I've been hiding in this dump."

"Only two weeks," Izzy corrected.

George lay back on the bed, staring at the wall for a long time, Izzy watching him.

"Boss, why did you do it?" Izzy finally said softly. "Everything was going hunky-dory. Nobody can figure out why you killed Rothstein."

George looked at Izzy for a moment, then swung his legs off the bed and stood up. He pulled a small leather satchel from under the bed and unzipped it, then opened a bureau drawer and transferred some socks into the bag.

"Get my gray suit out of the closet, Izzy."

"But Hines said—"

"To hell with Hines," George muttered as he folded a shirt. "If I lie low any longer I'll be tripping over my beard before I get out of here."

"Just a few more days, Hines said," Izzy protested.

George shook his head as he put on a tie. "No more days. He was supposed to cover up for me. Now I'm facing a murder rap. I'll take my chances outside."

Izzy brought the gray suit from the closet. He watched George change, brushing dust off his gray fedora.

"At least call Hines, boss," Izzy finally said. "He might be making some plans and you could screw him all up. I think you should call him."

George brushed his hair back carefully, then tossed the brush in the bag and zipped it up. "My mother didn't worry

396

about me the way you do." He looked at Izzy. "All right, stop with the long face. I'll call. Gimme a nickel."

Izzy handed him a coin, then opened the door and peered into the hallway. A red-haired boy played with a ball on the steps but he ran downstairs when he saw Izzy. Otherwise the hall was deserted. He led George to the telephone at the end of the hall, then moved away to watch the stairs as McManus dialed.

He was on the telephone for a long time, speaking in a hushed voice, before he finally hung up.

"It's set," George explained. "Hines wasn't happy, but he's arranging for Broderick to pick me up in the barber shop at the Plaza. I told him I need a shave before I see my public. I go into night court at eight o'clock. I'll be out on bail by eight-fifteen and halfway through a big steak by eight-thirty."

Izzy nodded. "Wait and I'll find us a taxicab. And please, do not shoot anybody while I am gone."

Izzy was halfway down the stairs when George called him back. "I need another nickel," he whispered.

Izzy tossed him the coin with a wary glance, then went downstairs. George walked back to the telephone, staring at the dingy wall for a moment. Finally he put the coin into the slot and dialed.

"Wainwright Construction," a female voice answered after the third ring.

George cleared his throat. "Let me speak to Elizabeth McManus."

"McManus? Oh, you mean Miss Wainwright. She's away from her desk for a moment, sir. Hold on and I'll try to locate her."

There was a quiet hum. Then he heard footsteps on the other side of the line.

"Hello. Can I help you?"

He recognized her voice immediately.

"This is Elizabeth Wainwright. Can I help you?" He listened to the sound of her breathing. She turned from the phone and spoke to someone else, then came back on the line.

"Is this a joke?" she demanded. "Is anyone there? Philip, is that you?"

For a second he opened his mouth to speak, but nothing came out.

"If this is a joke, it's not very funny. You'd better stop calling me every day like this, whoever you are. I'm warning you, I'll report you to the telephone company."

George slowly put the earpiece back on the hook.

Detective Sergeant John Broderick held the tall courtroom door open officiously, as befitted the man who brought in George McManus.

"Remind me to leave you a tip, Johnny," George whispered as they went down the aisle. Broderick gave him a short, vicious jab in the ribs as they reached the swinging gates.

"Yer a funny lad," Broderick muttered as he shoved Mc-Manus into his chair, then jerked George's hat off his head, threw it on the defense table, and sat down behind him.

Joseph Rosenbach looked up from where he was talking to the bailiff and came over to sit next to McManus.

"How are you, George?" he asked, shaking hands. "How does it feel to be a famous man? You've gotten yourself into a real mess this time."

McManus shrugged. "Just doing my part to keep you lawyers in three-hundred-dollar suits and good cigars. How'd you get on this case?"

"Hines had me dragged out of a saloon to represent you. I assume he's got everything arranged with this Judge Lenahan. A Tammany hack right down the line. If Hines told him to go to hell, Lenahan would be waiting for the next bus with a pitchfork in his hand."

George sat back and studied Rosenbach. The lawyer was a little thinner, had a few more liver spots and even less hair than when he had represented George in the Paradise Rehearsal Club injunction case. But the reedy old man still had the look in his eye of someone who had seen the worst man can do, and survived it all.

"Still, I got the feeling talking to Hines that he was a little perturbed with you, George," Rosenbach went on. "He didn't want you to come out of hiding?"

George tugged at his collar. "Hines does what Walker

wants. And Walker doesn't like the publicity over Rothstein's death. Too many waves, too many questions. Say, why is it so hot in here?" George noticed that a number of people were fanning themselves.

Rosenbach smiled. "One of Lenahan's idiosyncrasies. He gets chills easily so he orders the heat turned up in his court."

They were both silent for a moment, avoiding the obvious next question. "I have to ask you," George finally said. "Do you think you can get me off for Rothstein's death?"

Rosenbach's big head bobbed back and forth. He fiddled with the handkerchief in his breast pocket. "You want the truth?"

George nodded.

"It won't be easy. You're a hot potato," Rosenbach told him quietly. "But having Hines behind you means a lot."

There was a stir in the courtroom as the judge swept in, wearing a bulky black robe. He was a tall man, almost totally bald, with an ancient, wrinkled face. George could see the edge of a wool suit and a sweater under the judge's robes.

"Hear ye, hear ye. Night session of the Criminal Court of the County of New York will now come to order. The Honorable Francis X. Lenahan presiding," called the bailiff. "The first case is People versus. George McManus."

George watched two bored reporters talking in the press seats, their collars open in the oppressive heat. At the mention of his name they nearly fell off their chairs. One stared at McManus and began scribbling furiously in a notebook. The other hurried up the aisle to call his paper, George guessed. As he watched the reporter go out George noticed a fat, middle-aged man with a big, unlit cigar in his teeth sitting in the last row of the courtroom. It was Jimmy Hines, he realized with a start. They nodded to each other.

"You may proceed, Mr. Rosenbach," the judge began in a quavering voice.

"Your honor, this is a simple bail hearing for Mr. McManus," Rosenbach said, rising. "The charges against him are clear and serious, but I wish to point out that he surrendered himself to police custody voluntarily. Mr. McManus is also a responsible member of the community with substantial assets and a thriving business. Under the circumstances, the defense moves that he be freed on his own recognizance until such time as trial may be scheduled."

Rosenbach sat down and the judge looked at the prosecution table. The assistant district attorney, a pudgy man with a double chin, looked up with an expression of utter boredom.

"This is a capital case. One hour ago the defendant was indicted by the Manhattan grand jury on a charge of first-degree murder. Therefore the prosecution moves that Mr. McManus be denied bail," he droned desultorily.

The judge rapped his gavel. "Prosecution's motion is granted. Bailiff, you will see that Mr. McManus is escorted to the Tombs where he is to be held until trial. Next case."

George was stunned. Before he could react the bailiff was beside him, holding his arm, pulling out handcuffs. He looked at Rosenbach but the lawyer seemed equally surprised.

"I'll find out what's going on," Rosenbach promised. "I'll see you get out tonight. There's been some mistake."

The bailiff deftly slipped the handcuffs over McManus's wrists and squeezed them shut, the small connecting chain rattling. He ordered George to his feet. Broderick handed him his hat with a big smile.

"Don't bother," George told Rosenbach as the bailiff began to lead him away. "I think I already know what's going on and it's no mistake."

McManus looked at the last row of benches, where Jimmy Hines contentedly spun his unlit cigar between his fingers.

1929

Through all the drama—whether damned or not—
Love gilds the scene, and women guide the plot.

—RICHARD BRINSLEY SHERIDAN
The Rivals

52

SOMETIMES he would watch the machine for hours at a time, fascinated as the stream of yellow ribbon wound through the glass bulb and past the many cogs and sprockets until it came to rest curled like a snake on the floor. He would listen to the chatter and whir of the machine endlessly running the stiff tape easily through his fingers as he read the names and numbers punched into it. Sometimes, when the machine was running quickly, constantly revising and correcting itself, he felt he could sense the thousands of people around the country and across the world who hovered over similar devices, trying to divine the true message, the secret path, from this same tape. For the machine was indeed all things to all men, he came to realize.

The machine told him where his money was, of course. And what it was doing. But beyond that, he learned the subtle signs that meant companies were faltering, fortunes were being won or lost. He knew when the government handed down directives, when banks panicked, when a few bold men tried to corner the market on gold or silver or oil. The machine had no emotions itself, he knew. And yet he often felt a pulse beat through the tape, a quickening in its tempo, and he would become alert, forgetting to eat or drink.

So fascinated was he by the machine that after a while, during the days, George McManus almost forgot how incongruous it was that he and a stock ticker should be sharing a jail cell.

The nights were more difficult. After the machine clicked off for the day and the lights went out in the long cellblock that had been reserved for him alone, George McManus would lie on his bed and think. He would think of Jimmy Hines and the Paradise Rehearsal Club and Big Bill Dwyer, who was running the club while he was in his spacious cell with bars-to-bars carpeting, liquor, books, a radio, and his stock ticker. But mostly he thought of Elizabeth.

In March, when Izzy the Stub said Hines was about ready to release him, the ticker let George know that Studebaker stock was about to go through the roof. He made almost a million dollars, but he remained in his cell. Hines felt he should stay behind bars until after Governor Roosevelt endorsed Walker for reelection. It wouldn't take long, Hines promised. That month George dreamed often of the first time he had ever seen Elizabeth, in her wedding gown.

In June, the endorsement came through on the same day that the machine told George McManus that he should buy a lot of Houston Oil. He made a million and a half dollars. But Hines said just be patient a little longer. Wait until the primary. It was only logical, Izzy said. That night George dreamed of the way men would stand up straight, suck in their stomachs, and pat down stray hairs when Elizabeth came into a room.

One morning in September, mere hours after Jimmy Walker won renomination, George slept very late. The machine was already running when he awoke, chattering excitedly. He stared at the machine for a long time from his bed but he did not get up and look at the yellow tape as he normally did every day. Instead, he lay and tried to hold onto his latest dream. He and Elizabeth had flown in her plane, then picnicked beside a stream. After a while he remembered how they had made love in the water, the sun shimmering off her wet body. Now he recalled the smells of the nearby field, the wind in the trees, the soft splash of the water. He closed his eyes, hoping he would go back to sleep and dream again, perhaps remember more details of that day.

But every time he would doze off the machine would ring and clatter again, waking him, reminding him of the limits of his life. Finally he got up and went to the machine. It told him something was happening to Woolworth's stock; thousands of shares were changing hands. But he only dropped the tape and sat in his armchair—another luxury—and looked out the small barred window at a patch of blue sky, like every prisoner in every cell in every age.

53

STILL IN HIS PAJAMAS, George McManus padded to a small table holding several bottles of liquor and glasses. He poured bourbon into a glass until the bottle was empty.

"O'Toole!" he shouted, carrying the bottle to the cell door. *"O'Toole!"*

A bushy-browed policeman with slits for eyes came sauntering down the corridor, his hat pushed back on his head and his collar undone. He looked to be in his fifties and about George's size, though thicker in the waist. He carried a metal ring holding a dozen big keys.

"Yeah?" he said, only moving one side of his mouth.

"I'm out of bourbon." George held out a twenty-dollar bill. "Be a good flatfoot and run out and get me a bottle of the usual."

"Keep the change?"

George nodded. "And pick up the afternoon papers."

The policeman sighed. "That newsstand is another half block from the speakeasy, Mr. McManus. I shouldn't be leaving my post for so long a time."

George peeled a five off his roll of bills and handed it over. "O'Toole, you're the biggest crook I ever met. As there's a God in Heaven you should be in this cell instead of me."

The policeman stuffed the money in a pocket and clicked his heels in mock salute. He went away, keys jingling.

George sat on the bed and picked up the morning papers as the stock ticker chattered. He went through them restlessly, then dropped them on the carpet. He stood and walked across to the ticker, picking up the long yellow tape. Woolworth's was up four points since yesterday. He should have bought. George impatiently dropped the tape as he had the newspapers, pacing restlessly up and down the big cell. He should shave and dress, he knew, but he didn't.

Soon the jingle of keys heralded O'Toole's return. George went to the cell door and the policeman passed the newspapers and the bottle, wrapped in brown paper, through to him.

"You got a visitor." O'Toole pointed a thumb over one shoulder. Big Bill Dwyer was coming down the long steel corridor. The policeman unlocked the door, let Dwyer in, then relocked it and left them alone.

Dwyer looked at him critically. "It's noon and you're still in pajamas?"

"I wasn't expecting company until the cocktail hour," George said, unwrapping the bottle. "How about a libation?"

Dwyer shook his head.

George sat on the armchair, opened the bottle, and sipped from it as Dwyer sat on the bed. The shadow of the bars fell on the legs of Dwyer's well-tailored suit. He wore the same diamond stickpin George had seen the first day they met. The years in prison after the submarine crash hadn't seemed to age him at all, George thought. Dwyer's eyes were still clear blue and untroubled, the face strong and impossibly smooth for a man in his fifties. Dwyer held his derby and walking stick in one hand, his gray gloves casually in the other, as if being in a cell were the most natural thing in the world, like sitting in someone's parlor sipping tea.

"How are things at the club, Bill?"

Dwyer shrugged. "Pretty much the same as last week. Since Walker won the primary he doesn't need as much publicity. Broderick and the boys only raided the joint once this week. They gave us plenty of warning and only broke up two tables. Very civilized."

"I read about it in the papers," George said. "So much for the court injunction. Aren't there any laws in this city?"

"I showed the injunction to Broderick one night." Dwyer sighed. "He took the frame off the wall and read it. Did you know he moves his lips? Then he tore up the court order and took the frame home with him. He said we should sue Hines if we didn't like it. Tammany gives and Tammany takes away."

McManus stood and walked over to the stock ticker again. He tapped the glass cover impatiently and tore off the tape, examining the piece in his hand.

"Woolworth's is up another point. You ought to jump on

this one, Bill. My mechanical friend here says it should go lots higher."

"You know how I feel about the stock market, George. That's really gambling—without the fun. Anyway, I like to see my money, feel it make lumps in my mattress."

McManus came back to the bed and sat beside Dwyer. "Well, I can't complain. The market's made me the richest man behind bars." He gulped more bourbon.

"What the hell went wrong, Bill?" George finally said. "Where did we screw up? There we were on top of the world, then everything fell apart. You went to prison, I'm in here for months. I don't get it. We paid our bribes on time, we knew all the right people, we didn't stiff anybody at the club. So how come the world has decided to shit on us?"

Dwyer crossed his arms gravely. "I don't know. Maybe nobody is supposed to stay on top forever. Even Arnold Rothstein. But the important thing now is to get you out of here."

George rubbed his hand across his chin, feeling his ragged, bristly stubble. "Get me out of here? I'm beginning to wonder if I'll *ever* get out of here. And even if I do, then what, Bill? Those Tammany bastards have cut me loose."

"What are you talking about?"

"I'm talking about the electric chair," George said, emphasizing the last word. "I'm an embarrassment to Hines and Walker. An inconvenience. I've been doing a lot of thinking here in my gilded cage, and I've got a feeling they'd be happier to see me out of the way. Zap. Fifty-thousand volts. And you know what? That's the way I'd see it if I was in their shoes."

Dwyer shook his head. "It's not like that at all. They're not out for blood, George. They're only trying to stay on top, too. In fact, Hines is offering you a deal. A proposition."

George looked at him closely. "Well, I guess the least I can do is spare some moments out of my busy day to listen."

Dwyer carefully put his hat and cane on the bed before beginning. "Short and not so sweet, then. Hines wants you to plead guilty to manslaughter. He says he can guarantee you five to ten years, and with good behavior you'll be out in four."

George jumped to his feet and went to the cell door. He

leaned his forehead against the cold steel, then suddenly slapped the bars hard, four times, until his hands stung.

"Four years? Four years out of my life?" George turned back to Dwyer, flexing his red hands. "I'd rather be dead."

"Look, George . . ." Dwyer began.

McManus ignored him, pacing quickly back and forth across the cell. "I can see why Hines didn't come here and give me this 'deal' personally. An eyeful of spit can be very painful."

Dwyer sighed. "Think it over," he said quietly. "Then I think you should accept it. Four years isn't so bad. I just did three on the submarine business and it didn't kill me. You're young. You'll come out of prison a rich man, all set up." Dwyer's voice trailed off as he watched George pace angrily.

"They're not going to let you go," Dwyer added slowly. "They can't, George. You're in too deep—they're in too deep. The bad guys hate you for killing Rothstein. The good guys hate you for symbolizing Walker's corruption. You know there are still good-government pickets walking around in front of the jail demanding your skin? After all these months."

McManus held up his hands. "Just shut up, Bill. Shut up for a minute and let me think."

He went back to pacing, then finally threw himself into the big chair. For a long time the two men avoided looking at each other. McManus stared at the wall, the bars, the window. Dwyer fiddled with his cuffs, then his cane, waiting for the other man to speak. The silence was awkward, strained.

Finally George stood and walked over to Dwyer, looking down at the older man. "What do *you* think my chances are, Bill? If I don't deal?"

Dwyer shook his head. "Let me put it this way. There's a lot of money already bet on your trial—and the bookies are giving eight to five against you. Does that answer your question?"

George studied the other man, then said: "Lie down on the floor."

"What?"

"I said, lie down on the floor. Pretend you're having a heart attack or something."

"Are you crazy?"

George began to unbutton his pajamas. "I have to get out of here. I think maybe I can beat this mess. At least I have to try. But I can't do anything in here. Now will you help me by getting on the floor?"

"You'll get into big trouble," Dwyer warned.

George looked at him. "I'm already in trouble, remember?"

Dwyer paused. "Can I put a blanket on the floor? I don't want to get my suit dirty."

George took a blanket off the bed and spread it on the rug. Dwyer lay down stiffly on his stomach and closed his eyes.

"*O'Toole!*" George shouted, going to the door. "*O'Toole, get in here fast!*"

The policeman's heavy shoes thudded on the steel floor until he puffed to a stop in front of the cell.

"I think he's had a heart attack," George explained quickly.

Wide-eyed, O'Toole fumbled with his keys, finally unlocking the door. He knelt beside Dwyer and touched his shoulder. "What's the matter, buddy?"

George went to the corner of the cell and patted the stock ticker. Then he picked it up, stepped behind the policeman, and dumped the machine across his back. O'Toole collapsed over Dwyer with a surprised look on his face as pieces of the machine rolled across the rug.

"Help me get his clothes off." George began unbuttoning O'Toole's shirt.

They stripped the unconscious man and bound his hands with his socks. In a minute George was dressed in the uniform and pulling the visor of the blue hat over his forehead.

"What do you think? Too bad I don't have time to shave." George studied himself in the mirror hanging on the wall.

"I think you're nuts," Dwyer said, brushing dust off his knees. "But good luck."

George let himself out of the cell. "In about fifteen minutes you can have a miraculous recovery and untie our friend there. Thanks, Bill."

Dwyer waved, but George was already walking down the corridor, forcing himself not to run. Using O'Toole's keys he slid open two sets of doors. In the guards' room three men were playing dominoes, their uniform coats open to the waist. None of them looked up as George walked through. He went

411

down three flights of stairs and then across the busy lobby to the front doors. No one looked at him twice.

Outside, he stopped for a moment and breathed deeply. On the sidewalk two serious-looking young men and an old woman in a tired, ankle-length black dress carried signs as they walked to and fro. "Walker's Pals Get Away With Murder" and "Clean the Scum Out of Our Town," the men's signs proclaimed. The woman's sign said crisply: "Fry McManus."

George walked clumsily along the street, his feet suddenly feeling thick and heavy. He brushed by the old woman with a tip of the cap that covered his face and made for the subway entrance that glowed under the street light at the next corner.

But, finally, he couldn't stop himself. Almost against his will his feet began to move more quickly. He ran the last hundred feet and leaped down the subway steps three at a time.

Jimmy Hines was cutting into his roast beef when the maid bent and whispered in his ear. He looked up at her briefly, then dismissed her and looked about the table at his wife and three daughters, who were deep in conversation. He pushed his chair back and stood up, leaving his napkin tucked under his chin. With a nod to his wife he stalked from the dining room down the dim hall toward the front door, angry at the interruption in his meal. A uniformed policeman stood next to the coat rack.

"What's the meaning of this, officer? What ever's so important that it couldn't have waited until—McManus?"

George grabbed the portly man by his lapels, spun him about, and pushed him against the wall. "Yes, McManus. Surprised to see me?"

"Why . . . ? Where . . . ? What are you doing in uniform?" Hines gasped, his face turning red as he tried feebly to pry George's hands off.

"Shut up and listen, you little worm," George warned. "Now I'm out of the Tombs and I'm staying out. You're going to see to that, understand?"

"You're crazy," Hines sputtered, trying to push George away.

"People keep telling me that. Did you hear what I said, Hines? You're going to arrange for my bail until the trial, got it?"

"I don't know . . . if I can do that," Hines said wide-eyed. "You—you're an escaped prisoner."

George pressed him against the wall until the other man gasped and fought for breath. "I'll do it, I swear. I'll arrange bail," Hines coughed.

"And don't get any funny ideas when I'm gone," George warned. "I'm a killer. A desperate man. Remember?" He grabbed Hines under the armpits, hoisted him up, and hung the back of his jacket on a coat hook. The fat man kicked helplessly, his feet six inches off the floor.

George slapped Hines lightly on the cheek. "I'm warning you. If you cross me again, next time I won't be such a gentleman, you son of a bitch."

George took a cigar from Hines's pocket, broke it in half, and stuffed the pieces into Hines's mouth. Then he backed away and opened the door, leaving Hines squirming and spitting on the hook. He turned around to see Hines's wife and three daughters standing in a little group in the hall, staring at him.

"Good evening, ladies." George tipped his cap and watched all four women curtsey slightly as he went out.

"Get me down, woman," he heard Hines sputter through the door. "Goddammit, don't stand there like four fools. Find me a chair!"

54

THE ROOM was inky black but Elizabeth didn't turn on the lights. She carefully made her way through the darkness, avoiding the familiar furniture, until she found the vanity. She touched the low chair before it and sat down, staring into what she knew was the tall mirror. It reflected only darkness, as if she didn't exist.

She sat there for a long time, listening to her own breathing.

She found the darkness soothing and it eased her tired eyes. What a luxury to look, she thought, but not have to see.

Finally she moved her right hand over the shapes of the perfume bottles and make-up boxes, past the power puffs and pins and combs and brushes until she found the small lamp with the ruffled shade and turned it on. The lamp gave off a weak, yellow light, a little pool of color that left the corners of the big bedroom dark. Now the mirror showed her a thin, achingly-tired woman, her hair up, her clothes and face muted in color. In the mirror, in the low light, she could almost have been a man, Elizabeth thought with a start.

Her hand went to her throat, unbuttoned the high-collared blouse, then took the pins from her hair and let it fall about her face. Yes, it was a woman after all. She pinched her cheeks to bring some life back into them. So drab. Yes, that was better, she thought. That was Elizabeth Wainwright in the mirror. Or was it Elizabeth McManus?

She picked up the small clock on the table. Almost midnight. She tried to remember if she had had dinner, or even lunch, but the details slipped away from her. She realized that she wasn't even sure what day it was. Her life had become a blur of meetings and decisions and arguments, one day much like the next. She only knew that each night she sat alone like this, staring into the mirror.

She slowly began to undress, watching herself take off the jacket and blouse. She stood for a moment and pulled her skirt and slip over her head, then removed her underwear. Finally she rolled her silk stockings off and tossed them aside. She started to reach for her dressing gown, but stopped and sat down, drawn by the mirror again.

In the yellow light her body now seemed to glow softly, the edges diffused, her hair nearly lost in the darker shadows of the room. Unconsciously her hand went back to her throat and she let it fall, tracing a line between her breasts. Slowly, tentatively, her hands cupped her breasts, squeezing gently until she shivered, suddenly surprised and dismayed at her emotions. So long, she thought. So very long.

With one hand she opened a drawer in the side of the vanity and took out a small, framed photograph. She leaned it against the mirror, letting her hand linger on the photo for a moment.

She studied it closely, her eyes following the boxy lines of an airplane to the man standing casually with one leg on the wing and the other in the cockpit. The face of George McManus looked at her mischievously, full of secrets. The picture was grainy, the face slightly out of focus, but she stared at it for a long time, trying to bring back that day, to remember.

Then she looked up into the mirror again, meeting her own eyes. She sat straight, putting her shoulders back. Her hands touched her thighs, her stomach, then almost reluctantly came back to her breasts, tracing around each areola. She could feel her nipples grow, stiffen. She looked back at the photograph, excited, aroused, but angry, too. Her body was warm, flushed. In the mirror she watched the hands on her breasts, pinching her nipples—but almost as if they were the hands of another. She felt her legs quiver, her back arch. She fought to remember. So long. A moan came out of her almost grudgingly, then another. She closed her eyes.

"Very touching."

Elizabeth shot to her feet and spun around. Someone stepped out of the shadows, the lamplight glinting off brass buttons.

"Who is it? Oh, God!" She stood before George McManus naked, her face scarlet, a hundred questions running through her mind. But as she stared at his uniform, all she could ask was: "You're a policeman?"

"Let's just say I'm very close to the law." George stepped around her, put his hat on the vanity, and picked up the photograph. "Not a very flattering shot."

"What are you doing here?" Elizabeth stammered. "You're in jail. I mean, you're supposed to be."

He put down the picture and looked at her. "I got out for good behavior. And since I haven't been with a woman for months, who else would I go to but my loving wife?"

Anger, confusion, shame flooded through Elizabeth. Suddenly she remembered she was naked and her hands moved instinctively to cover herself. She reached for her dressing gown but he grabbed her shoulders, pulling her toward him.

"Not so fast, toots." His fingers dug into her. "I think I like you better like this, where you can't hide anything from me."

Elizabeth twisted out of his grip. "If all you want is a

415

woman, there's a hundred dollars in my purse. Take it and buy yourself what you need."

He reached out and slowly ran a finger from her shoulder down one arm to her wrist. Elizabeth could hear his breathing quicken but she did not move.

"That's right, your price is a lot higher, isn't it? What did it cost Arnold Rothstein—five hundred thousand? Six hundred thousand? Not to mention his life."

He laid one hand flat on her stomach, then rubbed slowly. She stiffened at the feel of his heat on her skin before pushing him away.

"Let me get dressed. Please, George."

But his hand came up again and brushed her hair back from her face. "My God, but you're beautiful. I'd almost forgotten." He couldn't help adding: "Do you think Rothstein died a happy man?"

"Stop this," she pleaded. "You don't know what you're saying."

Again she pushed his hand away, trembling with anger but aware of how near George was, of his breath on her brow as he stepped closer. His rough coat just brushed her nipples and she felt an electric surge—half revulsion and half longing. She forced herself to move back a step but he moved too, his hands now squeezing her hips.

"It wasn't like that, damn you. It was business," she said, surprisingly softly. "I only went to Rothstein to borrow money. And when you came—well, I needed that money. I couldn't think of anything else."

George stepped back and walked slowly behind Elizabeth, trailing one hand over her body. She could feel his breath on her neck as he pressed against her back and put his arms around her. His hands came up and cupped her breasts, teasing her nipples.

"Please stop," she whispered. "Let me get dressed."

He put his mouth close to her ear. "Only business? One man has already died for your business, and I spent nine months in a cell with half the city clamoring to put me in the electric chair." He squeezed her nipples harder until she squirmed. "Can you imagine what it feels like, to spend nine months in a cell?"

416

One hand came down and kneaded her stomach. "Now your business is going to cost me a fortune in bribes to beat a murder conviction. The club is being raided every week. Today I slugged a cop and escaped from the Tombs." She closed her eyes as he whispered harshly in her ear. His hand found her pubic hair.

"A couple of hours ago I left Jimmy Hines hanging from a coat hook. You remember Hines, don't you, Elizabeth—the most powerful man in Tammany? I'm depending on Hines for my life and I left him on a coat hook. What do you think my future prospects are, Elizabeth?"

His hand found her soft crease. She shuddered at his words, at what he was doing to her, but she couldn't help herself. She moved her legs apart, inviting his probing fingers. His lips were on her ear, teeth biting her lobe. She pressed herself back against him.

"The crazy thing is, Elizabeth, that I never stopped dreaming of you in that cell. Every night, weeks and then months at a time. I relived every moment we ever spent together. You never visited me, but I thought of you all the time. Isn't that crazy, Elizabeth?"

She moaned, shuddered. Her hand covered his, pressing his fingers more tightly into her. Her hips began to quiver involuntarily.

"Tonight I climbed up your trellis and sat in the dark waiting for you, Elizabeth. I knew it would be worth it. I thought about ways to hurt you, the way you hurt me every morning when I woke up from my dreams."

He could smell her desire now, feel the sweat on her skin. "And then, my pretty little wife, I saw you at the vanity. I watched you take out the picture. I knew you still wanted me."

Elizabeth twisted about and threw her arms around his neck. She pulled his mouth to hers fiercely as he dug his fingers into her buttocks. He picked her up and carried her to the shadowy bed.

"Shut up. Shut up and make love to me," she murmured, her face buried in his neck, her teeth scraping the skin.

He laid her on the bed and knelt next to her. She looked up at him, making little noises in her throat, then her fingers

417

pulled swiftly at the buttons of his uniform. For a moment he watched her, almost detached as she writhed naked before him. Then he grabbed her hands and pulled them away.

He stepped from the bed, rebuttoned his coat, then turned and went to the vanity. He picked up the policeman's hat and put it on squarely, looking in the mirror. In the glass he saw her raise up on one elbow on the bed.

"Come back to me," she called. "Don't go away."

George went to the bedroom door and opened it, checking that the corridor was empty. Then he walked close to the bed.

"You see, when I saw you with that picture, Elizabeth, I knew how I could hurt you," he said quietly. In the shadows he thought he saw tears streak her cheeks.

He went back to the door. He had expected this to be a moment of triumph. He had expected her to scream at him, wail in anguish. But as he shut the door behind him she said nothing and he suddenly felt very hollow. He stood in the corridor for a long time, almost hoping she would cry out. The night sounds of the big house and the city outside mocked him.

When he opened her door and came back to her, she was lying, still naked, on the bed.

55

"LET'S GO THROUGH IT one more time."

Izzy moaned, slumping in the straight-backed wooden chair.

"Where were you on the night of November fourth, nineteen twenty-eight?" Joe Rosenbach began again, standing in the middle of the rug with his hands clasped behind him.

"Jersey," Izzy replied mechanically.

"Where in New Jersey?" the lawyer pressed.

"Hoboken."

"And what were you doing there?"

"Business."

Rosenbach nodded. "It's about time. You're finally learn-ing. Don't volunteer anything, Izzy. Just answer the ques-tions. Now, what kind of business?"

"We were looking at a lady singer, for the saloon."

"The saloon? You mean Mr. McManus's social club?"

"Yes, that is what I mean."

"Was Mr. McManus with you that night?"

"Why not? He is the boss."

"And how long were you and Mr. McManus together?"

"The whole night and the next morning, also. We drove to Mr. Dwyer's farm after."

"After?"

"After we looked at the singer."

Rosenbach turned and picked a glass of red wine off the desk. "Okay, I guess he'll do all right on the stand. Just make sure he wears something quiet to court. If he testifies like that"—Rosenbach indicated Izzy's red sport coat with wide blue checks—"the jury will laugh so hard they won't hear anything he's saying."

Izzy stood and stretched, holding the small of his back. "Very nice. He makes me sit in this chair for two hours, then he insults my clothes."

Rosenbach sipped his wine. "It's your turn again, George." He motioned toward the chair.

McManus shook his head. "I've been through it enough times. I've been out on bail for six weeks and I'm already testifying in my sleep. I know what I have to say. Act confi-dent but not cocky. Stick to the story. Look straight at the jurors if somebody says anything damaging about me. Wear the same conservative suit every day. Not too cheap, not too expensive. Right?"

Rosenbach took his wine to the sofa and sat down. "That's it, then. I'll coach the other witnesses tomorrow in my office —the singer, some of Dwyer's stablehands, the bartender at this Jersey club, your chauffeur. It doesn't look as bad as I thought, George. As long as there's no eyewitness to put you in Rothstein's room at the moment of the shooting, it's our word against the prosecution's."

Rosenbach hesitated. "There are no eyewitnesses, are there, George? I mean, I hate surprises when I get to court."

McManus sat forward on his desk, resting his chin on his knuckles. "No eyewitnesses, Joe."

"I only ask because I'm hearing rumors," Rosenbach said, his big head cocked sideways over his ridiculously thin body, fierce eyes fixed on McManus.

"Rumors are a dime a dozen." McManus clicked two poker chips between his fingers. Outside in the club the band began to play the "Sugar Blues." It was a slow rag, gentle and melodious, for the early-evening crowd.

"We miss anything?" George looked at the corner where Big Bill Dwyer sat in an armchair, his legs stretched out before him, each crease in his pants carefully adjusted.

Dwyer stirred, resting the heel of one shoe on the toe of the other. "No, it sounds all right," he said thoughtfully. "There's just one thing I don't understand, George. I've been trying to figure it out for weeks. If you didn't kill Rothstein, why not just tell the truth? Who are you really trying to protect?"

"The truth?" Rosenbach snorted. "What has the truth got to do with the law? You should know how it works, Bill. You've made enough payoffs, done enough finagling. Our witnesses lie. The district attorney's witnesses lie. But this time we buy the judge before the other side does to help make sure the jurors believe our liars instead of theirs."

Dwyer and McManus looked at each other.

"Oh, no," Rosenbach complained, standing quickly. "I'm not going into a court of law to defend anybody with the truth. You can get yourself another lawyer if that's what you want. I've gone to a lot of trouble, stuck my neck out, to set up this alibi."

George came from behind the desk and calmed the old man with a hand on his arm. "You're the expert, Joe. We'll do it your way. This is no time to walk out."

Rosenbach sank tensely back onto the sofa.

"Now, how about the judge? Has he been picked yet?" George sat on the arm of the sofa, trying to soothe the old man's flare of temper.

420

"Of course." Rosenbach looked up. "I do things right, don't I? You've been assigned to Byron Rasmussen. I've already talked to him." Rosenbach paused. "But it's going to be even more expensive than I thought."

"How much?"

"He wants a hundred thousand now, six hundred and fifty thousand the night before the trial begins." The old man licked his lips. "Sorry. I thought he'd go for five. But when he heard whose case it was . . ."

George nodded to Izzy, who went to the squat safe in the corner and began twisting the dial. "It's all right, Joe. I can afford it. I'm a Wall Street tycoon now, remember? Strictly legitimate. I'll give you the down payment now. The rest—you let me know and I'll sell a few stocks."

Rosenbach watched Izzy swing open the safe. Several packets of money fell out onto the floor. Izzy picked them up and began counting.

"There can't be any screw-ups. I mean, when the time comes for the payoff," Rosenbach warned. "Maybe I didn't give you such good advice, telling you to get out of the rackets and put all your money in the market. I know it will look good to a jury—respectable. But the way the stock market is now, you could get hurt."

Dwyer watched the old man from his chair, wondering what he was really trying to say. He thought of his outburst of temper. "How much did you lose, Joe?"

Rosenbach looked at Dwyer sharply, then blushed. "You heard?"

Dwyer shrugged. "I guessed."

The lawyer took another sip of wine, looking from Dwyer to Izzy to George. "A once-in-a-lifetime tip. You know how it is—it's always the chance of a lifetime. But this broker never led me wrong before. So I went big, almost everything I could lay my hands on I converted to cash. A brand-new type of sewing machine, the broker said. The first all-electric. No more pumping pedals. A miracle."

Rosenbach drank again, then plunged on. "I bought six hundred thousand dollars' worth at ten A.M. Believe it or not, by two P.M. I was a millionaire. The next morning I was almost broke. The sewing machine didn't work. They ran away with the money. That's what the broker said, anyway. Who knows?"

For a few moments no one spoke. The band finished the rag and started on "Somebody Stole My Gal." There were more voices from the casino now.

Rosenbach stood up and began to struggle into his overcoat. "Well, easy come and easy go. Just watch out for yourself."

George crossed to the safe and knelt down. He came up with a handful of cash, then took the packets of bills Izzy held. He went to Rosenbach and pushed them in his coat pocket.

"There's the down payment for the judge, Joe. And fifty thousand for starters on your legal fee. Stay away from sewing machines."

Rosenbach looked at him, surprised. "It's not customary to pay until after the trial."

"I'll make a deal with you then," George said. "If you lose I get my money back."

Rosenbach pulled the coat about him as he went to the door. Then he patted his pocket. "It's even less customary for lawyers to return fees. In fact, it never happens. See you in court." Rosenbach opened the door.

Detective Sergeant John Broderick stood just outside, one uniformed arm raised, ready to knock. Behind Broderick's bulk George could see several other policemen. One officer with an ax was chopping up a chair while a bored photographer with a press card in his hatband took a picture. The band was no longer playing. Customers and waiters trooped resignedly out the club's big door.

"Dammit, you're early," George complained. "You said you weren't going to be here until midnight. This screws up half a night's take."

Broderick lowered his arm. "I had to come early, McManus. I promised the wife I'd take her to a wake later. She dearly loves to wail and moan with the other women. By the way. I've orders to close you down tomorrow night, too."

"What's going on?" Rosenbach demanded. "What happened to the injunction keeping the police out of the club?"

"Tammany gives," explained George, looking back at Dwyer, "and Tammany takes away."

She was as he had first seen her, wildly pretty as she pulled the hem of her wedding gown to her knees. She loped unsteadily through the streets toward him, her heavy train dragging behind like a ceremonial anchor. Again he could hear the screech of tires and the clash of gears as she moved, laughing, toward him. Now he could see the others chasing them, dark figures without faces but with their hands clenched angrily into fists as they ran. And then she was in his arms in an avalanche of white lace and flying hair and pale, smooth skin. He held her as tightly as he could, his fingers nearly ripping the gown. But there was a steady, booming noise, a crashing like church bells on a holy day, that somehow threatened to pull him away from her. He fought back, refusing to heed the bells, trying to hang on to her as long as he could. She smiled at him, moved her lips, but he couldn't grasp what she was saying. Gradually her image faded away as the clanging bells took on meaning, resolving themselves into the ringing of a telephone.

He opened his eyes slowly, feeling the grit of sleep in them. He blinked several times, looking toward the sudden noise from the gray window. Rain pelted against the glass in vicious spurts, almost drowning out the persistent ringing. Finally he reached across the bed and pulled the telephone to him, lifting the earpiece with thumb and forefinger.

"Yeah?" His throat was dry and scratchy.

"McManus?" The voice at the other end was hurried.

"Yeah."

"This is Rosenbach. Sorry to wake you so early but it's important. Rasmussen wants his money."

"What time is it, anyway?"

"It's nine-thirty, George. Listen, Rasmussen wants cash, and by noon."

"Nine-thirty? I just got to sleep." His head fell back on the pillow.

"Wake up, dammit. This is important. The judge said something's going on downtown. He wasn't making much sense but he sounded shook up. He said have the money by noon or it's no deal, George."

"Okay, okay. I'll be at the club with the cash before noon,

423

Joe. You can pick it up." McManus hung up before Rosenbach could say anything else.

He lay still a moment longer, savoring the warm sheets, listening to the rain on the glass. Finally he swung his legs off the bed. Scratching his head with one hand he rummaged around the nightstand for his address book. He found a number, picked up the telephone, and dialed. The busy signal yammered back at him. He hung up and tried three more times before putting down the telephone.

McManus rose and padded across the Oriental rug to the window, pulling away the red brocade curtains. Leaden clouds hung low over the buildings, obscuring the tops of the highest ones. Puffs of lighter cloud skittered beneath the gray cover. The streets were black with rain. He put his hand on the glass and felt the damp cold through the pane.

He went back to the telephone and dialed twice more, only to get the busy signal. Finally he went to the bathroom and shaved quickly, uncertain why he felt a growing urgency. He put on the suit he had worn at the Paradise Rehearsal Club the night before. He dialed the number once more without getting through before he left the apartment.

He tied the sash of the blue overcoat and pulled his fedora low over his eyes as the elevator descended. He considered sending for his car, but then remembered Rosenbach had said the time was short. The doorman hailed a cab under the dripping sidewalk canopy.

The streets were jammed with slow-moving traffic in the rain. George felt his stomach tighten as the cab crept down Seventh Avenue toward the financial district.

"There's an extra five in it if you get me to Wall Street inside fifteen minutes," he told the driver.

The cab immediately shot ahead, squeezing through tight spaces between other cars, as the driver worked his horn. For a while the cab raced along as the steady rain diminished to a drizzle. But below Canal Street the big buildings seemed to squeeze in, like collapsed trees only kept from falling by leaning on each other. Traffic slowed to a crawl, then finally stopped altogether.

The cabbie leaned heavily on his horn, as did the drivers of the cars and trucks around them, but nothing moved. People stopped on the sidewalk to stare at the useless machines.

After a few minutes George threw the cabbie a ten-dollar bill and stepped out. His shoes splashed in the rain puddles as he walked between cars, down the center of the street, toward the murky buildings far ahead in the mist. The rain began to pelt down again and George walked faster, pulling the collar of his coat tight. He passed City Hall and the little park that surrounded it, ignoring the knots of people gathered before the low, domed building in the rain. There were many people on the streets, as if it were a fine spring day instead of a damp and dreary autumn morning. But through the honking of traffic George realized that those around him seemed transfixed, their eyes glazed. Few said anything. They drifted past him in virtual silence as he turned off Broadway onto Wall Street.

McManus stopped, stunned. From sidewalk to sidewalk the narrow street was jammed. People filled the spaces around the stalled cars and trucks, crowded next to the stolid buildings, oblivious to the rain. A few men talked among themselves, but most stood silently, staring at the imperious, pillared building in the middle of the block, where the crowd was thickest. The building stood out like a confused Greek temple on the crowded street, the only break in its classical stone facade the carved words proclaiming it the New York Stock Exchange.

The silent crowds left George uneasy. Twice as he walked toward the stock exchange building he stopped to ask what was happening. But people only looked at him dumbly, as if he were an idiot not to automatically comprehend the misery that surrounded them all. And when he shook one well-dressed middle-aged man, the man turned his face and began to cry quietly, like a child ashamed of his tears.

George backed away from him, frightened, and ran across the street to a narrow brownstone building that stood next to the stock exchange. He pushed through the milling crowd in the lobby and rang for an elevator. But, impatient, anxious now, he turned and raced up the stairway to the third floor. He fought his way along the crowded corridor to a glass door

425

that bore the name "Martindale and Ward," and in smaller letters "Investment Brokers."

When he finally squeezed in he was almost relieved to find the office full of commotion, with workers rushing about feverishly. Sweating men too agitated to remember to take off their hats and coats crowded around several desks, while dozens of others stood before a lined blackboard the length of the room that reached from the floor to the ceiling. Clerks with rags and chalk in their hands raced up and down along the board, rubbing out old stock quotations and chalking in new ones as quickly as the long strings of ticker tape were brought in from another room. Each erasure was accompanied by groans and angry cries.

George stared at the board, incredulous. He saw that many stocks had dropped twenty, thirty, and even forty points already, and the clerks couldn't keep up with the ominous, furious chatter of the stock tickers. The fear in the faces of the men around him began to seep into George like a sudden chill. He could almost smell their desperation. He rubbed his hand across his face to find he was sweating now, too.

He broke away from the board and squirmed through the packed room to one of the desks where angry men shouted at an unhappy red-faced clerk in shirt sleeves. The clerk held up his hands, palms outward, in an appeal for order, reason. But the shouts drowned out whatever he was saying. Finally he stood and climbed onto the desk. He put up his hands again and the crowd slowly quieted.

"I'm sorry, but we just can't take your sell orders," he said loudly, dropping his hands. "There are lots of crazy rumors going around, but all I know for a fact is that the stock exchange's board of governors has halted trading by Martindale and Ward, and early this morning people from the district attorney's office confiscated most of our records."

His last words were obscured by the noise of the crowd. He held up his hands again until he could be heard.

"Don't ask me what's going on, because I'm not sure," he shouted. "I haven't seen Mr. Martindale or Mr. Ward since Friday. Now I know the story is that they've been selling off your stock to cover their own losses since Black Thursday— but it's only a rumor and I don't believe it. I urge you to . . ."

The loud, threatening crowd washed away the rest. The clerk shook his head, climbed off the desk, and sat down again, to be immediately surrounded. He held his head in his hands, his eyes closed, oblivious to the angry, frightened men around him.

With sudden strength born of panic George surged forward blindly, flailing through the crowd, pushing others away until he found himself before the desk. The clerk looked up as George grabbed him by the collar, lifting the sad man to his feet.

"My name's McManus," he shouted into the clerk's face. "I want to sell out my stock. I want my money, do you understand? I've got millions here."

The clerk's hands came up in the same supplicating gesture. "I'm sorry, but there's nothing I can do, mister. Let me go."

"My life depends on that money," George shouted over the crowd. "I need it now!"

"I can't even get my own money," the clerk pleaded quickly. "How can I get yours?"

George tightened his grip on the man's shirt. "What's going on around here? Is everybody crazy?"

The man looked at him. "That's it," he said with wet eyes. "Everybody's gone crazy. Maybe you can get your money next month or next year. Maybe never, mister. I wish I knew."

George released him and then slowly backed away as others pushed to the desk. He looked at the frantic, shouting men around him, then turned and made his way toward the door, suddenly needing to get out. He was nearly at the door when he heard a new chorus of shouts and groans. He turned to see one of the clerks—a young boy—on a stepladder chalking a new number in one of the high boxes on the blackboard. The boy was flushed, proud to be the center of so much attention. He scrambled down the ladder nimbly and moved on, leaving his legacy of lost fortunes behind.

McManus pushed out of the office and into the corridor. He leaned against the wall, shaken, and took a deep breath. The immensity of what he had seen, what the clerk had said, left him dizzy, confused. He found it hard to breathe as he walked unsteadily back down the stairs, wiping his dripping face with his coat sleeve. He stumbled through the jammed lobby to the street, stopping in the cool rain amid the thousands who stood wordlessly before the stock exchange. There were more police now, he saw, standing beneath the exchange building's pillars and on every corner on Wall Street, as if to guard the sanity that seemed to be slipping away. But even the police were silent.

George took off his hat and the rain fell on his face, ran off his chin. He wondered how many millions he had lost, the millions he had plotted and schemed and fought for. Otto would be able to tell him in a few days, he knew. Otto would soon have it worked out to the penny.

He began to run blindly in the terrible silence, crashing into other men, knocking some to the pavement. Bile flooded his throat until he felt he must be sick, but he had to get away from there.

It was blocks later, his lungs burning, that he finally stopped and leaned against a wall. The rain trickled down his neck when he straightened up and began walking.

Now he knew what he must do.

SOMEONE LAUGHED.

Elizabeth looked up, surprised. She hadn't known there was anyone left besides her secretary. She strained to hear if the laugh would come again, but it didn't. It must have come from outside, in the street, she decided. For there was nothing to laugh about here.

She sat back in the big leather chair. Always before in her father's office she had heard the clatter of typewriters, the murmur of voices, the shuffling of papers, the creak of chairs, phones ringing, footsteps. But all that was gone. Now there was just the faint rustle of her lone secretary, cleaning out the desk. She pushed her chair back and went to the window. The blustery November wind punched at the glass like a soft glove, rattling the weathered frame. Outside, the trees in the little park seemed to quiver as if reeling from some mighty blow. A trick of the light, she guessed.

"I'm ready to go, Miss Wainwright," the secretary said behind her. "Is there anything else?"

Elizabeth went back to the desk. "You've sent out all the severance checks, Betty?"

"This morning." There was a hint of emotion in the young woman's voice.

Elizabeth looked up to find an unexpected trace of red around her secretary's eyes as she fiddled with the buttons of her brown coat.

"Have you got your letter of recommendation?"

"Yes, Miss Wainwright. In my purse, and thank you very much. I'm very hopeful it'll help me find another job, even with all the layoffs now."

"You'll do fine, Betty."

The secretary started to turn away, then paused. "I just want to say, Miss Wainwright, that I'm sorry it's ending like this. I was hoping you'd be able to keep the company going. I mean, because we're both women as much as for my job." She looked at her toes. "I don't mean to be presumptuous."

Elizabeth stood and came around the desk. They embraced quickly, almost embarrassed. Without another word the secretary turned and walked out, putting her plain brown hat on her plain brown hair as she left. Elizabeth heard the squeak of the swinging gate, then the clicks of the hall door opening and closing. The secretary's footsteps trailed away down the corridor.

After a while Elizabeth came out of her office and walked slowly along the two rows of smaller offices that led off the reception room. They were nearly empty. Just a few bare desks and tables and office machines waited to be taken away. In a rear room someone had gathered all the plants near one window. Elizabeth found a pitcher and gave the plants water. She wondered who would do this after she was gone.

She was walking back to her office when she heard the door open, then the sound of footsteps. Jimmy Walker was leaning on the gate when she reached the reception room. A young policeman in uniform stood patiently by the door, holding the mayor's coat.

429

Walker tipped his derby when he saw her. Without a word she went past him and into her office. He followed, telling the policeman to wait outside. Walker closed the door as Elizabeth sat behind her desk.

"We'll have to make this quick. I have to appear at a campaign rally at a Polish retirees' home in a half hour." Walker checked his pocket watch.

"If I'm late a lot of them will already have started their afternoon naps." He snapped the cover of the watch shut. "I think you said something about having some papers for me? Your father's papers?"

"You don't waste time," Elizabeth said.

"You can't afford to when you're a public servant, Miss Wainwright. Especially when you're running for reelection. Every vote counts. Now, about those papers?"

Elizabeth opened the bottom drawer of her desk and took out a yellow envelope. "These are my father's notes on his political payoffs to your administration. I'm willing to give them to you, Mr. Mayor. But I want something in return."

Walker looked pained. "Of course you want something in return. Everybody wants something in politics. But not your damned subway tunnel. I won't even discuss that mess again. Besides, I have worse problems to worry about."

Elizabeth sat forward, laying her hands on the desk. "I'm not interested in the tunnel anymore. It's too late now, my father's company is out of business. I'm closing down the office today and all the heavy equipment will be auctioned off next week to pay off some of the debts."

"I'm sorry to hear that," Walker said with a stab at sincerity. He pulled up a chair and sat down, watching Elizabeth. "These are difficult times, with the stock market on the fritz and companies going under left and right. The whole country is going to feel the pinch."

Elizabeth shook her head. "Now who's wasting time? Please spare me your sympathy and campaign oratory."

Walker was a little taken aback by Elizabeth's vehemence. "All right then, if it isn't the tunnel, what the hell *do* you want?"

Elizabeth stood up and walked across the room, stopping

by her father's portrait. She studied it for a moment before turning around.

"Tell me, Mr. Mayor, how is the case going against my husband?"

Walker looked from her legs to her face. "Your husband? I think the city has a very serious case against him for murder. There's a good chance George McManus will go to the electric chair. But please, don't even think about asking me to let him off in return for your father's papers. It would be impossible for me. I'd be recalled from office. You've no idea—"

"I don't believe you," Elizabeth interrupted. "I read the papers. All the prosecutor has is circumstantial evidence—people who saw my husband around the hotel the night of the murder. But you don't have any eyewitnesses."

"There's only one eyewitness," Walker said very quietly. "And we both know who it is. Unfortunately, a wife cannot be forced to testify against her husband."

"You knew I was there?"

Walker shook his head. "Just because I'm a politician it doesn't mean I'm stupid. I sent you to Rothstein that day, didn't I? And I called George and told him what I had done. It didn't take much imagination to figure out what McManus found when he got to Rothstein's apartment. Besides, there was the money."

Elizabeth sat down. "How do you know about that?"

"The police found out Rothstein had won something over half a million in a poker game that day. The money wasn't in the room after the murder. But the district attorney found a deposit of over half a million in your company's accounts the next day."

They looked at each other silently.

"Oh, don't worry, your secret's safe with me. There's enough evidence without you. But in a way I'm sorry it's come to this," Walker said. "We offered him a deal, you know. Just a few years behind bars. But George wouldn't take it. So I have to let the district attorney do his job, don't I? Still, maybe George will get off with life in prison. I'd prefer that. But please, don't waste your time trying to bribe me into letting him off."

431

Elizabeth pushed the envelope halfway across the desk, keeping two fingers on it. "You don't understand. I don't want to save him. I want to testify against him."

Walker looked from the envelope to Elizabeth's expressionless face. He searched for a tic, a quiver of the chin. But there was nothing. "You're right," he said slowly. "I don't understand."

Elizabeth crossed the fingers of both hands to make a tight ball of her fists. "My husband is a clever man, Mr. Mayor. You know him well. Do you think he's going to calmly accept going to the electric chair or spending the rest of his life in prison? I'd bet he's got a plan to wreck the whole case against him. I can make sure, however, that he doesn't succeed. I saw what happened that night. And I want to tell it to a jury."

Walker ran a finger around his tight collar and found it damp. He cleared his throat, looked away, unable to meet Elizabeth's steady stare.

There was a light tap on the door. The policeman stuck his head in. "Your car's waiting, Mr. Mayor. You've only got ten minutes to get to your next rally."

Walker waved his hand and the policeman closed the door. He got up and went to the window, gazing out.

"You'd kill your own husband?" Walker finally said, turning. "Do you hate him that much?"

"George McManus destroyed my father, this business, my future. Everything I ever had," she said tonelessly. "Most people hate for a lot less."

For a moment Walker hesitated, then went to the desk, picked up the yellow envelope, and put it in his coat pocket. He turned his back on Elizabeth and walked to the door. He was halfway out when he stopped and looked back at her.

"Lady," he said softly, "I hope you never get mad at me."

"WHAT DO YOU THINK of the jury?"
"They look reasonably dishonest."

"Why did you kill Rothstein?"

"Rothstein? Who's Rothstein?"

"Did you get hurt in the crash?"

"Didn't everybody?"

"If you didn't kill Rothstein, who did?"

The reporters flew at George McManus like excited bees, hovering around. He tried to wave them away as two hefty policemen escorted him from his car and across the street, but they kept hurling questions, theories, insults, anything to get a quotable reaction.

"I'm not saying any more, boys," George called, smiling. But that only made the newsmen more insistent and they began shouting.

McManus looked up at the Manhattan Criminal Court Building, its stone facade chipped and cracked and covered with a brown, decades-old layer of soot and grime. On the steps another crowd had gathered. A handful, carrying signs, were chanting about Walker and murder and Wall Street. But most just came to see George.

"Good luck, Georgie," someone called.

"God is going to punish you, McManus."

"Hey, McManus, if I pay you five bucks will you shoot my mother-in-law?"

He ducked as someone tried to snatch his hat. More policemen ran out of the building to help him through the crowd. Two dozen more reporters waited for him in the courthouse's domed lobby, near the bank of telephones installed for the trial. They swooped toward George, but the policemen formed a wedge and pushed through.

The heat of the packed courtroom leaped out at George as he walked in. An excited whisper went through the jammed benches as he walked down the aisle. A few friends waved to him. George found Bill Dwyer, Otto Berman, Marie, and Izzy in the first row.

"Nice crowd," Marie said, looking around. "Too bad you can't put some slot machines in." George noticed Marie's hand held Otto's arm.

George took off his coat and hat and sat in a chair next to Joe Rosenbach. When he looked back, Dwyer held up crossed fingers.

433

Rosenbach was tapping a pencil on his legal pad, unhappily watching the long table on their right. Every once in a while he would sigh.

"Now what's the matter with you?" George asked. "Things are going fine."

"Uh huh. Look at the enemy," Rosenbach said.

George followed his gaze to the prosecution's table, where four men conferred, their heads close together. Three of the men were young lawyers he recognized from previous hearings. The fourth—a stoop-shouldered, long-nosed lawyer in his sixties with a patrician air and salt-and-pepper hair combed over to hide a bald spot—was new.

"Who's the old guy?"

"That," explained Rosenbach, "is Manhattan District Attorney Thomas Jefferson Reed."

"So?"

"So how come he wasn't on the case for jury selection but he's here today?"

"What do you think, Joe?"

"I think maybe Mr. Reed didn't want to be associated with this case as long as he thought you might get off. But maybe now he doesn't think you're going to get off and he wants to be in on the glory."

George straightened his tie. "I think you think too much. What could go wrong?"

A uniformed bailiff came out of the room next to the judge's bench. "All rise," he ordered loudly.

As the crowd noisily shuffled to their feet a thin, bald man in an unusually bulky black robe climbed up to the high-backed leather chair on the bench and sat down. The sleeves of two different colored sweaters protruded from the arms of the robe.

Rosenbach moaned. "That's what could go wrong."

"This court is now in session. The People of the State of New York versus George Michael McManus. The honorable Francis X. Lenahan presiding."

"Wait a minute, where's the guy we paid?" George mumbled, stunned. Rosenbach was already on his feet.

"If it please the court, where is Judge Rasmussen? This has been his case all along."

434

"Judge Rasmussen is incapacitated. I am now assigned to this case, if you have no objections," the old man said in his high-pitched voice, glaring at Rosenbach. There was a murmur in the courtroom but the judge silenced it with one rap of the gavel.

"Your honor, this is an unforeseen turn of events. I'm afraid I'll have to ask for a mistrial, or at least a postponement, on the grounds—"

"You can ask, but you won't get it from me, Mr. Rosenbach. This case has been delayed long enough. Now, let's proceed, shall we? Mr. Reed?"

Rosenbach sat down heavily. "You have to hand it to Hines. He doesn't miss a thing."

"That's great," George said. "When you get through complimenting Hines and Tammany, maybe you'll tell me how we're going to win with their judge on the case."

"The hard way, that's how," Rosenbach muttered. "The hard way."

The district attorney planted himself firmly before the jury box, legs spread, thumbs thrust into the waist of his pants.

"Gentlemen of the jury," Reed began in a deep, resonant, theatrical voice, "I won't waste your time with long speeches. This is a simple case. The state will prove beyond a shadow of a doubt that the defendant, George Michael McManus, did willfully, and with malice aforethought, murder Arnold Rothstein.

"We will present witnesses who will place Mr. McManus at the scene of the crime, who heard the fatal gunshot, who saw Mr. McManus fleeing the scene. We will prove that George McManus and Arnold Rothstein were sworn enemies, bitter rivals for control of every nefarious racket that has blighted this fair city. We will show how George McManus, fearful of the consequences of his actions, hid out for two weeks after Mr. Rothstein's death, despite knowing full well he was the subject of a nationwide manhunt."

Reed paused for a moment, then began pacing to and fro in front of the somber jury.

"Gentlemen, you have a grave responsibility before you. This is not merely a murder trial. We have just passed ten

435

years in which the world has gone insane. Corruption has seeped into our most valued institutions. Gamblers and boot-leggers like George McManus have become honored citizens. Our young men have become drunkards and wastrels. Our young women . . ."

Reed's voice trailed off, as though he couldn't quite bring himself to say what the women had become.

"There are men in this country, this city, who say the law means nothing. Morality means nothing. Even murder is like a parking ticket—to be fixed and forgotten. These men, like Mr. McManus, these men who even own many of our most trusted public officials—"

"I object, your honor," Rosenbach interrupted. "My client is charged with murder, not with defiling the virginity of pol-iticians."

"Objection overruled," the judge whined. "And watch your language, Mr. Rosenbach. Virginity has no place in a court of law."

Reed turned back to the jury.

"These men—and we all know who they are—have gotten away with virtual as well as literal murder again and again and again. But, my friends, I submit it is your duty to put a stop to this. At the end of this proceeding, I believe you will have only one alternative. And that is to find the defendant, George Michael McManus, guilty as charged of murder in the first degree!"

There was a smattering of applause as Reed sat down. Len-ahan peered sternly over his gavel. The clapping stopped.

Rosenbach stood and nodded to Reed as he approached the jury. "Much as it pains me, I must agree with Mr. Reed," he began. "This *is* a simple case—a simple case of harrassment. A miscarriage of justice. George McManus did not murder Arnold Rothstein. The defense will prove he was nowhere near the scene of the crime. And far from being enemies, we will also establish that Arnold Rothstein and the defendant were, on the contrary, friends."

Rosenbach smiled at a pink-faced, mustachioed man in the back row of the jury box. Establishing eye contact, Rosenbach called it. The man smiled back.

436

"Now, we will not venture to guess who did kill Mr. Rothstein. But we do know that there are other suspects, better suspects, men who profited greatly by Arnold Rothstein's death. Men in high places who would rest easy if George McManus were wrongly convicted for this murder.

"We will show that the prosecution's case against my client is nothing but a mass of circumstantial evidence based on half-truths, innuendo, and outright lies. I submit that the state can prove no motive. The state can present no eyewitnesses. The state, finally, cannot prove beyond a reasonable doubt that George McManus had anything to do with the death of Arnold Rothstein—because, gentlemen of the jury, my client is simply, and totally, innocent."

Rosenbach pounded his fist on the rail of the jury box for emphasis. A battery of reporters bolted out of the courtroom to the telephone.

"Now what?" George whispered when Rosenbach sat down.

"Do you remember how to pray?"

There was a stir in the courtroom as everyone exhaled, sat back. The judge rapped his gavel again. "Mr. Reed, you may call your first witness."

"The state calls Dr. Robert Bradford."

"Dr. Bradford, as the county medical examiner, what was the cause of death?"

"Extreme loss of blood and a massive infection caused by a single gunshot wound inflicted approximately forty-eight hours earlier."

"Can you describe this wound?"

"The bullet entered Mr. Rothstein's left side, a few inches above the hip bone, and traveled through the spleen, the liver, and a kidney. It lodged in the gluteal muscle."

"Can you tell anything about Mr. Rothstein's assailant from the wound?"

"Yes. Given the angle of descent and the bullet's final location, he was probably shot by a right-handed man taller than he was."

"How tall was Mr. Rothstein?"

"Five feet, nine inches."

"Tell me, doctor, have you been able to get medical records on the defendant?"

"Yes."

"And how tall is he?"

Rosenbach jumped to his feet. "Objection, your honor. That's privileged information between Mr. McManus and his doctor."

"Denied," the judge said. "Answer the question, doctor."

"As of an examination two years ago he was six feet tall."

"And do you know which hand he favors?"

The doctor looked at McManus. "Well, he's writing right now with his right hand, so I'd guess he favors the right."

George dropped his pencil as though it were afire.

"Your witness, Mr. Rosenbach."

"Doctor, is it possible that the fatal wound could have been self-inflicted?"

"Well, suicides rarely shoot themselves in the hip. But I suppose it could be possible, yes."

"And, despite your best estimate, doctor, isn't it also possible that the wound could have been inflicted by a much shorter man, possibly standing over a sitting Arnold Rothstein?"

"Yes, it could have happened that way. But—"

"Or by a left-handed man standing to Rothstein's left?"

"Well, maybe—"

"Or by a one-eyed Ubangi with a limp?"

"Um, what's a Ubangi?"

"Isn't the fact of the matter, doctor, that you just can't be sure from the wound exactly who shot Arnold Rothstein?"

"Objection," Reed called. "The witness has already answered that question to his best professional knowledge."

"Sustained," the judge replied quickly.

Rosenbach shook his head.

"Officer Delaney," Reed began, "where were you on the night of November fourth last year?"

"Walking my beat on Seventh Avenue."

"Did you see anything unusual?"

438

"Well, I seen a man staggering down the street holding his side and weaving around like he was drunk. But that's not exactly unusual. Anyway, he fell down and I ran over to help him."

"Did you recognize the man?"

"It was Arnold Rothstein. I've seen him often enough collecting on Broadway."

"What was his condition?"

"There was blood gushing from his side and his face was gray and sick looking. He had whiskey on his breath but I don't think he was plastered."

"Did he say anything to you, officer?"

"He asked me to get him a doctor."

"What happened next?"

"I asked, 'Who shot you?' and he says, 'Did somebody shoot me?' Then another cop came running and I left Rothstein with him."

"What did you do next?"

"I called for an ambulance. Then I walked over to the Park Central Hotel."

"Why the Park Central?"

"There was a trail of blood on the sidewalk. I followed it up the stairs to room four thirty-nine."

"What did you find in that room?"

"The door was broken in. There was more bloodstains on the floor and a table set up for a poker game. I also found empty whiskey bottles and two suits, a gray sweater, and a brown overcoat in a closet."

"Was there anything special about this overcoat, officer?"

"There was a name tag sewn inside."

"And what was the name on the tag?"

"George McManus."

"Did you find a gun in the room, Officer Delaney?"

"No, sir, but there was a hole in the window screen where I figure McManus musta shoved the gun out."

"Objection, your honor," Rosenbach called.

"Denied."

"This overcoat," Rosenbach began, "did you find it the first time you searched?"

439

"No, sir, I didn't look in the closet at first."

"When did you look?"

"Not until two days later, after Mr. Rothstein died."

"Why did you look then?"

"We got a tip."

"An anonymous tip?"

"Well, the guy sure didn't leave his name."

"Isn't it possible, then, that this coat bearing the defendant's name was planted, Officer Delaney?"

"Well . . ."

"Objection," Reed said.

"Sustained. Don't answer that question, officer," Judge Lenahan ordered.

"Did you find George McManus's fingerprints in room four thirty-nine?" Rosenbach went on.

"No, we didn't find his prints. Somebody must—"

"Thank you, Office Delaney. That's all."

"I was parked on Fifty-sixth Street next to the Park Central Hotel when somethin' hard bounces off the hood of my hack and lands on the street. It like to scared me to death."

"What time was this, Mr. Rooney?"

"Around nine-fifteen or nine-thirty."

"Did you investigate?"

"Hell, no. I just got out and looked to see what clunked my cab."

"And what was this object?" Reed asked.

"A rod."

"Is this the, uh, rod you found in the street?"

"Yep. See it's all broke up from where it hit. Banged the hell out of my hood. I still got two years to pay on the damn thing, too."

"Tell me, Mr. Rooney, why were you parked outside the Park Central Hotel that evening?"

"I had a fare. He told me to wait, so I was waiting."

"And who was your fare?"

"Why, him, over there."

"Let the record show that the witness is pointing to the defendant, George McManus," Reed said.

440

"When he was in your cab, Mr. Rooney, was the defendant upset?"

"Objection," Rosenbach called.

"Denied."

"Well, he was sure in a hurry. He told me to step on it."

"And did he have a gun with him?"

"I didn't see any gun, but he had a kind of lump under his coat."

"Objection," Rosenbach shouted.

"Denied," said the judge.

"Shit," Rosenbach muttered.

"The hour is growing late, gentlemen," Lenahan said, digging his pocket watch from under his layers of clothing. "I'm going to adjourn until tomorrow morning at ten A.M."

Reed stood up. "Your honor, in view of the severity of the crime Mr. McManus is charged with, and the atmosphere about this trial, I move that the jurors be sequestered for the remainder of this trial. I have heard disturbing rumors of plans being made to influence the members of the jury."

"That's bull," Rosenbach shouted, jumping to his feet. "If the prosecutor has evidence of wrongdoing, then let him present—"

The gavel sounded three times. "Sit down, Mr. Rosenbach," the judge ordered. "Motion to sequester is granted. This court is adjourned."

George was silent as the heavy-set waitress put down three thick, white coffee mugs. He drummed his fingers on the shiny table as she swiped a wet spot with a rag, then waddled back to the counter of the dim diner.

Rosenbach finally broke the heavy silence at the table. "Okay, so it looks bad. I didn't expect to have to fight this case in front of that Tammany bastard Lenahan. So sue me."

"Nobody's blaming you," George said, running a finger around the rim of his cup.

"Did you hear the bastard? He overruled practically every one of my objections. Reed could have spit in my eye and Lenahan would have charged me with contempt of court for

441

littering." Rosenbach was so angry his frail body shook. He put a spoon into his coffee but it clattered nervously against the sides of the cup until half the coffee was spilled on the table.

Bill Dwyer handed Rosenbach a handful of napkins and the old man spread them before him. Then Rosenbach poured coffee into his saucer and brought the saucer to his lips, slurping the hot liquid noisily.

"I just wonder what happened to Judge Rasmussen—and the six hundred thousand I loaned George to buy him," Dwyer said quietly.

"You'll get it back, Bill. Every penny," George vowed. "If worse comes to worst, you can have my half of the club."

Dwyer looked at him. "It's not the money, Georgie. You know that. I just hate being taken by anybody, much less a judge. Especially a judge."

Rosenbach put down his saucer. "I don't know," he said, slightly less jittery. "We can't get to the judge. We can't get to the jury. The way it went today in court, maybe you should make a deal with Walker and Hines. Right now a couple of years in prison don't look so bad. If we go through with this trial, anything could happen, George. Consider this a warning from your high-priced counsel."

"Uh-uh." McManus shook his head. "I'm a gambler, Joe, remember? I'll take my chances."

As he spoke George saw Izzy run across the street, dodging traffic. He came into the diner, looked around hurriedly, then headed for their table.

"It took a while, boss, but I kept my ears wide open and I heard two secretaries talking in an elevator in the courthouse. This Judge Rasmussen to whom you gave so much money. . . ." Izzy put his hands together as if in prayer, then made a motion like a diver going off a board.

"When?" George said slowly.

"Last night, this morning—what does it matter?" Izzy shrugged. "One secretary told the other secretary she heard he was broke."

"In the fall?" Rosenbach asked.

"No, no. In the stock market. You know—he went broke."

The four men stared at the table.

442

"Are the bookies still taking bets on me, Izzy?" George finally asked.

"Sure, boss. But the odds are now five to one against that you do not walk away as free as a bird."

"Then here's what I want you to do." George took a sip of coffee and put down the cup.

"I want you to call our friends in Buffalo and Miami and Philadelphia and Detroit and any place else you can think. Spread around two hundred and fifty thousand in very small bets. Get Otto and Marie to help you. I don't want anybody to get wise that there's a lot of money involved."

Rosenbach coughed. "Wait a minute. You're betting that you're going to lose?"

George leaned across the table and patted him on the shoulder. "No, Joe. I have confidence in you. I'm betting that I'm going to win."

McManus and Dwyer looked at each other as Izzy busily found a pencil and laboriously scratched notes on a napkin. When he was finished he stood up.

"You know, boss, this is *meshugge*. If you lose and you cannot pay off, they will divide you into little pieces and put them in different rivers."

"It doesn't matter, does it, Izzy? If I lose, I'm dead anyway."

58

THE NARROW-SHOULDERED policeman sat ramrod straight in the stiff chair, looking out at the far wall. He was not in uniform, yet he wore a tightly cut blue suit that closely resembled a uniform. All it would need was a badge and brass buttons, George thought.

"Now, Lieutenant Flynn," began the district attorney, "will you tell the court if there were any fingerprints on the gun found outside the Park Central Hotel that night?"

"Just the cab driver Rooney's, sir. We got a good set of those."

"Did the police laboratory test-fire the gun?

"Yes."

"And?"

"It was the gun that killed Arnold Rothstein, no doubt about it. The bullets were a perfect match-up."

"Did you ascertain if that gun had been in room four thirty-nine? Had it been pushed through that broken screen?"

"Yes, sir. There were tiny flecks of screen rust and wire scratches on the gun. These matched up with samples taken from the screen. There was also gun oil on the screen the same as on the gun."

"Your witness," said Reed.

"No questions," Rosenbach glumly replied.

Reed took a deep breath. "How long have you known the defendant, Sergeant Broderick?"

"Twenty, twenty-one years. I arrested him as man and boy."

"Is that why he surrendered to you?"

"He didn't surrender. I captured him. And quite a tussle it was."

"Then the defendant tried to resist arrest?"

"Sure, but I slapped the handcuffs on him too quick."

"Tell me, sergeant, did you know the deceased, Arnold Rothstein?"

"I saw him many a time. And I am well-acquainted with his criminal record, Mr. Reed. A very bad man he was."

"Since you've known Mr. McManus so long, sergeant, do you know if the defendant and Mr. Rothstein were friends?"

"Objection. Calls for a conclusion by the witness," Rosenbach called.

"Denied," the judge replied mechanically.

"Well, sergeant? Were they friends?"

"Like brothers."

"Brothers? Can you explain that more fully?"

"Like Cain and Abel, Mr. Reed. They were always at each other's throats."

"Can you tell the court why they hated each other?"

"Objection," Rosenbach complained.

"Denied," the judge said. "Go ahead, sergeant, answer the question."

"Business, you could say. McManus and his gang would bring in a load of liquor and Rothstein would try to steal it. It was a regular game. Or Rothstein would put the muscle on McManus's joint, as they say in the underworld. One time, Rothstein even had two buckos take McManus for a ride."

"Objection," Rosenbach shouted.

"Denied."

"A ride? Will you explain what you mean?" Reed asked.

"They forced George McManus into a car and were going to kill him. I hear McManus tricked his way out of it. He's a clever lad, but everybody knew he was boiling mad at Rothstein."

"Mad enough to kill?"

"Objection, your honor," Rosenbach demanded.

Lenahan sighed unhappily. "Sustained. That's one for you, Mr. Rosenbach."

"Do you know the penalty for perjury, Sergeant Broderick?" Rosenbach began.

"Surely. I'm a cop, am I not?"

"Do you know there are several witnesses who saw George McManus surrender to you?"

"Objection," Reed said. "Witness has already dealt with that incident."

"Sustained," agreed the judge.

"All right, then," Rosenbach went on, "tell me, sergeant, what do you earn a year? What's your salary?"

"About twenty-five hundred a year."

"Isn't it true, sergeant, that you have over two hundred thousand dollars in various accounts at—"

"Objection," Reed said. "Sergeant Broderick is not on trial here."

"Sustained."

"And isn't it true, sergeant, that you worked for Arnold Rothstein, performing many nefarious—"

"Objection."

445

"Sustained," the judge said quickly.

"And isn't it true that you have a long record of corruption complaints from merchants in the Times Square—"

"Objection," Reed demanded.

"Sustained."

"No more questions," Rosenbach sighed.

"Where were you on the night of November fourth last year, Mr. Richards?" Reed asked.

"I was working. At the front desk of the Park Central Hotel. I'm the regular night man, you see. Been the night man for four years."

"That's very interesting, Mr. Richards. Now, did you see the defendant, George McManus, that night?"

"Sure. I used to see him every night. He came in that night exactly quarter after nine."

"What did Mr. McManus look like, Mr. Richards? Was he angry, upset?"

"Objection," Rosenbach muttered. "Calls for a conclusion."

"Denied," Lenahan said. "Answer the question."

"Well, his face was red and he walked real fast. Didn't even say hello to me. I'd say Mr. McManus was pretty mad."

"Did you see him come back out through the lobby?"

"No. No, I didn't."

"Mr. Richards, how long has George McManus been living at the Park Central?" Rosenbach asked.

"Since nineteen twenty-five, I believe."

"And how often do you see Mr. McManus on an average day?"

"Oh, maybe three, four times."

"Do you keep a record of each time you see the defendant?"

"No."

"Then how can be sure you saw him at exactly nine-fifteen on November fourth, nineteen twenty-eight? Are you sure it wasn't eight-fifteen or ten o'clock?"

"Well . . ."

"Can you tell me your wife's birthday, Mr. Richards? Can you tell me what you had for lunch last Tuesday?"

"Well, let me think now. . . ."

446

"Isn't it a fact that you remember that day in nineteen twenty-eight so well because you were coached, Mr. Richards? Didn't the prosecution tell you what to remember?"

"Objection," Reed shouted, suddenly on his feet.

"Sustained. I'm warning you, Mr. Rosenbach."

The judge rapped the gavel three times to silence the crowd.

"Did you see George McManus leave the Park Central on the night of November fourth, Mr. Lamana?"

"Sure, I saw him from my newsstand."

"What door did he come out of?" Reed asked.

"He came out a fire door at the bottom of the stairwell on the Fifty-sixth Street side of the hotel. I know the hotel pretty well, you see. I've had that stand outside the hotel for almost ten years."

"And what did he do when he came out that door?"

"He looked around, then ran the other way, up the sidewalk toward Broadway."

"Were you surprised he went the other way? Was that unusual?"

"Sure. He always dropped by my stand before. Never missed. He'd buy a paper two, three times a day, and leave a big tip. I remember that night because there was no tip."

"Tell the court, Mr. Lamana, why you wear those dark glasses," Rosenbach said.

"The glasses? My eyes are very sensitive, that's all. I was gassed in Flanders, you know. In the war. My eyes have been sensitive ever since."

"Have you ever been arrested, Mr. Lamana?"

"Maybe once."

"Isn't it more like eight times, on bookmaking charges? And don't you face indictment right now on another charge?"

"It's just small potatoes. Little bets."

"Isn't it also true that you are legally blind as a result of your war injury, Mr. Lamana? That you couldn't have seen the defendant or anyone else that night who was more than six feet away from you?"

"My eyes ain't that bad."

"I'm holding a cane, Mr. Lamana. Will you tell the court if it's your cane?"

"No, that's not my cane. I don't use a cane."

"Thank you, that's all," Rosenbach said, noisily dropping the chair from his hands.

"Where were you on the night of November fourth, nineteen twenty-eight, Mrs. Higgins?"

"In room four-thirty of the Park Central Hotel. Just down the hall from Mr. Rothstein's room."

"Can you tell us what happened that night?"

"I was listening to the radio with a gentleman friend when I heard this pounding. I was afraid but I went to the door and opened it a crack. I saw him banging his fists on Mr. Rothstein's door."

"Let the record show the witness is indicating the defendant," Reed said. "Now, are you sure it was Mr. Rothstein's room?"

"Sure. We were friends."

"What happened next?"

"He—"

"The defendant?"

"Yeah, the defendant backed up and ran smack into the door. He busted it wide open. Then there was a lot of shouting and all of a sudden a loud noise like a car backfire."

"Tell the court what you saw next."

"Mr. Rothstein came staggering out of the room holding his side, all bloody. I slammed my door closed then. I didn't want to get involved in anything like that. I believe in minding your own business, see. But a few minutes later I peeked out again and saw the defendant come out. Then he went down the stairs."

"When George McManus went into room four thirty-nine, did he have anything in his hands?"

"Yes."

"What?"

"A gun."

"Mrs. Higgins," Rosenbach began, "what is your occupation?"

448

"I'm a housewife."

"Are you currently married?"

"No. My husband left me four years ago."

"But you're still a housewife?"

"Of course."

"Isn't it true, Mrs. Higgins, that you make your living providing sexual favors—"

"I object," Reed interrupted.

"Sustained."

"Mrs. Higgins," Rosenbach resumed, "are you being paid to testify?"

"Of course not."

"Not a penny?"

"No, nothing."

"Didn't you receive five thousand dollars from a representative of the Hearst newspapers to testify against George McManus?"

"Absolutely not."

"What would you say, Mrs. Higgins, if I showed you the canceled check?"

"That's impossible! They paid cash!"

"Your honor, I move for dismissal," Rosenbach shouted over the noise that burst out in the courtroom. "This whole case is tainted."

Lenahan rapped the gavel again and again but to no avail.

"I'll rule on your motion tomorrow, counselor. Right now I have a headache. Court's adjourned until ten A.M."

They ordered doughnuts with their coffee. Izzy passed a silver flask of bourbon around the table. Even Big Bill Dwyer drank.

"You earned your money today, counselor." George held up the flask in a toast. "You've got them on the run."

"You think so?" Rosenbach blew on the coffee in his saucer.

"But you destroyed a couple of their key witnesses," Dwyer pointed out, holding his cup with both hands. "They've been shown up as liars."

"So what?" Rosenbach shook his head. "Don't you see, they've still got the judge, the other witnesses that put you at the scene. And I have a bad feeling about what Lenahan is

449

going to do to my defense witnesses. It's going to be brutal. We might as well forget about putting Izzy or Bill on the stand. They're too close to you. I'm not even sure I'd risk having you testify, Georgie. Reed and Lenahan would tear you apart. There would be words coming out of your mouth you never heard before. They'd tie you in to Al Capone, the stock market crash, and the assassination of Lincoln, and you'd probably agree with everything they say, you'd be so confused."

"But they screwed up today, Joe," McManus protested.

Rosenbach dunked a doughnut into his coffee and let it soak. "Tell him, Izzy."

Izzy fumbled with his red and green tie. "Bad news, boss. I asked around among our friends. The odds against you today went from five to one to six to one."

"Then there's only one thing to do." George took another sip from the flask.

"What's that?" Dwyer wanted to know.

"Bet another hundred thousand."

59

THE COURTHOUSE STEPS and corridors were jammed as George pushed through the crowds behind seven policemen. Crushed beside him, Dwyer warily guarded his handsome suit and diamond stickpin from stray hands. Izzy and Joe Rosenbach lagged behind.

When they reached the courtroom, two policemen swung the doors open and the crowd rushed for seats. But George spotted two men standing together down the hall and, with a word to Rosenbach, bent and covered his face with his hat. While the crowd swept into the courtroom he pushed the other way until he was on its outer edge, then walked toward Walker and Hines.

Jimmy Walker smiled broadly when he saw McManus. Almost a smile of relief, George thought. They shook hands. But Hines pointedly walked away a few steps and busied himself reading a newspaper.

"I'm surprised you're here, Mr. Mayor."

"I had to see what all the headlines were about, Georgie. Anyway, you know politicians—we just can't stay away when there's a crowd."

"I suppose I should congratulate you on getting reelected," George said. "Even though I didn't vote for you."

Walker laughed. "Look, all this"—he waved a hand toward the courtroom—"if it was just up to me the whole case would have been dropped the minute the polls closed." His face suddenly became serious. "But now, with Hearst and the newspapers—well, everything has gotten out of hand. And of course, Hines is never going to forgive you for hanging him from a coat hook in his own house."

"It was almost worth it just to see his face."

The distinct rap of the judge's gavel floated to them down the corridor. The noise in the courtroom subsided.

"I think I'm on," George said softly.

They shook hands again. "Good luck," Walker said. "No matter what happens today."

A last awkward glance passed between the two men—a glance almost of affection—then McManus turned and walked slowly down the hall. He pulled open one of the doors and went down the aisle. As he took his seat next to Rosenbach, he saw that Chins Hamner, Rats Wolnik, and most of the club's waiters and croupiers and the band were sitting with Otto and Marie. They waved to him excitedly.

"Well, what did Walker say?" Rosenbach whispered harshly.

"Good luck."

"Bullshit." Rosenbach stood up.

"I apologize for the delay, your honor," he called. "The defense is ready to proceed."

Lenahan glared over his desk, pulling his muffler around his neck even though the radiators hissed and spat with heat in the corners of the courtroom.

"I believe you were making a motion when court adjourned yesterday, counselor," the judge said. "And keep it brief."

"Of course, your honor." Rosenbach consulted his notes, then looked up. "It seems to me that the prosecution has no case beyond some shaky circumstantial evidence purportedly placing my client at the scene of Arnold Rothstein's injury. But, you yourself, your honor, heard several prosecution witnesses as much as admit to perjury yesterday. Their testimony that they saw George McManus is worthless."

Rosenbach drew himself up, bouncing on the balls of his feet. "I further submit that the prosecution has failed to prove intent, motive, or opportunity to commit this crime, on the part of my client. Who saw George McManus pull the trigger? No one. No jury would convict my client on such shoddy circumstantial evidence. Why, even the officer who found Arnold Rothstein admitted that Rothstein denied being shot. Are those the words of a man who has been murdered?

"In short, your honor, there being no eyewitnesses to the crime for which my client is accused, I move all charges against George McManus be dismissed."

"Not very brief, Mr. Rosenbach," the judge said, holding his forehead. "Mr. Reed, do you care to respond to the motion before I rule?"

Reed stood beside his chair, glasses balanced precariously on the edge of his nose. "I certainly do, your honor. The fact of the matter is that I must apologize for the conduct of some of the state's witnesses yesterday. Criminal charges are being considered in cases where perjury may have been committed.

"But the prosecution would like to present one more witness in this case, your honor. A key witness."

"All right, Mr. Reed," the judge said. "Motion denied."

George watched Reed scribble something on a piece of paper. Then one of his younger assistants carried the paper up to the court clerk.

"I thought you said no surprises," Rosenbach whispered, sitting down. "Do you know who the witness is?"

"I'm not sure," George answered slowly, hardly breathing.

The clerk unfolded the scrap of paper, then handed it up to Judge Lenahan. Both men raised their eyebrows. But finally the judge nodded and the clerk stood up.

"The state calls Elizabeth Wainwright McManus to the stand."

It was almost five seconds, a stunned delayed reaction, before the courtroom exploded. Reporters ran for their telephones, people bounded to their feet, fell into the aisles.

Rosenbach was shouting. Policemen poured into the court from an anteroom and ran up and down trying to quiet the crowd.

The judge banged his gavel again and again until, gradually, the noise died away and people resumed their seats. Lenahan was red-faced and sweating by the time the courtroom was silent. He loosened his muffler and turned to the bailiff.

"Bring the witness in."

The anteroom door opened and a tall woman in a gray dress, gray hat, and a veil walked out, her head held high.

"Son of a bitch, McManus," Rosenbach hissed. "Why didn't you tell me your wife saw you do it?"

But George was watching Elizabeth, mesmerized, and didn't answer. He felt his pulse pound through his skull as she crossed in front of him and stood facing the judge. He began to rub the old scar on his temple.

"This is a farce, your honor," Rosenbach shouted, on his feet again. "This is inhuman. It violates the most sacred principle of Western jurisprudence. The state cannot force a wife to testify against her husband. You will destroy a bond only God—"

"Your honor," Reed interrupted, "Mrs. McManus is not being forced to testify. She is doing so at her own request. This court is obligated to—"

"Both of you sit down!" Lenahan ordered. Then he looked at Elizabeth.

"I want you to face me, madam. And remove that veil so I can see your face."

Elizabeth lifted the veil and looked at the judge squarely, aware that five hundred eyes were on her back. She could hear the scratching of the reporters' pencils, the breathing of the onlookers as they leaned forward on their benches.

The judge watched her in confusion. "Do I understand correctly, Mrs. McManus? You asked to testify against your own husband?"

"Yes," she said softly.

The judge turned one ear toward her. "I can't hear you."

"Yes," Elizabeth said more loudly. "I want to testify."

Lenahan looked up, uncertainty in his eyes. George

453

watched him search out someone in the back of the court-room. He looked over his shoulder to see Walker and Hines seated near the aisle. Walker seemed grave, his eyes down-cast. But Hines nodded to the judge almost imperceptibly, then looked directly at McManus.

"All right," Lenahan finally said, almost relieved. "Swear her in."

The bailiff held out the Bible and Elizabeth laid her left hand on it. She raised the other hand. "Do you solemnly swear to tell the truth, the whole truth, and nothing but the truth, so help you God?"

"I do," she said clearly.

Elizabeth stepped up to the witness chair and sat down, her shoulders tight, tensed. For the first time since she walked into the courtroom her eyes met George's. She quickly looked away.

"Can't you do something?" Rosenbach whispered. "Can't you control your wife?"

McManus only shook his head, staring at her.

"Then I'll tear her down on cross-examination," Rosenbach muttered. "I'll show how she hates your guts. We've got to wreck her testimony or you're a goner."

The district attorney stood and tucked a stray corner of his shirt into his pants. He walked around the table, toward Elizabeth.

"Mrs. McManus, how long have you been married to the defendant?"

"Two and a half years."

"Where do you reside, Mrs. McManus?"

"At eight thirty-seven Fifth Avenue."

"Does your husband live there, too?"

"No. We've been living apart for a year."

Reed paused for a moment. "Did you know the deceased, Arnold Rothstein?"

"Wait a minute," Rosenbach shouted. "Why don't you ask her why they're separated? I protest, your honor. I believe this woman has a grudge against the defendant."

Lenahan banged the gavel three times to quiet the buzzing in the room. "Be careful, Mr. Rosenbach, or I'll have you thrown out of this court."

He turned to Elizabeth. "You understand, Mrs. McManus, that you are under oath? Any personal feelings you may have about the defendant must be put aside in the interest of truth."

"I understand that," she said, looking straight ahead, her back stiff.

The judge nodded to Reed, who locked his hands behind him. "Now then, Mrs. McManus, let's resume where we were interrupted. Did you know the deceased, Arnold Rothstein?"

"Yes, slightly."

"And how did you meet?"

"Through my husband."

"Were your husband and Mr. Rothstein friends?"

"No."

"How would you characterize their relationship, then?"

Elizabeth thought for a moment. "I'd say they were rivals."

"Rivals? In what way?"

"Well, both professionally and socially. I know they took pleasure in cheating each other out of great sums of money. But over the years, from what my husband said, the rivalry became more serious—even deadly. I know that Mr. Rothstein tried to have my husband killed at least once. My husband never told me much about his business affairs, but I know this for a fact through George's associates."

"What else can you tell us about their affairs?"

Rosenbach jumped up. "I protest, your honor. Even if she is the man's wife, this is hearsay!"

"Objection denied. It seems to me a wife would be in the ideal position to know these things. Go on, Mr. Reed."

"So, you would say there was bad blood between the two men?" Reed went on.

"Oh, yes," Elizabeth agreed, nodding.

Rosenbach slumped down in his chair. "Kiss your ass goodbye, Georgie," he muttered. "Your wife is killing you."

But George hardly heard him. He was concentrating on Elizabeth, watching the tilt of her chin, the way she crossed her legs. His heart beat madly in his chest. His fists were clenched, every muscle taut with tension. Yet he could not tear his eyes from her as she sat before him, so emotionless, the soft eyes he remembered so icy now.

"Now, Mrs. McManus, I want you to think back to the evening of November fourth last year. Can you tell us what happened that day?"

"I arranged to meet with Mr. Rothstein at the Park Central Hotel."

"Why did you want to see him?"

"I needed to borrow a lot of money—money I couldn't get from banks—to keep my company going. I heard that Mr. Rothstein lent money."

"Did your husband know you were going to do business with Arnold Rothstein?"

"No. I didn't tell him because it was none of his business. We were separated by then, you see."

Reed looked closely at Elizabeth. "Was there another reason you didn't tell your husband, Mrs. McManus?"

"I didn't think George would let me go. My husband is a very proud man." Her voice broke for a moment, but she caught herself. "By that time I was sure George and Mr. Rothstein were enemies."

Rosenbach flew out of his chair. "Objection. That's a conclusion by the witness."

"Denied."

"What time did you arrive at Mr. Rothstein's apartment that night?" Reed went on.

"About nine P.M."

"And what happened?"

"The place was a mess. Mr. Rothstein told me he had just finished a long poker game. We talked for a while about the terms of a loan."

"And then what happened?" Reed urged.

Elizabeth looked directly at George, then at Reed. "My husband broke in. Broke down the door."

"I object," Rosenbach shouted again. "This woman obviously has it in for my client. I protest most strongly—"

"Denied," the judge said angrily. "I warn you, Mr. Rosenbach, many more such interruptions and you're out."

Reed went back to the prosecution's table and picked up his notes, aware there was not a sound in the room besides the hissing radiators and his flipping pages. Slowly he put the papers down and walked back to Elizabeth.

456

"Now, Mrs. McManus, think carefully. A man's life may depend on this. What happened when your husband broke into room four thirty-nine at the Park Central Hotel and found you and Arnold Rothstein together?"

"Objection," Rosenbach cried. "The prosecutor is implying my client saw some sort of sexual liaison."

The judge waved Rosenbach down. "All right. Rephrase your question, Mr. Reed."

Reed sighed. "What happened, Mrs. McManus, when your husband broke into room four thirty-nine that night?"

For the first time George thought he saw Elizabeth's facade crack. He leaned forward to see the slight tremble of her shoulders. Slowly she turned her gaze to him again. But this time she did not turn away.

"I'm not completely sure. It was all so fast. I know they fought. There was a gun."

"Try to remember, Mrs. McManus. Was the gun in your husband's hands?"

"It's very confused," she said. "My husband and Arnold Rothstein hit each other. He was screaming."

"Who was screaming?"

"Mr. Rothstein."

"And then what happened, Mrs. McManus?"

"I was pushed down. They struggled in front of me. Arnold Rothstein was kicking. Then there was a bang—a shot. I remember the smoke burned my nose."

Her last words were drowned out by the roar from the benches and the sound of heavy feet as reporters eagerly stumbled over each other to telephone a sensational new paragraph to their papers.

"This is the most disgusting display I've ever seen in a courtroom," Rosenbach shouted, banging on the table with each word. "This woman obviously hates the defendant and will say anything to—"

"Shut up," Lenahan shouted back in exasperation, crashing his gavel again and again over the rising tumult. "Bailiff, one more interruption and you will remove Mr. Rosenbach and clear this court of spectators."

Reed waited for a long time, until the policemen in the aisles had everyone seated again and the courtroom was

457

nearly silent, before he turned to Elizabeth again. For a moment Reed let himself admire her defiance and strength as she stared at George McManus. This was going almost better than they had rehearsed it, he thought. The dream case. This could even make him governor someday. Then he shook himself.

"Mrs. McManus, are you sure you can continue at this time? Perhaps the judge will allow a short recess."

Elizabeth shook her head. "No, I'm fine. I want to go on. I want to tell my story."

"Good. I'm sure the court admires your courage, Mrs. McManus. Now, can you recall what Mr. Rothstein did when he was shot?"

Elizabeth took a deep breath. "He staggered. His hand was covered with blood from his side. I remember, he had the strangest look on his face, surprise more than pain, as though he couldn't believe it was happening to him."

"And did he run from room four thirty-nine after your husband shot him?"

"I don't understand."

Reed looked from the judge to Elizabeth. "I said, did Mr. Rothstein run from room four thirty-nine after your husband shot him, Mrs. McManus?"

"I object." Rosenbach bounded up automatically. "He's leading the witness, your honor. This kind of interrogation has to—"

"But my husband didn't shoot Arnold Rothstein."

"What?" said Reed.

Elizabeth blinked. "I said my husband didn't shoot Arnold Rothstein. Rothstein shot himself as they fought for the gun. It was an accident. That's why he looked so surprised."

For a second there wasn't a sound, then the court erupted in shouts and shrieks and war whoops. In a moment everyone in the courtroom was on his feet.

"You heard her, you heard her," Rosenbach cried as two reporters suddenly vaulted over the rail toward Elizabeth. "I move for dismissal, your honor. There's no case. You heard her. Move for dismissal."

Judge Lenahan pounded his gavel but no one was listening anymore. The district attorney quickly scooped up the papers

458

on the table before him, stuffed them in his briefcase, and walked out of the room. A dozen more reporters rushed toward McManus. A phalanx of photographers burst into the courtroom. Their exploding flashbulbs released the rest of the crowd like a pistol shot at the start of the race. And now they all swarmed around George and Elizabeth, oblivious to the frantic rapping of Lenahan's gavel. Finally the judge gave up and threw the gavel over his shoulder, mopping his face with his muffler in exasperation.

He was shaking his head as he watched George McManus push through the crowd around Elizabeth, pull her from the witness chair, and sweep her into his arms.

60

THE SEA OF COLOR swirled and eddied, breaking against buildings and cars caught in its midst, re-forming endlessly into new waves and riotous combinations. Suddenly, illuminated by the blazing marquee lights, a detail would emerge —a flashing face, a bright scarf tossed high, a bottle being passed from hand to hand—and then disappear just as quickly. In the cool night the bodies that made up the sea swayed together, rank upon rank, friends arm-in-arm with strangers, shouting, pushing, laughing, drinking, roaming endlessly from one end of the great thoroughfare to the other while still more thousands streamed in to join them, ripples adding to the boiling maelstrom.

On one side of the huge crowd George McManus took Elizabeth's hand, hesitated for just a moment, then plunged in, leading her through the jostling mob. They clung to each other's hands tightly even as they laughed at the human folly that filled Times Square on this night. They were halfway across when a deep, sonorous bell sounded, reverberating off the buildings around them. The bell was greeted by cheers and dancing in the broad street and George explained to Elizabeth that the bell was Big Ben, heralding the new year in London and broadcast over big speakers. In the sudden new burst of merriment they lost each other for a moment, then George found her in the middle of a happy circle of dancers, but they had to drink mouthfuls of wine before she could be released.

The tide of bodies swept them along inexorably, as if they were in a real sea. But finally they reached the other side of the crowd, bursting out onto a sliver of bare sidewalk under a theater marquee lit by hundreds of white bulbs. Elizabeth took George's arm and under the warmth of the lights they skirted the edge of the roaring crowd, feeling its tremendous pent-up excitement, but the sadness, too, that always accompanies an ending—even one as ephemeral as the stroke of a clock that ends one year and heralds another.

At Forty-sixth Street they turned at the corner and walked down the block. A double line of big cars interspersed with busy cabs stood in front of the Paradise Rehearsal Club, and they could see Chins, with an exaggerated bow, holding the door for several couples. When he saw George and Elizabeth he trotted to them, folds of fat jiggling under his bright red uniform covered with swirls of icing-like piping.

Chins whistled through pudgy lips as he fingered George's tuxedo and top hat and stared at Elizabeth's long white fur coat. "Boss, youse two look like a million bucks. But where ya been? Big Bill's been down twice lookin'. He says everybody in town's askin' for youse."

"What are you doing here, anyway?" George asked. "Why aren't you upstairs at the party?"

For a moment Chins looked sad. "Well, the truth is, this being the last night for the old joint, I just thought I'd like to stay in the costume for a little while longer." He smoothed the coat over his bulges. "I kinda like the uniform, boss. It fits real nice."

"What are you going to do for a job after tonight?" Elizabeth asked. "Maybe George could find you something."

"Oh, I'll go back to the newsstand, make a little book. Don't worry about me, missus. But I'll sure miss the joint."

George looked to the club's tall, blacked-out windows on the second floor. Even above the noise from Times Square and the traffic on the street he could hear the hum of voices and snatches of music, like distant rumors. Three more cars pulled up and scrambled for space on the curb, women getting out and stepping daintily across puddles with their long gowns hoisted to the knee as men uselessly pressed their elbows.

"Gotta go," Chins called over his shoulder, oozing his mass toward the street. "I'd like to talk, but tips is too good tonight, boss. Go tell Big Bill youse is here."

Elizabeth smiled. "Yes, darling. Let's go tell Big Bill youse is here."

Arm in arm, George and Elizabeth walked by the window of the corset shop and up the narrow, creaking stairs. The walls were the same dingy gray they had been five years ago, George thought. The same smudges, pencil messages, handprints, and peeling paint.

"You know, I always meant to fix up this stairway," he told Elizabeth. "But people seemed to like it the way it was. Atmosphere, I guess."

"Some things shouldn't change," she agreed, squeezing his hand as they neared the top of the stairs. Elizabeth reached for the door, but George pulled her toward him.

"Did I say thank you today for saving my skin?"

She touched the stiff ruffles of his starched, snow-white shirt. "You haven't stopped thanking me since the trial three weeks ago, remember? I'm nearly worn out."

"But this is a big night, toots. New Year's, the last night of the twenties, the last night of the club." He slipped his hands under her heavy coat and rubbed her bare back lightly. "And I'm still very grateful."

"I only did what we planned. The hard part was staying away from you until the trial was over."

"It was just as hard for me." His lips brushed her cheek. "But you were my insurance card. And I couldn't have used you if anyone saw us together." He pulled her closer and nibbled gently on her ear. "Thanks for letting me use you."

Elizabeth sighed in mock resignation, looked around the shadowy landing. "Do you think this is the best place to show your gratitude? There's only about ten thousand people on the other side of that door, you know."

"All right, then, later. But I warn you, it might take all night to show you just how grateful I really am."

461

Then there were voices at the bottom of the stairs, laughter, the sound of footsteps. They looked at each other and laughed almost conspiratorially before George pulled open the door.

Noise and light flooded out at them like a physical assault, making them wince. Like Times Square, the broad wooden-floored room was packed, bodies crammed together everywhere they turned, three-deep at the bars, crowded around the slot machines. To add to the confusion a string of red-faced people wound through the room in a confused snake dance, raggedly singing their own music as they fell laughing, then re-forming the human chain.

It took George and Elizabeth a half hour to cross the jammed room. At every step they were happily jostled, pawed, pounded on the back, alternately congratulated and commiserated with. Halfway across a big man with cascades of sweaty red hair grabbed George, lifted him off the floor, wetly kissed both his cheeks.

"He owed Rothstein money," George explained to her with a shrug.

Finally they made it to the short steps that led up to the casino. The crowd thinned as they pushed down the hall and past the big refrigerator door. But if it was possible, the casino was even more crowded than the downstairs room. The air was already blue-gray with cigar and cigarette smoke. They could barely hear the band over the noise, just stray bits of music drifting to them like sunlight filtering through dense trees. And everywhere perspiring waiters dashed with trays of drinks held high while people drank too fast, laughed too hard, talked too much, as though every second were precious, something to be hoarded like gold.

They were taking off their coats when Dwyer found them.

"It's about time, Georgie. Some host, your husband." He helped Elizabeth with her coat and handed it to the pretty girl in the cloakroom.

George shook his head. "We'd have been here sooner but I had to shake twenty thousand hands downstairs. Are they drinking as much as they're yelling?"

"I just sent to the warehouse for a hundred more cases of whiskey and gin and forty of champagne." Dwyer looked

462

around the crowded casino. "But I'm not sure even that's going to be enough."

"Try putting a little more ice in the glasses."

"Who's using glasses?" Dwyer said with a straight face. "They're drinking right out of the bottle."

But George looked at him almost sadly. "No word from Walker? No last-minute reprieve?"

Dwyer shook his head. "Forget it. He wouldn't even answer my call."

"After all these years," Elizabeth said. "Why does he want to close the Paradise Rehearsal Club now?"

"It's all your fault, you know," Dwyer told her. "The reformers all think he fixed George's trial. No one believes the two of you did it all by yourselves. Even I still don't believe it. The mayor is in for some very bad days, I'm afraid."

George nodded. "So he closes the club in retaliation."

"More like insurance," Dwyer said. "Maybe it will buy him more time before the hounds of good government overtake him. Poor Jimmy. The first time in his life he wasn't in on a fix, and no one will buy it."

Elizabeth straightened Dwyer's crooked tie. "Why don't you take me out to the dance floor? I'm tired of talk."

Dwyer nodded, pleased. "You might check on Izzy in the money room," he told George as he took Elizabeth's hand. "He's been complaining all night."

"And you, my dear, can tell me again how you two worked out that lovely scam at the trial." Dwyer led her into the dense crowd. "But I'll still probably never forgive either of you for not letting me in on it. George makes a million and I'm shut out of the action. That's very cruel, madam."

George heard Elizabeth's high laugh even after she was lost in the crowd.

He grabbed a glass of champagne from a waiter and went toward the roulette tables as, far away across the room, a woman shrieked gaily when the band struck up the "Muskrat Ramble."

George wormed through the mob around the tables until the tightly packed bodies would let him get no closer. On the other side of one of the tables Rats Wolnik called for bets and

463

almost immediately a blizzard of green bills fell to the felt. Rats was sweating profusely, George saw, his collar soaked gray and wrinkled like his face as he tried to keep up with the dozens of hands pushing money toward him. For a second Rats looked up and, as George caught his eye, shook his head in bewilderment.

"No more bets, ladies and gentlemen," Rats called, pushing away handfuls of bills, then spinning the wheel. "Next time, next time."

He said something to the croupier beside him, picked up a small, bulging canvas bag, and pushed through the crowd toward George. They met near the bar.

"Do you see it, boss? They're betting like crazy." The bartender handed him a glass of water and Rats gulped it down.

"I got to get back to the table, boss. We're pulling in a fortune here." Rats wiped his face with a handkerchief and handed George the canvas bag. "Give this dough to Izzy, will ya? You believe it's the eighth load from that table tonight? It's like they're trying to get even for everything they ever lost in their lives." He ran off before George could say anything.

McManus tucked the bag under his arm and went toward the money room. Five times people grabbed him, pulled him into their little circles, pushed drinks into his hand. With nowhere to put the glasses, George drank the liquor and pushed the glasses into his pockets, hoping nobody reeled into him and shattered them. Finally he reached the money room and knocked quickly. There was a buzz on the other side of the door and George let himself in, slamming it quickly behind him.

Izzy the Stub sat at the long counting table surrounded by tall piles of bills on the table and floor. His hands were full of cash, his hat tilted back on his head.

George put down the canvas bag and began unloading the glasses from his pockets.

"Thank you very much. Just what I wanted—empty glasses," Izzy grumbled. "It would be nicer if maybe you put some hooch in the glasses, boss. I have been so busy counting your greenbacks I haven't had a second to touch a single drop."

"I'll have somebody bring you a pitcher of water. What are you doing in here anyway? Why isn't Otto counting the money?"

Izzy made a face. "You're asking me? Ask that worm Otto. You know how much fun this is, to sit and count somebody else's money? I could die from this kind of fun. The cash is coming in so fast I'm even out of spit for my fingers."

Izzy noticed the canvas bag George was opening. "Wonderful. More work. This could make a man hate money."

George poured the money on the table. "Okay, okay, I'll see if I can find somebody to help you. But where's Otto? He was supposed to pick up the last of the money I won on the trial and have it for me tonight. I told Big Bill I'd pay off what I owe him."

"I don't know about that," Izzy complained, looking at the new pile of bills. "I only know Otto went out with Marie Flynn maybe four hours ago. He said he was taking her to eat and I should do his job until they came back. He should only die from indigestion."

George thought for a moment, then quickly turned his back on Izzy and went through the side door into his own office. The cool darkness was soothing after the heat of the casino. He turned on the lights and went to his desk, as if searching for something. Then his eyes fell on the dull-black safe in the corner. George rushed to it and knelt. He spun the dial and in a moment had the door open.

For a long while he stared into it, not moving. Next to some papers and the tin box containing the IOUs he saw only an envelope with his name on it. He ran his hands across the shelves, but he knew it was fruitless. The money that should have been in the safe was gone.

George stood and tore open the envelope. Inside was a note in Otto's familiar, cramped handwriting.

Mr. McManus,
Marie Flynn and I are going to be married tonight and then are going away to start a new life together. It was what you'd call a whirlwind courtship. In fact, I didn't know there was a courtship until Mr. Dwyer told us the club was closing. But Marie says she loves

me and I love her. We took your winnings and the money from the safe. Marie said she earned it and that you'd understand. Tell Mr. Dwyer I will miss him very much, but love doesn't come to a man like me very often.

Yours truly,
Otto Berman

George took the tin box and the note and sat at his desk. After a while, he was surprised to find a rueful smile on his face. He tried to imagine how long it would take Marie to go through almost a million dollars, and what she would do with Otto when the money was gone. But Marie was right, he thought. She had earned the money.

He picked up the box of IOUs and emptied it on the desk. First the stocks, then the club closing, now Otto. He was broke again, George thought, unless he counted these pieces of paper. There had to be close to two million owed the club, but somehow he knew he would never see any of this money. Something had changed, the world had slipped a little on its axis. He could feel it in the useless scraps of paper. They were cold now, lifeless, where once they had somehow been warm with promise.

Almost without thinking he piled up the IOUs, shuffling them easily with his fingers. The agility with which he did it comforted him. He slid open a drawer and found a new deck of cards, feeling the familiar rectangular shape without seeing it. He dropped the deck into his pocket. At least, he thought, he'd still be able to make a living.

He was still staring at the IOUs when the door opened and he looked up to see Elizabeth.

"It's crazy outside," she said, her face flushed and alive. "Everybody's dancing like mad. You know there's a woman walking on her hands? And she's not wearing underwear."

George stood and went to her. He shut the door, closing out the noise. "I have something to tell you."

She lifted her face. "You going to thank me again?"

He ran a finger along her throat, smiling despite himself. "I'm broke."

Elizabeth looked at him blankly.

"Otto Berman ran off with my money and Marie. Though I've got a feeling it was really Marie who took Otto."

Elizabeth tilted her head quizzically. "They took the whole thing? The million dollars you won on the trial?"

George nodded.

"You're broke," Elizabeth said softly.

They were silent for a moment, then Elizabeth raised her eyebrows and shrugged. "Well, that makes us even. I'm broke, too, now that Wainwright Construction is gone. I guess we'll have to look for work."

"Work? What could either of us do?"

"I'm sure I could get a job behind the counter in a dress shop. I've had enough practice buying dresses—I ought to be able to sell them. But what will you do? Do you have any skill besides poker? I suppose you could always dig ditches. Any fool with a strong back can do that."

"You certainly make poverty sound terrific, Mrs. McManus. And then what? Back to Hell's Kitchen and a cold-water walk-up flat full of bawling brats in diapers?"

"And how many brats would you like? I'd like three."

George frowned. "Maybe you didn't hear me. I said we're broke. B-r-o-k-e. You want to be saddled with a penniless Irish gambler like me for the rest of your life?"

"Just try and get away," Elizabeth whispered.

For a long time they looked at each other, listening to the music and shouts from the casino, the honking of car horns in the street, the faraway muffled-waterfall roar of the mob in Times Square. Each knew midnight was approaching but neither moved as they quietly drew strength from each other. Perhaps because it was New Year's, a thousand images flitted through their minds—fading dreams, broken promises. Like the millions around them, each looked inward, asking what things would be changed if they had it all to do over, then making peace with their regrets, packing away, in dim, silent corners, the things that could never be again.

"It's almost time," Elizabeth said as George stroked her fine hair. "Let's go into the club. Suddenly I want to scream and yell and whistle and stomp my feet when nineteen twenty-nine ends. I want the world to know I was here to-night."

George hesitated, looking around the office, then went back to his desk. He picked up the box of IOUs as Elizabeth opened the door. The roar of the crowd that greeted them made the chandeliers sway and the very walls quiver. Just then the lights dimmed and George saw Dwyer rolling a huge cake on a cart into the center of the room. They pushed through the crowd toward him.

"What's this?" George twisted to read the words on the cake.

"Tonight our players are going to have their cake and eat it, too," Dwyer joked loudly, to happy cries.

The cake was five feet long and three feet wide and decorated in little red and black squares to resemble a roulette table. On it was written in icing: "Paradise Rehearsal Club—1925 to 1929—There are no sure things." A waiter brought Dwyer a bottle of brandy and he pulled the cork and poured the liquor over the center of the cake.

"Since this is the club's last night, at the request of the local authorities, I thought about burning down the joint for a big finish," Dwyer shouted over the growing roar from the street. "But I settled on this flaming offering to the gods of chance instead. Now, with my partner's permission, if you'll all step back—"

"Just a second," George called. "I've got something to add."

He held the tin box over his head and let the pieces of paper drift onto the cake.

"These are all your IOUs, my friends. Every single penny. But since I figure most of you won't be good for a free cigarette in coming days—much less a lot of cash—you're all off the hook. Let it burn!"

To the cheers of the crowd, Dwyer struck the match on his shoe and dropped it on the cake. The flames sprang up quickly, the glow dancing across every face, then died just as fast, leaving the cake virtually untouched. The charred bits of paper drifted up through the smoke.

"That was very noble, Mr. McManus." Elizabeth brushed a bit of ash off his coat as the crowd surged back to the bar, the gaming tables, and the dance floor.

468

"I always wondered what it would feel like to burn up a fortune," George said. "It felt lousy."

Suddenly the band played a crashing fanfare, quieting the room again. Then, very distinctly, over the giant speakers that had boomed out Big Ben, they heard an amplified voice counting:

"*Sixty. Fifty-nine. Fifty-eight . . .*"

In the casino the people took up the chant, scattering across the room looking for husbands, wives, mistresses, lovers, friends, no one wanting to be alone at midnight.

"*. . . Forty-one. Forty. Thirty-nine . . .*"

Each second the noise grew louder. People screamed to hear themselves over the uproar. They held one another, drank last toasts. Eyes were wet with excitement and sadness.

"*. . . Eighteen. Seventeen. Sixteen . . .*"

George drew Elizabeth to him. He could feel her trembling, sense the excitement and anxiety of the thousands around them through her body. The noise seemed to crush them together with its intensity, rising higher and higher. They held each other tightly, anchors against the pandemonium, now trying to hold the moment, reluctant to let the seconds go.

"*. . . Five. Four. Three. Two. One. . . .*"

The casino, Times Square, the world, erupted in noise—church bells, car horns, sirens, the clap of hands, cries from hundreds of thousands of hoarse throats. The lights flashed off and on as George pressed Elizabeth to him fiercely, covering her face with kisses.

And then, slowly, the shouting and cheers died away. Quietly at first, then louder, the band began to play "Auld Lang Syne" and gradually everyone joined in, singing the old words.

"Listen, toots," he said as the last strains of the song died away, surprised to find his throat raw. "I've still got about a hundred bucks in my wallet. Let's go have a caviar and corned beef. Then afterward maybe we can start working on one of those bawling brats."

Elizabeth took his hand and they pushed through the suddenly muted crowd toward the checkroom. They were putting on their coats when Dwyer came up to them.

"Quite a night." Dwyer leaned against the door frame watching them as the band began playing again.

"The fun isn't over yet," George said. He took Otto's note out of his coat pocket and handed it to Dwyer.

"I don't believe it." Dwyer chuckled as he read it. "God bless the little bastard. I just hope Marie doesn't eat him alive."

George turned up the collar of his overcoat. "Look, Bill, I don't know what the casino take was tonight, but Izzy said the tables were paying off like crazy. So you keep my half of the profits from tonight. And if that doesn't add up to the six hundred thousand I owe you, well, then I'll find some way to pay you back. It might take a while, but I'm good for it."

"I know you are." He looked from George to Elizabeth. "You two have any plans, now that the club is finished?"

George shrugged. "Elizabeth says she'll recommend me for a ditchdigger job. And she's going to sell dresses. We ought to have your money in . . . say, a hundred years. But not a day more, I swear."

Dwyer scratched his chin. "Well, maybe I've got a better deal for you." He took his own coat from a hook and slipped it on.

"I've had my eye on some interests in Florida for quite a while, Georgie. But I haven't been able to find the right partner down there. I need a man with finesse."

"Someone who knows his way around people," Elizabeth added.

"Exactly. But somebody I can trust. Just between us, I think the time is ripe to open a bigtime casino down there, George. It's a shame, all those millionaires on their yachts with nothing to keep them out of mischief."

Elizabeth stepped between the two men and took each one's arm as they strolled through the club's big door.

"You'd need some important local connections, of course," George pointed out.

"No problem. I'm acquainted with several aldermen who'd sell their sisters to the Arabs for a dollar. And the mayor of Miami would sell his mother."

"Well, then," George said as the three of them went down

470

the hall, then across the big noisy room past the slot machines, "here's a way we could work it. . . ."

They walked together down the Paradise Rehearsal Club's creaky stairs, Elizabeth listening as the two men plotted. On the street a gentle rain fell, blurring the gray sidewalks, dark cars, and bright lights with a hazy mist. Papers, streamers, even a few hats blew about their feet as they strolled toward Broadway where the New Year's Eve crowd was beginning to break up, little groups drifting toward their separate destinies.

But at the corner all three suddenly stopped. Was it a trick of the wind that carried a few bars of jazz music to them, an echo of laughter? For a moment they looked back down Forty-sixth Street to the painted-over windows above the corset shop, remembering.

"The casino in Florida, will it be just like the Paradise Rehearsal Club?" Elizabeth finally asked.

"Better," said Dwyer. "Bigger and fancier."

"I don't know. Suddenly there are things I'm not sure about."

George turned to her, his face serious. "I won't pressure you, Elizabeth. Not after all that's happened, after what you've been through. If you want to walk away, just say so, and we'll leave Big Bill standing right here on the corner. And I swear I'll never look back."

Dwyer looked concerned as Elizabeth shook her head.

"Just answer me one thing, darling."

"Anything," George told her.

"I can never get it straight. Does a straight flush beat a full house?"

"We're going to be just fine." George laughed as the three of them locked arms again and began walking toward the bright lights ahead. "Just fine."

About the Authors

Alan Fisk is a journalist who has worked for the *Detroit Free Press*, *Newsday*, and the *Star*. Born in West Germany, he grew up in Detroit, Michigan. Margaret Cronin Fisk, also from Detroit, is a writer whose articles have appeared in many publications, including *Woman's Day*, *Cosmopolitan*, and *Turf and Sport Digest*. She is the author of *The Gambler's Bible* (Drake, 1976). She has also worked as a professional racing handicapper for the *Hartford Times*. When not at home in Brooklyn, New York, the Fisks can usually be found at the racetrack.